Deadly Whispers

RICHARD L. HATIN

Publisher Page
an imprint of Headline Books, Inc.
Terra Alta, WV

Deadly Whispers

by Richard L. Hatin

copyright ©2014 Richard L. Hatin

Turn Around Look at Me lyrics used with permissionof Alfred Publishing L130412-9006. Words and music by Harry Chapin and Sandy Chapin, 1961 renewed-All Rights Reserved.

To order additional copies of this book,
or for book publishing information, or to contact the author:

Headline Books, Inc.
P.O. Box 52
Terra Alta, WV 26764
www.headlinebooks.com
Tel: 800-570-5951
Email: mybook@headlinebooks.com

www.RichardHatin.com

Publisher Page is an imprint of Headline Books

Cover Design by Aaron Hatin

ISBN 978-0-938467-75-5 Paperback
ISBN 978-0-937467-80-9 Hardcover

Library of Congress Control Number: 2013950122

Deadly Whispers / by Richard L. Hatin
        p. cm.
ISBN 978-0938467-75-5 pb
ISBN 978-0938467-80-9 hc
1. Mystery-thriller

PRINTED IN THE UNITED STATES OF AMERICA

For my sons Joel, Aaron and Brady;
My love and prayers are always with you!
And for my parents, Reginald and Rose Marie;
Miss you both very much!

Chapter 1

Even though he survived death many times, he isn't invincible and he knows that. He is however, very, very strong and lives with a curse. He is descended from others who ate human flesh so very long ago, and were cursed for their transgression. Now, it must be said he has devolved and is now a curse unto himself.

Ever since the original curse was first uttered, his kind became driven by a fierce hatred for the human race, a hatred that was all consuming.

Inflicting pain is ordinary. He has perfected torture until it is almost his own art form. Killing is only slightly satisfying.

Yet, now his need is much more.

This special need has arisen in him; he has become single-minded and driven. Nothing can stop him. No one can deny him.

Once, long ago, he had a mother, a father and a sister. He did his best to learn all that was taught to him.

He learned to hunt, to slaughter and most of all he learned of his legacy, this curse that forever binds him to darkness.

His great grandfather was the first. Now as his descendant, he vows he will not be the last of his kind.

For his entire life he had to live deep underground. It is here he is lord over absolute darkness and the dozens of caves and endless miles of tunnels that connect them.

If the moon is dark, he may venture out to hunt but not always for food.

His flesh is pallid and almost completely devoid of color. When standing fully erect he is over six and a half feet tall. His eyes were removed long, long ago. They were a useless vestige, a reminder of what his kind once was, human. His hands are immense and more powerful than any man who ever walked the earth. He has thick powerful legs and long pure white hair. His teeth have yellowed and sharpened over the years. The soles of his feet and the palms of his hands are thickly calloused. His ears are oversized and somewhat pointy in shape. His remaining senses of hearing, smell, and touch are nothing short of extraordinary.

His voice, though seldom used, is thick and coarse sounding. His mind, the source of all his power, is always engaged, driven by his principal needs to survive, to kill and to mate.

These dark and deadly forces driving him are both powerful and needful.

Strangely, he would give anything to be human but at the same time he is compelled to destroy humans. This conflict defines him.

He is soulless and wanting.

Slowly, his special need to mate takes hold of him once more. Over the next several days it begins to propel him to fulfill a destiny instilled in him at birth, nearly two hundred years ago.

Chapter 2

Lenny Drew was small for his age. At thirteen years old he stood barely four feet-three inches tall. He wore black horn rimmed glasses broken at the curve of the left ear stem, held together by a generous wrap of clear tape. Glancing down at his watch Lenny noted the time of 6:30 a.m. He had just finished serving mass for Father Campbell and now he was quickly removing his cassock and surplus. Lenny carefully hung them up in the altar boy's closet just off to the side of the sacristy, here at St. Francis Xavier Church.

"Catch you later, Father," said Lenny as he half-ran for the door.

"Lenny, will you be able to serve for me at tomorrow's 6:00 a.m. mass?" asked the priest. "David Hunter is sick and unable to serve as altar boy for that mass."

"Not a problem, I'll be here," answered Lenny from over his shoulder as he bounded out the door.

Father Francis Campbell smiled at the carefree spirit of this young boy. After all his family had gone through over this past year, Lenny deserved to be a happy young boy off to take on the day. Lenny's father had regular drinking episodes along with beating Lenny's Mom and Lenny or tearing up some local bar. This often led to Father Campbell being called to intervene at odd hours of the day or night. It was the priest who first suggested Lenny become an altar boy. Father Campbell could relate to Lenny, after all, his own Father was also a drunk and a wife beater.

"May our Lord Jesus Christ keep him safe and bring him closer to the one, true God, Amen," whispered Father Campbell as he continued to remove and fold his vestments.

Lenny ran to his bicycle. He left it outside leaning against the sacristy wall. The bike was a new black, three speed Columbia. It had the latest handlebar mounted gear shifter. Lenny bought it just two weeks before with money he earned returning soda pop bottles at two cents a bottle. It took Lenny nearly two years to find enough bottles to save up the twenty-eight dollars and thirty-two cents. He felt ten feet tall the day he placed his hard earned money on the counter at the Aubuchon Hardware Store as they wheeled his "Black Beauty" from out of the back storeroom. It was indeed a mighty moment, the kind that becomes a lifelong memory for a young boy.

Slung over the handlebars was a drab canvas backpack. Lenny unzipped the old canvas Army surplus bag he had "borrowed" from his father's Army "stuff." Lenny rummaged through his dad's stuff last night when he secretly searched his father's foot locker which was pushed to the rear of the loft over the garage.

Now his precious bag was full. Everything was there, flashlight, matches, approximately a hundred feet of old rope, candles, one small folding shovel, extra batteries and his lunch. Lunch consisted of one peanut butter sandwich, one devil dog, and a hefty chunk of Velveeta cheese wrapped in wax paper and a bottle of root beer. The old canvas bag also contained a change of clothes, his oldest jeans, and a pair of black Converse sneakers, a sweatshirt missing its sleeves and Lenny's trademark Red Sox baseball hat, his "old red, white and blue."

Lenny swung his right leg over the cross bar and carefully pushed himself up on the right side pedal as he coasted down the walkway alongside the Church. It was a Saturday morning, late June 1962, the first day of his summer school vacation. Lenny was going to be in the eighth grade next year at St. Francis Xavier School. It would be a time for some serious "ass kicking" for all the eighth grade boys. After all they had suffered at the hands of the eighth graders for the past couple of years. It was now their turn to "rain some pain" as Lenny's Dad use to call it when he took off his belt to exact some of his parental justice.

Lenny looked down at his watch and noticed it was now nearly quarter to seven. He agreed to meet his buddies at Tony Fredette's house no later than seven. Today, he and his friends were going to explore the "Cave to Hell." It was the name they had given it last weekend when they discovered it and claimed it for their "Pine Street Gang." It was the name they settled on, after a fiercely fought over game of hearts played last Sunday in Mark Pushey's back yard tent. Lenny had plenty of time so he eased up on his pedaling.

* * * * *

"Hey guys, guess what ol' Karl is bringing on this expedition?" said Karl Sweeney.

Karl was almost fifteen years old. Karl had repeated second grade because he had a "bitchin fever" according to Karl. It lasted over several months when he was just seven years old. Karl also had a serious acne problem.

"Some of your Dad's homemade beer?" asked Tony Fredette. Tony, who was thirteen, had a round faced and liked to pick his nose.

Chapter 3

Lenny Drew was sitting at his desk on the 26th floor of the Hancock Tower in Boston, Massachusetts. It was a cold, windy February day. It was Monday the 24th and he had just returned from one of his supervisor's insufferable staff meetings. Lenny Drew was a Senior Financial Analyst for Wellington Trust Services, one of Boston's most prestigious financial management firms. They handled "old" money. The morning mail sat in the middle of his desk. He was sorting the envelopes to open them when he stopped at one particular envelope. It was addressed to "Lenny-the-Turtle-Drew." He had not heard his nickname since grade school. There was no return address. He opened it and withdrew a single sheet of yellow notepad paper. Unfolding the paper he noticed that its message was written in a child-like scrawl. It read, "The BONES are back, Lenny. They're back!"

He pushed the paper away.

Lenny Drew began to feel a headache coming on. It was going to be a major migraine. Suddenly, he could swear that he could smell the damp, dank odor of the Cave-to-Hell. He felt sweat run down his underarms. Who could have sent this note? Lenny had his suspicions. A prank by a childhood friend! If so, he was prepared to unload his anger. Lenny Drew was not amused by this in the least; he was plain old pissed off! Now the back of his neck throbbed with tightness.

Yessiree! Someone's just pissed me off. They won't get a second chance, thought Lenny. He suspected one of his childhood friends. "I've still got Karl Sweeney's phone number at home. I'll give him a call tonight and give him a piece of my mind!" grumbled Lenny.

Lenny went to the door of his office and peeked around the corner into the adjoining office.

"Sylvia, could you spare some ibuprofen? I've got a screamer of a headache," said Lenny. Sylvia was on the phone with a client, her long shapely legs resting on the corner of her desk.

Without interrupting her telephone conversation she pulled open her top side drawer, took out a small bottle of pills and tossed them over to Lenny. He blew her a kiss. She smiled back at him. He went into his office and pulled open the bottle.

Chapter 4

"It's a picture of your naked sister," said Mark Pushey who started to laugh. His infectious laugh got everyone laughing.

"Cr.....unch....squeeeeeee," was the sound of Lenny's tires braking as he fishtailed into Pushey's gravel driveway.

Tony was laughing so hard he didn't notice Lenny's grand entrance until the small stones were kicked up and hit the back of his legs.

"Hey, asshole, watch what you're doing," said Tony as he pointed his right index finger at Lenny. Lenny took one look at that finger and exploded into his own laughing jag.

"Tony you shouldn't point that thing when it's loaded," said Lenny.

"Oh yeah, why's that, Turtle?" demanded Tony.

"Cause you've got a long loogee hanging on the end of your finger, you doofus," said Lenny with a smirk.

With that everyone broke into some serious side splitting laughter.

After a while Lenny went into Tony's garage, changed clothes, and then pushed his new bicycle to the back of the garage where he pulled an old blanket over it. Lenny closed the garage door. Soon the Pine Street Gang headed off to the woods to revisit their recent discovery, the Cave-to-Hell.

It was still early morning as they entered the woods at the northern end of Pine Street. The morning dew on the tall grass wet their sneakers as they marched single file, moving deeper into the woods. The boys often speculated that many years before, early Indians probably explored these very woods in much the same way. They had each heard their fathers tell assorted campfire stories about the Indian spirits which still traveled these same woods.

"Hey, Karl, did you bring your father's kerosene lantern?" asked Mark.

"Yeah!" replied Karl.

"What was it you said you were bringing that was so special?" said Tony from the back of the line.

Karl stopped in the path and turned to his buddies and smiled his biggest shit-eating grin.

"I stole my old man's July *Playboy Magazine*," said Karl.

Lenny let out a small whistle. "Phew."

"Does the centerfold have big boobs?" asked Tony.

"Does Tony pick his nose in the woods?" replied Karl.

"Shit," said Mark, "I gotta have a look?"

"All in good time, all in good time," said Karl as he turned and resumed leading the trek deeper into the woods.

After a hike that lasted about a half hour, the boys descended into a thickly covered hollow. Next, they carefully went around a small moss covered bog. The woods here were dark and cool. There were occasional sounds of birds fluttering through the trees as they kept a safe distance from the intruders. The boys headed over to a pile of thick brush at the base of a ledge that stood approximately fifty feet high. They put down their packs and together they pulled the brush back to reveal a small hole in the base of the rock-faced hill. The hole was about five and a half feet across and not much more than three feet high. From where they stood, it didn't look like much, but it was their discovery.

Karl took out a small black flashlight from his backpack and knelt down at the opening to the cave and shone his light inside.

"What's it look like?" asked Lenny.

"It looks like there is a hole, about seventy-five feet in, at the back of the cave", said Karl.

"I can't see much else."

"Mark, get your ass over here, crawl in there and see if you can reach that hole in the back," demanded Karl.

"Not me," said Mark. "I ain't going in there unless everyone is going in."

"Lenny, you go," said Karl.

Lenny looked at his friends. He was as scared as he could be but he had a thought, *If I go in there when they won't, then maybe I will have showed them I'm tougher than they are.*

"Well, we don't have all day, Turtle, what's it going to be?" huffed Karl.

"I'll go," he said, as he adjusted his glasses.

Lenny could see by the look in their eyes he had scored some major points on the pecking order scale. Their eyes spoke of more than awe, they also revealed relief.

Lenny removed his overloaded backpack. He retrieved the flashlight he brought. He put his Red Sox hat in his backpack. Lenny approached the entrance to the cave. He sat down, and then laid on his back as he started to slide himself, feet first, into the cave. His friends were standing nearby.

"Wait," Lenny said suddenly. "Mark, get the rope from my bag."

Mark scooted to Lenny's bag and returned with the rope. Lenny tied the rope around his waist and handed the end of the rope to Karl.

"Hold on to this. You guys can pull me out if something happens, okay?" said Lenny.

Karl nodded his agreement.

Lenny then looked down at his left elbow which was braced against the surface of the large flat rock which he was laying on at the cave entrance. He noticed several long brown streaks etched about an inch apart which covered the surface of the rock. The streak lines seemed to point into the cave's opening.

"Hold the rope tight, Karl," said Lenny as he slid into the cave.

He travelled about ten feet when he noticed it began to slope gently downward. It was nearly four feet high at this point. Lenny repositioned himself so he was able to squat. The air was much cooler in the cave. It was also much quieter. Lenny could hear his own breathing. He panned the flashlight around the cave and saw that it grew very shallow at the far end but there was no mistaking it, there was an opening that went further, much further.

"Lenny, what do you see, man?" asked Karl.

"Not much," shouted Lenny as his own voice boomed back at him from the cramped walls of the cave. Just then, his mind picked up on something.

Was that an echo of my voice coming from that hole over there, or something else? thought Lenny.

He took another look around and then noticed something white sticking out of the dirt to the left of the hole at the far end to the cave. He started to crawl over to it when he felt a tug at the rope tied around his waist.

"Give me some slack," said Lenny in the direction of the lighted opening to the cave. With his flashlight he saw the rope had now gone slack. He turned and headed over to the white object that caught his attention earlier. He pulled at it but it wouldn't budge. Lenny began to dig out the object with his bare hands. He was determined to extract it from the compacted damp dirt that covered the cave floor.

Meanwhile outside the cave Tony sat on a nearby rock.

"What's taking him so long?" asked Tony. Just then Tony leaned to his right and grimaced as he let loose one of his famous farts, a real sheet splitter. Mark and Karl chuckled at Tony's shenanigans.

"Oh man, now I've got to take a shit," said Tony.

The boys now broke into some intense knee-slapping laughter.

"Did you bring some toilet paper, stink face?" said Mark.

"Yeah and you ain't going to get any if you need it yourself, you little ass kisser," responded Tony.

Tony took a roll of toilet paper from out of his backpack and headed across the hollow to a clump of thick bushes. After several minutes he returned.

Inside the cave Lenny had finished digging. He was able to pull the long white object loose. He shone his flashlight on it. It was a bone, about twenty inches long. It was about as big around at its middle as the thin end of a baseball bat. It was some kind of bone alright, but just what kind he could not tell. The ends of this bone were as big around as a softball. Lenny moved back to the front of the cave. He couldn't wait to show his buddies what he had uncovered. Near the entrance, Lenny had to lie down on his back in order to push himself upward and out. His flashlight swept across the low overhead ceiling to the cave. It was wet. He noticed that on the ceiling there were some of the same dark brown streaks that Lenny had seen earlier at the outside entrance to the cave. Digging with his heels, he pushed himself completely out of the cave, his flashlight in his right hand and the bone in his left hand.

Lenny was pulled to his feet by Karl.

"Holy shit, Lenny, what is that?" asked Tony.

"I think it's a bone of some kind. It feels real," said Lenny.

"Let me see," said Karl as he took it from Lenny. He wiped some of the dirt from around the ends.

Mark didn't say a word, he just stared at the bone and then back at the cave entrance, and then back to the bone.

"Well, Karl, what do you think? What kind of bone is it?" said Lenny.

"Can't really tell. Were there any more?" asked Karl looking back once more at the cave entrance.

"I didn't see any others but there could be more," said Lenny.

"Okay, then let's get to it boys, time to break out the shovels and coffee cans and get to work," said Karl. He handed the bone back to Lenny. Lenny went to his backpack and tied the bone to the outside. He took out his folding shovel.

One by one, they slid on their backsides and entered the cave. After a short while, the muffled sound of digging and scraping could be heard coming from the cave. Every few moments an arm extended from the mouth of the cave to dump a coffee can full of dirt at the entrance to the cave. The digging went on for a couple of hours.

The June noonday sun had settled high above, yet in the tree-shrouded hollow, it remained dark as dusk. Only a stiletto of the sun's rays pierced the hollow's canopy to send a finger-like light beam straight down to the moss-covered ground.

The boys exited the cave, one-by-one, sliding out on their backs. They each slowly stood holding their lower backs like old men suffering from arthritis. Tony and Lenny also brushed at their jeans to remove the caked layers of dirt and clay. Mark pulled his pants at the waist and watched as dirt drained from under his pants down onto his sneakers. Karl stretched his fingers on both hands in and out to try and release the cramp that was threatening to start at any moment.

Mark looked over at the pile of dirt at the entrance to the cave. It didn't look like very much from out here.

"I'm so hungry I could eat a horse," declared Tony.

"You mean a horse's ass," said Karl, who immediately set off a round of laughter and some good-natured pushing.

They each sat down to the side of the cave entrance and leaned against the rock wall, opened their backpacks and started to have their well-deserved lunch.

Chapter 5

Lenny Drew put his key into the door lock, unlocking the deadbolt. He stepped into his condominium on the fourteenth floor of Charles River Park —a rich upscale development set in the northeast end of Boston. It is adjacent to Storrow Drive and alongside an ungodly snarl of an intersection behind the new TD Bank Center formerly known as the Boston Garden. He set his briefcase on the foyer chair and turned on the overhead light. He placed his overcoat in the foyer closet. Loosening his tie, he headed straight for the den. Lenny went over to his wet bar and poured himself half a glass of bourbon. He went into the kitchen, turning on lights as he moved about. He pulled out his private phone book from the wall rack next to the phone. The large black leather-bound book held hundreds of phone numbers of clients, friends, family and important numbers like the Aer Lingus stewardess he met at Killigan's Pub last St. Patrick's Day. Maggie Colleen O'Rourke captured his heart with her smile. He managed to meet her on her overnights to Boston at least several times since that day. Their relationship was growing with each visit.

He looked up the telephone number of Karl Sweeney. Karl had never left Vermont. As far as Lenny knew, Karl was working as a middle school teacher in Milton, and was still married to his college sweetheart, Linda Miller. They had met when Karl was working on his Master's Degree in Teaching at Johnson State Teacher's College. Karl taught History and Linda became a Special Education teacher. Later, they adopted two children when their fertility efforts were unsuccessful. They adopted a girl named Sherrie and later they adopted a boy and named him Bart after Bart Simpson. Karl still had a twisted sense of humor. Bart was nearly twenty-four by now.

Lenny found the number and dialed it... It was 6:35 p.m. It rang several times. By now, an answering machine should have kicked in.

"Come on, Karl, answer the damn phone," groused Lenny as he took a swallow of his bourbon.

"Hello," said the voice from Vermont. It was spoken softly. "Hello," said the voice once again.

"Hi, this is Lenny Drew, a friend of Karl's, is he available?"

There was a long pause, then, "You're calling for Karl?"

"Yes it's important. I need to speak to him about some mail he sent to me. I received it today," said Lenny.

"Mr. Drew," replied the soft voice.

"Yes!"

"I could be mistaken but I don't think Karl sent you something recently," the voice was definitely female. "You see, Karl committed suicide over a week ago."

Lenny suddenly felt perspiration in the hand that held the phone. He took another swallow of bourbon from his glass. His throat felt very dry.

"Mr. Drew, are you still there?"

"Yes, I am, I... uh.... didn't know. I thought maybe Karl had uh...oh my God!" said Lenny, his voice cracking. "He was one of my best friends. We grew up together. May I ask where Linda, Sherrie and Bart are? I would like to maybe express my, oh Jesus!" said Lenny as he began to feel tears come to his eyes.

"My name is Marta; I'm a good friend of Linda's. I remember them talking about you. Karl always talked about his childhood friends. I'm looking after the house. Linda, Sherrie and Bart went to stay in Wisconsin with Linda's parents for a while. I am sure you understand. Would you like for me to give you her telephone number at her parents' house? I'm sure she would love to hear from you."

"Sure, sure go ahead," he said as he wrote the number down. He was beginning to get a grip on himself. "Uh, Marta, could I ask you how…. you know, how"?

"How he died? I suppose so; it might make it less awkward when you talk to Linda. It was really a shocker to everyone who knew Karl. As you know, Karl was just a carefree, fun-loving, guy. There was no indication he was, you know, depressed or anything. Over a week ago, he apparently started talking sort of weird. Linda and Sherrie said he was very upset about something but he wouldn't tell them specifically what it was that was bothering him. Then he would stay up all night pacing the floor. Sherrie lives nearby but Bart lives out of state. One night Linda took something to help her to sleep. She was exhausted. When she woke up the following morning, he wasn't in the house. She went out to the garage, which was on the far side of the house. She found him, sitting in the car. The windows were rolled shut. There was blood everywhere. There was a hole in the roof of the car on the driver's side where Karl was sitting. He had used his shotgun. There wasn't anything she could do. She was sleeping so soundly she never heard the shot. It's been very hard on her, she didn't just love Karl, he was her best friend," said Marta with a sigh.

"Such a tragedy!" declared Lenny. "Did Linda ever figure out what Karl was upset about, or what he was grumbling about? I mean, she must have some idea.

"Yes, she told me Karl kept talking about some bones," said Marta.

The bourbon glass slipped from his grip and shattered on the kitchen floor. "Oh no, oh my God," said Lenny.

Lenny, now in a daze, half-heard her condolences and his own response. They exchanged good-byes as he hung up the phone. Now drawn to his computer, his mind filled with an urgent summons, *Message, message, I've got to send...*

Chapter 6

"Hey, Karl, when are you gonna let us see the *Playboy*?" pleaded Tony.

"Yeah, Karl, dig it out of your backpack and let us have a peek at the boobs-of-the-month," said Mark as he tossed his half-eaten sandwich into his backpack.

"Come on, Karl. We need some," pleaded Lenny.

"Okay, okay," said Karl with a big-ass grin stretching across his face. "You're gonna have to let me finish my lunch first," he remarked slyly.

"Besides, I'm the only one who's going to hold it. I don't need you goofballs smearing your finger prints on the pages or my old man will know I snagged his *Playboy*. If he finds out, my ass will belong to his for a good month of extra chores, not to mention his kicking my ass upstairs to my room for extra punishment," said Karl.

The guys all knew the reputation of Karl's Dad. He was known to be a mean son-of-a-bitch when he set his mind to the task. They all nodded their agreement. Karl then reached into his backpack and removed the brown paper wrapped magazine. He slowly slid the magazine out onto his lap. He wiped his hands twice on the sides of his dungarees and then checked them over to see if they would likely leave any traces on the pages of the magazine. Satisfied that they would not, he slowly lifted the cover open. Each of the other boys knelt down next to Karl. Wide-eyed wonder and a reverence for the roundness of a naked woman's flesh bordering upon worship characterized their initial reaction to each new sight. Then, after a moment passed as each boy's breath grew shallow, someone would make a crude remark or whistle. This would break the sexual tension each boy keenly felt but barely understood.

"Holy Moses, she's too beautiful to be real, I mean I've never seen anyone that beautiful," said Mark.

"Yeah," sighed Lenny, his eyes never leaving the glossy pages.

Karl closed the magazine and while carefully holding the edges he slid it back into the plain brown wrapper sleeve it was mailed in.

"Karl, your dad has a subscription to *Playboy*. That is so cool! My old man has a subscription to *Life Magazine* and to *Reader's Digest*. Shit, I wish my dad got *Playboy* instead," said Tony.

"Yeah and if wishes were turds we'd be up to our necks in shit," said Karl which immediately set off a good round of laughter.

With that ice breaker, the boys put their backpacks to the side and were getting ready to re-enter the cave when Lenny said, "I'm feeling tired, maybe we should come back tomorrow and bring garden spades or something to help with the digging. I think we might need more rope, too."

No one argued with Lenny. They all embraced the idea of calling it a day. They grabbed their backpacks and started to walk across the hollow back towards home. As they departed, something inside the cave, hearing their departure slowly descended away from the small hole at the far end of the cave where it had been sitting, silently listening, watching.....and waiting.

Chapter 7

Tony Fredette was sitting at his small desk staring at his computer screen and its blinking cursor. He was very tired and had removed his glasses to rub his dry, sore eyes. He had been working on his third novel for the past seven hours, and had made little progress. The words weren't working for him tonight. He pushed himself away from the computer and slowly stood up while pushing his lower back with his hands to try and straighten himself out. He went down the stairs and heard the soft music, which was playing from the new surround sound system he had bought with some of the money he received when Hollywood bought the movie rights to his second book. The music was Mozart and the second book was titled, *Falling to Pieces*. It was a horror fiction work about a psychotic murderer who hacks his victims to pieces. Tony was a "hot" writer at the moment. His first work entitled, *No More Daddy,* sold more than 4 million copies and the movie rights also sold. Work on the film version was already underway. His first book was about a little girl who had been molested as a child and grew up to become a serial killer preying upon men who tried to pick her up at singles bars up and down the east coast. His second book was still on the *New York Times* Best Seller list at number two and had sold 3.7 million copies. His latest book was tentatively given the working title, *Pain Killers.*

He had settled down in Logan, Utah, a mid-sized community about an hour and a half north of Salt Lake City. He chose this area because he and his wife loved to ski and explore the natural wonders Utah offered.

Tony quietly tiptoed to the couch and kissed his wife on the top of her head. His wife, Kelly, was five months pregnant. His first wife, Cynthia had died from breast cancer eleven years ago. They had been married for nearly twenty-four years. It had been a beautiful but childless marriage.

Kelly, thirty-one years his junior, had her legs up on the ottoman; her shoes were off and she was in the middle of some serious crocheting. She was radiant. Tony loved her with all his soul. This was going to be their first child after years of trying. The fertility center at UCLA had given them hope and helped them overcome his reluctant sperm. Tony moved around the side of the couch and sat down next to her.

"Are you okay?" she said as she put down her crocheting and stroked his thinning hair.

"Yeah, I'm alright, just a little tired I guess."

"Anything I can do for you?" she said with a smile on her lips.

God, she's got the sexiest lips, he thought. He leaned closer and kissed her firmly. He could smell her hair, her hand lotion, her perfume and he let his kiss linger just a bit so he could take in the whole experience.

As their lips parted, she looked deep into his eyes and said, "Tony I've got dinner in the oven, it will be ready in an hour." She took his left hand and placed it upon her left breast.

"I've got the time if you've got the time big guy," said Kelly as she offered him her sexiest smile.

Tony was aroused by this sexy pregnant woman who wanted him. Besides, she knew how to get his attention. "Once a breast man, always a breast man," responded Tony.

"I've got to save my work upstairs," said Tony.

"Hurry up, I'll be waiting for you," she said as she raised herself from the couch. Looking over her shoulder she winked at him for good measure then turned and headed for the master bedroom.

Tony went back upstairs, taking them two at a time. He sat down at his computer to save his work on his latest novel when his eyes fixed on the computer screen. The screen was filled with the words, Cave from Hell. Cave from Hell. Cave, cave, cave, cave, cave, Cave, Hell, Hell, Hell.

On and on and in a random pattern scrolled the words. The words soon filled the screen. Tony's stomach was suddenly filled with knots. His mind flashed back to a suppressed memory he had from long ago. Terror gripped him. His hand reached for the computer's keyboard. He hit the page-up button. The message from the screen was the same. He hit the page-up button again and again, still the same message. Finally after several more hits upon the page-up button the text of his novel was displayed on the screen. On the bottom right hand side of his computer screen was a blinking icon which noted that he had an urgent e-mail message.

"Tony....Tony....Hurry up!" said Kelly from downstairs. "It's not nice to keep a lady waiting."

"I'll be right there," said Tony trying not to show the fear in his voice. The e-mail message was going to have to wait.

Chapter 8

The portable transistor radio was blaring with the voice of "Crazy Eddie," the morning Deejay at WJOY; "It's the latest and greatest dance craze sweeping the nation. It's Little Eva's big hit song, Locomotion."

It was the third day the boys had been digging in the cave. Their progress was slow and they were already tired. It was five minutes before ten o'clock in the morning. Karl and Lenny were standing outside the cave's entrance discussing the need for additional tools that they could use that would speed up their progress. Tony and Mark were inside the cave digging out the last of the dirt. The hole at the far end of the cave was not any larger than the first day they had entered the cave. At least now, they could stoop inside most of the cave rather than be forced to move around on their stomachs or backs, or in a squatting position. To enter or exit the cave one still had to lie down on one's back and slide in due to the large flat stone which butted up against the cave's entrance.

"You know what we need? We need a crowbar," said Lenny.

"Yeah, that's a good idea. My old man has a couple in the garage. He won't miss one for a few days," said Karl.

"What about a small sledge hammer?" asked Karl?

"Sounds good to me," said Lenny.

"Are you two going to talk all day or are you going to get your asses back in here?" asked the faint but unmistakable voice of Tony from deep inside the cave.

Just then Karl and Lenny heard a distant blast of a horn. After a short pause they heard it again. They looked at one another. Neither boy recognized the sound. Then they heard a third blast of the horn.

"What's that?" asked Lenny.

"Beats me," replied Karl.

Karl bent down and was about to slide back down into the cave when he and Lenny heard a loud bang. The sound startled the birds in the hollow, who noisily took flight. Suddenly the ground shook and Lenny had to reach out to the rock face of the cave's entrance to steady him self as Karl fell on his backside, his legs slipping out from under him. In the cave there were screams of absolute terror.

"Karl..........!"

"Lenny.......Jesus we're going to die."

"Help us, Jesus help us," said the terrorized voices from within the cave.

Inside the cave Mark and Tony had both been thrown down to the floor of the small cave from the violent shaking of the ground. A lantern placed on a small ledge near the middle of the cave had fallen over. Its light was extinguished. Small pieces of the ceiling broke free and fell on Tony and Mark. They became tangled as they quickly scrambled to exit from the cave. Their ears were ringing from the overwhelming concussion of sound which had pressed around them from the walls of the cave. They kicked their way out the cave's entrance knocking Karl down just as he was trying to stand up.

Tony and Mark stood up and looked at Lenny. They both had a wide-eyed look of terror. Tony's lower lip was quivering. Both of the boys' legs were shaking. They each also felt chilled to the bone. Tony swallowed hard and tasted stark fear for the first time in his young life.

Mark spoke first. "What the hell was that, an earthquake or something?"

"Yeah, was it an earthquake?" asked Tony.

"I don't know what it is," said Lenny.

"I think I know what it is," said Karl as he stood up. "It must have been some dynamite set off over at Bremer's Quarry."

"Jesus, we could have been killed in there," said Mark. "That cave could have crushed us both."

"The quarry is almost a mile away and it hasn't caused the cave to collapse yet," said Karl. "What's the matter, are you boys chicken shit or what?"

"Oh yeah, I don't see you sticking your ass in the cave," said Tony.

"Maybe we shouldn't go in the cave any more," said Lenny. "Maybe we should give it up."

"Look, I'll prove to you butt kickers that it's still okay." said Karl as he sat down in front of the cave and began to slide in. "I'm going in and get our stuff and I'll be back out in a minute." He soon disappeared inside the cave.

All three boys looked at each other and didn't say a word but each one silently said a prayer for their friend Karl.

Inside the cave Karl's eyes quickly adjusted to the limited light which barely illuminated the cave's entrance. He quickly began to gather up their tools and hand them out to the boys. After all the tools and the lantern were handed out Karl carefully crept forward, deeper into the cave, to the small hole at the far end of the cave. Karl squinted and noticed there was a crack line stretching outward from the hole. He then noticed several smaller fissure lines radiating away from this crack. Karl realized what this meant. They could now probably break open the hole and make it larger. He looked to the cave's floor and picked up a piece of the fallen ceiling. He tossed it into the small hole and listened for the sound of it hitting somewhere inside. "One thousand one, one thousand two" he whispered aloud.

"Click, click, tick" and then followed by the faint sound of a splash.

Karl turned and headed out of the cave. The boys were waiting anxiously for him to emerge.

"I've got some good news, I think we can break open the hole back there," said Karl as he stood up.

"Are you out of your friggin' mind Karl?" said Mark.

"Look we've all worked our asses off here and I, for one, want to see how deep it is and what's in there" said Karl as he looked into each boy's eyes. They tried to look away but couldn't avoid that look. It was a look that said, "Are you a man or a pussy?" A guy just couldn't back down now.

"Okay! Okay!" declared Tony, "I'm in."

"Me, too," said Lenny.

Now everyone was looking at Mark. He felt their stares. "We just need to be careful that's all. I guess I'm in, too," said a nervous Mark.

Karl slapped Mark on the back. "That's cool Mark, we all knew you wouldn't let us down, right guys?"

Tony and Lenny nodded their agreement.

"How do you think we can make that hole bigger?" asked Lenny.

"Let's grab our stuff and head over to my house and I'll tell you along the way. We're definitely going to need some different tools and a whole lot more rope," said Karl.

Each of the boys picked up their backpacks, tools, rope, and lantern. They all began to head across the hollow when Lenny realized that he left his flashlight inside the entrance of the cave.

"Wait, I forgot my flashlight. I've got to get it," said Lenny as he dropped his backpack and ran back to the cave.

He quickly sat down at the cave entrance and slid inside. Looking to his right he spotted his flashlight. He grabbed it and began to push himself out of the cave when he suddenly had the overwhelming feeling he was being watched from deep inside. He looked towards the hole but couldn't see anything. He still felt he was being watched and the thought terrified him. He quickly kicked himself out of the cave, jumped to his feet and ran to his waiting friends. He decided not to tell them about what he had felt. A guy can't be too careful around his buddies. They wouldn't let up on him if he was showing signs of fear since they all had agreed to continue exploring the cave. He would just put it out of his mind. Quickly joining his friends, he put his backpack on as they all headed away from the cave and out of the woods.

Meanwhile, deep inside the cave from beyond the hole at the far end, something sniffed the air. The now familiar odor of the boys still hung in the dank air of the cave.

He had waited a long time, a very long, long time. He was patient. He would wait; after all they were coming to him.

Chapter 9

Checking the altimeter and his air speed, Captain Mark Pushey adjusted the Boeing 747's angle of descent.

"Miami, this is Delta Heavy, flight 1206 making its final approach," he said.

"Roger Delta Heavy, flight 1206, you're cleared to land on runway 45 E, I repeat cleared to land on runway 45 E, over," said the monotone voice from the flight control tower for Miami International Airport.

"We copy that control tower, we are at 3500 feet, and descending, wheels down and locked, over," said Mark. His co-pilot toggled the passenger cabin bell alarm to ring three times, notifying the flight crew that the plane was beginning the final descent to land.

The co-pilot turned on his cabin microphone and announced; "Flight Crew, please prepare the cabin for landing."

The landing was routine, after all Mark had landed 747s for over fifteen years now. He admired the ease at which this huge plane maneuvered and, above all, he was confident of his ability.

He pulled the huge aircraft into its landing gate, C-34, as his co-pilot shut down the engines. Now he would begin the post flight rundown with his co-pilot before they would exit the plane. Mark was about to remove his headset when he heard a faint voice. It seemed to be calling to him. He couldn't quite make out what it was saying. He reached up and pressed the headphones closer to his ears. The voice of his co-pilot was fading into the background. He recognized this voice as his mind flashed back to a summer day in 1962. In his mind he was standing with Karl, Tony and Lenny across the hollow from the cave they had been working on for nearly a week. The girl was screaming and pulling down on her hair. She was standing in front of their cave and calling out the name of one of her two companions who disappeared into the cave just moments before.

"Eddie, Eddie, please don't scare me like this." No answer. "Come on this isn't funny anymore," said the girl.

The four young boys were hiding across the hollow, behind some low growth scruff pine trees, as they watched her in silence. They cautiously glanced sideways at one another. They could hear each other's breathing.

"Don't go in there," whispered a nervous Mark.

* * * * *

Mark sat in the cockpit and went through the motions of his post flight checklist review. He even responded in the proper manner but somehow his mind was drifting back in time to the start of his worst nightmare.

"Captain", said the Senior Flight attendant, as she placed her right hand upon his right shoulder, "The flight crew will be leaving now."

Her remark and gesture broke Mark's daydream. *Or was it a dream?* he thought. It certainly felt like he had been dreaming. His co-Pilot, Frank Spellman, closed his flight log, removed his headset and hung it overhead on its flight hook. Mark removed his headset and did the same. They stood up and gathered their flight bags, which were stowed in the flight crew's forward storage area. Frank was telling Mark about his daughter's soccer team's success as they exited up the flight ramp. Mark nodded and smiled a lot but his mind was drifting in and out of focus. The daydream was calling to him and he felt a growing need to respond.

Chapter 10

It rained on Thursday. The boys stayed home and played a game of Canasta at Tony's. Later when the rain stopped they rode their bikes over to Karl's house and searched his garage for more rope. They found more than eighty feet of rope sitting on an old trunk in the garage's loft along with an old crowbar and a small sledge hammer. Mark had earlier located some highway flares in his attic. His Dad stored a lot of weird stuff up there according to Mark.

They set out early on Friday for the cave with their new gear.

The boys arrived at the cave around ten thirty in the morning. They quickly set their backpacks down and laid out their tools. Karl lit the lantern.

"Here, you hand me this when I get inside," said Karl as he passed the lantern to Tony.

Karl sat down at the cave entrance and quickly slid inside. He reached out for the lantern Tony handed to him. The other boys took their shovels, small pails, flashlights and candles as they followed him into the cave. It was damper than ever. The rain washed some of the soil they had removed back inside.

"Shit, we're going to have to dig this stuff out again," said Lenny.

"While you guys do that I'll see if I can open that hole back there with the crowbar and the sledge hammer," said Karl.

Karl, squatting down, moved deeper into the cave. For the last ten feet he had to crawl on his belly. He took out his flashlight and examined the rock around the fractured opening. Sure enough, it was just as he remembered; it was cracked in several places. He got to work with the crowbar, poking and prying the rock. His fellow explorers organized an assembly line as they worked to remove the re-deposited dirt. Their voices were muffled by the closeness of the cave. Their work proceeded for the next hour.

Karl worked open a crack in the hardened granite on the right side of the hole. He wedged his crowbar into the crack but he found that he couldn't exert enough leverage to the bar's long handle. He slid back and approached the hole again, this time while lying on his back. He grabbed the crowbar and extended his legs until he could pin them against the cave's wall. Now he had leverage. He strained and pushed the bar with all the strength he had. At first it didn't move. Then Karl could see the fissure opening slightly. He pushed harder. He grunted from the strain. The other boys stopped their digging and turned to look at Karl.

"Come on you son of...," he grunted once more.

A surprisingly small, cracking sound emanated from the fissure as it broke open and a piece of rock tumbled into the darkness beyond the hole. From where the boys were they couldn't hear the rock tumbling down deeper into the cave. But they all heard the faint sound of a splash as the rock struck water deep inside the cave. Karl slid away from the hole and squatted down near the others. Mark shined his flashlight over towards the hole and they all saw that the hole was enlarged by the piece that Karl had broken off. The hole was now about fifteen inches across. Not yet large enough to crawl through but larger nonetheless.

Tony was sticking his stained left index finger into his left nostril when Lenny noticed and said, "Tony we ain't digging enough dirt in this cave, you've got to go nose prospecting, too."

Everyone looked at Tony and started to laugh. Tony was embarrassed so he removed his finger and wiped it on his soiled dungarees.

Mark headed for the cave's entrance.

"I'm hungry. I'm going to have lunch."

"Me, too," said Lenny.

"I'm with you," said Tony.

Karl crawled over to the hole at the back of the cave and left his tools there as he grabbed his flashlight and then the lantern which was on a small ledge on the left side of the cave. He blew out the lantern and exited the cave.

Inside the cave a long pale, white skinned arm came through the hole at the far end of the cave. It was covered with hair. It had the shape of a human arm, but the hand on the end of that arm was somehow different. The fingers were all nearly the same length, and the palm was much darker, heavily creased and thickly padded. The hand reached around the surface of the cave near the hole. It was searching, touching, and then the hand and arm withdrew. From the deep darkness a sniffing sound could be heard coming from just beyond the hole. Yet no one was inside the cave to see that arm, that hand or to hear the sniffing. The boys were outside the cave enjoying their lunch.

Chapter 11

Mark sat in his hotel room at the Doubletree Inn just off the airport beltway. The flight from London to N.Y. then on to Miami had been routine. He loosened his tie and sat down in the deep padded chair near the writing desk in his room. He felt very tired. Perhaps he would just watch a little television and relax. He pointed the TV remote, which was in his right hand at the television. The TV screen quickly displayed the Doubletree greeting screen which announced the dining specials offered for that night in the Caribbean Room restaurant located across the street. He clicked his remote controller until he found the CNN channel. He turned up the volume and then placed the remote on the writing desk as he settled deeper into the chair.

The last thing Mark remembered is the CNN announcer's voice saying, "And now in our lifestyles report we will take a look at ...." Mark was fast asleep. It wasn't long before his earlier daydream returned.

"Don't go in there," he whispered to no one in the hotel room.

* * * * *

The boys picked a sunny spot several feet from the cave's entrance to sit down and have their lunch.

Lenny turned on his portable radio. The announcer on station WHDH was delivering a sports report.

"The Red Sox will be playing an afternoon game today right here on WHDH. The Sox will be facing the Baltimore Orioles who are in Bean Town for a three game visit to Fenway Park. The Sox will be starting Bill Monbouquette in today's afternoon game. Hear all the action brought to you by Red Sox announcer, Curt Gowdy, starting with the pre-game show, beginning at twelve forty-five."

Lenny turned down the radio's volume.

"How big do you think the cave is beyond that hole, Karl?" asked Tony.

"Don't know."

"Did I hear a splash when that rock fell into the hole?" asked Lenny.

"Yeah, I heard it, too," said Mark.

"I think there's some kind of pool of water at the bottom of the area beyond the hole," said Karl.

"Is the cave beyond the hole deep?" asked Mark.

"How would I know Sherlock, I ain't never been inside there before, in case you hadn't noticed," said Karl mockingly.

"Karl, did you find out about the blasting at the quarry?" asked Lenny.

"Uh, huh, my old man says the quarry blasts every Wednesday morning. He says they blow up a huge chunk of the quarry wall so they can break the rocks down in their stone crusher. He also says he is a good friend of the guy who sets the dynamite charges. They were in the National Guard or something. He says the guy knows a lot of neat shit about the rocks and underground stuff around here."

"We sure as shit don't want to be in that cave when they're blowing stuff up at the quarry," said Tony.

"Damn right," said Mark.

The boys all agreed on this point. Soon they were discussing the latest exploits of the Boston Red Sox, Lenny's favorite team. Tony said he was a New York Yankee fan just to tweak his good friend Lenny. Eventually their conversation drifted to a favorite topic, girls.

"Hey, Karl, who's going to have the biggest set when we go back to school?" asked Tony.

"I don't know but I sure hope all the girls add a few inches."

"I bet that Angela Weddington leads the pack," said Mark.

"No way, if anybody is going to bust out it's going to be Charlene Leclaire," said Lenny, oblivious to the obvious pun.

"How can you be so sure?" said Tony.

"Easy, I just look at their older sisters and Charlene's older sister, Gloria, must be a 44 something, I mean she's huge."

"Geeze, I never thought about that, man you're probably right," said Tony.

"What do you say we get back to work guys and save the hornies for later? When we go back home tonight I'll see if I can sneak an old copy of my old man's *Playboy Magazine* and bring it over to Mark's house when we tent out tonight," said Karl.

Everyone's eyes lit up at the prospect of exploring another *Playboy*.

"Man, summer just can't get any better than this," said Mark, as the other boys nodded their agreement.

They soon re-entered and finished diggingout the remaining soil from the dank, cave floor. Karl now crept deeper towards the hole. Taking the crowbar he left nearby, he began to explore the remaining crevices around the hole. He chipped away at some smaller cracks in the surface opening the hole just a small bit. Soon Karl, despite the cool damp temperature of the cave, was sweating profusely. He crept back and sat down. Lenny took the crowbar and took Karl's place as he, too, tried to widen the opening.

"Hey, Karl, hand me the sledge hammer will you?" said Lenny.

"Here!"

Lenny took the hammer. Lying on his back near the hole he swung the hammer overhead into the left side of the hole. Two, three times he struck the hammer firmly against the rock surface. Sparks emitted with each strike of the hammer. The noise reverberated around the cave.

"Man, did you smell anything coming out from this hole?" asked Lenny.

"Nothing unusual," said Karl.

"Well, it smells like dog shit or something."

"I can smell it now, too," said Mark.

"Yeah, like dog shit," said Tony.

Lenny gripped the hammer and gave it a mighty swing as he struck at the left side of the hole again. A piece of rock gave way and fell into the hole. They all heard the now familiar splash.

Karl took the lantern from the small ledge, on the right side. He crept up towards Lenny while holding the lantern up to shed more light on the hole.

"Mark, can you see how big the hole is?" asked Karl.

"Yeah, I can, so what?"

"Do you think you can squeeze into it?"

"Are you nuts? I'm not squeezing into that hole!"

"I don't mean all the way in, just enough to look inside and tell us what you see."

Mark looked at the other guys and felt his stomach tighten with a knot of fear. He felt a chill run up and down his spine. However, Mark wasn't going to show any fear, not now, not ever.

"Yeah, I'll check it out. Just get out of my way," said Mark.

He reached for the coil of rope setting near the cave wall and tied a loop around his waist. He handed the coil to Karl and said, "Here, I want you to hold this tight in case something happens."

Karl understood, and took the rope from Mark. He wrapped it around his waist and tied it firmly twice for good measure. The other boys moved out of Mark's way and Tony handed him his flashlight. Hitching up his dungarees, Mark headed for the hole at the rear of the cave. He crept up to the hole on his elbows. He turned on the flashlight and shone it into the darkness beyond the hole—nothing but darkness. Mark inched closer. He reached his right arm into the hole and pushed his body forward in a kind of crawling motion propelled only by his feet. Soon his head and shoulders were through. They filled the hole. There was nothing but silence. Mark said nothing.

"What do you think he sees in there?" asked Tony, his nose filled to the second knuckle by his favorite finger.

"Shush," said Karl as he signaled for quiet.

They could see Mark's body moving as he shifted his feet.

Mark looked around slowly. The flashlight could only clearly illuminate about fifty feet into the darkness. Mark noticed just inside the opening and about five feet below it was a ledge about three feet across jutting out from the wall of this inner cave. The ledge descended around and down from the inner wall of the cave and disappeared into the darkness below. It resembled a kind of circular stairway. This new cave had a ceiling about twenty feet above Mark's head. It was covered with stalagtites of various lengths. The light from the flashlight barely reached across this inner cave. Mark guessed the cave was around eighty or a hundred feet across. Mark shone the light down to see if he could see the water the falling rocks splashed into. His flashlight couldn't even reach to the bottom of the cave. This was not a good sign.

Mark noticed how quiet the inner cave was. *Except, what was that sound?* Mark tried to concentrate on the sound as he moved the flashlight's light about.

Wait, what is that? he thought. *About fifty feet down the spiraling ledge it looks like something white. No, several things. They're all white. I can't quite make them out. Are they bones?* he thought.

"Karl, what could be taking him so long?" asked an increasingly nervous Tony.

Before Karl could answer Mark suddenly seemed to be moving more vigorously. They all just stared at Mark's back.

Mark now realized that what he was looking at was a small pile of bones. As his eyes fixed on the bones his ears picked up on a distant sound. The sound seemed to be coming from below. To Mark it sounded like slow, deep breathing. He didn't dare shine his light down. Mark now wanted to get out of this opening and out of the cave. A wave of fear was setting in and Mark could feel himself tighten up. He wiggled himself back out of the hole.

"What did you see?" said Karl as Mark turned to look into the faces of his friends.

"It's huge in there, its deep and it looks like there's a kind of ramp or path that leads down into the bottom. I saw something else. I saw a pile of bones!"

Karl saw in his friend's eyes...this was no bull shit, Mark was telling the truth. Karl took the sledge hammer from Lenny and slid up to the hole. He began to whack away at the crevices around the hole. Finally, after several good strikes a huge chunk broke away and tumbled into the hole.

"Splash," came back the familiar sound. Now everyone stared at the hole. It was much larger. Any one of them, even a large man, could now easily fit through. Karl turned back and looked at his friends. They were looking ahead stunned except for Mark. He was motioning to Karl to move outside the cave. He held his index finger up to his lips. He didn't want to say out loud why he wanted to leave the cave but Karl could tell that Mark wanted to leave immediately. Karl took the hint.

"Hey, guys, let's take a breather outside for awhile," said Karl.

Lenny had left his portable radio next to his backpack. As the boys headed out of the cave they could hear the radio playing.

No one needed to be persuaded as they each headed out of the cave. Lenny was the first to notice the three pairs of legs standing at the cave's entrance. He stood up squinting into the light as he noticed two older boys and a girl were standing there looking at the cave's entrance. The boys were at least seventeen and the girl was older than Lenny and his friends so he guessed her age to be maybe sixteen. One of the boys was smoking a cigarette, which hung loosely from his lips.

In a moment all of the guys were out of the cave. They looked quite the sight. Karl immediately noticed some of their backpacks had been rifled through. He figured it had to be these two dorks and their main squeeze. These older boys wore blue dungarees and white tee shirts and black Converse sneakers. They each had their hair slicked back into duck's ass hairdos. The girl was a shapely blonde with a cold sore on her lower lip. She wore a madras blouse pulled up and tied off high above the waist, cut off dungaree shorts and white canvas tennis sneakers with no socks. She had a good tan and a "come hither" smile.

The taller and meaner looking of the two boys spoke first.

"What are you pussies doing in our cave?"

"Yeah, who said you could explore our cave and leave your shit everywhere?" said his partner.

The girl said nothing but she was plainly looking over each of the boys with a lingering look.

Mark spoke up. "We didn't see anybody's name on the cave so we decided to check it out."

Karl was about to say something that would get them all into trouble with these older boys but Lenny shot him a glance that said not to. Tony was clearly quaking in his sneakers.

The boy smoking the cigarette dropped it to the ground and stomped it out.

"I'd better check the cave out and see if you assholes messed it up. Eddie here is going to keep his eye on you, so don't think you can run away. If we have to chase you, we'll catch you and maybe cut your nuts off or something," he sneered.

Eddie laughed and the girl even smiled.

He sat down and was about to slide into the cave when he reached over to Mark and took the flashlight out of his hand. He then entered the cave. They all could hear him moving deeper into the cave. A muffled sound followed by a crash reverberated towards them.

Several moments passed and there was no further sound coming from the cave. Eddie bent down and shouted into the cave.

"Johnny....hey Johnny....what do you see in there, man?"

No answer from inside the cave.

"Johnny..... c'mon, speak to me man!" said Eddie. There was a tinge of nervousness in his voice.

The girl looked concerned but not overly anxious. Perhaps these two had played pranks on her before.

"I'm going in, you wait out here," he said to the girl. He sat down and began to slide into the cave when all of a sudden he just vanished into the cave, like he had been pulled into the cave. He screamed at the top of his lungs.

"Jesus, What are you, oh no......oh shit...." He screamed again only this time it was a scream of utter terror.

"Ayeieeeee......." a loud scream echoed from deep inside the cave followed by a fading, dragging noise. Suddenly, even that noise stopped.

Lenny and the other boys backed away from the cave's entrance. Tony turned and started to run. The others quickly followed. They sprinted across the hollow.

The girl shouted at them.

"Please help me....help my friends.... Please...." her voice trailed after them.

When they reached the low growth pine stand at the opposite side of the hollow they all stopped and looked back at the girl standing in front of the cave entrance. She was pacing back and forth in front of the cave. She was saying something into the cave. She pulled at her hair. She looked across the hollow in their direction. They each believed she couldn't see them from where they now were hiding.

"Eddie, Eddie, please, you have to stop scaring me like this." No answer. "Come on, this isn't funny anymore," said the girl.

"Don't go in there," whispered a terrorized Mark.

Chapter 12

Their lovemaking was something very special to Tony and Kelly. They each had read dozens of books on the subject. They were both into body massages, oils, scented candles and saunas. Kelly liked her love making to be spontaneous and to last a long, long time. She wanted to make love sometimes in public places. She enjoyed the risk. She needed a tender lover and she rewarded Tony for his tenderness with a passion that knew no boundaries.

Tony felt their sex life was beyond a ten. Tony responded to her needs because he liked her to be in charge. At first Tony was uncomfortable making love in the car outside the movie theater at the mall, which was the first time they made love in a public place. He just couldn't relax. Later on, after episodes in their back yard, on a hotel balcony, on the deck of the cruise ship last summer and that time at the 4th of July fireworks under that blanket, with all those people around. Well, Tony had to admit it was very good, no, it was damn good!

Tony's greatest sexual pleasure was derived from giving Kelly pleasure. He oftentimes wondered if he was good enough for her.

And now they were going to have a baby. Tony Fredette was going to be a father at age sixty-three. Tony felt his life was complete.

He was about to step into the bedroom. Kelly lit several candles. Their faint light flickered across the room. Kelly was standing with her back to him in front of the full length mirrors which covered the outside of her closet doors. She wore white lace-topped stockings, a white garter belt and white patent leather heels, and nothing else!

She was humming a song and gently swaying her hips as she slowly caressed her body with her exploring hands.

Tony stood in the bedroom doorway and watched Kelly for a moment. He listened to her humming and after a moment he recognized the tune. She was humming the Madonna song, *Like a Virgin.*

Tony slowly stepped towards Kelly. She saw him in the reflection in the mirror and smiled that sexy smile of hers.

"Here's my lover. The look on your face is priceless," whispered Kelly. His aroused look was serving as a huge turn on for her.

He reached around her from behind and pulled her close to him. He kissed her on the nape of her neck several times as she tilted her neck back and forth. She continued to move her hips and softly hum the tune. They were bound this way for nearly a minute when she turned around.

"Am I still sexy, Tony? Do you still find me attractive even though my stomach is so swollen?" she whispered. "Will you still find me sexy after the baby is born when I lose my shape and my hips are wider than a doorway?" she pouted.

Tony looked deep into her eyes and smiled.

"Kelly, you are my lover, my wife and my best friend. You will always be sexy to me. I just hope that you'll have time for me, I mean us, you know, after the baby."

Kelly pushed him back towards the bed and made him sit down. She knelt down and removed his shoes and socks and then tugged at his belt, she went on to remove his pants. Kelly stood up and reached over to the pillow and from beneath it she removed a can of whipped cream. Tony took one look at the can and began to laugh. Kelly laughed along as she now stood before Tony.

"Tony, have I told you about this story I read in......"

Their love making was slow as each watched out for the other's needs. Kelly was full of energy tonight. As for Tony, he was lost in bliss.

Meanwhile, the candles had burned down quite a bit.

Tony began to feel a little light headed. The room reminded him of something from his past.

Where is he? It's dark. He's sweating scared. He can see a girl standing over near the… the…..Cave! But what is she doing there? His mind is in a swirl. *She's screaming but Tony can't hear her. She is looking around. She is looking in his direction. Does she see him?* His powerful thoughts are quickly consuming him.

She looks terrified. Tony feels helpless.

She kneels down in front of the cave opening. She shouldn't do that.

Tony's mind is blaring. *Get Away, Get Away! Hurry up. Run!*

She reaches an arm into the cave. Suddenly his mind slows everything down. Tony sees an albino white and powerful hand take her arm and now she is slowly being pulled into the cave. She tries to stop from being pulled inside. She reaches out with her other arm but it, too, is grabbed by another evil, menacing hand. She turns her head and Tony can see her scream but still he hears nothing. She is being dragged on her stomach down into the cave. Her legs bend as her heels slam against the rock at the cave entrance. Blood splatters as her white canvas sneaker ricochets off her left foot and tumbles to the ground several feet in front of the cave.

Breaking through his haze, Tony barely hears a voice calling to him. He knows this voice. Suddenly the words are coming through loud and clear, just as the cave and the dreamscape rapidly fade from his mind.

"Tony, please stop, you're hurting me. Tony, please you're hurting me. Tony, don't you hear me?" Kelly shouts at him.

Tony looked down at her and saw that he was pushing down on Kelly's shoulders and that his fingers were pressing into her flesh. The look in her eyes was clear. Tony had scared her. He released her and rolled to the side of the bed. He sat there with his head in his hands trying to hold back his tears. He felt ashamed. He couldn't look at Kelly right now.

She moved quickly to his side.

"Hey, Tony, it's okay. You kind of scared me. I've never seen you like that. You were screaming; "Get away. Get away!" It was like you were having a nightmare or something. Are you all right?"

Tony shook his head, no.

"Tony, what's the matter?"

"I don't know, Kelly. I'm sort of confused right now. It felt like a panic attack or something."

Kelly placed her arms around Tony and kissed his ear.

"Maybe we could," but before she could say any more he had picked up his pants and shirt and headed out the bedroom door. She heard him head up the stairs to his computer. She reached up and massaged her neck muscles. They were tender and sore.

Upstairs Tony hit his keyboard's enter key and noticed the e-mail icon still blinking. He sat down and typed his way into his e-mail directory and called up the new message.

It was from his old boyhood friend, Lenny Drew. He hadn't heard from him in years. His mind momentarily caught a fleeting memory from the past—a memory that had been hidden for many years.

The message was simple and ominous.

"Mark says, don't go in there.....Don't go in there."

* * * * *

All of the boys stood frozen with fear.

They saw the girl kneel down and reach into the front of the cave when all of a sudden something reached out for her arm and pulled her violently into the cave. They saw her struggle and kick her feet about as she quickly disappeared from their sight. The last thing they saw was the heel of her left foot strike hard against the flat rock at the front of the cave. Now a splash of blood darkens her white canvas sneaker, knocked from her foot as it rebounded away from the cave's entrance.

From across the hollow the sound of music coming from Lenny's radio could be heard. The Red Soxs game must have ended and Bobby Vinton's hit song "Roses are Red" was playing.

Lenny felt like he was suffocating, his chest was tight and he couldn't quite draw a breath. He looked at his friends and saw that they were experiencing the same distress. Suddenly from the cave came a scream, a scream of absolute unbridled terror. The gut-wrenching scream reached all the way across the hollow and pierced their frozen daze.

There was no mistaking that scream, it came from her.

Now only silence from the cave!

The only sound that each boy now heard was the sound of each other's breathing. There wasn't even a breeze to stir the trees. The tension was unbearable.

Finally Lenny spoke.

"Do you think they're faking it, like you know a joke or something?" His voice trailed off.

"I don't think this a joke," said Mark.

"Me either," said Tony.

"It's no practical joke," said Karl. "It's real all right."

"What in hell is going on?" asked Lenny.

There was no answer from any of the boys.

Suddenly Karl stepped forward and pushed the bushes aside. He slowly crept towards the cave.

"Are you friggin' crazy?" whispered Tony.

Karl looked back at the boys and put one finger to his lips signaling them to keep quiet and then he gestured for them to stay put.

"He is crazy, the son-of-a-bitch is out of his mind," whispered Tony.

Mark gave Tony a firm and unmistakable stare and then he whispered, "Shut your asshole, Tony."

Karl crept closer, stopping every few steps and listening, never taking his eyes away from the entrance to the cave. He was very close now. Without looking down, he reached and picked up the sneaker that the girl had been wearing just minutes ago. He then slowly moved diagonally over to left side of the cave's entrance. Karl then picked up a flashlight which had been dropped earlier and pointed it into the cave.

His friends stiffened when they saw him shine the flashlight into the cave.

Karl quickly grabbed the boys' backpacks, then Lenny's radio before he sprinted across the hollow. He kept stealing glances over his shoulder in the direction of the cave's entrance as he ran. It seemed that he might be afraid that something or someone might just slither out of that cave and begin to chase after him.

Huffing and puffing he dropped the backpacks to the ground after reaching his friends. He also handed Lenny his radio.

"Let's get the fuck out of here, pronto," said Karl.

No one needed further prodding. They each grabbed their backpacks and immediately broke into a full run along the path that would take them clear of the woods. They looked over their shoulders frequently as they ran from the terror they had all just experienced at the cave. After nearly a half hour they exited from the woods at a point just beyond the unfinished end of Pine Street. They stopped and bent over with cramps from the running and from the fear that was still with them. As they panted, they turned to face the woods. They were just being cautious.

Karl pulled the soiled and formerly white sneaker from under his belt where he had stuffed it just before the exodus from the hollow.

"Look, it's stained with blood, her blood," said Karl as he handed it to Lenny.

Lenny took it from Karl and slowly turned it over to look at it from every possible angle. Lenny then handed it to Mark who after a moment handed it over to Tony who didn't want anything to do with the sneaker as he tossed it at Karl like it was a "Hot Potato."

"They're all dead, aren't they?" said Mark looking at the others.

No one disagreed.

Chapter 13

Mark awoke from his troubled sleep. He had a splitting head-ache. The TV was still on, turned to CNN. Picking up the remote control, he turned the TV off.

Mark turned on a nearby light and began to look for his shaving kit. He spotted it in the corner. Retrieving it, he opened it and re-moved a small bottle of aspirin. Mark took out one tablet. Heading into the bathroom, he turned on the faucet and filled a drinking glass with cold water. He swallowed the pill with one small sip. Mark looked into the bathroom mirror and saw his own face staring back at him. But wait—there's something else. Over his right shoulder, he detected a shape slowly coming into focus. Mark rubbed his eyes and then splashed some water onto his face. When he looked up again the shape is still there. Mark now recognized the mysterious specter. It was his childhood friend, Karl Sweeney.

"Mark, we need to talk man."

Mark heard Karl's voice clearly. "This must be a dream," Mark said out loud.

"So you think this is a dream, do you?" asked Karl. "Well it's no dream old buddy. I've come to warn you. You, Tony and Lenny are in some serious danger."

"You're not real. This is just a nightmare and I'll wake up soon....," argued Mark.

"Don't interrupt me. I don't know how much longer I can hold on here. You see, the cave has been opened again, and we both know what that means. That monster is back on the loose. You do remember Ne Wha Ta?"

"Yeah, I remember Ne Wha Ta. The old Indian told us the name of that beast. Ne Wha Ta, one who is cursed to live underground because he ate human flesh."

"You remember all the things he did?"

"You bet I do."

"Well, he's back and this time he's really pissed off."

"Look," said Karl's specter as he slowly turned his head. Mark didn't want to turn around so he fixed his eyes on the bathroom mirror. Karl's top back portion of his head was blown away exposing bits of his scalp with shreds of hair and dried blood hanging down like stains of sweat soaked hair.

"He made me do this, Mark."

"Are you telling me you're dead and that monster killed you?"

"I'm dead all right and he made me do it to myself."

"When, how? What happened to your eyes?" asked Mark.

Karl's image was starting to fade away. Mark turned around and only saw a faint mist lingering in the air in front of the shower curtain.

Mark looked down at his watch. It read 1:47 in the morning. He was still unsure of what just happened. He headed out of the bathroom back into the bedroom. There, over by his bed on the nightstand, was a blinking red light. It was the telephone light telling him he has a message. Sitting on the side of the bed, he turned on the nightstand light. Mark picked up the phone and dialed seven, then his room number in order to listen for the phone message. There is a momentary pause.

"You have one message," said the recorded voice.

"The message was received at 1:45 a.m. If you wish to listen to the message dial one, now."

Mark touched the number one on the telephone pad. There was a click and then the message began. "Mark, It's back, you've gotta believe me, man."

It's the voice of Karl.

Mark listened for a moment longer but the line soon went dead. No dial tone, nothing. He pushed down on the disconnect button several times, still no dial tone. He hung the phone up. He then picked it up again and dialed 0 for the front desk. It was no use, the phone was not working. Mark now realized the phone was not going to work tonight. He decided he didn't want to go to sleep tonight. He had a lot on his mind right now. His adrenaline was dialed way, way up. Sleep was out of the question.

Mark reached for the TV remote control to turn the TV back on.

"That's good," said Mark to the empty room.

He flipped through the TV channels as he leaned back against the headboard of the bed. This was going to be a long night. Mark knew he was going to have to call the airline before five a.m. to tell them that he was not feeling well and they would have to assign a replacement pilot to take his flight assignment for today. He knew he couldn't take a chance he would experience spectral apparitions during his flight. His passengers were his responsibility and he would never knowingly put them at risk.

I think Karl still lives in Vermont, or maybe he's moved! thought Mark. *I'll call Dad in the morning. He'll know.*

Mark hadn't spoken with his dad in over two months. He missed his father, especially after his mother died two years ago. He tried to call as often as he could but somehow he kept forgetting. Being single and an airline pilot was at times a lonely way of life. He had his circle of friends but nothing like the friends he had when he was young. Friends who would do anything for one another, no questions asked. As for women, Mark found it difficult to establish any kind of relationship. Usually he kept people at a distance. His pilot's career had been extended twice before due to his exceptional flight record. Now he was approaching sixty-two years of age. He decided to retire when he reached 62. His birthday and retirement were less than two months away. Time felt like it was speeding up but now these messages were changing everything.

Although he valued his privacy, Mark had secrets, dark, deadly secrets. Mark was not about to allow anyone to learn what happened to him during the summer of 1962. His nightmares were his burden, one he carried alone.

Yes, sir, all mine! thought Mark.

* * * * *

"Listen guys, we can't tell anyone what we saw back there," said Lenny.

"Lenny's right," said Karl, "If we tell anyone what we saw, they'll blame us."

"What about our stuff we left behind? Sooner or later someone's going to be looking for those two guys and girl. When they find their bodies they'll find our stuff and that's when the shit's going to hit the fan for all of us!" said a panicked Tony.

"Look, I didn't want to say anything to you guys just yet, but you know when I used the flashlight to look in the cave? Well, I didn't see any bodies. There were some drag marks on the floor of the cave but I sure didn't see three bodies," said Karl.

"Where did the bodies go, if they're not in the cave?" asked Lenny.

"They were taken into the back cave through the hole we've been working on, that's the only place they could be," said Mark.

"Look, we need some time to think this through," said Karl as he hitched up his backpack. "Let's meet over at Mark's house after supper. We'll camp out in his tent and try to figure out something, okay?"

Without a word each boy nodded their agreement. They picked up their backpacks and set off for home in different directions, each carrying a heavier burden than when they left for the cave that morning.

Chapter 14

Lenny returned home and quietly went to his room. On the way he grabbed a bath towel from the hall closet. In his room he removed his dirty clothes, balled them up, and tossed them on the floor at the foot of his bed. He wrapped himself with the bath towel and headed into the bathroom and began to fill up the bathtub with warm water.

Lenny's mother entered the house from the back yard through the door off the kitchen. She had been outside hanging up clothes. She heard the water running in the bathroom. Putting the empty clothesbasket down on the kitchen table and wiping her hands out of habit, she headed for the bathroom. The bathroom door was closed. Lenny's mom decided a couple of years ago she needed to respect her son's privacy. She listened at the door for a moment and then she gently knocked on the door. After a moment the door opened just a crack. Lenny looked up at her from behind the door.

"Lenny, you're home early today?" asked his mother.

"Uh-huh," answered Lenny.

"You're taking a bath in the middle of the day is a bit of a surprise. Is everything all right?"

"I'm okay."

"We'll then, if you're okay and you want to take a bath, I suppose that it's quite all right. Now young man, just where did you leave your dirty clothes?"

"In my room, on the floor!" said Lenny as he gazed down at his feet.

"Just as I imagined, Lenny you know I expect you to help around this house in any way you can. I shouldn't have to remind you that dirty clothes belong in the clothes hamper. After your bath, I want you to march back into your room, pick up those dirty clothes, and put them into the hamper."

"I will Mom, I promise. Oh, Mom, the guys and me are going over to Mark's house to sleep over in his back yard tent. I told him it would be okay. It is okay, right Mom?"

"You'll have to take that up with your father when he gets home from work. If it's fine with him it will be fine with me."

Lenny closed the bathroom door. He could hear his mother's steps lead away from the bathroom. He checked the bathtub. It was nearly filled to the level he wanted. Next he checked the temperature. The water was too cold. Lenny adjusted the tub water handles to draw warmer water. It was going to be ready any moment now.

Lenny's mother went to her bedroom and tiptoed over to the baby's bassinet. She looked in on the newest member of the Drew household, a baby girl named Karen. Karen was seven months old. The baby was sleeping soundly. Mrs. Drew smiled warmly. She didn't know it yet but Karen and Lenny were going to have another sibling, an as yet unnamed boy. Lenny's Mother was a couple of weeks pregnant.

She left the bedroom and quietly walked over to the bathroom door and knocked quietly.

"Father Campbell called earlier asking if you could serve at a wedding mass this coming Saturday."

Lenny was already into the tub.

"I'll call him after I get out of the tub."

"Call him after you pick up your dirty clothes," reminded his mother.

"I will," replied Lenny.

She turned and headed back to the kitchen.

Lenny sat in the warm water of the tub on a seasonably warm day and yet he shivered from head to toe. His lips quivered and his teeth chattered. Lenny turned the hot water faucet on to try to further heat up the water.

Lenny's mind now drifted back to the events of the week. What had started out to be a lark, exploring an unknown cave, had turned into something horrifying.

The water kept slowly filling the tub.

Lenny tried to focus upon what he and his friends had seen today. He tried to find an explanation but none could be found except what his eyes and ears had plainly etched into his memory.

There was something else that drifted in and out of focus on the very edges of his memory. Something that would add to his understanding of what he had witnessed today. The faint memory eluded him.

The water level of the tub continued to rise.

Lenny heard a voice. Not a voice in the room with him. Not a voice in the hallway or even outside. This voice came to Lenny from the inside, the inside of his mind. Lenny kept trying to focus on this voice like one who is trying to pick up a distant radio signal. With effort, the voice came into focus.

"You were in my cave again today." The voice was gravely. It felt angry and willful.

Lenny didn't try to answer but he somehow knew that the voice understood.

"You brought me an offering. I am pleased. You and the others are under my protection now. Nothing of this earth, beneath it or above it can harm you. Your enemy will be my enemy. Your friends will be my friends."

"I don't know what you are talking about," said Lenny in a loud whisper.

"I will reveal myself to each of you in time. For now I only need you to know that I am here and I will be watching, listening and learning, especially learning. I have been out of contact with you humans for a long time. I must leave you now, one of the male humans is about to awaken. I haven't eaten such flesh in a very, long, time."

Lenny now felt a new terror more frightening than anything he had experienced yet. There was a creature, a menacing monster that reached across a large distance, perhaps three miles or more and visited Lenny in his mind. Lenny knew beyond a shadow of a doubt that what he heard or thought, whichever it was, was real.

"Did this creature also speak to the guys?" whispered a nervous Lenny.

Lenny suddenly noticed that the water level of his bathtub had risen to the brim of the tub and was about to spill over. Lenny shut off the hot water and just sat in the tub staring straight ahead. His mind was bouncing off the walls.

"What have we done?" he stammered.

* * * * *

It was early Tuesday morning.

Lenny's radio alarm clock kicked into gear at 5:45 a.m. The radio personality was droning on that lucky caller number seven would win a free pair of tickets to see the Stones 50th Reunion Tour. The show was coming up in just a few short weeks at the TD Bank North Center. Lenny reached out from under the covers and hit the snooze bar to receive five more minutes of twilight sleep before the radio alarm clock kicked into gear once more. Eventually the snooze bar interrupted several abbreviated sleep cycles before Lenny decided to get out of bed.

Lenny rubbed his weepy eyes as he dragged himself off to the bathroom. After showering, shaving and brushing his teeth, Lenny exited the steamy bathroom and headed to the kitchen in search of some coffee. With coffee cup in hand and wearing his favorite bathrobe, he opened his front door and picked up today's edition of the *Boston Globe* from the floor.

Lenny barely scanned the newspaper while he dressed and packed for his trip to Vermont. He called his office and dialed into his voice mail. He changed his voice mail message to indicate he would be away on unexpected business and would be back on the following Monday. He would have nearly a full week to carefully check into things. He was about to embark upon a trip that would have him revisit some of the most horrifying memories a young boy could have kept secret.

Lenny also dialed into his boss's voice mail and left him a message he had to be away on family business. Something personal had suddenly come up that required his immediate attention. Lenny promised he would check in each day for messages from his business clients.

Later, Lenny locked the door to his condo and took the elevator to the basement where his car was parked. Lenny hardly ever had the need to drive a car in Boston, yet he kept his car more out of attachment then anything else. Lenny drove a fully restored 1957 Ford "Baby" Thunderbird. It was a hardtop, black with a black and white leather interior.

Lenny carefully pulled his classic car out onto Storrow Drive heading towards the upper deck of Interstate 93, leading north into New Hampshire. Just south of the City of Concord, New Hampshire, Lenny picked up Interstate 89 and followed it northward, straight into Vermont.

Lenny was going home.

Chapter 15

Lenny decided he would leave his bicycle at home and walk to Mark's house. He filled his backpack with extra socks, a couple of comic books, Red Sox trading cards, some candy he had been saving, along with his new transistor radio his grandmother bought him last Christmas and of course, his toothbrush. He left his backpack in the front hallway and went off in search of his mother and baby sister.

Lenny played with his new baby sister while his mother did the dishes from supper. In a rare instance, his father wiped the dishes, then headed out to the back yard with a six pack of beer to read the paper.

Lenny stood at the screened back door and said, "I'll be seeing you, Dad. I'm heading over to Mark's house to sleep over in his back yard tent tonight."

"Uh huh," said his Father as he opened his first can of beer and took a long swallow.

Lenny knew his dad was going to put away a six pack and more tonight. His dad usually drank heavily when he was quiet and tonight he hadn't said a word at dinner or even after he helped with the dishes. Lenny was glad he wouldn't be home so his father could find an excuse to beat on him.

Lenny went to the bathroom door to look in on his mother, who was changing the baby's diaper. It smelled really bad. Lenny wrinkled his nose at the foul odor.

The baby's legs were kicking furiously. His mother was struggling with the diaper and the diaper pins.

"Mom, I'm going over to Mark's house now. I'll see you some-time in the morning, maybe around ten o'clock."

"Did you clear this with your father, young man?"

"Dad said I was to say hi to Mark's parents." He had just lied to his mother. Lenny hated to lie to her. He knew he had to regroup with his buddies and tell them about what happened during his bath. They just had to make a plan, and soon.

"That is not what I asked you, Lenny Drew."

"Ah, Mom," he said with his most favored hound dog look.

"Come here and kiss your little sister," said his mother with a fresh, warm smile.

Lenny poked his head in the door and kissed his sister on the side of her chubby little cheek. She smelled baby fresh. She looked up at Lenny and broke into a wide smile as she began to kick away once more. She made sounds like, "yeh, yeh, yeh...."

"She loves you very much, Lenny"

"I love her bunches and bunches and more," said Lenny.

With that, Lenny stood upon his tiptoes to kiss his mother. She bent down and took his kiss on her left cheek. Lenny then scam-pered down the hallway, grabbed his backpack and burst out the front door. Lenny's mom held the baby in her arms as she looked out at Lenny skipping down the street. She touched her left cheek where he kissed her just moments before. Lenny always touched her heart in a special way.

After a short walk down the street, followed by a turn through a shortcut through old man Gauthier's yard, Lenny reached Mark's house.

Lenny waved to Mark's mom and dad who were sitting on the front porch.

"My parents said to say hi, Mr. and Mrs. Pushey."

"Say hello for us to your parents will you, Lenny?" answered Mark's parents.

"I will."

Lenny hurried out to the Pushey's back yard. He entered the tent and found Tony and Mark were already there. They had worried looks on their faces.

"Guys, what's the matter?"

"Karl's father found out Karl was using some of his stuff for our work in the cave. He wanted Karl to put it back. He can't cause some of the stuff is still up at the cave; maybe even inside," said Mark.

"Karl's father thinks Karl lost the stuff or sold it or something—anyway he beat the shit out him," said Tony.

"How do you know all this?" said a worried Lenny.

"I was going to pick up Karl on my way over here but when I got to his house I could hear the hollering from outside. I heard some whacks and something crash or break on the floor. His Dad called Karl some really bad names and then I heard Karl hollering for his dad to stop. It got real quiet then. Except for the whacks like Karl was being hit by his old man's belt. You know his old man takes a belt to him sometimes. I guess this is one of them times," said a saddened Tony.

"Sheeeeeit," whistled Lenny.

"What do we do now?" said Mark.

"We do nothing until we can meet with Karl," asserted Lenny.

"But what if he's grounded for a week, or a month, or something?" said Mark.

"Knowing Karl, he'll figure out something," said Tony.

"You're right. All we have to do is be cool and wait for Karl, and then we can figure out what to do next," said Lenny.

Lenny didn't want to say anything to his buddies but the fact that Karl had been given a beating by his Father reminded Lenny of his own Father's hair-trigger, violent temper, and the fact that he, too, had "borrowed" some of his Father's stuff.

Man, things can't get any worse, thought Lenny.

They all sat on the chairs around the card table in the center of the tent. On three sides were arranged four beds. The tent was an Army surplus officer's tent. It was even hooked up with electricity.

The boys sat in silence for a while before Lenny spoke up.

"I think that there's a monster in that cave."

No one responded.

"It tried to talk to my mind this afternoon when I was taking a bath. It was like in a science fiction movie. I heard this really mean sounding voice."

Mark expected his friends to laugh or tease him based upon this revelation. Ordinarily they would have, but not now.

"Well, aren't you guys going to say something?"

Tony looked at Mark then back to Lenny.

"It talked to us, too," said a worried looking Tony.

* * * * *

Mark sat in the overstuffed chair near the small table in his hotel room. He just skimmed through the complimentary copy of the *USA Today* newspaper left by his door. He picked up the telephone and sat it on his lap and dialed his father's house back in Vermont. The phone rang several times. Mark was about to give up when a familiar voice was heard on the end of the line.

"Hello, hello, this is Mr. Pushey. Who's calling?"

"Hi, Dad, it's me, Mark, calling from Miami, Florida"

"Why, hello, Mark. It's always good to hear from you son." Mark's father's voice came up a notch upon noting it was his son calling him.

"So, Dad, how are you doing these days?"

"I'm doing fine I guess, although the gout in my left toe has been acting up the past few days." Mark's father was pushing ninety years old.

"I was beginning to wonder if you were home."

"I was outside checking on the bird feeder when I heard the phone ring. It takes me a bit longer to get to the phone from the back yard than it use to, you know."

"Gee, Dad, what about that cell phone I bought you last Christmas?"

"Mark, did it ever occur to you that I don't want to be taking phone calls in my back yard. That's not what back yards are for, son! Back yards are a place you should be able to go to get away from things, to find some peace and quiet."

"Maybe you're right, Dad!"

"Of course I'm right and I'm still handsome, too," said his father with a chuckle.

"Dad, you'll never change," laughed Mark.

"Say speaking of change did you hear what happened to your friend, Karl Sweeney?"

"No, I didn't," replied Mark. He didn't want to share his early morning apparition with anyone, least of all his Dad.

"Poor man, he committed suicide a few weeks ago. It is a real tragedy. From what I heard no one thought he was having any problems. Your friend Karl was a good man. Your mother and I always liked Karl from the first time he came over to play back when you boys were young."

"How did he, you know, commit suicide?"

"With a shotgun, I think."

"Jesus, why didn't you get in touch with me? I would have wanted to go to the funeral and pay my respects."

"I was going to, but his family wanted a quick and small funeral with no wake. It was a very private funeral; that's why I didn't bother calling you."

"Makes sense I guess. It just comes as a shock."

"Will you be stopping by any time soon?" asked his dad.

"I don't know, maybe, I was sort of thinking I could use a vacation. I haven't spent time back home in a while."

"You know that sounds good to me, son. You're welcome to stay here with me and Pokey." Pokey was the Black Labrador that he had rescued from the dog pound five years ago.

"I'll get back to you on this."

"No problem, son. Oh, and before I forget, did you hear the news about the old quarry?"

"What news?"

"It's been in all the papers and even on TV. Some big out-of-state company bought up the old quarry. They were taking out some rock and it seems one day after they blasted a huge chunk out of the north side of the quarry on some of the extra land they bought up, they found something. It was a cave that had a pile of bones inside and quite a few of the bones were human. The police have been investigating the cave and the quarry. The new quarry owners are frustrated because they want to get their quarry business up and running."

Mark's palm holding the receiver was suddenly very sweaty. He felt a huge headache slamming into gear. His heartbeat jumped to a chest-pounding pace. This was not good news.

"Have the police connected any of these bones to anything?"

"Well, it seems that, wait a minute, there's a story in today's paper. Here it is! It says here that state police spokesman, Lieutenant Theodore Murphy, has indicated that some of the recovered remains from the Bremer Quarry cave site are, in fact, human remains. Police believe they are connected to several cases of missing persons that have been unsolved for perhaps fifty years or more. The state police crime lab is working literally around the clock on this case. It has been revealed by persons closely connected to the case that the remains may contain parts of over fifty humans. The Attorney General and the Commandant of the state police will be holding a press conference this afternoon when more details are expected to be revealed about this puzzling case."

"Jesus, Dad, how could I have missed that story?"

"Don't know. Everyone's talking about it. There are some pretty strange theories. Even Geraldo Rivera is supposedly going to come here to do a show on this."

"Dad," said a clearly exasperated Mark.

"Yes, son."

"I've changed my mind. I'd like to come home for a short vacation. I think I can be there tonight. I would like to take you up on your offer to stay at home with you."

"Mark, you come on home and don't you worry about the time either. Pokey and I will get the place ready. Hear that Pokey? Mark is coming home tonight."

"Ruff...Ruff..."

"Come on home, son!"

"I will. Dad."

Chapter 16

Each of the other boys, in turn, told his story about the strange but scary voice talking to them earlier in the afternoon. Tony was reading a Batman comic when he had a conversation just like Lenny's. Mark's conversation took place while he was praying in his room. Mark was praying for a miracle to get them all out of the mess they were now in.

To pass the time they tried to play cards but their hearts were not in it.

They next tried reading comic books. That didn't work, either. Tony suggested maybe they could listen to the radio. However, Lenny reminded Tony the radio might be blaring about the murders of three people and right now they didn't want to have to listen to that if they could help it.

"Maybe we could sneak over to Karl's house and toss a stone up against his bedroom window and see how he's doing," said Tony.

"That's not a bad idea," said Mark.

"Oh yeah, well what are you two going to do if his old man catches us?" said Lenny.

With that declaration, their collective spirit dropped another notch.

They settled down on the beds and stared into the shadows near the top of the inside of the tent. Time passed slowly. It was beginning to settle into twilight time.

"I'm going into the house to take a leak. Anybody else need to go?" asked Mark, as he sat up.

"Yeah, I'll go," said Tony.

"Me, too," said Lenny.

They made their way to the house, up the back steps and into the house. Meanwhile, someone moving through the shadows crept into the tent.

After several minutes, the boys came back outside, each armed with several homemade cookies. They were making small talk as they entered the tent to a surprise. Karl was sitting at the foot of one of the beds.

"Jesus, Karl, we sure are glad to see you!" proclaimed Tony.

"Yeah, man, we heard about the beating your old man gave you. We all figured you were seriously grounded." said Mark.

"So, are you?" asked Lenny.

Karl stood up, but not without wincing and holding his right side. He faced his friends. Even in the faint light cast by the single sixty watt bulb mounted near the top of the tent, they could see the swelling on Karl's face. Both of his cheeks were swollen. His left eye was nearly closed shut by the swelling. There was a streak of blood coming from his right ear. His lower lip seemed swollen and mis-shapen.

"Karl, your old man did this to you?" asked an incredulous Tony.

"Yeah, my fucking father beat me and kicked me like I was some dog or something," said Karl through clenched teeth.

Karl was sniffling back his emotion. His nose started to run. Mark gave him the handkerchief his mother always made him carry.

"Karl, I'll go get my mom and dad, they'll fix you up," said Mark.

"No, no fucking parents! I'm not supposed to be here. I snuck out of the house through the hall window. If my old man finds out I snuck out, he'll fucking kill me. I can't stay here for long. All I know is we've got to get our shit out of that fucking cave before the cops come looking for those three assholes and then find our stuff. Damn it, the police will pin the murders on us for sure!"

It had clearly sunk in. Each boy was stunned at the beating Karl had received and now, to be possibly blamed for murder, well what else could go wrong?

"You forgot something, what about that friggin' monster, the thing that really killed those kids?" said Lenny.

"Lenny's right. Oh man, we are in some deep shit," said Mark.

"Karl did the monster try to talk to you?" asked Lenny.

"What?"

"You know, did it talk to your mind or something? It talked to all of us this afternoon."

"No, I was too busy getting the freaking crap beat out of me, remember! So, what did it say?"

"It said it was our friend and our friends were its friends and our enemies were its enemies. Something like that," said Mark.

"And you guys believe that shit?"

"We don't know what to believe," said Lenny as he glanced sideways at the others.

"Look guys, tomorrow morning we've got to go back to the cave and get our stuff out of there. If I have to I'll go alone. But I could use your help. I'll sneak out of the house right after my father goes to work. I'll meet you guys here in the tent around seven thirty. Now are you with me?"

After a momentary glance around the tent they each nodded their agreement.

Karl stood up to leave. He wobbled for a moment, then gathered himself and stood up straight.

"One of these fucking days I'm going to beat the shit out him especially for the times he beat my mom. I'm telling you there are times I wish he was fucking dead. My mom and I would be better off without him," said a still angry and defiant Karl.

Karl now headed out of the tent and set out for home.

"Man, that was some beating Karl took," said Tony.

"Yeah," said Mark.

Lenny just nodded his agreement. He knew all too well the feeling of a brutal beating at the hand of one's father. After all, Lenny had been beaten several times, only his buddies didn't know how bad things could get between a father and his son.

Meanwhile, Karl crept up to his own house. It was still quiet.

That was good because if his father had discovered he snuck out on him he would be ranting and tearing up the house right now. Karl carefully climbed the post of the back porch and boosted himself up onto the roof of the porch. He tiptoed across the roof and carefully poked his head into the upstairs hallway window. He could hear the TV playing downstairs. Karl slowly climbed into the window and tiptoed down the hall to his room. He grasped the door knob as quietly as he could. He entered his bedroom and closed the door. He slid the chair from his desk over to the door and propped it up against the door knob. He didn't want any surprises during the night.

Exhausted, Karl dropped down on his bed and stared at the ceiling. *Yessiree! Life around the Sweeney household would be a whole lot better if my father weren't around anymore,* thought a bitter and angry Karl.

Back at the tent, the boys were settling in for the night. Each of them expected it was going to be a nightmare kind of night. They each just wanted to get it over with, and above all, show no fear.

Later that night Karl's father exited the bathroom and settled into his side of the bed. His wife was already into bed and was pretending to be fast asleep. He knew she was pretending, but he didn't care.

Fuck her for raising that juvenile delinquent of a boy. I work my ass off to put a roof over their heads and decent food on the table. All I want is some respect and for that lying asshole of a son to leave my stuff alone, thought Bob.

Bob was still percolating with anger as he pulled up the bedcovers.

Betty Sweeney was lying in bed tensed from her head to her toes. Her married life with Bob had been a series of beatings and explosions of blind rage—often times for reasons she couldn't re-member. Today, Bob had savagely beaten their son. She wanted to intervene but knew her efforts would give Bob an excuse to beat her and he would have beaten Karl even more severely then before. Perhaps she could get her parents to take Karl for the summer. Put Karl out of Bob's reach. She would call them in the morning. Yes, she had a plan, a good plan. After Karl was out of the house maybe she and Bob could get their marriage back on track. Betty soon drifted off to sleep.

It was now two o'clock in the morning. Bob, a chronic light sleeper, thought he heard someone in the room. He opened his eyes and tried to pick up any movement or sound. Bob slowly pushed the bed sheet off, and began to sit up when he felt two cold hands around his neck. They were squeezing his throat. Bob suddenly couldn't breathe. He looked to see who would be doing this to him and in the darkness of the room he could only make out a shadowy shape. The guy was huge.

Bob struggled. He reached up with his own powerful arms and tried to grab hold of the hands around his neck in order to break free. He couldn't find any hands. No arms.

No fucking arms, thought a now panicked Bob. He was beginning to black out from the lack of oxygen. He would have to kick his way out. Bob now realized he couldn't lift his legs. It was as if someone was sitting on them.

Why isn't Betty screaming or something, or has this fucking person already killed her?

His chest felt like it was going to burst. His heart was beating furiously.

"What the fuck is happening?" he managed to say through clenched teeth.

A voice entered his mind, *Karl is my friend and you are his enemy, and now, my enemy.*

Bob's last life experience was seeing a horrific face, breathing into his face, a foul breath coming from an oversized mouth with many sharp white teeth.

"What the fuck are you?" were the last words spoken by Karl's father.

Around six o'clock that morning Betty climbed out of bed and tiptoed to the bathroom. She quietly closed the bathroom door and used the toilet. She then took a brief shower. After drying off she went back into the bedroom. It was then she noticed the foul odor. It smelled like someone had emitted, at the least, a fetid and horrid fart. She went to her husband's side of the bed to wake him up.

"Bob it's...," she stopped in mid-sentence. Her husband's pallor was an ashen grey. *Something is wrong,* flashed instantly into her mind. She suppressed the thought as she put her right hand on his shoulder to give him a shake. His shoulder felt unnaturally cold.

It was then she noticed several flies buzzing around Bob's face. One was crawling around in the corner of his wide open bulging eyes. Drool was running from his open mouth. A fly landed on his right ear and appeared to be exploring the dried blood streak running down his neck from his ear. A small fly flew out from his nose.

Betty screamed a blood-curdling scream and fainted at the side of the bed.

Karl sprang from his bed. He shoved the desk chair away from his bedroom door and ran down the hall to his parents' bedroom. His mother was lying on the floor. Karl knelt down next to her and saw she was breathing. He now set his eyes on his father. There were more flies now.

Karl was shocked and scared.

Chapter 17

Lenny had been driving for two hours. He needed a bathroom break. He also needed to stretch his legs. He pulled into the I-89 Rest Area about twenty miles south of Lebanon, New Hampshire. It was a beautiful rest stop with a picturesque view looking down into the valley below. There were a couple of small ponds in the valley. It was a bright, cloudless February day. It was twenty-five degrees and the wind was biting and coming out of the north. Lenny was only the fourth vehicle in the rest stop parking area.

He felt a blast of warm air as he entered the building. It was coming from a small but highly efficient wood burning stove which hosted a roaring fire. Lenny admired the fire for just a moment, then turned to his left and entered the men's room. There were two men washing their hands at the nearby sinks. Neither said a word. They appeared to be in a hurry as they stepped past Lenny and out the door. He was now alone in the restroom. He relieved himself at one of the urinals and stepped over to a sink to wash his hands. When he was done he looked up into the mirror. The reflection was not his. In fact the reflection suggested that Lenny was not in the men's room at a rest stop on I-89. It suggested Lenny was in a tent.

The image of the tent was deeply familiar to Lenny. He immediately recognized it as Mark Pushey's old back yard tent. Lenny looked thirteen years old in the image reflecting from the mirror. Lenny then heard a familiar voice from his haunted past. It was the voice of the creature. The voice seemed to be emanating from the empty air behind him.

"You are returning to me. After all these years we will be meeting once again."

"Why can't you leave me alone?"

"It's not just you that I want, I also want the one called Mark and the other one, Tony."

"They're going back?"

"Very soon you will all be together once more!"

"What do you want from us?"

"You each thought you entombed me many years ago. I was loyal to each of you. I served you. Yet, my reward was to be locked away again while the four of you failed to fulfill your part of our bargain."

"How many more will you kill this time?"

"I remember the past very well, but I will not predict the future."

"This has got to stop."

"It will not. You are all part of my most important quest."

"What quest?"

"Have you forgotten? I deeply yearn to walk the surface of the earth as my ancestors once did. I also wish to see the wonders of your world for myself. But this can never be! It was my grandfather who was the one originally cursed. He managed to foster a child, my father. I am his only son. Now, I also seek a mate so that I, my father and his father before him can defeat the curse by extending our bloodline."

"I won't let that happen. I won't stand by and let you kill again. You deserve to die and to be exterminated from this world."

"Lenny, will you kill for me?" he asked mockingly.

"You son-of-a-bitch," answered a very angry Lenny.

Lenny tried to close his mind to the mirror image, to drive away this monster. He wanted to hurry to Vermont. He willed with all his might that when he opened his eyes he would only see his own image reflected back at him from the mirror. Lenny's fingers were sore. Throughout this encounter he had been gripping the edge of the counter top with all his strength. He had to concentrate on releasing his grip. Lenny slowly opened his eyes and now only saw his own reflection staring back at him.

Lenny's upper lip glistened from perspiration. His hair was matted down to his scalp, also wet from heavy perspiration. He looked at his watch. He had been in the men's room for thirty minutes. He turned on the cold tap of the faucet and splashed some water on his face. It felt refreshing. He ran a comb through his hair and exited the bathroom. He saw no one as he left the building. As he strode past the racks of tourist information pamphlets, something out of the corner of his eye caught his attention. Sitting on the sill above the racks was a left behind copy of a Vermont newspaper, the Burlington Free Press. The top of the front page displayed an oversized headline, "Mass Gravesite Mystery." Under that banner was a smaller headline trailer, which read, "Police Still Baffled: Seek Public's Help."

Lenny quickly picked up the paper. He hurried to his car and settled inside, started the engine and began to read the front page story.

"Damn....Damn....Damn," he repeatedly muttered to himself.

"When I find Tony and Mark, this time we're going to end this fucking nightmare once and for all."

Lenny put the car in gear and pulled out of the parking lot and onto I-89 heading north into Vermont.

* * * * *

The sound of distant sirens began to slowly break through Mark's subconscious. The wail of the sirens grew louder and louder. Mark began to open his eyes just a crack.

Am I dreaming? thought Mark.

Just then he was shaken by Tony, who was standing over him.

"C'mon Mark get up. Let's go check out the sirens."

Mark noticed that Lenny was standing next to Tony.

"We both have been awake for a while," said Lenny.

"Yeah, we both had to take a whiz," said Tony.

Mark kicked off the covers and felt a layer of cold early June air cascade across his half-awake body. He shivered as he swung his legs over the side and began to slip into his sneakers.

"Hurry up, Mark," said Tony.

"I'm moving as fast as I can. Jeeze, what time is it anyway?"

"Around seven I guess," said Tony.

"I've got to go."

"Can't it wait until after we find out what's going on," said a frustrated Tony.

"Let him go do his thing, it can't take that long," said Lenny.

Mark dashed out of the tent and bounded up the back steps into his house to use the bathroom. His mom was up and wearing her favorite yellow terrycloth bathrobe. She was beginning to organize breakfast.

"Mark, do you and your friends want some scrambled eggs and bacon for breakfast."

"Not now, mom, we're going to see what the sirens are all about," said Mark as he rushed past her and into the bathroom.

He closed the bathroom door and fumbled with his zipper, getting it undone just in time.

After a few moments Mark opened the bathroom door and made a bee line for the back door.

"Mark, I didn't hear you washing your hands young man."

"Later, Mom," replied Mark as he leaped out the back door and tumbled to the ground.

Mark's mother watched him receive a friendly backslap from both of his friends as the three of them scampered around the corner, chasing after the sirens they all heard just a few minutes before. She noticed Karl Sweeney wasn't with the boys this morning. She thought Karl was going to be sleeping over just like the rest of the boys. After all, the four of them had become inseparable since school let out for the summer.

Mark's father shuffled into the kitchen. He stretched and began a long yawn.

"Was that sirens I heard a while ago?"

"Yes, the boys just ran off to see what it's all about. From the sound of them I think they stopped over on North Street near Orchard Terrace."

"I wonder what could be going on. I'll take a look out the front door and see if there is any smoke. Could be a fire," asserted Mark's father.

"I'm sure the boys will be back with all the details," she said over her shoulder as he headed to the front door.

She heard him open the door.

"There's no smoke."

"That's good."

"Can you see anything?"

"Not a thing. Maybe it's a false alarm."

Chapter 18

Tony sat at his computer gathering his thoughts to try to respond to Lenny Drew's e-mail message. He was trying to focus upon the computer screen.

Odd, there's no return e-mail address.

Tony didn't understand how Lenny could have sent him an e-mail message without his computer recording the e-mail address of the sender.

Suddenly his computer's mouse slipped from his hand and the right mouse button clicked as the cursor exited him from his e-mail. Tony tried to grab his mouse but there was a force that prevented him from touching it. He looked at the screen and watched as his computer selected Programs from his menu screen and opened up his word processing software.

The keyboard keys began to click. A message appeared upon the screen.

"Hello Tony. Can you guess who I am? I know it has been a long time, but you do remember, don't you?"

Tony reached out for the keyboard. He was now able to type a response.

"Is this someone's idea of a sick practical joke? I'm not finding this funny."

"Lenny and Mark are coming back to me Tony."

Tony just stared at the screen. *I must be hallucinating*, he thought.

"Karl won't be joining them. Karl's dead."

"Who are you?"

"I like playing games. Are we playing a game, Tony?"

"All right," typed Tony. "How am I supposed to know who you are?"

"Tony don't you remember? You and your friends many years ago tried to imprison me in my cave. Tony, I even know that you still have the white sneaker that Karl gave you."

Tony sat frozen in the sudden grip of fear. Tony knew full well who or what was communicating with him now.

"I've been watching, listening and learning for a very long time, Tony. Isn't this new technology wonderful?"

"Where are you now?"

"I could be anywhere I choose to be."

"Underground?"

"Yes, underground, for now."

"What if I don't go back?"

"Tony, I'm much stronger now. Stronger than you can possibly imagine."

There was a long pause as Tony's mind raced wildly with the upside down events that were now confronting him.

"Tony, you have a woman. She has a little one inside her. Maybe you should tell her about me, or should I?"

"YOU FUCKING MONSTER, YOU LEAVE HER ALONE," he typed with a pounding fury.

"Tony, come back to me, now. Remember what I told everyone long ago. Your enemies will be my enemies and your friends will be my friends. Well, for your information, your mate can be mine, too."

Tony ripped the key board from the computer as he flung it across the room to smash against the wall.

"You bet I'll go back, only this time we'll do it right, you fucking freak!" sputtered Tony.

* * * * *

The boys cut through a couple of back yards in their haste to reach where they last thought the sirens ended. As they came around the corner of a house onto its front yard on North Street, they saw immediately to their left, two houses up, an ambulance and a police car with their lights flashing. The vehicles were parked right in front of Karl Sweeney's house. The boys could hear loud sobs coming from inside the house.

The boys walked slowly up the sidewalk towards Karl's house.

A couple of neighborhood women dressed in their bathrobes ran towards the house. They went in through the front door. A police officer pushed them back outside. He spoke to them. They retreated and now stood at the edge of the front walk whispering to each other. The policeman went to his car and sat inside. It appeared he was using his radio.

Just then a sedan pulled up behind the police car. A man quickly got out of the car and headed for the Sweeney's house. He was carrying a small black bag. The boys recognized him. It was Dr. O'Reilly. He was the family doctor for just about everyone in Winooski. He nodded to the women out front and then hurried in the front door of the Sweeney's.

The boys couldn't figure out what happened. They stood in front of the house as a small crowd began to gather. Everyone was whispering.

"I'll bet he beat his wife again," whispered one woman in a blue bathrobe.

"Maybe this time he killed her," said another in a lime colored bathrobe. Her hair was in rollers.

A second police cruiser pulled up. This one held the police chief and another officer who was the driver. The Chief said nothing as he headed straight for the house. The other officer stepped between the small crowd and the house and began to try to push them back.

"C'mon now. Let's move back please. Don't block this front walk."

A man in a pickup truck pulled to a stop and shouted from his open window, "What happened?"

A woman in curlers shouted back, "We think it's a stabbing."

Her friends shushed her, telling her not to spread gossip at such a time.

Someone tooted his car horn at the pickup driver. He pulled away as the driver of the car pulled into the Sweeney's driveway. His driver's side door had a seal painted on its side. It read, "Chittenden County Coroner, for Official Business Only."

The small crowd grew very quite. The Coroner walked past the crowd and was greeted at the door of the house by the chief of police. They shook hands briefly as the Chief gestured to the inside of the house.

Lenny pulled at Mark's shirt sleeve and nodded that they should move back away from the crowd. Mark pulled on Tony's arm and gestured for Tony to join them. The boys stood next to the curb.

"What do you guys think happened to Karl?" Mark said.

"I think Karl's old man killed Karl or something. He probably found out that Karl skipped out last night," said Tony.

"Shit, man, don't say that," said Lenny.

"Well, what else could it be?" asked a worried Tony.

"I don't know. Maybe there was a big fight or something. Maybe someone's hurt, I mean we don't know, right?" asked Mark.

"Whatever happened can't be good. Did you guys see that car with "Coroner" painted on the door?" said Lenny.

Twenty minutes passed.

At that moment the boys heard a murmur rise from the crowd. The boys turned and saw two ambulance medics carefully carrying a gurney down the front steps. They dropped the gurney legs down and began to wheel the shroud-covered gurney to the waiting ambulance. Everyone's eyes followed their every move. The boys moved closer to get a better look. It was not possible to tell from the shape on the gurney who it was.

The woman in the lime colored bathrobe, clutching it close to her, approached one of the medics after they closed the back door of the ambulance. She whispered in his ear and he leaned over and whispered something back.

The ambulance slowly pulled away from the curb. It went a short distance when the flashing lights were turned off.

"Mrs. Beaudette, could you come here please?" said Police Chief Santerre from the opened front doorway.

A short, quiet and unassuming woman stepped from the back of the crowd and headed up the front steps.

"Could you stay with Mrs. Sweeney for a while?" said the Chief.

"Why, yes, I could," agreed Mrs. Beaudette.

The crowd began to break into several whispering groups. The boys stood to the edge of the crowd. They happened to be standing next to the woman who had spoken to the medic a moment ago. She spoke not in a whisper but in a voice that all could hear.

"I found out what happened. The medic told me," she said with a degree of certainty.

"Well, don't keep us all in suspense," said a woman in a powder blue bathrobe.

"He had a massive heart attack. He died early this morning. The medic said his body was stone cold."

"That poor woman, she lay next to a dead husband and didn't know until the morning," said an elderly man at the back of the crowd.

"Jesus, Mary and Joseph," said someone in the crowd. This immediately caused many to do the sign of the cross. Winooski was a blue collar community of predominately French Catholic descendants. Many in the crowd now bowed their heads in silent prayer.

A hand touched Lenny on the shoulder. Lenny jumped at the touch. He turned to face Father Campbell. The priest walked over from the Church rectory, which was a block and a half away. He was carrying a small black bag.

"Lenny this isn't something you should be hanging around to see," admonished the priest.

"Father, I think my best friend's dad just died. Me and the guys are worried about him," said Lenny.

The priest looked into the eyes of the three boys and flashed a small smile.

"It is good that you care about your friend. I'll check up on him. Why don't you stay here for a while? Later I'll come and let you know how he's doing?"

"Thanks, Father," said Lenny.

The priest walked through the crowd speaking quietly to some as he went. "The body's been taken to the morgue, Padre," said someone in the crowd.

The priest acknowledged the information with a nod and then turned and headed into the house. The police chief met him at the door.

"Sorry we had to move him Father. We couldn't wait for you to perform the last sacrament. He was dead already. He was drawing flies. If you'd like I'll drive you later to the funeral parlor after they release his him so you can bless the body."

"That won't be necessary, Chief Santerre. I'll go later by myself. Thanks anyway. What exactly happened here?"

"My officer, the medics and the Coroner all say he had a massive heart attack. The wife found him dead this morning when she tried to wake him up. He must have died in his sleep. She doesn't remember him tossing around or anything that would have suggested to her he was hurting, if you know what I mean. She's a mess, Padre."

"There's a boy?"

"Yup, he's not in too good shape either. Seems like he and his Father got into an argument yesterday. The father beat the boy real bad. The strain might have caused the father's ticker to tense up. Who knows what might have brought on the heart attack! The man was a wife beater, too. Say, the Sweeneys aren't Catholic are they, Father? I mean I don't see them at church."

"I believe they are Catholic. They apparently stopped attending church some years ago."

"Too bad they didn't stay with it—might have cut down on the beatings."

"We'll never know, will we now, Chief?"

"Guess not."

"I need to see Mrs. Sweeney."

"She's in the kitchen. The boy is sitting on the back steps."

"Excuse me, Chief, Father" said the Coroner.

"Chief, I need you to sign as witness to the death certificate."

"If you'll excuse me," said the priest as he ducked away to minister to the living.

Chapter 19

"Tony, what was that noise?" said Kelly from downstairs.

"Nothing, Kelly, it was nothing," said Tony.

Kelly came up the stairs as Tony was picking up the broken keyboard. Kelly stepped into the office doorway and saw Tony standing near the far wall with a keyboard that was in two pieces. Behind him was a dent and scrape-marks on the wall.

"I thought you said nothing happened. First I hear a crash and now there is a dent in that wall behind you. You're standing there with a broken keyboard."

Tony tossed the keyboard pieces onto the desk and went to his wife and gave her a big hug. She warmed to his embrace and hugged him fiercely in return.

"I've got to take a short trip back east," he said while whispering in her ear.

"Has that got to do with you throwing your computer around the room?"

"Not really, I was just upset the keyboard was jamming up on me, and I just sort of snapped."

"Well, Tony Fredette, don't think you are going to behave like that after our child is born. If I have to, I'll take you across my knee and give you a spanking." She stuck her tongue into his ear and gave it a lick.

She pulled away from him, giggling like a school girl.

"Hey, you know, I don't like that wet ear thing you keep doing."

"I know. That's why I keep doing it. Well, when do we leave?"

"Leave, for where?" he asked.

"Back east, you said."

"Vermont. I need to go to Vermont, and I can't take you along. It's sort of a guy thing. I've been invited to a reunion with some guys I use to know when I was a teenager."

"Sounds like fun. You could use a break. You've been working on your books now for nearly three years without a vacation. But why can't I go along? You can have your reunion and I can meet some of your relatives and do a little shopping."

Tony couldn't let her and his yet unborn baby get anywhere near Vermont. He had to try and keep her as far from the reach of that creature as possible.

"Kelly, I…..uh...can't take you along because, well it's not like a real school reunion."

"What are you trying to say?"

"One of my friends from long ago when I was twelve or thirteen just committed suicide. Me and the other guys are getting together to pay our respects."

Tony tried to tell the lie with as much conviction as he could muster. He hoped she bought his story.

"Tony, I had no idea. I'm sorry, honey. Which friend was it that died? How did he die? Does he have any family? Oh, Tony, we should send flowers right away."

The last thing Tony needed right now was to have to answer a lot of questions. He knew he was not an accomplished liar. Sooner or later he would trip himself up.

"Look, Kelly," he hugged her close to him. "He was one of my very best friends. His name is Karl. I think he has family. I don't have any more details than that. I just know he's dead and the other guys want to get together and sort of, maybe you know, remember the guy."

"Well, of course you should go. I'll be fine here. I'll get together with some of my girlfriends. We'll find something to do."

"It will be only for a few days. I promise I'll be back before you know it."

Tony turned off the computer power switch at the surge protector while Kelly turned off the office lights. They left his office and headed back downstairs. Tony noticed that Kelly was holding her lower back.

"Are you hurting?"

"Me?"

"Yeah, I noticed that you're holding your back."

"Oh that! Yeah, my back is just a little sore tonight."

"Was it the love making?"

"No! It just hurts from time to time. I'm carrying an extra load in the front lately in case you haven't noticed."

"Oh, I noticed all right."

"Careful Tony, you're skating on thin ice right now," she said with a smile as she climbed under the covers.

Tony climbed in on his side of the bed and quickly scooted to her side as she turned her back to him. He wrapped his arms around her and pulled her closer to him.

"When are you leaving?"

"Tomorrow!" he replied.

"Be careful."

"I will."

"I love you."

"I love you, too."

"Goodnight."

* * * * *

The back screen door swung open with a slight screech. Police Chief Santerre, a very big man, who tipped the scales at well over two hundred and seventy five pounds, stepped outside. He carefully went down the back steps. Karl, sitting on the stairs, pushed aside to allow the Chief to pass. The Chief pulled one of the wooden back yard chairs over to the back steps. He sat down in it facing Karl.

"How are you doing, son?"

"I'll be fine."

"You found your dad?"

"Yeah, I found him. So what?"

"My officer tells me you're the one who called the police. Is that right?"

"Uh-huh."

"Look at me, son."

Karl looked up slowly at the police chief. The Chief's eyes were soft and kind. His round face was a friendly one. The Chief removed his hat and stroked his balding head with his right hand.

"It's going to be a hot and sticky day."

"What do you want with me?"

"Look, Karl, I know about the beatings."

"Big deal, so my old man beat me."

"Did he beat you yesterday?"

"You think I had something to do with his dying?"

"No, I don't, Karl. I just want to help you. Your mom's going to need you now, more than ever, you know?"

"I know."

"Karl, let me put it to you this way. I've seen young men, boys, whose father beat them or their moms, sometimes both. When we know about it we try to put a stop to it. Anyway, sometimes the boy is angry and has no place for that anger. Do you know what I mean?"

"I think I do."

"Well, these boys suddenly find themselves getting into trouble. I want you to know that's the wrong way to go with your anger. Try to be strong and good for your mom's sake. If you need someone to talk to or you think I can help you, I want you to feel you can talk to me."

"Thanks, Chief, I appreciate the offer."

"I sure hope so. Here comes Padre. Hi there, Father! Me and Karl, we've been having a little chat. Care to join us?"

The priest sat down next to Karl. He patted Karl on the head. Karl winced a little at the priest's touch. The priest had touched a side of Karl's head where his father had slapped him hard the day before.

"Karl's had a tough time, Father."

The priest looked down at Karl and could see the swelling around the eyes and the purple and red swollen left cheek. Karl didn't like the attention, so he looked away.

Just then, at the back door to the house, another police officer appeared.

"Chief, we got a call. It seems like we've got an accident at the corner of Main and Lafountain Streets."

"You go ahead. I'll be right behind."

Karl looked at the Chief as he extended his big soft hand.

"You take care. I'll stop by some time and see how you're doing."

They shook hands. The Chief turned and left. He walked around the outside of the house along the shrubs as he went to his car.

The priest moved to the chair vacated by the Chief. He sat down and looked at Karl. Karl looked back at him with moist eyes.

"You loved him, didn't you?"

"No way could I love him. I hated him. He was mean. He sure as shit didn't love me or my mom."

"Karl, you need to let go of this anger. You will find it easier on yourself if you do."

"Look Padre, my dad is dead. I'm not sorry he's dead. My mom's going to miss him a lot but I won't miss him at all. You don't know what it was like to live around here. He never had anything good to say to me or my mom. He made fun of religion, too! We're just better off without him. I'll take care of my mom and me just fine!"

Karl got up from the steps and walked into the back yard with his back to the priest. He stopped with his hands in his dungarees.

"Do you believe there really is a Hell?" asked Karl in a subdued and controlled voice.

"Yes, I do," said the priest.

"And is the devil real?"

"Yes, he is real, but......"

"Then I hope my Dad sees them both."

The priest stood up and walked over to Karl, knelt down on one knee next to him and said, "Karl, do you have any close friends or family living nearby?"

"Yeah, I'm buddies with Tony Fredette, Mark Pushey and Lenny Drew. Why?"

"Do you have any other family?"

"None around here. My parents moved here from Massachusetts when I was born. We never hear from anyone down there. My mom sends some relatives Christmas cards I think. Why are you asking?"

"I'll be right back. Just wait here."

The priest stood up and headed into the house. The family Doctor was in the kitchen making a phone call. He hung up the phone.

"I just called in a prescription for the mother, something to help her sleep. She's taking it hard. Mrs. Beaudette is with her now. She's offered to stay with Mrs. Sweeney for a while. How's the boy?"

"He's an angry young man right now. It seems his father beat him and his mother regularly. Did you have any idea about these beating?"

"I didn't see these people hardly at all except maybe when the boy was little for an ear ache or chicken pox. I never saw the father, not once. I believe the mother came in once a couple of years ago with a broken arm. She said she broke it when she fell down the back stairs. I just didn't see them often enough to pick up on the beatings."

"I know. I didn't see them either. They didn't attend our church or any church that I'm aware of. It appears they kept their family nightmare a secret."

"Well, now it's over."

"Say, Doc have you checked the boy over yet?"

"Not yet, I'll take a look at him now."

"Good."

"I'm going to make a call or two to see if I can find a place for the boy for the next few days. The mother can stay with the

Beaudettes until after the funeral. The Beaudette family and I will organize the neighbors to help out. I'll get the ladies church auxiliary to lend a hand as well."

"If you need my help just give me a call. Now I'll go have a look at the boy."

He went to the back door and called out to Karl.

"Karl, could you come in here, please?"

The doctor took Karl into the bathroom and closed the door.

Father Campbell made one call and struck pay dirt immediately. He had a place for Karl. Next he made other calls, one to his rectory, another to the head of the ladies auxiliary and yet another to the funeral director. Winooski was a small community and it had only one funeral parlor, Lavigne's. Father Campbell called Oscar Lavigne, who it turned out had already heard the news. News travels fast in a small community.

Meanwhile, outside in front of the house Karl's friends sat on the curb. They didn't know what to do. They wanted to see Karl and give him their support but they didn't think they should just walk up to the house.

Lenny had a small stick and was drawing in the sand in the gutter. Tony was on one of his usual booger hunts. Mark sat there in silence with his head in his hands.

"Mark?"

He looked up and had to shield his eyes from the early morning sun. It was his mother and father. His mother knelt down to him and stroked his hair.

"Would it be all right with you if Karl came and stayed with us for a few days?"

"Of course it would be all right, Mom."

"Your mother and I were asked to help out. We know how close you guys are so we figured it was the least we can do. Karl will have to bunk in your room with you, Mark."

"That's fine with me. Anything we can do to help is cool with me."

"Good. Now why don't you head on home with the guys and get your room picked up. Your mother and I are going to see Karl and help him pick out some of his things. We'll be along in a while," said Mark's father.

The boys didn't have to be asked twice. They bolted from the curb and ran quickly back towards the Pushey's house. Mr. and Mrs. Pushey, walking hand-in-hand, went up the front steps of the Sweeney's house. They had never been there before.

The crowd began to thin out now. A car pulled up to the curb. An elderly man got out of the car. He was the Plant Manager of the furniture factory where Bob Sweeney worked. He loosened his neck-tie. It was already a hot and sticky morning. The temperature was seventy-four degrees and was headed towards the low nineties, with above average humidity. It would be an unbearable day. On top of the weather he had a most unpleasant task to perform. He hated this part of his job. The company death benefit was a paltry five hundred dollars. Later, he would organize a factory-wide collection, but it wouldn't amount to a whole lot. He just had to walk his way through this and get back to the factory. News reached the plant within minutes of the police arriving at the Sweeney's home. As Plant Manager he took exceptional pride in expediting payment of the company's modest death benefit. He had sole authority for the payment out of the benevolence fund. And so it is that he was able to arrive at the Sweeney household in less than an hour with the "death check" in hand.

The company check was in his coat pocket as he climbed the front steps.

He was soon followed by the local insurance agent. He had somewhat better news. Several years ago Bob Sweeney had invested in a couple of policies which totaled nearly fifty thousand dollars. Bob also was a veteran and there were some modest benefits there as well. The life insurance agent would help with all the paper work. It was part of his service commitment to his customers. He would encourage her to sell the house, and save the insurance money to help her get back on her feet. She was going to have to get a job to help support herself and her son. The sale of the house might bring her additional assets but not much more. He took great pride in his job. He did it well. It was always better to get these things settled quickly. Working through these issues often helped the survivors get over the tragedy by focusing on the here and now.

Later, there would be a steady stream of visitors for the rest of that morning. There was much to be done and there were people ready to help. The community pulled its resources together during times like this.

Chapter 20

Eddie Martin was still dazed. He hurt in several places. He tried to recall what happened to him. He vaguely remembered heading out into the woods with his friend, Johnny Savoy and Johnny's girl-friend, Gloria something or another.

What was her name? thought Eddie. It flashed into his mind, Gloria Swett. They were going to do some exploring and if Johnny got lucky, maybe he could talk Gloria into letting him into her pants. Eddie would get to watch.

Eddie tried to sit up, but his stomach hurt quite a bit. He felt his right side, where his wet tee-shirt stuck to his side. Right now he simply hurt in so many places.

"Why is it so fucking dark?" mumbled Eddie. "Jesus it's cold," His teeth were chattering.

The sound of his voice echoed back at him from several directions. He heard some faint screeching sounds.

He reached out to either side and despite intense pain he pushed himself into a seated position. As he pushed himself up, his hands felt what seemed like sticks. It felt like he was lying on a bed of sticks of varying sizes and shapes. He felt around, grabbed one and passed his hands over it.

"It feels like....a bone," he whispered. "I'm lying on a pile of freaking bones."

He tried to roll over onto his knees to stand up. He instantly felt sharp pain shoot up his legs. He reached down to both of his legs and could feel tremendous swelling. On his lower left leg he felt what seemed like a piece of his lower leg bone protruding through his pants leg. He suddenly felt sick and light-headed, with his stomach in full revolt. He turned his head to the left and vomited.

Eddie also felt terrified. He didn't know where he was or how he got there. He now knew he had two broken legs. Suddenly, his senses went on full alert. He tried to sit as quietly as he could. Despite the incredible pain and his gripping fear, he listened.

He heard a single, simple sound.

Then it repeated.

There was a steady dripping sound which seemed to come from several places all around him. He was shivering from the cold and the gripping effects from the shock was now overpowering him.

He listened some more and thought he could hear the delicate flapping of wings.

The blackness was total. Eddie sniffed at the air. It smelled dank and fetid. He thought he could smell something rotten, something spoiled.

It was starting to come back to him now. There was a cave. He and Johnny wanted to explore it. There were some other boys, too. Those boys seemed scared. Johnny disappeared into the cave. Something pulled Johnny into the cave. Eddie tried to come to his friend's rescue.

Suddenly, Eddie heard the faint sound of a stone tumbling down over other rocks and then a small splash. Eddie froze with fear. He listened with all his might. Was it someone coming to rescue him? Was it Johnny? He wasn't sure who or what it was, so Eddie chose to sit as quiet as he could until he knew who or what made that sound.

Eddie's heart beat was racing. He felt himself struggling to breathe. He was shivering with chills which racked his bruised and battered body.

Eddie heard steps, steps that were coming closer. He also began to hear breathing coming closer.

Sniffing, something is sniffing near his face. He can feel the breath of whomever or whatever is doing the sniffing. He doesn't dare to move.

There's a voice, a strange throaty voice.

"Your male friend is gone."

"Gone where?"

"Does it matter?"

"I don't understand. Are you someone who can help me?" stammers Eddie.

"I might be able to help."

"You can help me?" asked Eddie pleading in a soft whisper.

Suddenly, Eddie felt himself being pulled up by his shoulders. His hands reached out as he tried to feel something about who might be helping him. He felt powerful long hairy arms. He couldn't reach anything else. His body had been lifted quickly and easily off the pile of bones and Eddie realized he was now suspended in the air.

"What have you done to me? Why can't I see anything?" cried Eddie. His voice echoed and rebounded back at him

The purely evil voice spoke, "Because, I ate your eyes."

Eddie was barely able to reach up to his own face and feel for his eyes. In the place where his eyes should have been were two sunken depressions beneath his eye lids. They were stuck shut.

Eddie screamed at the top of his lungs, "You ate my fucking eyes. You ate my eyes!"

He screamed in absolute terror "eiyeeeeeee" as he flailed away at the creature holding him. Despite the pain and shock, Eddie's deep desire to live instantly consumed him. He tried to kick and punch, but he struck little while the pain in his broken legs was becoming overwhelmingly intense. The noise and motion stirred up the northern long eared bats that clung to the roof of this cavern deep inside the cave. They took flight and fluttered about, screeching as they did.

The creature pulled Eddie to him, and in one powerful lunge with his enormous jaw, the creature took a bite of the boy's neck and nearly decapitated him. Blood gushed from the open wound. Eddie was now silenced as the creature sat down cross-legged and proceeded to eat the choice parts of the now dead Eddie Martin.

In another chamber a couple hundred feet away sat Gloria Swett, the girl who was dragged into the cave along with her friends, Johnny and Eddie. She was conscious. She had two badly sprained and bloodied ankles. Her hands were tied behind her and she was tied to a piece of rock. She had something tied over her eyes so she couldn't see but she could hear.

She clearly heard the echo-distorted voice of her friend Eddie, scream out, "You ate my eyes" followed by a blood-chilling scream. It was now very quiet where she was. She listened and only heard dripping sounds. A large drop of cold water dripped on her head. The water ran down the side of her face. Her hair was wet and matted to her head. She wanted to scream, but found she was too frightened to even try.

* * * * *

Lenny Drew pulled his Thunderbird into the parking lot of the Sheraton Hotel. The hotel was on the west side of I-89 located on the eastern edge of Burlington, Vermont. It was large and attached to a convention center. It was much larger than the Sheraton he remembered as the location of Winooski's Class of 1967's Senior Prom.

He checked into the hotel and unpacked in his room. He sat on the bed and looked up the phone number for Mark Pushey's parents. He found the listing with Mark's father's name only. He dialed the number and after a few rings a familiar voice answered.

"Hello."

"Hi, is this Mr. Pushey?"

"Why, yes it is. You sound like Lenny Drew. Is that you Lenny?"

"It sure is Mr. Pushey. How have you been?"

"I'm fine, Lenny, just fine. I lost the Missus a few years ago— she died of breast cancer. It's just me and Pokey my dog. Say, what a coincidence. I heard from Mark today and he is coming to visit me for a few days."

"That's nice. I sure would like to catch up with Mark and kind of go over old times."

"Why don't you come to Vermont for a few days, too? I'm sure you could use a vacation from that busy job you have, making money all day long."

"Well, as it turns out, I'm already in Vermont. I've got a room over at the Burlington Sheraton Hotel. I came back to pay my respects to Karl Sweeney's family. I just heard about it a couple of days ago."

"Now that's a real tragedy. Poor Karl. Karl was a good man. From time to time, he would stop over and visit with me. He liked to talk about you boys and how close you all were. I sure miss him."

"Yeah, I do, too."

"Listen, Lenny why don't you come and stay with Mark and me. There's plenty of room. We could use the company. It would be like old times for you two."

"I'll think about it, Mr. Pushey. Anyway, here's my room number. It's 255. Give it to Mark when you see him. By the way, when is he getting in?"

"He said he was going to be here tonight. He's flying in from Miami, Florida."

"Well, he'll be tired from his trip I'm sure. Just let him know where to reach me."

"I will, Lenny."

"Goodbye."

"Goodbye."

Chapter 21

Gloria was holding her breath, her mind was racing wildly. "Where am I?" kept repeating in her head. She was becoming more lucid with each passing moment. She remembered being dragged kicking and screaming into the cave. She also remembered hearing someone groaning from a distance. She vividly recalled being carried on the shoulder of what she believed to be a very large, hairy man. He moved with considerable speed. She lost sight of the faint light from the cave's hole she had been dragged through. The next thing she was able to remember was waking up here, being tied up and having a splitting headache.

She didn't know how long she had been tied up, but her leg and arm cramps indicated it must have been for a while. She was also very hungry. Finally, Gloria realized, she also wet her pants.

The agonizing scream she just heard reminded her how terrified she was.

That had to be Eddie, she thought. *Is he dead? Am I alone in this hellhole? God, somebody help me, please.*

She felt a slight breeze coming straight at her.

Where is the breeze coming from? she wondered.

"Is someone here with me?" she whispered.

She felt another drip from above as it struck her left shoulder.

She now heard a new sound, a flutter above her head. There were increasingly more fluttering sounds. Something brushed her head. Gloria felt the tension mount with each passing moment.

"Screech ...screech," was the sound that now echoed across around the chamber. The sound made Gloria flinch.

Wait, what's that? Footsteps, I hear footsteps. Who could it be? she kept these thoughts to herself out of mortal fear. The steps were coming closer.

She suddenly detected a breathing sound which could clearly be heard in addition to her own. Someone or something was close now and its breath was pushing towards her. Now there was a new smell, a sickening fetid odor. Her stomach cramped up with dry heaves.

She tried with all her might to remain still in the darkness.

A raspy, guttural male voice spoke to her.

"Female, are you hungry?"

She didn't want to answer.

"Here, I brought you some food."

The creature reached towards her with a hunk of meat. He pushed it to her mouth. She could smell the meat. It was not cooked, it was raw. Gloria tried to turn her head away. He pushed this meat at her again, trying to force it into her mouth. She resisted but some of the meat entered between her lips and she could taste it. She turned her head and with all her might, let out a scream.

"No.....no, no, just leave me alone."

The creature knelt down in front of her. He tossed the meat to the ground at her feet. He reached up and touched her face with both of his heavily callused hands. She pulled away. He again reached towards her and touched her hair.

"You don't want meat. I thought all humans were flesh eaters. I brought you a very choice piece I could have eaten myself."

Gloria found her strength was ebbing. She was weak and tired.

"What do you want from me?" asked Gloria, desperately trying to sound defiant.

Before she could ask another question her legs were quickly pulled apart. She lets out a full-throated high-pitched scream no one except the creature would hear. She heard sniffing coming from the creature. The creature now released her legs.

Her sprained ankles lit up with new pain from the sudden, forced movement.

The creature sniffed all around her. She could feel its breath in her face. It removed the material that was covering her eyes. It took a moment for her eyes to adjust, but she noticed there was a faint light coming from above and behind the creature, who was kneeling directly in front of her. She couldn't make out any features, just his shadowed outline.

"Please, can't you let me go?" she pleaded. She was crying.

The creature now reached out and touched her face. She tried not to pull away this time.

"It has been a long time since I have had a female." The creature's voice, spoken in a menacing growl, struck her with a fear greater than she had ever experienced.

He pulled her to her feet by her hair.

"I offered you the flesh of the male called Eddie. His flesh was still warm. You should have eaten."

"No.., it can't be. Oh, my God, let me die, I want to die," she sobbed.

"I can't use you to mate. You are not a suitable mate. You are spoiled. I must have a mate! My friends who walk above the ground will find me one. You, you're now just food to me."

He lifted her higher with his left hand. Suddenly he tore into her chest with his oversized and powerful right hand and pulled out her still-beating heart.

* * * * *

It was a Thursday morning. Tony used a shuttle door-to-door service to commute from his home in Ogden to the airport. Tony eventually boarded United Flight 3908 out of Salt Lake City heading for Chicago's O'Hare Airport. There, he would switch planes and take a United Commuter Flight for Burlington, Vermont. He was scheduled to arrive in Burlington at 9:05 p.m. He said goodbye to his wife Kelly earlier that morning and promised to call her every day. Their goodbye kiss was long and passionate. He was going to miss her dearly, but he knew he had no choice.

Once in the air, Tony took a small black book from his coat pocket and looked up the telephone number for Lenny Drew's office. It was 8:10 a.m. in the skies over Utah so it would be 10:10 a.m. in Boston. Tony used the in-flight telephone. He entered his credit card information and waited for the digitized approval code before he dialed his good friend's office number. It rang several rings before a recorded message picked up telling Tony the usual, "Lenny was not available at this time but to leave a message," which he did. At the end of his message, Tony hit the 0 key to reach Lenny's Executive Assistant. A very pleasant-sounding woman's voice came on the line. After a brief conversation, Tony advised her he was not only a client of Lenny's but a childhood friend who urgently needed to reach him.

She mentioned Mr. Drew had urgent family business back in Vermont. If Tony needed to speak to him she would be glad to contact Mr. Drew for him. She couldn't give out Mr. Drew's cell number but she understood that Tony was anxious to reach Mr. Drew. She assured Tony if Mr. Drew called in to the office she would immediately forward his message.

"Is there a number where Mr. Drew can reach you, Mr. Fredette?"

"I'm in transit to Vermont myself. I've made arrangements to stay at the Radisson Hotel in downtown Burlington. Please advise Len, (as he was now called in the business world.) he can reach me there."

"I will be certain to pass along your message. I will call him as soon as we hang up."

"Thank you."

"Goodbye, Mr. Fredette."

"Yes, goodbye," replied Tony.

Tony looked up the telephone number for Karl Sweeney's house. He thought, to possibly speak to Karl's widow but changed his mind. Calling from the airplane would be too tacky and besides these on-board telephone devices were very expensive. He would go see her when he got to Vermont.

Lenny's going to Vermont was good news. This meant no time would be lost getting together and figuring out just what was going on.

Tony next looked up the phone number for Mark Pushey. He dialed Mark's apartment in New York City. It rang several times and just like with Lenny's office there was a recorded message. Tony left a message on the answering machine. Tony was anxious to reach Mark so he called Vermont telephone information and asked for the number for Mark's father's house. He knew Mark still stayed close to his father and maybe his father could help speed up the process of tracking down Mark.

After two rings, a familiar voice answers the phone.

"Hello."

"Hello, Mr. Pushey?"

"Yes. Who is this?"

"Mr. Pushey, this is Tony Fredette calling. How are you?"

"Tony, I don't believe it. What a coincidence."

"What do you mean?"

"Tony, Mark's coming in tonight to spend a few days with me. And the amazing thing is, I heard from Lenny Drew and he's here in Vermont, too. He might be staying with Mark and me. Where are you calling from?"

"I'm calling from an airplane. Right now I am on the way to Chicago and then on to Burlington, Vermont. I just heard about Karl's passing and I wanted to visit and pay my respects to the family."

"Look, Tony, I've got plenty of room here. Why don't you stay here with us? It will be just like the times when you boys spent the summers in the back yard. I know Mark would just love to have you stay with us."

"I don't know, Mr. Pushey. Maybe I will. For now please tell Mark and Lenny that I'll give them a call tonight when my flight gets in, okay?"

"Sure, Tony. Say, how's that lovely wife of yours?"

"Thanks for asking. She's fine. She's not with me on this trip. This is a sort of business trip and I didn't think it would be a good idea to bring her along. She's expecting, I mean we're expecting a child and the traveling would have just worn her out."

"Tony, you're going to be a father? That's great news. Does Mark or Lenny know?"

"No, we haven't gotten around to telling folks back east. You can tell them for me though."

"No, I wouldn't want to spoil it for you. You can tell them when you see them. I just want to see the looks on their faces. I'm going to get a picture of that moment, that's for sure."

"Well, I've got to go for now so I'll give you a call sometime tonight, agreed?"

"Sure!"

"Goodbye, Mr. Pushey."

"Goodbye, Tony."

Today's on-board calls would cost him a pretty penny but for Tony, it was worth it. Soon they would be all back together once more and this time things would be different. They just had to be!

Chapter 22

Mark, Lenny and Tony heard the front door open. They scooted from Mark's bedroom and ran down the stairs to the first floor where Gene and Ida Pushey, Mark's parents, stood next to Karl. He looked away from the gaze of his friends. He was carrying a small scuffed brown luggage bag. He put it down and put his hands into the back pockets of his dungarees.

"Why don't you boys take Karl out back while we put his stuff upstairs," said Mr. Pushey.

"C'mon, Karl," said Mark. He turned and headed down the hall towards the back door.

Lenny slapped Karl on the shoulder and followed Mark. Tony did the same.

"Karl, go on now," said Mrs. Pushey.

Karl shuffled down the hall and slowly headed out the back door.

"The poor kid, I know he'll be better off with his friends for the next few days. Listen, I've got to get to work. I'm already late. Will you call the store if you need me?" asked Mr. Pushey.

"We'll be fine. You go on now. Give me a kiss and scoot," said Mrs. Pushey.

They hugged and kissed warmly.

He headed out the front door. She stood in the doorway and blew him a kiss as he waved at her from the car. She watched him drive away.

She turned and picked up Karl's luggage and headed up the stairs.

Meanwhile, in the back yard the four boys stood outside the back yard tent, saying nothing. They kicked at the ground. Someone needed to break the tension.

"Karl, we're sorry, man," said Mark.

"Yeah, me too," said Lenny.

"Me, too," said Tony.

Karl picked up his head and looked at his friends. His eyes were moist. He went past them into the tent and sat on the edge of a bed. They followed him inside.

"Thanks, guys. I'll be okay. It's no big deal. He's dead. Me and my mom will get by," said Karl.

"What happened?" asked Tony.

"Ease up, Tony," said Lenny.

"No, it's cool. I can talk about it. They think it was a heart attack. I heard the cops and the doctor talking. They were saying it had to be his heart."

His friends sat down in the chairs around the card table. He stood up and joined them at the table.

"How is your mom doing?" said Lenny.

"She's staying over at the Beaudette's. She'll be okay. The doctor gave her some medicine stuff and the priest guy spent a lot of time with her. She looked better after he left."

"The priest is a nice guy," said Lenny.

"Yeah, I guess so," said a somber Karl.

Tony turned on the radio, which was set on top of the apple crate next to the card table. The Red Sox were playing on the radio. The Sox would also be playing an evening game against the Baltimore Orioles according to the radio announcer.

"The Red Sox won yesterday's game for Bill Monbouquette when Dick 'The Monster' Radatz, the Sox's top relief pitcher, came in at the top of the ninth and struck out all three batters he faced."

Mark reached into the apple crate and took out a deck of cards. The afternoon was a hot one and the tent flaps were pulled and tied wide open. There was a gentle breeze drifting through the tent from the west. Soon a game of hearts was dealt out. The baseball game on the radio began. The game on the radio droned on in the background as the card game picked up everyone's spirits.

Later, Mark's mom brought out a pitcher of grape Kool-Aid and some fresh Tollhouse cookies.

Thoughts of the mysterious creature drifted away.

* * * * *

Beyond the cave, deep inside its bowels, in a cavern several miles from the cave entrance stood the creature. He was filled with the flesh of three humans. It had been years since he tasted human flesh. It tasted so good! He should have made it last. He rushed because of his excitement. He knew he needed to be more in control. He had been taught by has father, long ago, to be patient. He was also taught to not take too many human lives at a time because it would stir the humans to hunt him. His parents and their ancestors learned long ago to carefully choose their victims. With him, the curse was now into its third generation.

He had been catching and eating humans for over a hundred and eighty years. He had been separated from his kind for over one hundred years. He found his senses grew stronger with each passing year. As long as he could have a regular supply of humans, he could live for quite a long time. The underground passage he used to reach another of his kind had collapsed in the fall of 1895 during an earthquake which struck the northern New England region. He tried to reopen the passage. For nearly a week he pulled and lifted boulders that at times weighed several hundred pounds. He tried to call with his mind to his kind beyond the collapsed tunnel but there was no response. He could not reach his own.

He eventually gave up his efforts to reopen the passage. He returned to prowl the caves and tunnels of northern Vermont and northeast New York for the animals and occasional humans he could get his hands on. He also worked to develop his abilities. He believed he was the strongest and most cunning ever. As time wore on, he found in himself a need to somehow connect with humans. He envied them their numbers, their ability to move about. He listened to their love making. He envied that the most.

This female he had just killed would have been the wrong choice for his mating. His grandfather, one of the original of his kind, had told him he could only mate once. It had to be a human female who would willingly mate with him. She would be the only one who could deliver to him a young one of his kind. To catch and mate with a human and then to keep her until she gave him a young one was something he knew would be difficult. It had been done before, not often, but it had been done.

These boys could be used to find him a mate. He would need to be very careful. One wrong move and humans would rise up and hunt him. This, too, had happened long ago. That is how he lost his parents. He lost contact with his sister over one hundred years ago. While he couldn't be completely sure, he believed, from all he knew, he was the last of his kind. He must mate. The survival of his kind was at stake. Survival was the only revenge left for the curse that had been placed upon his ancestors. He sat down and picked up a thigh bone and picked at the meat that still clung to the bone. He would find a way to use these cave hunting boys. But first he would be patient.

He chewed slowly.

High above his head there was a fluttering of wings as thousands of bats began to fly about. They flew as one, up the shaft and down the tunnel and out the cave entrance. This cave was hidden from view by a thick bush which grew at its entrance. This particular cave entrance faced to the west. It was situated half way up a thirty foot ledge outcropping on Vermont's eastern shore of Lake Champlain in the Town of Georgia.

* * * * *

It was getting dark now. All of the boys agreed to stay over for supper. They had cold meatloaf sandwiches and macaroni salad. Earlier, they learned Mrs. Sweeney decided she would bury her husband on Monday. Tonight his body would be available for viewing at the funeral home. After supper, Tony and Lenny went home after saying they would see Karl and Mark later. Mark and Karl got dressed to go to the funeral parlor.

The funeral parlor was hot. The room Bob Sweeney was laid out in was the smaller of the two available. The other room was occupied with the wake for Mrs. Goodrow. She died at the age of ninety-three. Her descendants were numerous. She had been a teacher for forty-five years. Her funeral parlor room was filled to capacity.

Bob's Sweeney's was filled, too, even though he had few friends. His neighbors and other strangers came to pay their respects to his family. His wife was too distraught to stand and greet people. She sat and silently accepted their condolences. Karl stood quietly at her side. He shook hands and nodded occasionally. His friends Tony, Lenny and Mark stood with their families. The boys were very uncomfortable with the crowd and the heat. The sweet smell of flowers hung in the humid air.

Several of the men went outside to stand or sit on the front porch. Some lit up cigarettes. They stood aside and mumbled a greeting to Father Campbell as he walked up the front steps of the funeral parlor.

"I don't know how he can wear black and that collar on a hot day like this," said a tall thin man, smoking a cigarette, who was sitting on the top step.

"I wouldn't want his job either," said another.

"Why not? He doesn't have to get his hands dirty? He knows where his next meal's coming from. He doesn't have to worry about paying bills. All you God-fearing Catholics pay his bills. Shit, he even gets to hear all the juicy stuff about who's screwing who when all the freaking buggerers in this fucking town need to clear their consciences."

Several of the men laughed at the sarcasm. The sarcastic one was Lenny's father. Lenny had been standing just inside the door and heard every word his father said. Lenny was embarrassed his father would speak so crudely about Father Campbell. Lenny liked the priest. He could talk to the priest. He couldn't talk to his own father.

The chatter on the porch next turned to other matters. The Red Sox were brought up. Lenny turned and headed back inside the funeral parlor. The priest was visiting with some of the people in Mrs. Goodrow's parlor.

Lenny went over to Karl and whispered, "Do you want to go out back and get some fresh air?"

"Yeah!" said Karl, as he leaned over to his mother and whispered into her ear. She nodded and smiled at Karl. She patted him on the hand. He left with Lenny. Soon Mark and Tony followed them outside.

When they got outside they all sat on the back steps. There was a warm breeze blowing which quickly cooled them off from the scorching heat of the funeral parlor.

"Your dad looks good," said Tony nervously.

Karl looked at Tony and then burst into a laugh. Soon Mark and Lenny were laughing, too. Tony didn't know what was so funny so after a pause he also started laughing.

"Tony, you're too much," said Karl.

"Why? What did I say?"

"My dad looks good? It sounded like you were talking about a piece of pizza. All I could think was how you always say when we have pizza at Mark's house, "Man that sure looks good." We all know how much you love pizza, right guys?"

"I didn't mean it that way," said Tony.

"I know, I know, it just struck me as funny that's all."

"It's good that you can still laugh, Karl," said Lenny.

"Listen, guys. Let's get it straight, okay! I'm not upset my dad's dead. He was a bastard and you guys know it. I'm sad for my mom. She still loved him even though he beat on her once in a while. We'll both be better off now that he's gone."

"But Karl, he was still your dad," said Mark.

"Yeah, Mark he was, but that's no excuse for the kind of jerk he was. End of story."

From inside the funeral parlor the boys could hear the murmur of hushed voices reciting the rosary.

"Karl, you should get back in there and be with your mom," said Lenny.

"You're right."

The boys headed back inside the overheated funeral parlor. Lenny noticed his dad wasn't inside. He must still be out front on the porch. Lenny joined in the prayers with everyone else.

"Hail Mary........"

The prayers went along quickly as the faithful responded to the prayers led by Father Campbell.

Several minutes into the prayers Karl heard a strange raspy voice resonating inside his mind.

"Are you pleased?"

Karl mentally fought the voice.

"I am your friend. I promised your male friends your enemy would be my enemy. This dead person hurt you. He was your enemy."

What are you telling me? thought Karl.

"I killed him for you. Are you pleased?"

He died of a heart attack. My mother didn't hear anyone else in the room. You're lying. Karl was very tense. He looked at the other boys. They were all praying. They obviously didn't hear what Karl was hearing.

"I held his heart in my hands. I squeezed it until it stopped beating. He fought for his life but he was scared as well. He knew he was going to die. He felt great pain before he died. I kept my promise."

Karl looked around the room. It was soon obvious the creature was only speaking to him. Karl looked at his father lying in the coffin. He noticed that his father's chest was moving. He next saw a hand attached to a hairy powerful arm reach into his father's chest. His father's face became contorted with a look of terror.

Karl watched as his father's arms pulled out of the inside of the casket and fought the hairy and monstrous arm gripping his chest.

Doesn't anybody see what's going on? thought Karl. He was panicked as he searched the room for anyone who could see what he was seeing.

Karl's father called out to him.

"Karl, help me. Jesus, I'm your father. Help me."

His father was growing increasingly angry.

"You little bastard, you won't help your father. Who in the fuck do you think you are?"

Karl couldn't look at him anymore. Karl was growing white with fear. He was sweating profusely.

Tony noticed that Karl didn't look too good. He got Lenny and Mark's attention and directed them to check out Karl.

Karl's legs were quaking now. He started to feel light-headed. He shot a sideways glance at his father's casket. Nothing! He was laying there just like he should. After all, he was dead.

Karl looked at him a while longer. Something was different after all. What was it? Some small detail was nagging at him. Something he should be noticing, but what could it be?

He focused on his father's eyes. His eyelids were closed but they weren't rounded and raised like they should have been. They were sunken in. It was like he had no eyeballs. That couldn't be.

The voice taunted Karl, "I killed him for you."

Karl fainted.

Chapter 23

Tony unfastened his seat belt. He looked out of the plane window at the well-lit Burlington, Vermont International Airport terminal building. It had been quite a while since he had been in Burlington. This was his first time flying into Burlington. He noticed there were signs of construction activity on the south side of the terminal building. It appeared they were adding onto the terminal. He waited for some of the other passengers in the rows ahead of him to gather their things from the overhead luggage compartments. Soon it was his row's turn to exit. He stiffly rose from his seat and shook the weariness from his legs. He reached into the open overhead storage compartment and pulled down a small overnight bag. He headed up the aisle then out the connecting ramp up into the terminal building. He went to look for the luggage area to pick up his other bag.

Tony's commuter flight, United Flight 2240, had arrived right on time, 9:05 p.m. Tony had already adjusted his watch to Eastern Standard Time, which was two hours ahead of his home back in Logan, Utah.

Standing just beyond the boarding gate area were several clusters of family or friends waiting for the departing passengers from United Flight 2240 to come through the boarding gate. In this area there were three people awaiting the arrival of Tony Fredette.

"Here's Tony now," said Lenny Drew.

"Where? I don't see him," said Mr. Pushey.

"Is that him in the corduroy sport coat?" asked Mark.

"Yeah, that's him all right. Hey, Tony, old man, it's good to see you," said Lenny.

"Well, I'll be damned—a welcoming committee. I guess this must mean I've reached true celebrity status, even here in Burlington," said a surprised Tony.

"I'd go easy on that celeb bullshit if I were you," said a smiling Mark.

"Tony, have you got any bags to retrieve at the luggage carousel?" asked Mr. Pushey.

"Yeah, I do, just one."

"This is really special, having you boys back home," said Mr. Pushey.

"Home?" asked Tony.

"My old man insisted I stay at his place while I'm here in Vermont," said Mark.

"Yeah, the same for me," said Lenny.

"And he wants you to stay there also. When he came out here to pick me up from my flight he had already picked up Lenny at his hotel. He made Lenny check out of the hotel. My flight arrived forty minutes ago and these two were here waiting for me. They said your flight was right behind mine so we decided to wait for you to arrive," said Mark.

"Isn't this the damnedest coincidence, having all three of you boys coming back home to Vermont the same day. No matter what, it sure is a treat for me. Now, let's get going," said the elder Mr. Pushey.

"Coincidence, huh?" said Lenny with a glance at his boyhood buddies.

The other two friends looked at each other and nodded their acknowledgment. Their knowing looks conveyed this was no coincidence, no coincidence indeed!

The foursome moved on and gathered up Tony's luggage. They soon exited through the automatic doors of the passenger terminal, into the biting cold night air. Heading out to Mr. Pushey's car, none of the friends said a word as each bundled up against the cold. Soon, they were all in the car. Mr. Pushey talked non-stop all the way to his house. No one interrupted him, since they each preferred to be gathering their thoughts. The drive to Winooski took only a few minutes. Mr. Pushey complained about the recent proliferation of stop signs in Winooski. The numerous stops the car had to make before they reached the Pushey house added considerable weight to Mr. Pushey's complaint.

As they entered the house, Pokey barked to protect his territory, the Pushey residence. Mr. Pushey soon quieted the dog. In a matter of moments the dog had been introduced to everyone. He received a generous scratch behind his ears from each. Now contented, he padded off to lie back down next to the wood stove.

"You boys can go upstairs and pick out a room for yourselves. I sleep downstairs now. It's easier on my legs, you understand. Anyway, go on ahead. I'm going to make a fresh pot of coffee. It shouldn't take but a few minutes. I'll give you boys a shout when it's ready."

Mr. Pushey headed into the kitchen.

The three guys picked up their respective luggage and headed up the stairs to drop the luggage off and perhaps use the bathroom.

Pokey rose from his spot in front of the wood burning stove and followed Mr. Pushey into the kitchen. Mr. Pushey opened a cupboard and took out a treat for the dog. He gave it to Pokey, who now sat in the middle of the floor, gnawing on the dog treat.

"What do you think, Pokey? It's going to be nice having these boys around for a few days."

The dog looked up from his chewing for just a moment. He seemed to agree.

"It sure is one damn coincidence though!"

The dog didn't look up this time. He focused upon the task at hand, which was to enjoy his dog treat.

Soon the enticing aroma of freshly brewed coffee wandered upstairs.

The guys were still in their rooms. They hadn't spoken a word to each other since the airport. They were each pondering how to bring up the subject, the return of Ne Wha Ta.

* * * * *

Karl didn't remember very much at first. He was still light-headed from his fainting spell. After a few moments his head began to clear up. He now realized he was sitting on the back step of the funeral parlor with a cold cloth pressed to the back of his neck. A neighbor was sitting with him. She asked Karl if he was all right. He nodded that he was feeling better. Standing straight in front of him were his three buddies.

They each had a worried look.

"Hey, guys, I guess I fainted, huh?" said Karl.

"Yeah, you fainted. You collapsed on the floor in there. It scared all the old ladies," said Tony. "Sorry, Ma'am!"

"Well, it appears you are going to be fine Karl so I'm going to go back inside now," said the lady who had helped Karl.

"Thanks," said Karl.

She rose and went back inside. The low murmur of praying voices could still be heard as the solemn praying continued.

Karl removed the cold cloth that had been resting upon the back of his neck. He twisted it and watched the water drip out onto the ground.

"That friggin' monster in the cave killed my old man," said Karl.

"How do you know that?" asked Lenny.

"Do you guys remember telling me the thing talked to you? You know, how it sort of spoke to your mind. Well, I think it was talking to me in there. He said he killed my old man to show me he was my friend and that any enemy of mine was his enemy or some shit like that."

"So you think he killed your old man because your old man beat you, is that it?" asked Tony.

"What do you think?" said Karl.

"I think you're right. I think that friggin' thing can do anything it wants to, including killing somebody," said Mark.

"That must mean it can even kill us if it wants to," said Tony.

"I don't think it wants to do something like that. If it wanted to kill us it could have done it already, right? Listen, it says it wants our friends to be its friends and our enemies to be its enemies. If that's so then it must think of us as its friend," said Lenny.

"Lenny's right, but for how long?" said Karl.

"This is a friggin' nightmare. There's some fucking monster out there—it kills people, that we know and it thinks it's our friend. Shit, that's just too much!" said Mark.

The back door to the funeral parlor opened just then. Father Campbell stepped through the door.

"Hello, boys! How's Karl doing?" he said, as he patted Karl on the head.

"I'm doing okay." said Karl.

"Your mom's inside saying good-bye to some of the visitors. Do you..."

"I know, I know, I'm heading back inside," said Karl.

"I'll meet you out front," said Mark.

"All right," replied Karl.

Mark and Tony broke away and headed around the side of the porch, towards the front of the funeral parlor. Lenny stayed back. He wanted to talk to the priest.

"Father, I am worried for Karl" said Lenny.

"How so?" asked the priest.

"Karl's one of my best friends and I don't want to see him taken from his mom and have to go to some reform school or something," said a worried Lenny.

"Lenny, you are both wise and thoughtful. Caring to be with your friend and help him in his time of need is a true corporal work of mercy. Indeed your unselfishness and concern for your friend is special. I am quite sure he will not be taken from his mother. She needs him and he needs her."

"Are you sure he won't be sent away?"

"I am very sure. That sort of thing happens when both parents are no longer around and no relative is around who can look after the child."

"I guess," replied a still-worried Lenny.

"I understand. I tell you what I'll do. How about if we plan a trip to Ausable Chasm for a week or two from now? Consider it an adventure to help cheer up your friend."

"That would be great. Could Tony and Mark go, too? You see we're close buddies and ......"

"No problem, Lenny. I think having them along is a good idea, provided we get their parent's permission first."

"Thanks, Father Campbell."

"Lenny, Lenny where are you?"

It was Lenny's father calling for him. Just then Lenny's father pulled into the back parking lot next to the funeral parlor's back porch. He rolled down his car window. He looked like he was in a foul mood.

"Hey, Padre, if you're done with my boy there, we would sure like to get going," he said sarcastically. "Lenny, get your sorry ass in the car. You know you shouldn't wander off and not tell us where you're going."

Lenny sheepishly headed to the car and climbed into the back seat. His father smiled at the priest. It was not a friendly smile. It was more like a "kiss my ass" smile.

His father turned the car around and laid a little rubber as he sped out of the parking lot.

The priest said a silent prayer for Lenny's father's soul.

I wouldn't mind kicking his ass once or twice either, thought the priest, at which point he assigned himself three, "Our Father's" as a sort of self-imposed penance. He walked to his own car with a smile on his face.

Chapter 24

Deep in the woods, about a mile north of the cave, a squirrel began scampering around in search of food. It was dusk and squirrels don't usually search for food this late in the day. But this squirrel had a need to search that overpowered its natural instincts.

It jumped from bush to tree, from tree to rock, not turning up any useful food. Nervous, it stopped and sat perfectly still on its hind legs. Its eyes searched the immediate landscape for movement. Nothing! Cautiously the small creature moved step by step across the stony ledge surface.

It poised to leap over a large crack in the rock's surface. It sprang forward and in an instant it was snatched in midair by a large hand that snapped shut. The hand was attached to a hairy, albino, muscular forearm. The squirrel kicked and squirmed inside the hand. The arm and hand with the acquired squirrel withdrew into the crack in the rock.

In the twilight of the woods a nearby owl sitting on a branch of an old oak tree surveyed the scene it just witnessed. It no longer saw the familiar small creature moving along the ground. The owl decided it would look elsewhere for its dinner tonight.

It hooted and flew away.

* * * * *

Lenny's father looked over his shoulder at Lenny. His look telegraphed his anger. Lenny tried to look away. When his father had his pissed-off look on, it was best not to give him an excuse to tee off on you.

His father glared at Lenny while he fixed his stare at the rear view mirror so he could keep an eye on his boy. He was not paying attention to his driving. He sped through a stop sign at the intersection of North and West Spring streets. Another driver, looking to pull through the intersection, had to hit his brakes to avoid hitting the Drew family's car. The other driver honked his horn at Lenny's father who in turn offered an obscene finger gesture in response.

"Fucking asshole," said Lenny's father.

"Please, Rudy, can't you slow down?" said his wife Carol.

He didn't even look at her when he swung his right hand and hit her across the face. She had seen it coming but there was little room to pull away. The sound of the slap startled Lenny. He jumped at the sound. His mother put her hands to her face and began to quietly sob. Her left ear dripped blood on to her dress from a small cut on the side of the ear.

"See what you made me do?" he said as he shot a glance back at Lenny.

"Me?"

"Yeah, you, you little ass kisser. I saw you sucking up to that priest. I don't like him. I don't want you getting near him. Do you hear me?"

"But, dad I'm an altar boy. I..."

"Don't interrupt me when I'm talking! You stay away from that priest. I want you to quit this altar boy shit. Fucking priests are all queer."

"Dad, please don't make me quit," said a scared Lenny.

Carol Drew tried to regain her composure and speak to her husband.

"Rudy, Father Campbell is a good man. Lenny is proud to be an altar boy."

"Are you disagreeing with me in front of the boy? Are you? If you are, you are stepping into some serious shit!"

"All I'm trying to say..."

He quickly pulled the car over to a screeching halt at the curb. He grabbed her left arm and twisted it so hard that she cried out in pain.

"Stop it, Rudy. Oh God, don't, it hurts."

Lenny didn't know what got into him at that moment, but he felt compelled to try to help his mother, so he reached from the back of the car and tried to pull his father's arm off of his mother. His father smiled at Lenny's bravado and let go of her arm. Lenny fell back onto the rear seat.

"You've got some balls, Lenny. Maybe you will turn out okay after all. Yes sir, my boy is developing some balls. Hot damn!"

He slapped the steering wheel and laughed as he put the car back into gear and continued heading home.

Lenny's mom didn't know what to make of his reaction to Lenny's intervention. She half-expected him to crawl into the back seat and slap Lenny around. Lenny feared something worse. When he realized what he had done without thinking he expected his father to get out of the car and take Lenny by his ankles and screw him into the ground.

I've got to watch myself, thought Lenny.

Lenny sat at the rear passenger side, as far away from his father as he could. He began to plot how quickly he could exit the car when he got home and where he could hide when he got there.

Lenny's father pulled the car into the driveway and turned off the engine. Lenny jumped out of the car and ran inside as fast as he could. Carol Drew stepped out of the car and was still stroking the left side of her face. She heard the car engine start up again.

He hollered out his driver's side window. "I'm going to get some beer. I'll be back in a little while."

Without waiting for a response, he backed the car out onto the street and sped away, leaving his wife standing in the driveway. She climbed the steps to the house and went inside. The babysitter was sitting at the kitchen table reading a movie magazine. Lenny's mom, while positioning herself so the babysitter couldn't see her bruised face, opened her purse and gave the babysitter a dollar and fifty cents.

"Thanks, Mrs. Drew. I'll be going now. The baby was fine. She's sleeping in her crib."

"Thanks for baby-sitting on such short notice."

"No problem. It sure was a surprise that Mr. Sweeney died so young. It sort of makes you think, you know? Oh well."

The babysitter picked up her magazine and headed out the door. Carol Drew opened the freezer and took out an ice tray and popped out several ice cubes onto a wash cloth. She rolled up the wash cloth and placed it against her left cheek. She sat down at the kitchen table and started to cry.

After a few moments Lenny appeared in the hallway off the kitchen. He was peaking around the corner to see if his father was anywhere to be seen. He didn't see his father but he saw his mother holding a cloth to her face and quietly crying. He went to her and put his arm around her. She reached up and touched his arm. They stayed this way for a while.

"Your father didn't mean to hurt me, Lenny. I shouldn't have spoken up like I did. It's not a good idea to distract a driver when he is driving."

"Mom, he almost had an accident. He was driving too fast."

"I know honey, but he's a good driver and he's just upset about Mr. Sweeney's death, that's all."

"Mom, he never even mentioned Mr. Sweeney. He's just pissed off about Father Campbell being nice to me."

"Don't you talk like that about your father!" she admonished. "Now please get me a tissue for my nose."

Lenny retrieved a tissue box from the bathroom for his mother. She put down the wash cloth and took out a tissue to blow her nose. Lenny noticed that the left side of her face was turning blue. There was only slight swelling but the bruise was unmistakable. She blew her nose.

"Where's dad?"

"He's gone for some beer. He'll be back soon."

"Great, that's all he needs, more beer."

"Lenny, sit down."

Lenny sat in the chair opposite his mother.

"Now look at me. Your dad is a good man, it's just that he's got a temper and we all know that don't we? Don't we?" she insisted. "Since we know about his temper it's not right to say or do things that upset him. Can you understand that?"

"Mom, we don't say the kinds of things or do stuff that he should beat us for. Mom, it's wrong. Can't you see that? I love you, Mom, and I hate it when he hurts you or when he says bad things to you."

Lenny started to cry. His shoulders shuddered with the power of his sobbing.

"Oh Lenny, I love you, too. You're a good son. You're all a mother could ask for. We just need to love your father and pray for him. We should pray for God's help to control his temper."

"Mom," said Lenny between sobs, "I pray for God's help with Dad for both of us, all the time. God hasn't answered my prayers."

"You just keep on praying, Lenny—God will answer our prayers. He always does." She gave Lenny a big, loving, mother's hug.

He broke away from her and headed to his room. He knew when his father returned home with more beer he'll probably get drunk and look for an excuse to beat either Lenny's mom or Lenny, or both. Tonight was going to be long and hot. It was also going to be a nightmare, Lenny just knew it.

* * * * *

"Boys, the coffee is ready," said Mr. Pushey, as he hollered upstairs to Tony, Lenny and Mark.

"Pokey, go on upstairs and tell the boys that the coffee is ready."

The dog looked at him and then slowly climbed the stairs. When he got to the top, he barked, "Gruff....Gruff."

"Good boy, Pokey. You can come back down now."

The dog slowly turned himself around and climbed back down the stairs.

After a few moments, the three friends left their rooms and came downstairs. They all headed to the kitchen where the aroma from the freshly brewed coffee proved to be mouth-watering to each of these weary travelers. They sat down at the kitchen table. All the fixings for their coffee were set out on the table including a plate full of snack cakes.

"Sure smells good, Mr. Pushey," said Tony.

"Thanks, Tony."

"You bake the cakes, too?" asked Lenny.

"Nope, not me. I can't bake a lick. I bought those fresh at Louie's Bakery this afternoon."

"Dad, how are you feeling these days?"

"Oh, I feel good. I walk as much as I can. Pokey keeps me on my toes. My back gets stiff once in a while. It's the only thing I have left that gets stiff anymore."

Everyone laughed. This caused the dog, which was lying down near the wood stove, to lift his head and raise his ears. His curiosity satisfied, he put his head back down.

"Dad, you have one weird sense of humor. Jesus!"

"Mark, we forgot what a character your dad is," said Lenny.

"Say, have you boys heard the one about the guy who raises peaches in all sorts of flavors?"

"No, but I've got a feeling we're about to," said Mark.

His father sat down and began telling a string of off-color jokes that stretched on for the next half hour. They all had a good time laughing and teasing one another.

* * * * *

In a deeply-darkened chamber over two miles away sat the creature. He sat up and raised his ears to satisfy his curiosity. He listened to the conversation unfolding in the kitchen. He felt pleased with himself. His mission to bring back these three succeeded sooner than he could have hoped. They would still be formidable but weaker now that one of their own was dead. Karl was always a threat. He was someone who could face his fear and that made him one who was difficult to control. He was also instrumental in trapping him inside the cave over forty-five years ago.

He listened and waited. He had proven he could wait a very long time.

Chapter 25

Karl and Mark came downstairs together. They could smell breakfast cooking all the way upstairs. They sat down at the kitchen table while Mrs. Pushey poured some orange juice. She placed a plate filled with eggs and bacon in front of both boys. In the center of the table she deposited a plate filled with toast. The boys dug in with gusto.

"How are you two feeling this morning?" asked Mark's mom.

"I'm fine, Mrs. Pushey. This food is great!"

"I'm not feeling too good, mom," said Mark slyly.

"Oh dear, do you have a fever?" she said as she placed a hand on Mark's forehead.

"No, I've got to fart," said Mark bursting with laughter as he ripped off one very loud fart.

"Mark, please, not at the table."

The boys kept laughing.

"Morning, boys," said Mark's father.

"Morning," replied the boys in unison.

He went over to Mark's mother and gave her a hug and a kiss on the cheek. He sat down at the kitchen table. He had been outside to retrieve the morning paper, the *Burlington Free Press*. Mark's mom put a cup of coffee in front of him along with a plate filled with a steaming omelet.

"Thanks, dear."

He opened the newspaper and folded it into a quarter of its size. Part of the front page faced towards the boys. They both noticed the headline of one of the front page stories. "Police Seek Answers."

Under that headline was a smaller one which read, "Three Area Teens Missing."

They shot sideways glances at one another. They both recognized the story. It had to be about the three teenagers who had disappeared into the cave. What did the police know? They knew they just had to read the story.

Mark's father put the paper down and began to eat his breakfast. Mark's mom joined them at the table as they all continued eating breakfast over assorted small talk.

After a while Mark's father rose from the table and took the newspaper with him.

"Well, I'm off to work. I'll be seeing you boys later. Don't get into any trouble, okay!" he said with a wink directed at Mark.

"Here's your lunch, dear," said Mark's Mom.

He took the lunch pail she had prepared for him and headed out the door.

"Can we be excused, Mom?" said Mark.

"Yes, dear. You boys go on now, but please make your beds first."

"We will, Mom, c'mon Karl."

The boys hurried from the table. They had barely entered the living room when Karl spoke.

"We've got to get a newspaper."

"I know. I was thinking the same thing. Let's get dressed. We can go to the Vic's Market and get a paper."

They ran up the stairs and quickly dressed, made their beds and ran back downstairs and out the front door. In a matter of moments they were at the store and purchased a newspaper. They both sat down on the sidewalk in front of the store and quickly read the story about the missing teenagers.

"So the police think they may have run away. That's good, right?" asked Mark.

"I don't know. It also says they were last seen driving a blue Ford Falcon. That means they left a car somewhere near the cave.

Shit, if the police find their car I just bet they will track them or something and probably even poke around the cave."

"But what about that monster, won't it scare away the police? Maybe the police will even kill it."

"We can't take a chance the monster has left and the police find our stuff where those kids were taken and killed. They'll think we had something to do with the murders."

"What do you think we need to do?"

"Like I told you guys before, we need to get our stuff out of there somehow, and fast."

"Shit, all I know is that I don't want to go back there. Lenny and Tony won't either."

"Well, we've got to do something. Look let's get Tony and Lenny, head back over to your place and talk this thing through."

They stood up. Karl folded the newspaper and stuffed it into his back pocket. They headed off to hook up with their friends.

Somewhere in the neighborhood a June bug's buzz resonated. It was going to be a scorcher of a day.

* * * * *

Mark's father poured the remains from his coffee cup into the kitchen sink.

"If you boys don't mind, I'm going to go to bed. I don't usually stay up this late anyway. Besides, I'm sure you fellas have things you want to chat about. You must have plenty of stories to dig up from the past that you don't want this old man to eavesdrop on, so I'll be seeing you in the morning. Good night," said Mark's father.

"Good night, Mr. Pushey and thanks for inviting me to stay here," said Lenny.

"Me, too," said Tony.

"Good night, dad," said Mark.

"Feel free to help yourselves to anything you need."

"Thanks again," said Mark.

His father headed out of the kitchen and down the hallway towards his first floor bedroom. Pokey got up from his spot in front of the wood burning stove and stretched out for a moment, yawned and headed after his master. He would settle in for the night, on the floor, at the foot of his bed. After a moment Mark's father's bedroom door could be heard softly closing.

"I think I'm going to call home and check in with my wife!" said Tony. He pulled out his cell phone and swiftly selected her number from his phone's contact list. He stood up from the table and wandered down the hallway to have some privacy.

As he dialed her number Lenny turned to Mark. "It sure is a pisser that Karl took his life."

"Yeah," nodded Mark.

Lenny poured himself another cup of coffee.

"Did your father tell you about the strange behavior that Karl exhibited before he committed suicide?" asked Lenny.

"No. What do you mean strange behavior?"

"I spoke yesterday with a neighbor friend of the Sweeneys who is house-sitting for Karl's widow while she recuperates with her family somewhere."

"And what did she have to say?"

"Well, it seems that he was upset and wouldn't talk with anyone about what was bothering him. She said he was going around muttering something about bones!

"No shit, bones?"

"Yeah, and I've got today's *Free Press*. It's got a story about the old quarry north of the city. It seems that someone is trying to re-open the place. When they did some initial blasting, guess what they uncovered?"

"Let me guess, bones!"

"You guessed it. They found a shit load of bones. Most were human ones. The police believe the remains of over fifty people were in the cave. They've opened a big investigation. The state police have been brought in and maybe even the FBI will get called in on this one."

"Do you think it's the same cave?"

"Yeah, I do."

Just then Tony snapped shut his cell phone and sat back down at the table. Mark and Lenny brought Tony up to speed on what they had been talking about.

"Did either of you guys send me a letter about this bones business?" asked Lenny.

They both shook their heads no.

"Did you guys send me an e-mail message pretending to be that fucking Ne Wha Ta?" asked Tony.

Same response!

"Look, this monster has been sending me mind messages and other shit. That's why I had to come back. I want to put a stop to that son-of-a-bitch once and for all," said Mark.

"If it's any consolation, he's been fucking with me, too," said Tony.

"Yeah, he's been getting after me as well," said Lenny.

"He's got some damn reach! He was sending me mind messages all the way to Logan, Utah," said Tony.

"Yeah, well, he was sending me stuff down in Florida. What scared me was the thought that he could take over while I was piloting a 747. Jesus, he could cause me to crash one of those. I just can't take a chance piloting while he's still alive. His reach and powers are too fucking deadly. I won't risk innocent people's lives," said Mark.

"Well, we've got to do something guys and we may not have a lot of time. This fucker threatened to take my wife. He still wants to mate, can you imagine that? He eats humans to extend his life and now he wants to make baby monsters," said Tony.

"I know. He's pissed off that we didn't deliver him a mate the last time. For all these years we thought we had been successful, that we had killed him. It's obvious when the new quarry operators accidentally opened that cave they also unleashed him again. I'll bet the first thing he did was reach out for the closest one of us that he could locate and it happened to be Karl. He took out his anger on Karl. He probably made him kill himself," said Lenny.

"So, now he's managed to get us all here. We have got to do it right this time. We can't let this Ne Wha Ta live. Remember what he did to those kids and all the others?" said Tony.

"Yeah, we remember. Remember the Indian who helped us, Louis St. Germain? Remember what he did to him?" said Mark.

"And the priest?" said Lenny.

They sat quietly now, each remembering in his own way the horror Ne Wha Ta had brought into their lives. The old fears were being resurrected along with the tightness in the stomach. This time a pounding headache was added to each for emphasis.

After a while Lenny spoke up.

"We'd better turn in. We've got a lot to think about. Goodnight, guys," said Lenny.

"Yeah, I guess I'll turn in, too," said Tony.

"I'll head up in a little while. I'll see you guys in the morning," said Mark.

After Tony and Lenny left the kitchen and headed upstairs, Mark got up and cleared off the dishes from the table and put the milk and sugar away. He turned out the kitchen light and he, too, headed up to bed.

As he headed for the stairs Mark thought, "We're in our sixties now. Older, wiser, but much less fit to take on this fiend. How in the hell can we stop him this time?"

A very weary Mark headed up the stairs off to bed.

The fire in the wood burning stove lit up the kitchen in a soft yellow reddish glow. It cast shadows that flickered about the room from its amber window. The fire in the stove flared briefly and then settled back.

Outside it was bitter cold. The chilling north wind pushed against the house as if seeking to gain entry. It was too cold to snow.

* * * * *

Karl and Mark picked up Tony first. He was sitting on his front porch eating dry cereal straight out of the box. He was happy to see his buddies. He put the cereal box away and the three of them headed over to Lenny's house. They went around back to knock at the back door. Before they could reach the porch, Karl held his hand up to motion to the others to stop and be quiet. It was then the others noticed Lenny's dad sleeping in the chaise lounge chair. There were two empty six packs of Genesee beer scattered on the ground around the chair. The zipper to his pants was half unzipped and his shirt was out of his pants. One shoe was on and the other was nowhere to be seen. The boys were about to turn and head to the front of the house when Lenny appeared behind them. He had come from around the front of the house. He motioned to them to be quiet and to come to the front of the house. They followed his signal. In the front of the house Lenny sat on the first step and put his head in his hands.

"What's happening Lenny?" asked Mark.

"What do you think? My father got shit faced last night. He's sleeping it off in the back yard. My mom and he got into an argument last night after I went to bed. She threw him out of the house because he pushed her into the bedroom door. He pounded on the back door for a few minutes, then drove off and came back later with some more beer. I guess he drank himself to sleep."

"How's your mom?" asked Karl.

"She's okay. She's got a bruise on her face and it's a little swollen, but I don't think anything is broken."

"What's going to happen when he wakes up?" asked Tony.

"It's hard to tell. Sometimes he's all right and other times he's angrier than before."

The front door to the house opened and Lenny's mom was standing there. She stood behind the screen door.

"Lenny, you can go play with your friends if you want. I called in to your father's work and told them he won't be coming in today. You go on. Your father and I will be fine. Now go, Lenny."

Lenny stood up when he heard his mother's voice. He was concerned for her, but felt in his mind that if he were not around when his father woke up, it might be one less thing for his father to focus on, particularly if he were in a bad mood.

"Okay, Mom, we'll be over at Mark's house if you need me. Just call and I'll come home right away."

"Don't worry, Lenny, just be good for Mom. Now send me a kiss."

Lenny blew her a kiss and turned and left with his buddies. She watched them head up the street from the behind the front screen door. She watched as Karl pulled a folded newspaper out of his back pocket, unfolded it, and gave it to Lenny. For just a moment she wondered what was in the newspaper the boys could be interested in, but before that thought could develop, the baby began to cry from inside the bedroom. She closed the door and went to look after the baby. The last thing she wanted was for her husband to wake up to the sound of a crying baby.

The boys walked at a brisk pace back to Mark's house. They headed straight for the back yard tent. Soon they each settled on a bed.

"We've got to come up with a plan to get our stuff back, and quick," said Karl.

"Karl, we can't just crawl into that cave like there's no big deal," said Tony.

"I know that. Look, this monster says it is our friend right?"

"Yeah," said Tony.

"Well, if it's our friend, maybe it will let us get our shit out of the cave."

"How can we be sure?" asked Lenny.

"I know how!" said Mark.

The other three boys looked at Mark with obvious curiosity.

"Just what in hell are you talking about?" asked Karl.

"Wait here and I'll show you," said Mark as he sprang from the bed and headed for the house.

"What do you think he's got in mind?" asked Lenny.

The other boys just shrugged their shoulders.

Several minutes later Mark returned carrying a brown grocery bag. He entered the tent and put the bag on the table. Then he reached up and closed the front flap to the tent so no one could see inside from the house. Mark was obviously taking security precautions, which just heightened the interest of his buddies in what was in the bag.

He pulled a long thin box from the bag and tossed the bag on the ground. The box was yellow and in large black letters it was marked with the words, "OUIJA BOARD."

"Well, guys, what do you think?" said Mark boastfully.

"What is it?" asked Karl.

"Yeah, how is this supposed to help us with that monster?" asked Tony.

"Isn't it a game?" asked Lenny.

"You mean you guys don't know what this is? Man, it's a freaking Ouija Board. You can use it to talk to the dead and stuff. I think you can even get it to tell the future, at least that's what the instructions say."

"How do you know about this board thing?" asked Lenny.

"Late one night, last year, when I was at my uncle's camp in North Hero, my parents and other adults played with this board. They thought the kids had gone to sleep but I was still awake. Anyway, I watched them play with this thing. It gave them answers to questions. It scared the shit out of my aunt because she started crying. The adults decided to stop playing with the board and my uncle made my dad promise to take the board home and burn it in the trash. I snuck it out of the trash and hid it in the attic. I forgot about it until Karl mentioned we need to find a way to see if we can figure out if the monster will let us get our stuff back. I just thought maybe we can use this thing to talk to the monster. You know, check things out before we get near the cave. So what do you guys think?"

They briefly looked at each other and then hopped off the beds and sat around the table.

"So how does this Ouija thing work." said Lenny?

"It's easy—I'll show you," said Mark.

Chapter 26

Julien Dufresne pulled his pickup truck off of U.S. Route 7 onto a dirt road heading west. The dirt road was located near the bottom of Sunderland Hollow. He drove on the road for a distance of about five hundred yards where the road opened in to a wide clearing. The clearing was a favorite among area teenagers as a place to hang out, drink, have a little sex and listen to some rock and roll.

Julien was planning to do a little hunting. He loved to rabbit hunt and west of the clearing was a series of grassy open patches which presented some fine hunting opportunities. He brought his favorite shotgun and a full box of shells.

At the far edge of the clearing he noticed a car parked in the shade of a large oak tree. He pulled his truck over towards the car coming to a stop next to it. He wondered if perhaps someone had discovered his hunting range and might be out there now. He shut the truck off. Its engine made a ticking sound as it began to cool down. He got out of the truck and stood alongside the car, scratching his head. Something was familiar about this car, but what could it be?

He decided he couldn't remember what made him think that this car was familiar. He went around to the passenger side of the pickup truck to roll up the window. He opened his door and was about to roll up the window when he noticed the morning newspaper lying crumbled on the truck's floor along with this morning's coffee cup.

He was drawn to the newspaper. He picked it up and began to scan the front page stories looking for something he could connect to this car. There it was. He folded the paper and pointed his right index finger repeatedly into the page.

"There it is, right here. I was right! It says the police are looking for a blue Ford Falcon in connection with those missing kids. I'll just bet this is the car they're looking for."

He walked around the car and noticed the windows were rolled down. He touched the hood of the car and it was cold.

"It hadn't been run this morning, that's for sure."

He took a pencil from the dash of his truck and wrote down the license plate of the car on the newspaper. He got back into the truck and started it up, backed away from the car, turned and headed back out of the woods. He set out for the local police station to tell them what he found. He wondered if there could be a reward. He might even get his picture in the paper. The rabbits could wait. This was important.

* * * * *

Mark and Lenny sat across from each other. They each rested the tips of their fingers lightly upon the tear-shaped Ouija Board planchette.

"Karl, go ahead and ask the board a question?" directed Mark.

"Like what?"

"How should I know? Just ask it something!"

"Okay, how about, is this monster real?"

The piece with their fingers lightly attached zipped straight to the place marked YES.

"That's fucking cool," said Tony.

"Did you guys push it there?" asked a skeptical Karl.

"No way," said Lenny.

"All right, how about, what does the monster want?" asked Karl.

The piece moved haltingly across the board stopping at letters along the way, the letters spelled T-O-L-I-V-E.

"What does that mean?" asked Mark.

"It spelled out, to live," said Lenny.

"I've got one. Would the monster let us get our stuff and not hurt us?" asked Mark.

"That's two questions," said Tony.

"Sh......," motioned Karl as the piece moved across the board. It first went to the "YES" space then it spelled out the word "Friend."

"Can we trust that thing?" asked Tony.

It answered by moving quickly to "YES," then on to spell out, once again, the word "Friend."

"Let me try this," said Karl as he took Lenny's place.

"Did the monster kill my father?"

"YES."

"Why?"

"Your enemy is my enemy."

"Am I talking to the monster now?"

"Yes."

"Holy shit," said Karl as he bolted to his feet.

"I told you this OUIJA Board is weird stuff," said Mark.

"What can we ask it now?" asked Karl.

This time no one was touching the piece. It started to move on its own. It spelled out a message, "Get your things, police coming soon."

"Well, what are we waiting for?" said Karl.

"Wait, let me hide this thing," said Mark. He quickly folded the board and put it and the planchette back into its box. The box was returned to the brown bag. Mark put the bag under one of the beds up against the side of the tent. It was now well out of view.

The boys quickly headed out of the tent and set their sights on the woods at the end of Pine Street. In a few moments they entered the woods.

Not far behind them was a too familiar figure. This person had noticed the boys were fully focused on heading into the woods. He had been coming down Cote Street where he was going to turn onto Pine Street, head into the woods, and do a little shooting. He had seen the boys before they could see him. He waited near a tree which grew near the street. He decided to follow them. He might even get a chance to try out his new piece, a Smith and Wesson, 357 Magnum. He shifted his pants as he, too, headed into the same woods, to follow the four boys.

* * * * *

"Hey, Dad, me and the guys need to run a couple of errands, do you mind if we borrow the car?" asked Mark.

"Of course not. Pokey and I need to take a walk anyway. It looks nice out there this morning. We like to take a little walk every day, rain or shine. Here are the car keys. Oh, and before I forget, here is a spare house key. I've got another key," said Mr. Pushey.

"We'll be back by lunch time," said Tony.

"No problem. Just enjoy yourselves. C'mon Pokey, let's go shake a leg."

"Ruff...Ruff."

Right after Mark's father and the dog headed out the door, the boys left the house themselves. They were soon heading off in the car. The car was cold and their breath left a vapor in the air.

It didn't take long to reach their destination, St. Francis Xavier Church cemetery. Mark pulled the car into the cemetery entrance and turned onto a side road. In the distance there was a funeral going on. There was a small group huddled over a casket. A priest was sprinkling holy water on the coffin. They sat in the car watching the burial.

"How do we know he's buried here? I thought if a Catholic committed suicide he couldn't be buried in his church's cemetery," said Tony.

"Maybe they looked upon his suicide as a result of his unstable mental state, sort of like he couldn't be responsible for his actions," said Lenny.

"I'm going to ask the cemetery attendant over there by the tractor," said Mark. "You guys wait in the car."

Mark got out of the car, pulled his collar up and headed over to the cemetery attendant. They spoke for a moment and the attendant pointed in the direction of the burial that was going on. Mark turned and headed back to the car. He got back inside.

"Did he say if Karl's buried here?" asked Tony.

"Yeah, he says Karl's buried in the row beyond the funeral that's going on now, four plots over to the right. It's the one without a headstone. He said the headstone was removed because it misspelled his name and the new one isn't back yet."

"Shit, Karl's got no headstone," said Lenny.

"Yeah," said Mark.

They waited in silence as they watched the burial break up and the people return to their cars. Soon the funeral procession moved out of the cemetery. Mark backed the car up and turned onto the road that would take them back to the area where Karl was buried. Mark stopped the car and they all piled out.

The cemetery attendant stopped his tractor near the casket, now sitting poised above its final resting place. He turned a crank and the casket began to lower into the barely frozen ground.

They walked a few feet ahead of the car and stopped in front of a fresh looking burial plot. It was obviously a recent burial and it was the only one on the row without a headstone. They approached in silence. They stood there for a while.

"Karl, we're going to miss you. You were the strong one among us. You were the first to know the monster is back," said Lenny.

"Yeah, Karl, we could have used your help," said Mark.

"Karl, we won't let you down. We're going to put an end to this nightmare," said Tony.

"Excuse me, fellas, I was wondering if you'd like to use this wreath?" said the cemetery attendant, who had walked over to them.

"The other party has quite a few, and well, I figured maybe you'd like to have this for your friend."

"Thanks, that's really thoughtful of you. Are you sure it's okay?" said Lenny.

"Oh, sure, I'll be coming by tomorrow and have to remove the flowers. They will be dead anyway. It's early winter, cut flowers don't last too long out here, especially this time of year."

"Thanks," said Mark.

"Don't mention it. I've got me a casket to cover. So long."

Mark took the wreath and laid it down on top of Karl's grave site.

"Let's say a silent prayer," said Lenny.

The three of them stood there for a couple of minutes in silence. The only sound was the sound of the tractor pushing soil on top of the nearby casket. They turned and headed back to the car. Their eyes were moist. As they pulled away in the car, the attendant raked the soil over the new grave site into a neat mound. He picked up chunks of sod and spread it carefully over the newly buried grave. He then straightened out the flowers around the grave and repositioned the small American flag. He climbed aboard the tractor, put it into gear and slowly made his way around the cemetery road back to the storage shed.

Tony, Mark and Lenny later made their way to the old water tower which was an integral part of their long struggle and battle with the creature. They had to leave their car and climb the old snow covered road. They spent a moment in the cold wet snow and bone chilling winds at the base of the green metal water storage tank. They came here to honor a mentor, a fellow warrior and a legend.

* * * * *

The boys reached the hollow across from the cave quickly this morning. They stopped and looked at the cave. After a moment, Karl started across the hollow with the other three boys right behind. He carefully approached the cave from the left side. He slowly stepped forward until he was next to the entrance. He knelt down on one knee and looked around the side of the cave opening—so far so good. Their hearts were pounding.

"Look, I'm going in, and as fast as I can, I'm going to toss everything out. You guys grab everything. Don't leave anything. When everything's out I'll get out real quick. Then we can get out of here," said Karl.

"What if the monster grabs you?" asked a plainly frightened Tony.

"You guys will have to run for your lives, forget about me, just get far away fast," responded Karl.

"Ready?" said Karl.

"Yeah," said Mark.

Karl took a deep breath and signed himself with the sign of the cross. He had seen Lenny do it often and he figured he could use all the luck he could get. Karl lay down on his belly and went into the cave head first. He wasn't in there more than a moment when things came flying out: shovels, flashlights, candles, coffee cans, used in removing dirt, a lantern, and a length of rope.

The boys scurried around, picking things up as fast as they could, before more stuff came flying out. All of a sudden, Karl came scampering out. He quickly stood up and began brushing off his pants.

"I've got an idea. Help me grab up some pine branches. We're going to cover up the cave's entrance—hurry!" said Karl.

The boys quickly headed to a clump of low-hanging pine trees and pulled down branches, which they dragged over to the cave's entrance.

"What the fuck are those pussies up to?" thought the person who had followed them into the woods. He had been watching them ever since they first reached the cave. Now he stepped out of the shadows and strolled across the hollow. The boys didn't see him approaching. They were busy covering the cave's entrance and consequently, they had their backs to him.

"Just what are you boys doing to my cave?" he bellowed.

The four boys were so startled they later would swear that their hearts skipped a beat or two.

"Turn around slowly so I can see your 'skuzzy' faces."

They did as they were told and came face to face with Chucky Letourneau, the craziest, meanest, and cruelest son-of-a-bitch that ever walked these woods. He shot indiscriminately at anyone he happened upon in the woods just to scare people. He tortured animals that he hunted. He deliberately wounded his prey so he could torture the animal before he killed it. He hated little kids and had been known to drop lady-finger fire crackers down guys' pants. He was even questioned once by the police as a suspect in the killing of some breeding hogs at the Longe Brother's Pig Farm over on the east side of the woods. He was someone you didn't want to mess around with, least of all, to piss off.

"What are you boys hiding in there?" said Letourneau.

"Nothing Chucky, it's just a cave—that's all," said Lenny.

"It looks to me like you boys are hiding something. Maybe I should check it out."

"I wouldn't do that if I were you," said Karl.

"Why's that suck face?" He pointed his shot gun under the chin of Karl.

"Uh, well..., there's something in the cave, and it may be dangerous, that's all," stammered Karl.

"Oh yeah, well, you pussies may be scared but I ain't scared of nothing! Now why don't you guys just move these branches out of my way? I'm going to check the cave out for myself."

They did exactly as they were told.

"Listen. I'm going to leave my shotgun out here with you guys. Don't get any funny ideas. Nobody touches my gun, got that?"

They each nodded their agreement.

"Remember, I still have my 357 magnum and I will drop the first one stupid enough to touch my shotgun. Now step aside while I check this place out."

He slowly slid down, on his back, into the cave. The boys waited outside. He climbed to the rear of the cave and poked his head inside the opening at the back of the cave. He could smell a foul odor. He decided to head back outside. He turned and crawled back to the front of the cave. He pulled himself part way out of the cave. The boys were standing there looking down at him.

"This is nothing but a fucking bear cave and Eiyeeeeeee.....!

Something's got my legs! Help me, help me," he screamed at the top of his voice.

The boys jumped back in total terror. Their eyes were ready to pop right of their heads.

Chucky Letourneau laughed so hard he thought that he would piss his pants. He had fooled these punks and their reaction was priceless.

"You fucking little twerps, I'll bet that you're all scared of your weenies," said Chucky Letourneau.

The boys looked at each other. They had to agree that he had got them good.

He reached out with his right hand, when all of a sudden, the expression on his face changed to its own reflection of terror.

"What the fuck?" he said.

In a flash he slipped back inside of the cave.

This time his screams were unmistakably real.

"Jesus, what are you. Let go of me." His voice was growing more frightened. "I've got a gun, you bastard!"

Two shots rang out.

The boys didn't wait to find out what else was going to happen next—they already had a good idea what was happening. Instead, they quickly grabbed up their stuff and sprinted across the hollow. After a short pause to look over their shoulders they kept right on moving out of the woods as fast as they could.

* * * * *

Julien Dufrene pulled his pickup truck into the parking lot of the Town of Colchester's police Department. He got out of the truck and strolled into the police Station with a folded newspaper in his right hand. He pulled open the front door and walked right up to the glass window.

He cleared his throat. "Ahem... Excuse me ma'am. May I speak to the police chief?"

"Can I have your name, please?" she said. She was the town's police Dispatcher. She was married to one of the town's Selectmen. In her younger days she turned quite a few heads. She was now in her early fifties but didn't look her age. Indeed, she looked several years younger. She dyed her hair black and she wore a police uniform, which fit her younger looking shape rather well.

"My name is Julien Dufresne."

"Uh-huh," she said as she wrote his name on a sheet with lines showing the time of day down the left side of the paper.

"And what do you need to see the chief about?"

"You see, I remembered something that I had read in the paper this morning. You know those missing kids? Well, I was out rabbit hunting this morning like I -,"

The telephone rang just then.

"Just a moment please," she motioned to him to hold on telling his story. She picked up the telephone and in a moment she was involved in a conversation with someone named Violet.

He looked around the lobby and sat down on a gray metal folding chair. He didn't like waiting, but what could he do? He picked up a magazine from a small side table and started to thumb through it to pass the time. It seemed he had been waiting for quite a while. She had been on the phone all this time. He looked at his watch. Approximately fifteen minutes had passed when the front door suddenly opened and a very large man stepped through. This man had to be six foot four and weighed at least two hundred and twenty five pounds. He was wearing a white short sleeve police shirt with dark blue pants. The leather from his belt and holster creaked as he walked. He nodded at Julien Dufresne. The dispatcher pressed a hidden button which buzzed and it was accompanied with a click at the lower half to a Dutch door to the left of the dispatcher's glass entrance.

The officer went through the door and around to the dispatcher who, by now, had hung up the telephone. The officer leaned forward and she whispered something to him. He then briefly disappeared for a moment then reappeared at the Dutch door.

"I hear you're looking for the chief. I'm the chief—the name's Jack Seltzer. Why don't you come on back here?" He reached out his hand as he opened the Dutch door and shook Julien's hand vigorously.

"My dispatcher says your name is Julien Dufresne, did I get that right? Mr. Dufresne, please have a seat," as he motioned for him to sit down next to the chief's desk. The chief's desk was well worn and scarred. It was also piled high with papers. The chief sat down and leaned forward, putting his elbows on the desk and his chin in his folded hands.

"Thank you for seeing me. I'm a little nervous."

"Don't be nervous, unless of course you just robbed the local bank." He let loose a laugh that helped to relax Julien, who managed to laugh just a little.

"Well, as I said earlier to the lady, I read in the morning paper the police are still looking for those three kids that disappeared. I said to her that this morning, as usual, I headed to my favorite rabbit hunting place. I go rabbit hunting two, maybe three times a week. I've got me a couple of good spots. I just about get a rabbit every time I go."

"Mr. Dufresne, if you have some information about those kids, I would sure like to hear it?"

"Yeah, yeah, those kids, I know, I'm getting to that. Well, this morning I headed over to the old sand pit west of Sunderland Hollow off of Route 7. When I got there I noticed this car parked at the back end. Now, I've been there plenty and I never see a car there during the day except during deer hunting season. I thought maybe someone found my secret hunting spot. So I pulled my truck right next to the car. Right away I noticed there is no one around the car."

"Please, Mr. Dufresne what makes you think this car is connected to these missing kids?"

"I knew you'd ask me that, so I brought the newspaper that was on the floor of my truck. I wrote down the license plate number right here next to where the story says you're looking for a blue Ford Falcon."

He handed the folded newspaper to the chief, who took it. The Chief turned the paper around and located the hand written numbers. He wrote the numbers down on a note pad next to his phone. He handed the newspaper back to Julien. He pulled a sheet of paper out of a tray on the top right side of his desk. He glanced at the paper and back down at his note pad and then stood up.

"Will you excuse me for a moment?

The Chief went out of his office and went straight to the dispatcher. He spoke to her quietly for a moment. She picked up a microphone and began to speak into it. The Chief returned to his office and closed the door behind him.

He sat down again and said, "Mr. Dufresne, could you please tell me again what you saw this morning and don't leave out anything, okay?" The Chief took a yellow legal pad out of his side drawer and nodded for Julien to begin.

Chapter 27

There was a tunnel that weaved underground south from the quarry. It had several branches. In some places it was only four feet high and no more than five feet across and in some places fifty to as much as a hundred and fifty feet below the surface. The creature knew every inch of this passage. He spent his entire life roaming throughout the miles and miles of tunnels and caves that spread out like a spider's web. He now reached a spot where he stopped and listened. He could hear a machine working at the surface. He strained, then detected the conversation of Mark, Tony and Lenny. He waited and soon they left.

He began to dig. While he dug, he did so at an angle, digging in the direction of the surface. He removed small to mid-size boulders which he deposited further inside the narrow tunnel, gradually back-filling as he went. It took him nearly an hour of digging before he reached the bone chilling frost- permeated ground which had taken hold three feet below the surface.

Suddenly, he pulled aside a wide, flat rock and dirt cascaded down. He now smelled what he was looking for. He quickly put the rock inside a side tunnel which he used to deposit the material his digging had produced. He returned to the tunnel he was digging. He sniffed the air.

"Yes, this is it!" he said to no one.

He reached up and punched a hole into the bottom of the wooden casket. He ripped at the wood and opened half of the bottom. He pulled down stuffing and silk fabric. Soon a semi-rigid body dropped down while still partially hung up inside the casket. He pulled on the shoulders and removed the body. He dragged it down the tunnel and put it on the ground. He then began to put back many of the boulders he had earlier removed during his excavation. He was back-filling the short tunnel to the surface to ensure it would not collapse and reveal his latest theft. He was enjoying this work.

It struck him as strange that the underground, which humans were so much afraid of, was the place they chose for themselves after death. While he listened and studied humans he knew he could never fully understand this foolish ritual.

Soon he was done with his refilling of the recently excavated tunnel. He returned to the human body he had just removed from its casket. He sniffed at the body of Karl Sweeney. It smelled foul to the creature. From his earlier efforts at grave robbing, he had learned that many years ago humans began to use some strange liquid to fill the body and this liquid gave off a foul odor to him. Worst of all—it ruined the meat, such a waste. There wasn't even a drop of blood.

Well, this time it didn't matter. He wasn't after the flesh to eat. He merely wanted the body for another purpose. He needed it to complete the surprise welcoming he was planning for his friends. He hoped they would be impressed with his resourcefulness, but he would settle for just plain intimidation.

He put the dark blue suited body of Karl Sweeney under his left arm and then began the trek back to his favorite cave.

* * * * *

The door to the Chief's office opened and the Dispatcher poked her head inside.

"Chief, excuse me. Officer Coulon is on the radio. He wants to talk to you.

"Please excuse me, Mr. Dufresne."

The Chief left the room, closing the door behind him. He was gone for a few minutes. He returned shortly and closed the door again.

"Mr. Dufresne, we found the car where you said it would be and it checks out. It looks like the car we've been looking for. Now I've got a few more questions and then I think you can go. I'll also need your address and a telephone number."

Julien gave the Chief the information he requested and answered a few more questions.

"Chief, can I head over to the sand pit now and go rabbit hunting?"

"I don't think so, at least not for a while. We're going to begin a search of those woods and I wouldn't want any hunting nearby. You understand?"

"I sure do, Chief. I'm just glad that I could help."

"Mr. Dufresne, you've been a very big help. Right now we need to do our jobs and hopefully find those kids safe and sound."

"Okay, Chief."

Julien rose and the Chief did likewise. They shook hands. Julien headed out to the lobby, and before he headed out the door, he nodded and tipped his cap to the dispatcher, who smiled at him. He climbed into his truck and turned it on. Slowly backing up, he pulled out of the parking lot.

The Chief put his hat on.

"I'm heading out to the sand pit to meet up with Officer Coulon. Give State Police Sergeant Miller out at Post 5 a call and get a message to him. Have him meet me out at the sand pit. Tell him what we found and tell him I would like to have him stop by."

"Will do, Chief. Anything else?"

"Nope, that's it for now!"

He turned, headed out the door and was soon on his way to the abandoned sand pit. He always hoped for the best but was seldom rewarded with that as the outcome. He turned on his cruiser's lights but left the siren off. He pushed the speed of the cruiser up to fifty. He reached down and took the radio microphone and put in a call to Officer Coulon.

* * * * *

Mark pulled the car into the parking lot of the Red Onion Diner located on a hill overlooking U.S. Route 7 to the east and the quarry to the north. The diner was located next to Interstate 89 just north of the Winooski-Colchester border. The three guys got out of the car and headed into the diner. It was decorated to resemble an authentic 1950s style diner with plenty of chrome. The floor was covered with large black and white linoleum tiles. The tables were basic formica to complete the look. The sign at the entrance said, "Self Seating -Breakfast."

They chose a table in the northeast corner. They sat down and put their coats on the empty fourth chair. A waitress approached the table with a pot of coffee in hand. She had a warm and friendly smile. She was wearing a red and white striped uniform which was clean and crisp.

For ten o'clock in the morning the place was rather busy. It was easily eighty percent full.

"Coffee, gentlemen?" asked the waitress.

"Yes," said Mark and Lenny.

"Do you have decaf?" asked Tony.

"Yes, I'll be back in a moment with the decaf."

She poured two cups of steaming coffee. In a moment, as promised, she returned with a pot of decaf coffee for Tony. She poured him a cup.

"Will you gentlemen be having breakfast?"

Lenny looked at the others and answered for them all. "Yes, I believe we will. Just give us a moment will you?"

"Of course, if you need a refill, just give me a wave. Refills are free."

"Thanks, we will," said Lenny.

"She seems real nice," said Tony.

"Yeah, and this place must be pretty good to be packed like this in the middle of the morning," said Mark.

"It was kind of interesting to drive around the city this morning and see some of the changes. In some neighborhoods, though, it hardly seems like anything changed," said Mark.

"Where we grew up seems pretty much the same except where the woods use to begin at the end of Pine Street. Pine Street has been extended and there are many new homes that have been built deeper into the woods," said Tony.

"Yeah, I noticed that, too. The new homes seem to stop about five hundred or so yards from the cave's entrance," said Lenny.

"Look at that quarry over there. It sure looks pretty big from here," said Mark.

They turned and took a long look at the quarry through the one north side window of the diner.

"Are you ready to order now?" said the waitress.

"Oh, sure, ah, do you have some apple pie?" said Lenny.

"Yes, we do, and it's still warm. We make our own."

"What do you say guys, apple pie all around?" said Lenny.

"Sure," said Tony.

"Sounds fine. By the way, is this place always this busy at this time of day?" asked Mark.

"Not really. I mean, we're usually busy, but not like this. Most of this crowd is part of the big investigation going on at the quarry over there," she said nodding in the direction of the quarry. "Some are reporters. Some of them come in several times a day."

"Is that the investigation of the cave with all those bones in it?" asked Lenny.

"It sure is. It's real creepy if you ask me. I'd better get you that pie before it cools down," said the friendly waitress as she left to retrieve three orders of hot, homemade apple pie!

"Can't see much of anything from here," said Tony.

"I know. I wonder if there is a way we could get closer and check it out," said Mark.

"I doubt it, especially if the place is crawling with investigators," said Lenny.

In a few moments, the waitress brought them their pieces of pie. The aroma was mouth-watering. She moved on to attend to other tables. They began to enjoy the pie. It was every bit as good as promised. They ate in silence. The waitress returned and offered to refill their coffee cups, but they weren't quite ready yet.

At that moment two men walked over to their area and sat at a nearby table. The men removed their blue winter parkas and hung them on their chair backs. They were dressed in police uniforms. One had a shoulder patch which noted he was a member of the Winooski Police Department. The other had a patch which noted he was a member of the Town of Colchester Police Department.

The waitress soon approached their table and poured them cups of coffee. The men were talking quietly to each other. Just then a man came out of the bathroom located on the west side of the restaurant. He spotted the two police officers and headed straight for their table.

"Chief Contois and Chief Merrill, it's good to see you again," said the man. He vigorously shook their hands.

The Colchester police chief identified as Chief Merrill asked the man to join them.

"Why don't you sit down and join us, Special Agent Joyce?" said the Chief.

"Don't mind if I do," said the FBI Agent. He pulled out a chair and sat down. The waitress came by and offered him a cup of coffee, which he accepted. They began an animated conversation full of stories of past cases and past inside jokes.

The three guys couldn't believe their good fortune.

"Let's hang out here for a while. Maybe we can pick up on something in connection with their investigation," said Mark. The others nodded their agreement as they sipped their coffee. They strained to catch any snippet of conversation they could.

Police Chief Ed Contois began his career as a police officer in Colchester. He was the son of former Colchester Police Chief, Tom Contois. Winooski Chief Ed Contois was a fierce looking man. He was totally bald and had a small dark mustache which was neatly trimmed. He was at least six foot two and weighed two hundred easily. He appeared to have large muscular arms which stretched the sleeve fabric of his shirt. His eyes were small and animated, as he seemed to be constantly looking about, never stopping on anything for very long.

Police Chief Merrill had a flat top despite his obviously thinning hair. His hair was salt and peppered in color. He, too, was tall. He was slightly taller than Chief Contois and he was also heavier. He appeared to weigh somewhere near two fifty. He also had a mustache which was more white than black. He possessed powerful looking, large hands. He smiled a lot. He seemed more relaxed than Chief Contois.

Special Agent Joyce was not only dressed differently than the two chiefs, he was built much differently than they. He was about five foot ten and weighed perhaps one hundred and seventy pounds. He wore a dark blue suit, white dress shirt and a dark blue striped tie. His hair was reddish brown. He was wearing highly polished black wing tipped shoes. His hands were slender.

Agent Joyce took a note pad out of his inside jacket pocket and quietly read something from it to the police chiefs. They both nodded their agreement to whatever he just said. He sat back in his chair. He turned and looked across the restaurant and gestured to two other men who were sitting at a table in the corner to come over. They stood up, buttoned their suit jackets, and walked over to the table where Agent Joyce and the two chiefs were sitting.

Agent Joyce introduced the two men to the chiefs.

"Gentlemen, this is Winooski Police Chief Ed Contois and Colchester Police Chief Stockton Merrill. Chiefs, let me introduce my associates, Agent Dunfey and Agent Corsey. They will be working with me on this joint task force investigation. You'll find them very helpful. We're heading over there now to do some preliminary work. Are we still on for this afternoon for your office, Chief Contois?"

"Yes, at four p.m. sharp. The state Medical Examiner and County Coroners will be joining us as well," said Chief Contois.

"I'll be heading over to the quarry in a short while," said Chief Merrill.

"Good. See you soon, gentlemen," said Agent Joyce. He turned with the other two agents. They went back to the corner table and left a tip, picked up their overcoats and headed out of the restaurant.

The two chiefs resumed drinking their coffee.

Nearby, Mark, Tony and Lenny relaxed as they continued their conversation.

Chief Contois' eyes suddenly focused on Tony. He had stopped his glancing about and now eyed Tony from head to toe.

"Don't look now, Tony, but it seems that you've gotten the attention of Chief Contois. He's staring at you. No, no don't turn around," said Lenny.

"What are you, Tony, some kind of escaped rapist or something?" said Mark.

"Cut it out, guys, this isn't funny," said Tony.

Chief Contois whispered something to the other chief. He then got up from the table and headed over to Tony. He stopped next to Tony, who tried hard to act like he didn't notice the police chief.

"Excuse me, are you Tony Fredette?" asked the Chief.

Tony turned slowly and looked up at the intimidating presence of the Chief.

"Uh...yes I am, officer. Is something wrong?" said a nervous Tony.

"No, nothing's wrong. I'd just like to shake your hand. I've read your books and my wife has, too. We're both big fans," he said as he extended his right hand to Tony.

A greatly-relieved Tony stood up and shook the Chief's hand. The Chief turned and said to Chief Merrill, "I told you it was him. Come and meet the guy."

The two chiefs were smiling and seemed quite pleased to meet a famous author.

"Uh... Chiefs, I almost forgot my manners here. Let me introduce you to my two friends," said Tony.

Greetings were exchanged all around. Soon the five men pulled two tables together and ordered coffee refills.

"So you fellas have come back home to pay your respects to Karl Sweeney. That's real nice of you guys. Suicide is such a waste," said Chief Contois.

"We were all good and close friends. We hung around together and spent our summers hunting and exploring the woods around here. Of course there were fewer houses back then and the woods were not yet chopped up by the interstate highway," said Tony.

"We heard about this cave thing over at the quarry. It's all over the news. Mark even heard about it down in Miami," said Lenny.

Mark nodded his agreement.

"Is that so? It's no wonder. This case is just beginning. We've got a lot of investigating to do yet," said Chief Merrill.

"So, who's in charge of the investigation?" asked Mark.

The waitress quietly stopped by and discreetly slipped the checks onto their tables. She didn't want to disturb them from their conversation.

"The Attorney General has taken over the case and he has given the lead responsibility to the state police. We're helping as much as we can. Until there is certain evidence of a crime in either jurisdiction we will be expected to take a support role. The FBI has come onboard at the request of the Attorney General to help with specialized forensic analysis. They're also interested in the possibility of kidnapping across state lines," said Chief Merrill.

"That's all off the record!" said the Chief, with a firm look.

Changing subjects, Chief Contois said, "Listen, Tony, I was wondering if I could arrange to have you meet my wife. She would be so thrilled to meet you," said Chief Contois.

"I'd be happy to meet your wife, Chief. You can reach me at the Pushey residence on Pine Street. We're all staying there," said Tony.

"Chief Contois, I was wondering if you could do us a favor. We'd like to have a chance to see the cave site, at a distance, of course. I'm considering the possibility of doing a book on this story. It would help to actually see the site. Years ago we hung around the quarry and the surrounding woods as youngsters, and, well, frankly, we're also curious tourists," said Tony.

"Well, you fellas understand that it's an active crime scene and we shouldn't bring you guys out there. But I'll tell you what. We could head over there now if you guys agree to stay in my car. We can park pretty close. We'll only stay for a short while, and then I'll bring you all back here to your car," said Chief Contois.

"Thanks, Chief. We sure do appreciate it, don't we guys?" said Tony.

"Sure do, Chief. If either of you guys take a flight on a Delta 747 when I'm piloting, you can come up to the flight deck and I'll show you around," said Mark.

"That would be really interesting. Listen, let's get going. Chief Merrill, I'll take them over in my car."

The five of them rose and tossed their tips on the tables and grabbed their overcoats and headed for the door. The waitress greeted them with a smile as they paid their checks at the checkout register.

"That was brilliant Tony," whispered Lenny.

"I know," said Tony before sliding into the front seat of the police chief's cruiser. Mark and Lenny sat in the back. They noticed the back inside doors didn't have any door handles to open the doors and there weren't any handles to raise or to lower the windows.

The Chief started the car and quickly slipped it into gear. He maneuvered it expertly and quickly out of the parking lot and down onto Route 7. He turned left and went maybe a hundred yards when he turned left again and headed up a hill onto the quarry property. At the top of the hill was a police cruiser which was left running. An officer was standing outside in the cold. He waved at the Chief, who waved back as they drove by. The Chief turned right onto a service road which wound itself around and down into the quarry. The road was rough and the ride a little bouncy.

At the bottom of the wide open quarry the cruiser turned and headed to the west side of the quarry. The wall of the quarry rose from the quarry floor at least two hundred feet straight up. Near the far west wall was a construction trailer and several police cars. There was a large unmarked van with several antennas sticking up from its roof. There was also a large motor home with the State of Vermont seal on its side with the words "State Police Crime Scene Command Center" stenciled underneath.

The Chief pulled the car up as close as he could. He left the car running.

"Now remember, we agreed you fellas would stay in the car. I've got to check on a couple of things. I won't be gone long. I'll leave the car running so you guys can stay warm. Now just for your information that motor home is a mobile command center. The other large van over there is where we secure the evidence. The rest of these cars belong to different investigators. You can see the cave entrance right there. It opened up when they dynamited this area. The cave goes in maybe a hundred and fifty feet to where it apparently collapsed when the new dynamiting opened up this side of the cave. The bones that were found were located about fifty feet inside. The bones stretch all the way back to the collapsed part. Well, anyway, I'll be right back."

The Chief got out of the car and walked over to the cave entrance. He disappeared from view as he descended into the cave.

"Tony, this is fucking incredible!" said Lenny.

"Tony, what a great idea," said Mark.

"Yeah, I surprise myself sometimes," said Tony.

* * * * *

The four boys exited the woods, panting for air.

"Fucking-A, my lungs feel like they're on fire," said Karl.

The other boys nodded, since none of them wanted to waste any air on trying to speak. They sat down in the tall grass. Their breathing slowly began to come down to manageable levels.

"We got all of our shit back thanks to you, Karl," said Tony.

"Yeah, now the cops can't connect us to any missing kids," said Mark

"That may be true, but what about Chucky?" said Lenny.

"What do you mean?" said Karl.

"Don't you guys remember that he had a shotgun? He left it on the ground in front of the cave before he went in. I think it's still there," said Lenny.

"Shit, you're right. How could we forget the damn gun." said Karl.

"How's that going to connect us to anything?" said Mark.

"By itself it doesn't. But think for a minute. If the police search the woods they may stumble on the gun. Then they're going to want to check out the cave. Who knows what they might find. Maybe we forgot something inside the cave, they'll find it and then they'll think we had something to do with all those dead people," said Lenny.

"So what do we do?" asked Tony.

"How about if me and Karl go back and get the gun. We'll also cover up the front of the cave again. You guys head back to the Mark's tent?" said Lenny.

"That won't work. My mom will wonder where Karl is—we're supposed to be together, remember?" said Mark.

"I don't want to go back," said Tony.

"Go on, Tony. This is too important to leave to one guy. Look, I'll tell you what. If you go and help Lenny, I'll get you one of my old man's *Playboy* magazines to keep," said Karl.

"Okay, okay. I'll go, but Lenny carries the gun," said Tony.

"Deal," said Karl, as he shook Tony's and Lenny's hands. They handed over their stuff to Mark and Karl and turned and headed back to the cave.

Mark and Karl then picked up everything and headed for Mark's house. They were half way to Mark's house when a bright yellow pickup truck with the words Bremer's Construction Material painted in black on the door's side slowed up next to the boys. A somewhat familiar face peered down on the boys.

"Say, you're the Sweeney boy?" asked the driver.

The boys stopped walking and the truck stopped moving.

"Yeah, my dad is Bob Sweeney. Why?"

"I knew your dad. We were in the army together. I'm sorry about what happened," said the man.

"Thanks."

"Say, mister do you work at the quarry?" asked Mark.

"I sure do. I'm the dynamite man."

"The dynamite man?" asked Karl.

"Yeah, boys, I get to play with dynamite all day. It's kind of like playing with firecrackers only these can do a lot of damage. Dynamite can kill you if you're not careful. It's not something to fool with, I can tell you that."

"So you knew my dad in the army?"

"Yeah, we were in World War II together, towards the end of the war actually. We were demolition experts. We knew how to use every kind of explosive there was. So, what are you boys up to?"

"We've been playing in the woods and now we're heading to Mark's house," said Karl.

"Well I've got to get back to work. I just came home to get my wallet. I forgot it when I left for work this morning. Tell your mom I'm sorry about your loss."

"You didn't tell us your name," said Mark.

"Gees, you're right. My name's Benjamin Mackenzie, but my friends call me Bud."

"Well, so long mister," said Karl as he and Mark set off again for Mark's house. The truck pulled away and Bud looked back at the boys and waved. They waved back.

Chapter 28

Lenny and Tony moved quickly and quietly into the woods. It was hot and humid and all this running about raised a good sweat on both boys. Soon they were standing in the familiar location across the hollow from the cave entrance. They retraced the steps Karl had taken earlier when he crept up to the cave's entrance. The gun hadn't been disturbed. It was still on the ground just as Chucky Letourneau left it before disappearing inside the cave.

They stood to the left of the cave's entrance. Lenny turned to Tony and whispered to him.

"I'm going to run and pick up the gun and stop on the other side. If nothing happens then I'll move the gun over to that bush over there. After I leave the gun there, we toss these branches across the entrance as fast as we can and we get the hell out of here. Ready?" said Lenny.

Tony nodded in the affirmative. He was sweating profusely. He was wide-eyed and ready.

"On three, one, two, three," said Lenny.

He sprinted across the front of the cave and scooped up the shotgun. He stopped on the opposite side and listened. There wasn't any unusual sound. He moved to put the gun near the bush at the edge of the hollow. He came back. He signaled to Tony. Now they both moved as fast as they could. They reused the branches that they earlier gathered to cover the cave's entrance, before Chucky interrupted their efforts to disguise the cave's entrance.

After a couple of minutes they were satisfied with their efforts. They hurried over, retrieved the shotgun and once again headed out of the woods.

When Lenny and Tony reached the edge of the woods, Lenny stopped.

"Help me break up a few branches to carry with this gun, that way nobody will notice I'm carrying this thing," said Lenny.

Tony and Lenny soon had several sticks gathered up. As a result, they calmly walked from the woods with the gun in hand, heading straight for Mark's house.

* * * * *

They were at the quarry for about a half hour when the Chief returned to the car.

"I've got to head back to City Hall. I'll drop you off at your car on the way."

"How's the investigation going so far?" asked Lenny.

"It will go a lot better now that the FBI has joined up. We really need their help in doing some of the more complicated forensic analysis."

"Where did all the bones come from? I mean the news says you've discovered human remains from something like fifty people, right? Was it a mass suicide thing or a mass murderer?"

"You know the Chief can't answer that, Mark," said Tony.

"He's right. I can't answer that, but what I can say is some of those bones are real, real old, yet some of them are maybe a few years old," said the Chief.

"Is it just bones or is there other stuff in the cave?" asked Lenny.

"Same problem, I can't directly answer that, but what do you think?" retorted the Chief.

Changing subjects, Mark asked, "What do you think is beyond the collapsed part of the cave?"

"Don't really know. We haven't been able to get past that collapsed part. It's too unstable.

"Thanks, Chief for taking us along. I really do appreciate it. Please give me a call when you want to get together with your wife. I always look forward to meeting a fan," said Tony.

"Thanks, Chief," chimed in Mark and Lenny.

"I'll give you a call tonight so we can arrange to get together. Here you go!"

The three guys got out of the cruiser and waved to the Chief as he pulled away. They got into Mark's father's car and headed back to the house.

* * * * *

Meanwhile, deep beneath the earth's surface about a mile away, the creature reached his destination. His new nesting spot was just about a hundred and fifty feet from the old cavern just beyond the cave the boys first uncovered in 1962. The recent dynamiting uncovered the part of his systems of caves and tunnels he considered his home. It was a place he occupied for the past hundred and twenty-five years. He had not anticipated the reopening of the quarry. He would now use all his powers to shut down this effort. He would wait until the humans now exploring his home and removing the bones had left.

He propped the stiff body of Karl Sweeney against the wall. He sat down on a flat rock. He was hungry. He had not eaten in nearly a month.

Looking over at the corpse of Karl Sweeney, the creature said, "I would have preferred killing you with my bare hands. That way I would have something to eat along with satisfying some of my revenge." The creature spat on the ground.

The creature turned and headed off through a nearby tunnel in search of food. He traveled for several minutes. His stride was long, powerful and above all; purposeful. He sniffed the air while stopping at a junction in the tunnel system. He took another route which was smaller and steeper. It led near the surface. He could smell the sweet odor of flesh, not human, but at least coursing with warm blood. He crept quietly forward, stopped and sniffed the air.

He was real close now. He reached through the small hole directly ahead and felt the coarse fur. The body it covered was breathing slowly and surely. He felt around and found two other fur-covered bodies. He found the pointy faced small head of one of the smaller bodies and in one powerful crush of his hand he snapped the neck of the small creature.

He carefully pulled the body towards him through the hole. He soon had the small limp dead body of the year old bear cub in his full possession. He slipped back down the tunnel and made his way back to his nesting cave. The dead bear's body was beginning to slowly cool down.

He sat back down on a flat rock and tore off the bear's head. He put it aside and lifted the body up so that the blood would flow out of it. He held the back legs of the bear as he tipped his own head back. He drank the warm sweet blood of the bear. Some of the blood spilled down on his own hairy chest. It was sticky to the touch.

He ate slowly. He tore at the bear's flesh and ripped limb from limb. He stripped the furry skin off with his powerful hands and tossed it in the corner behind him. Small rodents, having smelled the blood, couldn't resist as they came out of their own hiding places and began to tear into the carcass remnants. The creature didn't mind the rodents sharing in his meal. He wasn't totally cruel. He didn't kill all living things. Killing for him had to have a purpose. It had to be necessary. He killed to eat. He killed humans to sustain his life force to survive. It was his destiny, and it had been handed down to him by his ancestors. He also killed as a means of control. He needed to control his environment to survive.

Now he had an unmet need that was urgent and greater than any other. He didn't know how long his life would be. He had not seen another of his kind in over a hundred years, even though he at times felt something or someone calling to him. But one thing was clear; he felt a strong urge to mate. He must ensure that his kind lived on. Perhaps his kind would one day walk the surface of the earth again as they once did hundreds of years ago.

He was, by far, the strongest of his kind, of that he felt sure. His power of mind control over humans was immense. His reach extended for well over a thousand miles, perhaps much more. He didn't really know its outer limits but he was sure that with his mind power over humans, and with the technology humans controlled, his own reach was perhaps global.

He lay down on a bed of moss he had assembled and soon was asleep.

* * * * *

Lenny and Tony arrived in Mark's back yard. Lenny had Tony hold open the tent flap as he slipped inside. He immediately hid the shotgun under one of the beds. He stepped outside just as Karl and Mark were exiting from the back door of the house. They each held a glass of Kool Aid.

"Hey, guys, want some? My mom just made it," said Mark.

"Sure," said Tony.

"Sounds good to me," said Lenny.

They went up to the back door. Mark came back out with two tall glasses filled with clinking ice and freshly made Kool Aid. The boys sat on the back steps and sipped the refreshing ice cold drink.

Leaning over to Lenny, Mark whispered, "Where'd you put the gun?"

"I hid it under one of the beds inside the tent."

"We can't leave it there. It needs to be hidden somewhere else," said Karl.

"I know. We can hide it in the garage loft for now. Nobody goes up there to get stuff. All we ever do is put stuff up there," said Mark.

"You should wrap it in something, too," said Tony.

"Good idea!" said Karl.

"How about an old army blanket? We've got several in the basement. Nobody will miss one," said Mark.

"Sounds like it would work," said Karl.

"Okay, here hold my drink. I'll be right back," said Mark as he handed his drink to Karl and ran inside the house. In a moment, he returned with a well worn brown Army surplus blanket.

The boys all headed into the tent. Lenny pulled the gun out from under the bed and Karl wrapped the gun with the blanket. After checking to see if anyone was looking, the four boys left the tent. They went inside the garage. Mark pulled down the ladder to the loft. Karl and Mark climbed up. Lenny and Tony could hear their steps from down below. It sounded like they walked to the front of the loft. There was a scraping sound like something being dragged across the floor. After a moment, Lenny and Tony heard Mark and Karl's steps returning to the ladder at the rear of the garage. They climbed back down and pushed the ladder back up into place.

"There, I'm glad that's done!" said Mark.

"I think we all are," said Lenny.

"Mark, Karl. Where are you?"

"It's my mom," said Mark.

The boys ran out of the garage and over to the back porch. Mrs. Pushey was standing in the doorway of the back door.

"There's a phone call for Karl. I think it's your mother," said Mark's mom.

"Okay," replied Karl.

Karl went inside the house to take the call and the other boys went back inside the tent.

"Did you guys see anything when you snatched the gun?" asked Mark.

"Naw...it was quiet. We even covered over the cave's entrance with branches," said Tony.

"You can't tell if there's even a cave there, right, Tony?" said Lenny.

"That's right."

Karl entered the tent and sat on the edge of the empty bunk bed. He looked sad.

"What's wrong Karl?" asked Mark.

"Nothing....it was just my mom. She wanted to tell me that my old man's funeral will be on Monday at nine in the morning. She was crying. She says she misses me but she's glad I can be with my friends."

"Is she going to be okay?" asked Lenny.

"I think so. There are a lot of people stopping by to see her. That would drive me up the wall. But I guess she needs all that visiting stuff."

"Do you miss your mom?" asked Tony.

"A little, but at least I know she's safe now."

"Do you miss your dad?" asked Tony.

"No fucking way," said Karl.

* * * * *

A rather impressive collection of police vehicles had assembled in the sand pit off of Sunderland Hollow. There were two state police cars, three Town of Colchester police cars, a City of Winooski police car, a Chittenden County Sheriff's car and two pickup trucks.

The Colchester police chief was talking to two State Police Troopers and two men with dogs on leashes. One man had one dog on a leash and the other man held onto two dogs leashed. There were three officers conducting a search of the blue Ford Falcon including taking finger prints.

"Let me spread out this map of the surrounding area," declared Chief Seltzer.

He spread the map out on the hood of his police car.

"The sooner we start the search the better the chances are of finding those kids," said the Chief.

"How do you know they're in the woods somewhere and not gone off with friends?" said the man with one dog.

"Because we found the girl's purse under the front seat, that's how. You know any woman who would leave their purse behind like that?" said the Chief.

"I guess I don't."

"All right now. Look, we've got a shirt from the back seat that must have belonged to one of the boys and we got the girl's purse. We let the dogs have a smell and see if they can pick up a trail. Then we split up and do some looking. Lesage, you take your two dogs and concentrate on the bottom of the Hollow, then head west. Blondin, why don't you take your dog and head south from here towards Bremer's Quarry. Officer Coulon will give each of you a two-way radio so we can communicate. The sooner we get started on a search the better. The trail, if there is any left, may already be too cold for the dogs. We already know this area is a lover's lane and a pretty popular hunting area as well, so there are too many footprints to track. If we find anything it'll be because of the dogs or because of a large scale search. I'm hoping we get lucky with the dogs first, otherwise, we mount a large scale grid search of the area starting first thing tomorrow. Are there any questions?"

Fred Lesage let his two black Labrador retrievers sniff at the shirt and the purse. He took the radio from Officer Coulon and headed off down towards the ravine at the bottom of the hollow.

Grant Blondin knelt down next to his four year old dog, a large cross breed mix of golden retriever, black Labrador and German shepherd. This particular dog was very successful locating missing persons. He had located nine missing persons in the past two years alone. The dog's name was Elvis.

"Come on, Elvis. Here boy. Okay, now take a good sniff. That's it, boy. Yeah you smell that, huh? Sniff it good now. Okay, Elvis, it's just you and me boy. Can you do it?" asked Grant.

The dog's tail wagged vigorously back and forth. His eyes were wide and friendly. He turned and strained at his leash. Grant and his dog began to move out. The dog, nose close to the ground, led his master around the car and then after a short pause, the dog headed straight to the south.

"Stay in touch," said Officer Coulon to Mr. Blondin, who waved back to the officer with his free arm.

"Alright, now let's have a look at the map again. See if we can organize search areas for tomorrow morning. We need to figure out how many searchers we'll need and then put the word out," said Chief Seltzer to the other law enforcement officers.

Meanwhile, Grant Blondin and his dog, Elvis, were making good progress. After about fifteen minutes, and after several tracking and back tracking searches, the dog seemed to settle down on one path that was slightly worn but noticeable to his owner. Elvis suddenly stopped and even more carefully sniffed the ground. He strayed off the path a few feet and then back and then back to a spot perhaps ten feet off the trail.

"What do you have, Elvis?" asked his owner.

He followed the dog and looked at the ground. He didn't see anything at first. He knelt down and lifted some low branches and spotted a crumpled pack of cigarettes. He took a paper bag out of his back pocket, and using a small twig, he lifted the crumpled empty pack of cigarettes and dropped it into the bag. He stood up and looked around at the area. Nothing seemed out of place. He listened carefully and could not detect any unusual sounds.

Cupping his hands to his mouth he hollered, "Anybody here?"

No answer. The woods seemed completely normal to him.

Grant Blondin encouraged his dog to resume his search. The dog responded enthusiastically and continued along the previous path, heading southward traveling perhaps nearly a mile. The ground at this location began to climb steeply upward. Grant Blondin stopped and took a drink from his canteen he carried in his backpack. He poured some water into a cup from his backpack and let Elvis have a drink, too. The dog lapped up the water quickly. Grant took out the two way police radio. He raised the antenna and turned the radio on.

"Blondin to base. I repeat, Blondin to base. Over!"

After a moment of static a voice came back.

"Blondin, this is Officer Coulon. We hear you loud and clear. Have you got anything for us? Over!"

"We're following a trail. The dog seems to behave like it's a good one but it's got to be few days old. We did find a pack of cigarettes. Did these kids smoke and if so, did they smoke Luckies? Over!"

"We'll check that out. Anything else? Over!"

"Nope, there is nothing else to report. Roger and out."

Grant Blondin pushed the antenna down into the radio. He put the radio back into his backpack.

"Come here, Elvis. I'm going to let you run off leash for a while. Now you be a good dog and let's find them kids."

The dog shook his head a few times as if he was relieved to have the leash removed. He turned around, and with his nose tracking close to the ground, he headed off up the trail, with his tail wagging.

The climb up the hill along this stretch of the trail was taxing Grant's endurance. He would call out to his dog every few minutes to keep the dog within view. The dog would bark and sit and wait for a short while, and then he would soon resume his hunt.

It was around two o'clock in the afternoon and it was hot and sticky. June bugs sang out their familiar buzz, otherwise the woods seemed to quiet down as if the creatures that inhabited it were taking a break from the oppressive heat and humidity.

Elvis found the scent getting stronger. It spurred his hunting instincts. He was heading along a part of the trail that was the beginning of a long, gentle downhill stretch. He quickened his pace. He was getting close. He broke into a full run.

"Elvis, stop boy! I said stop!"

The dog was focused on his hunt, didn't hear his master and thus didn't yield to his master's command. He kept running along. He was perhaps five hundred yards ahead of his master. He turned a corner along a rocky ledge that rose some fifty to seventy feet from the hollow's floor. He stopped in the hollow. There were many smells. These were the smells he had been following. The tracking smells were now mixed in with many others. He circled and doubled back over the smells. This was it all right. The trail seemed to head straight at a bush in front of the large ledge. He approached this bush and then came to an abrupt halt. He sensed another smell. This smell signaled danger. He crouched down as if he was preparing to leap and attack. A low growl formed in his throat. He let out a low bark. Something was in that bush. He barked louder.

He could hear Elvis barking. Perhaps the dog found something. Grant Blondin was exhausted and tried to speed himself up. He hollered to his dog to stay.

"Elvis, good boy, stay. Stay boy!"

The dog couldn't hear his master. Something moved inside that bush. The dog crept closer growling as he went. He sniffed the air. He was hot on the trail. What he had been tracking for the past couple of hours was straight ahead. He crept closer. There was an opening behind the bushes. He crept under the bush. He poked his head into the opening.

"Yelp."

The dog was whisked from under the bush and disappeared into the darkness beyond. There was a momentary muffled bark. It was a bark of fear. Then there was nothing but silence. Suddenly an albino, powerful hand extended from the darkness and pulled at the bottom of the branches covering up the opening of the cave. The fingers on this hand were nearly all the same length. The pad of the hand was thick. The hand and attached forearm were covered with thick, whitish hair. The dark opening was now all but invisible from outside.

"Elvis, I'm coming boy! Elvis stay!"

There was no answer from his dog. Grant hollered as loud as he could. Still there was no answer. He whistled as loud as he could, still no answer. Grant began to look at the ground for some sign of his dog's footprints. The ground was compacted and covered with pine needles which didn't favor a dog leaving any visible tracks.

Grant was getting worried for Elvis. This had never happened before. His dog seldom went too far ahead on a hunt or search without doubling back every few minutes. He decided to stop and wait. He stopped in a shady hollow. Perhaps the dog had just gotten way ahead. As soon as the dog realized he had lost contact with his master, he would likely double back to re-establish contact.

Fifteen minutes went by with no sign of Elvis. Grant hollered and whistled for several minutes still with no response.

From behind the bush next to the ledge the creature sat and listened. He sniffed the air and could smell fear in the human who was standing no more than seventy-five feet away. He already had killed the dog. He'd already eaten four humans over the past several days, the most he had eaten in many years. The dog was not as tasty as the human. The creature didn't want to attract humans hunting for the kids, which might end up hunting him instead.

Grant Blondin took off his backpack. He removed the police radio and raised the antenna. He was crying now for his lost dog. Elvis was his very best friend. Grant was not married and his extended family lived mostly in New Hampshire. Elvis was all he had. He was very worried that something had happened to his dog.

"Grant to base, Grant to base, come in. Over!"

"This is Chief Seltzer, Grant. We've got some good news. The boys both smoked. They smoked Luckies. It looks like your trail may be the hot one. Over!"

"Chief, I've lost my dog."

"Come back. Did you say that you lost your dog? Over!"

"He's gone. Elvis is gone. I can't find him Chief."

"Grant, give me your location. Over!"

Grant couldn't speak right now. He was too overwhelmed to talk. He began to sob.

"Grant, do you copy?"

* * * * *

Late that night, a moonless night, Ne Wha Ta crawled out of the cave. He stretched to his full height. In his left hand he carried a dead raccoon. He sniffed the cool night air and then knelt down to sniff at the ground. His ears were alert to any unusual sound. He needed to be alert to the possibility humans might be lurking somewhere in the darkness of the forest.

His extraordinary sense of smell picked up the trail the search dog had taken to find its way to the cave earlier in the day. He back tracked over the dog's route until he was about one hundred and fifty feet away from the cave's entrance. He ripped off the head of the raccoon. He stomped it into the ground and then he slowly squeezed the raccoon's lifeless body as he backed up. He was spreading blood and guts over the trail. Then after several feet he reached up into a nearby tree where he crammed the badly crushed remains of the raccoon into a crevice of the tree. He was careful to retrace his steps. The floor of the forest was heavily covered with pine needles, which didn't allow for any footprints. At last, he decided that he had done enough to create a diversion for any other tracking dog that might attempt to follow Elvis' path.

He carefully crawled back into the cave, pulling into place the pine branches the boys had earlier used to cover up the cave. The cave entrance was disguised once again.

Chapter 29

Tony, Lenny and Mark got out of the car and entered Mark's house. Pokey barked once, and upon seeing who they were, padded straight to the guys to receive a welcoming scratch behind the ears.

Mark's father came into the kitchen from the living room and smiled at the warm reception Pokey was receiving.

"You fellas are going to spoil him with all that attention. Pokey, go lay down. Leave the boys alone."

The dog turned and lowered his head. He padded over to the front of the wood stove. Pokey turned himself around a couple of times before he settled on his favorite small rug.

"You boys have a good time?"

"Yeah, we drove around the city a little bit. We stopped for some coffee at the Red Onion Diner. It's quite the place," said Mark. "All the new buildings downtown have dramatically changed the whole look and feel of the downtown area."

"We even bumped into some of the police investigating the cave filled with bones up at the old Bremer's Quarry," said Lenny.

"It seems Tony here is quite the celebrity. The police chief and his wife have read Tony's books. Apparently, they're big fans," said Mark.

"Come on guys. Cut it out," said an obviously embarrassed Tony.

"Yeah, and the Chief's thinking of having Tony over for dinner," said Lenny.

"Well, Tony, I guess I haven't been a good host. I haven't read your books yet," said Mark's father, breaking into a gentle laugh.

"Will you guys let up?" said Tony.

"Okay. By the way, Lenny, there's a message on the answering machine from your office. Mark, you have a message also from the airline. There were no messages for you Tony," said Mark's father.

"Where's the answering machine?" asked Lenny.

"It's in the living room on the stand next to the recliner," said Mark's father.

"Thanks," said Lenny.

Lenny and Mark headed into the living room to check their phone messages. Tony headed into the bathroom. Mark's father checked the wood burning stove and decided it needed another log. He used his oven mitts and opened the side door to the stove. He slipped a small chunk of dried hardwood inside. The fire immediately swarmed and engulfed the log as it crackled and burst into flames. The dog looked up at his master with his pleading eyes. Pokey then closed his eyes and laid his head back down.

Mark went to the answering machine and noticed the answering light blinked three times in sequence, then repeated. Mark thought back to what his dad just said about two messages, perhaps he didn't listen to all of the messages.

Lenny noticed it, too.

Mark picked up the small note pad next to the answering machine and pressed the message button. It beeped twice and then began to replay the messages.

The first message was for Lenny. It was from his associate, Sylvia. Her telephone voice was soft and sultry. She asked Lenny to get back to her because she had a client who needed investment advice on a buyout of his company by a friendly suitor company. Lenny was the firm's expert on takeovers and arbitrage. Sylvia asked if he could please call. She suggested perhaps they could set up a brief conference call.

The second message was for Mark. His flight scheduler needed to get a better fix on his return date. It seemed they were short on pilots because several were taken ill with the flu. They wanted to shore up the assignment schedule before calling in other pilots.

Then there was the third message. It was the creature. There was no mistaking the voice. Lenny and Mark were familiar with the voice from before. The call started out with heavy breathing. Then the creature spoke.

"Greetings to each of you. I have been looking forward to your return for a very long time. We have some unfinished business to settle. I have been patient, but you should not expect me to be patient for much longer. Did you enjoy your visit to the quarry? The old man you are living with, he seems very interesting, very interesting indeed. You will hear from me again, soon."

Lenny and Mark looked at each another; their mouths were wide open.

Mark turned around to see if his father might be listening and noticed that he wasn't in the doorway. Mark motioned for Lenny to check to see where his father was. Lenny went to the doorway, pointed into the kitchen and gave Mark the all clear sign. Mark pressed the message button down for a couple of seconds, which activated the command to erase all of the messages.

Lenny and Mark went into the kitchen just as Tony was coming out of the bathroom.

"Got your messages all right?" asked Tony.

"Yeah, we did," said Lenny.

Both Lenny and Mark looked indirectly at Mark's father to see if there was any kind of reaction. There was none. Perhaps he hadn't heard or noticed there was a third message. Lenny and Mark weren't about to approach him about it unless it was absolutely necessary. They concluded he hadn't noticed the third message.

Lenny and Mark would wait until they could be alone with Tony to tell him about the message from the creature.

Privately Mark was upset. This creature had contacted him at his father's house. Mark felt he had put his own father at risk. He wanted to end this cat-and-mouse nightmare as soon as possible. Mark's motive took on a renewed urgency.

"We'll never be safe until we kill that fucking thing," thought Mark.

Meanwhile, the creature was listening in on the conversations at the Pushey residence. He smiled. They would come to him soon and they would help him. They would yet bring him a mate. His species would live on. He was increasingly sure of that.

* * * * *

The boys sat inside the tent even though it was very warm outside. With the shade from the tree and with the flaps open, the slight summer breeze made it rather comfortable in the tent.

Lunch consisted of peanut butter and grape jelly sandwiches, sliced cantaloupe, potato chips and iced tea. They started a card game of hearts but nobody really seemed in the mood to play. Tony kept shuffling the deck of cards, over and over.

"Guys, I don't want you to think I'm a wussy. But I'm really scared. That monster has killed at least four, maybe five people that we know of," said Mark.

"I'm scared, too," said Lenny.

"I know I'm scared of that thing, whatever it is," said Karl.

Tony hadn't said a word. He was just staring straight ahead.

"Tony, hey Tony, are you still with us man?" said Lenny.

Tony wasn't mentally with them at all. His body was in the tent but his mind was inside the cave, deep inside the cave. He was crawling on his hands and knees in the dark. His hands hurt from grabbing at the sharp edged stones. His knees ached. He was laboring to breathe. He heard a noise behind him. Tony heard something running in the darkness. It was some distance behind him but moving quickly. Tony was frantic to hide, but where? He didn't know where he was. He didn't know where to hide. He couldn't see anything in the pitch-black darkness of the cave.

Now he heard the flapping of small wings. There were many small creatures flying overhead. Whatever was chasing him from behind was gaining ground quickly now. Tony was paralyzed with fear.

"How can I hide? I can't fucking see, I can't see!" he screamed.

Tony awoke from his daytime nightmare. His friends, with worried looks on their faces, were standing over him shaking him.

"Tony, are you all right? Tony, talk to us, man," said Karl.

Tony was confused and still in a daze. He looked at his friends but still couldn't quite recognize them.

"We have to hide. Where can we hide? He's coming, he's coming!" pleaded a desperate Tony.

"C'mon, Tony, you're freaking scaring us. Cut the shit," said Lenny.

Tony was sweating heavily. His eyes were darting about. He was shaking all over. He put his head in his hands and started to sob.

Mark massaged the back of Tony's neck. He looked at the others and they each looked frightened, too. The terror was getting to them. The pressure was mounting. Where and when would this monster strike next? Could they stop him? Did they dare?

After a while Tony stopped sobbing and raised his head.

"My head hurts," said Tony.

"It's no wonder, you just had a friggin' nightmare," said Karl.

Tony looked at Karl and seemed to not believe him. He looked at Lenny and Mark. Their expressions convinced him that something had happened to him.

"What happened?" asked Tony.

They told him everything he said. Now he began to feel chilled even in the heat of the June afternoon.

"What's going to happen to us, Karl? What's going to happen to all of us?" asked Tony.

"I don't know, but one thing is for sure. If we don't put our heads together and come up with a plan, that monster will keep on killing and it will be our fault. We've got to find a way to stop it," said Karl.

"We're only kids Karl. What can we do against something like that?" asked Mark.

"I don't know. Maybe if we knew more about it we could find a weakness," said Karl.

"Can't we tell some adult, someone who can help us?" asked Lenny.

"Like who?" asked Mark.

"I don't know, but there has to be somebody," said Lenny.

"Look, that monster has to have been around for a long time, right? Well, we need to find somebody who knows the woods and the history of the woods. They might have heard of something in the past," said Karl.

"I know. Let's ask the OUIJA Board. It's worth a shot," said Mark.

"I'm game. Let's give it a try" said a hopeful Lenny.

Tony was still a bit unsettled, so he only nodded his agreement.

Mark pulled the OUIJA Board out from its hiding place underneath and behind one of the bunks. He set the board up on the table. He and Lenny sat down and held their hands over the game piece, letting only the tips of their fingers touch the planchette.

"All right, here goes. Is there anyone who can help us learn more about this monster?" asked Karl.

The game piece slid quickly to the "yes" space on the board.

"All right, will this person help us?" asked Lenny.

The game piece moved to the letters spelling out the word "friend" then to the space marked "yes."

"What is this person's name?" asked Mark.

The game piece moved slowly but deliberately spelling out the name "Louis Germain."

"Who in the hell is Louis Germain?" asked Karl.

The piece moved to spell out one word, "Indian."

"Do any of you guys know a Louis Germain?" asked Mark.

They all shook their heads no. It seemed to all that the OUIJA Board hadn't been much of a help after all.

Mark put the game board away. He went into the house to go to the bathroom and returned with a fresh pitcher of grape- flavored Kool-Aid. It seemed to pick up their spirits. They even played cards for a while. Tony eventually joined in and began to seem like his old self. The afternoon wore on. Each boy tried mightily to have fun but despite their efforts they each harbored dark menacing thoughts in the recesses of their minds.

Individually they felt the pressure mounting. They needed to find someone to share this burden with—but whom?

Chapter 30

It was the middle of the afternoon. The guys spent the early afternoon playing cards with Mark's father. The card playing was getting pretty intense. They were playing Hearts and Mark's father made several successful runs against the guys. He won four of the six games they had played.

The phone rang and Mark's father got up to answer it.

"Tony, it's for you."

"Don't you guys deal the next hand until after this call," teased Tony.

"Are you accusing us of cheating?" mocked Lenny.

"Just don't deal the cards until I get back," insisted Tony.

"Okay. It's a good time for a stretch anyway," said Mark.

Tony went into the living room and picked up the phone in that room.

"Hello, this Tony Fredette."

"Mr. Fredette, this is Police Chief Ed Contois. Do you remember our meeting this morning at the Red Onion Diner?"

"Of course I do," said Tony.

"Well, I told my wife about meeting you and she insisted I give you a call and invite you and your friends over to dinner tonight. If you can make it, of course," asked the Chief.

"I'd be delighted. Let me check with my friends and see if anyone's made any plans with Mr. Pushey. After all, I should check with my host first. You understand?"

"Please bring him along as well. We've got plenty of room and we'd enjoy his company."

"That's very nice of you. I wouldn't want to impose on your wife."

"It's no imposition at all."

"All right. If you'll hold, I'll be right back."

"I'll wait."

Tony put the phone down and then went into the kitchen to extend the Chief's invitation to everyone including Mark's father. They all thought it would be quite a treat. Mark's father noted he hadn't planned anything for dinner. He commented he would enjoy somebody else's cooking besides his own.

"Chief, I've checked with everyone and we'd be delighted to join you and your wife for dinner. Is there anything we could bring?"

"Not a thing. My wife prides herself on her cooking and I'm sure she is looking forward to preparing the entire menu."

"What time should we come by?"

"Six-thirty would be just fine. We live at 436 Florida Avenue. Do you think you need directions?"

"Chief, I'm a Winooski native, remember?"

"You're right, of course. Well, we'll see you tonight. I've got to run now."

"Good-bye."

Tony hung up and returned to the kitchen.

"How about we go to a flower shop or a wine store and pick up something for our dinner hosts?" said Tony.

"Wait, I've got the perfect gift," said Mark's father. He quickly went down to the cellar. In a moment he came back upstairs. His arms were full of jars.

"What is all that stuff?" asked Mark.

"I've got some very special homemade goodies that I know they'll enjoy. I've got some homemade brown molasses beans, some sweet pickled cucumbers. Here's some piccalilli, some pickled beets and some sweet corn relish. And of course a jar of my personal favorite, maple flavored butter spread."

"Where did you get all this?" asked Tony, as he examined the various jars.

"I'm proud to say I made all this myself," said Mark's father.

"Get out of here! Dad, you couldn't boil water when I was a kid."

"That may be true, but when your mom died I needed to fill my time, so I took up gardening and, well, one thing led to another. I learned how to can and make preserves."

"Remarkable," said Lenny.

"I'm sure all this homemade food will please our hosts but I'd still like to bring some wine and flowers," said Tony.

"That's fine. I tell you what, why don't I take you up to Shaw's grocery store and you can get your flowers and wine there," said Mark's father.

"Great, let's go now," said Tony. "You guys don't mind, do you?"

"No, of course not. You go with Dad. Lenny and I can hang out here with Pokey," said Mark.

"Mark, you can get to know Pokey even better! You can take him for a walk. I'll get you his leash, his pooper scooper, and a small plastic bag for his business."

"Dad, you're too much," said Mark sarcastically.

"I'll take that as a compliment," said Mark's father with a sly sort of grin.

"Lenny's going to help me, right, Lenny?"

"That all depends. What part do I have to help with?" said Lenny.

"You can hold the leash," said Mark.

"That, I can do! I was afraid you might have assigned me the pooper detail."

"It's yours if you want the job," said Mark.

"No thanks. I wouldn't think of depriving you of this chance to bond with your father's faithful companion," said Lenny.

"Thanks. You're all heart!" said Mark.

"Hey, fellas, there is no need to quarrel. If you want, you guys can take turns walking Pokey. Right, Pokey?" said Mark's father.

"Woof, Woof," responded the dog, accompanied with his usual vigorous tail wagging.

* * * * *

Lenny had to go home for supper. When he arrived he could smell his mother's cooking well before he walked into the house. From the familiar aroma he knew she had made his favorite meal, spaghetti and meatballs. When he opened the front door, he could smell the mouth-watering aroma of freshly baked garlic bread.

He went into the kitchen and stopped to enjoy the picture before him. His mom was humming a tune unfamiliar to Lenny. She was stirring the spaghetti sauce. His little sister was lying in the portable play pen that he himself had explored several years before. His father never threw anything away. He felt the old playpen still had some mileage left on it. The baby was making cooing sounds and was playing with her feet She was trying to pull her right foot up and stick in into her mouth.

"Hi, Mom. Can I help you with anything?" asked Lenny.

"Lenny, yes you can. Please take out the trash. You know it is your chore. Your father would have a fit if he came home and found out you hadn't done it."

"I know, Mom. I'm sorry."

He pulled the garbage-loaded bag out of the kitchen waste basket. He went out the back door and over to the back yard garbage barrel, an old oil drum. He put the paper bag down and removed the heavy metal lid of the garbage barrel. He tossed the paper bag filled with garbage into the barrel. He put the metal cover back on. He went back inside and put an empty paper bag in the kitchen waste basket.

"Better go and wash your hands for supper," said his mom.

Lenny went to the first floor bathroom to wash his hands.

While he was washing his hands, he heard his father pull up. The car came to a screeching halt in the driveway. From the sounds of his slamming of the car door, followed by his heavy footsteps into the house, it was evident to Lenny that something was wrong.

"Why isn't supper on the table yet?" said an angry Lenny's father.

Lenny's mom was somewhat startled by his anger.

"I, uh, I thought we'd be having supper at the usual time, at five-thirty."

"Look, I'm home now and I'm hungry, so what's the hold up?"

"Well, I, uh, I have to cook the spaghetti and I still have to make the salad. You know how you like your salad to be freshly made," she said defensively.

"Just hurry the fuck up. I'm going out back to have a beer. Give me a shout when it's ready."

He opened the refrigerator and removed three cold bottles of beer before he went out back in a huff.

Lenny ventured out from the bathroom. He avoided his mother's eyes just as she, too, wanted to avoid eye contact. Her eyes were watery.

"Lenny, dear, could you help me with the supper?"

"Sure, Mom, what can I do?"

"Well, how about if you stir this sauce? I want you to be careful not to spill any on you. It's very hot. Hold the sauce pan handle with your left hand. That's it. Now you can use your right hand to stir the sauce."

"Okay, I think I've got it."

"Good. Now I'll make a fresh salad."

She went to the refrigerator and removed all the salad vegetables. She washed the tomatoes and cucumbers. She began to peel and cut up an onion. She was half way finished with cutting up the onion when the baby began to cry. Its cry grew rapidly urgent. She looked at the baby and then she looked out into the back yard.

"Damn," she muttered.

Lenny's mom washed her hands and picked up the baby. She pulled at the back of the baby's diaper and took a sniff.

"The baby needs to have her diaper changed. You just keep stirring the sauce and I'll go change this diaper."

"Okay, Mom."

She went into the bathroom to change the baby's diaper. Meanwhile, Lenny continued to stir the sauce as he was told. His father came into the kitchen unexpectedly, startling Lenny.

"I've got to take a whiz," said his father.

"Mom's in the bathroom changing Karen's diaper. I think she took a dump. At least that's what it smells like," said Lenny.

"What did you do all day?" said his father.

"I hung around with Karl, Tony and Mark at Mark's house."

"You know, it's time you get your ass out there and find yourself a job. It's a long summer and a job would be good for you. It'd teach you responsibility. In fact, I want you to start looking tomorrow, and that's an order."

"I know, Dad. I'll try."

His father went right up to Lenny. They were nearly chest to chest. Lenny could smell the sweat on his father which clashed horridly with his father's beer breath. Lenny felt trapped.

"I said," poking an index finger into Lenny's chest, "Get a job. I don't want to hear any slacker's excuses. You hear me?"

"Yes, sir."

Just then Lenny's mother came out of the bathroom with young baby Karen in her arms. She looked at Lenny and his father standing face to face and her face quickly filled with dread.

"I hope you washed your hands, woman," said his father, as he turned away from Lenny and moved past his wife and daughter to enter the bathroom.

She put the baby back into her play pen. She hurried to the sink and began to wash her hands. Lenny's father left the bathroom and went immediately to the back yard.

Lenny's mom silently finished preparing the salad and boiled the spaghetti.

"Go tell your dad it's time for supper."

Lenny went outside to the back yard to tell his dad supper was ready. Meanwhile his father had already consumed all three beers.

"Toss these into the garbage barrel for me," said his father, who tossed the empty bottles at Lenny. Lenny caught one bottle but dropped the other two. He quickly picked them up and did as he was told.

His father was already in the kitchen and seated at the table. His mother had taken out another beer and placed it in front of his father. Lenny and his mother then sat down to eat supper. No one spoke for several minutes. The baby amused herself in the playpen.

"Uh, Dad, I was wondering. The guys were asking me if we knew anyone named Louis Germain. Do you know anyone by that name?" asked Lenny.

His father, who had been playing with his salad, put his fork down. He took a long swallow from his bottle of beer.

"Yeah, I know somebody with that name, only it's Louis St. Germain. He's an Indian. He's a fucking crazy old Indian. Me and some of the guys, when we were your age, use to play tricks on the son-of-a-bitch to see if we could piss him off. What do your little shit-for-brains friends want to know about that old Indian anyway?"

"I don't really know, Dad," said Lenny. He was telling a lie. The top of his ears always turned pink whenever he told a lie. Right now, the top of his ears turned bright pink.

"That old Indian is still around. He lives in that old run down shack on the Winooski-Colchester line at the top of Main Street. He claims to be a medicine man. Humph! I think he's just some old used up Indian. He doesn't have any friends and I don't think he has any family either. Jesus, I'm thirsty, get me another beer will yah, Carol?"

Lenny's mother went to the refrigerator and placed another bottle of beer in front of her husband. She removed the empty bottle and placed it into the trash. His father had not taken one bite of solid food. He took another swallow of beer.

"The boy's going to get himself a job, Carol. Starting tomorrow he's got to go find himself a job for the summer."

"Oh, that sounds like a good idea," she said with very little enthusiasm. She looked at Lenny, but he didn't return her look.

"There's a rumor going around the plant down at good old Generous Electric that there's going to be a longer layoff this summer than usual. My boss told me today that it might go a month. How about that, you'd have the pleasure of my company for a whole...month?" he laughed sarcastically.

"But it's a rumor. You just said so," said Lenny's mother.

"I know what I just fucking said. You don't have to tell me what the fuck I just said." There was rising anger in his voice. He just sat there, silently for a long minute.

Suddenly he bolted to his feet and picked up his plate of spaghetti and threw it against the refrigerator door. The plate broke in two and fell to the kitchen floor. Spaghetti and deep red tomato sauce were splattered in a large pattern on the door. The baby was startled by the sudden noise and began to cry. He grabbed his beer bottle and stomped out of the house. In a moment they heard the car start up and race out of the driveway as Lenny's father drove away.

No one spoke until they heard the car pull away.

"I hate him," said Lenny.

For the first time in Lenny's memory, his mother didn't correct him. She didn't even try to pick up the broken dish or clean up the mess. Instead she picked up the baby and went out into the back yard and walked around the yard with the baby held close to her in her arms. Lenny watched her from the kitchen window. He could see she was crying.

Lenny picked up the broken dish. He tossed it into the garbage. What had once been a place setting for eight was now down to five. Lenny used a large spoon to pick up the spaghetti that was on the floor as best as he could. He used a dish towel to wipe the refrigerator. He had to rinse it several times. He used the same towel to wipe the floor. Every few minutes he looked out into the back yard and saw his mother was still walking the baby.

He was wiping the last of the tomato sauce off the floor when his mother came back into the house. The baby was sleeping in her arms. Quietly and gently she laid the baby down in the playpen. She went over to Lenny and gave him a big hug. She was no longer crying but her eyes were red and swollen.

"Lenny, you're a blessing. I love you very much," said his mother.

"I love you, too."

"Lenny, I want you to call Tony's house and see if you can sleep over at his house tonight."

"Why?"

"Just because, that's all"

Her face said it all. She didn't want Lenny around when her husband came home. He was an unpredictable man, and right now he was a drunken and angry man who was looking for someone to take out his anger on. She wanted to give him one less target.

Lenny called over to Tony's house and made up a flimsy excuse to get Tony to invite him over. Tony didn't need much of an incentive. Soon the invite was extended and accepted. Lenny agreed to come over in a half an hour, which was fine with Tony. The two of them would later head over to Mark's house for the evening.

"Are you sure you want me to go?"

"Yes, Lenny."

"Do you want me to get Father Campbell? Maybe he can talk to Dad? You know, calm him down or something! He's helped before!"

"Right now, I think seeing Father Campbell would just make your father even more upset. Everything will be fine, Lenny. Now you go pack your toothbrush and some clean underwear. I want you to check back here no later than ten o'clock tomorrow morning. I want you to call from Tony's house, okay?"

"Sure, Mom, but if you need me for anything make sure you call me. Promise me!"

"All right, Lenny, I promise. Now get going."

Lenny went to his room and quickly packed his things. He returned to the kitchen where his mother was washing the dishes. He gave her a big hug and a kiss. He then blew a kiss at his sleeping baby sister. He went out the back door and headed to the front of the house. He cautiously looked around to see if his father was parked nearby just in case. Not seeing him, he set off for Tony's house.

Chapter 31

Tony rang the doorbell. Before the door chimes even had a chance to ring, the front door swung wide open.

"Hello, Chief Contois!" said Tony.

"Hello, Tony. Everyone come on in, please," said the Chief.

"Chief, I'd like you to meet Mark's father, Mr. George Pushey. We're all staying at his house while we're visiting."

"It's nice to meet you, Mr. Pushey," said the Chief as he shook hands with Mark's father.

"Please, call me Gene."

"Okay, Gene! And you can call me Ed."

"Can I take your coats?"

They gave their coats to Chief Contois, who carried them into a small first floor bedroom where he placed them on the bed. He returned to the foyer and led everyone into the living room. Ed's wife, Ellie, soon entered the living room as greetings and introductions were exchanged all around. She appeared nervous. Tony presented the bottle of wine, bouquet of flowers along with several homemade canned goods; Gene Pushey specials to her.

"Mr. Pushey grew these in his own garden and canned them as well," declared Tony.

"You didn't have to bring anything. Didn't my husband tell you gifts wouldn't be necessary?" protested the Chief's wife.

"Yes, he did, but we're four men whose mothers raised us to always show our appreciation whenever someone shows you a kindness," said Tony.

"Well, thank you all very much, and Mr. Pushey, the canned vegetables and relishes look absolutely delicious. You really shouldn't have."

Mark's father beamed at the generous compliment. "Thank you for having me over for dinner with these young boys."

"Dinner will be ready in a few minutes. If you'll excuse me, I should check on things in the kitchen."

Ellie Contois left and headed to the kitchen. Tantalizing aromas from the food cooking in the kitchen drifted into the living room. The Chief and the four guests sat down in the living room and visited with one another as they exchanged pre-dinner small talk. Everyone's attention was really focused on the aromas which emanated from the kitchen. These aromas were also beginning to stimulate mouthwatering reactions.

Ellie came out from the kitchen and asked her husband to help her put the meal out on the dining room table. He excused himself and went along to help his wife.

Soon he returned to announce dinner was ready. He led the guests into the dining room. As everyone was sitting down, the Chief asked what everyone would like to drink. Mark and Lenny choose to have a small glass of white wine. Tony and Mrs. Contois chose to have tea. Mark's father chose to have milk, as did Chief Contois.

"The dinner looks and smells wonderful Mrs. Contois," said Mark's father.

"Indeed it does," agreed Tony, which was quickly echoed by Mark and Lenny.

Dinner began with a large fresh garden salad garnished with small shrimp. The dinner went on to include large baked potatoes, fresh baked bread, steamed mixed broccoli, carrots, and scallions. The main course was Chicken Marsala. The table also held garnishment dishes filled with pickles, relishes and sour cream and even homemade bacon bits. Later, dessert consisted of homemade pineapple upside down cake served with real whipped cream. Everyone enjoyed the food and many compliments were proffered in favor of Mrs. Contois' excellent cuisine.

After dinner everyone retired to the living room with fresh cups of coffee in hand.

"We really should help, Mr. and Mrs. Contois, with clearing the table and washing the dishes, after all you've done preparing such a wonderful meal," said Lenny.

"Nonsense, my husband and I will take care of it later. You're our guests and we'd much rather spend this time visiting with you," said Ellie.

"Ellie, I told Tony we're both big fans of his."

"I'm flattered you've both read and enjoyed my books," said Tony.

"I can't imagine writing a book. But I know a good one when I read it and your two books were exciting. I couldn't put them down," said Ellie.

"Mrs. Contois, you're very kind, really," said Tony.

"My wife's right. We both read a great deal. You could say it's our hobby. You're the only current author that we both agree is exciting to read and who writes a book intelligently. You know, to us, you sort of invite the reader to anticipate the climax of your stories. Your dialogue is tight and believable. I especially enjoy the clarity with which you sketch your characters," said Ed.

"Geeze, both of you should take up writing book reviews. I could always use some favorable press," said Tony.

"Tony, would you mind autographing our copies of your books?" asked the Chief.

"Not at all, I would be honored."

Ellie retrieved several copies from the bookcase in the dining room, all of which were first editions of Tony's books.

"I hope you don't mind signing all these—I bought extra copies. I am planning to use them as gifts," said Ellie.

"Of course not. How would you like me to inscribe them?" said Tony. He obviously enjoyed their attention.

Ellie soon replaced the books on the bookshelf before returning to the living room to rejoin the others. The conversation shifted away from Tony's books and settled, for the time being, on the ongoing investigation into the horrible discovery at the former Bremer Quarry.

"You say there are also a large amount of animal bones mixed in with the human bones?" asked Mark.

"As I said earlier, this shouldn't be repeated. This is after all, an ongoing investigation. The way I see it, we're going to need all the help we can get solving this. So, yeah, there are a lot of animal bones. I'd say there are easily bones and carcasses of thousands of animals," said the Chief.

"Wow, that many! Jesus!" said Mark.

"Yeah, I know, mixed in we've also uncovered the remains of approximately fifty or more humans. The number keeps climbing as we continue sifting through the evidence."

"So the FBI is helping out on this one?" asked Tony.

"Yeah, Special Agent Joyce is up from the New York City Field office and two resident agents from the Burlington Office are assisting him. We are also sending evidence to their crime lab in Washington, D.C. for analysis."

"I was wondering about that. Besides bones, there has to be other evidence such as clothes, jewelry, you know stuff you can use to identify the victims," said Lenny.

"I know, and believe me there is a huge amount of other physical evidence we are going through. We're getting inquiries from all over the country. People are sending us information on all sorts of missing persons. Since the news wires picked up on the story we've been buried with calls from all sorts of cranks, psychics, and people who want to confess. We haven't begun to form any theories yet."

"I think you're going to find all those dead people are from around here," said his wife with a knowing look.

"Right now I don't know what to think. Is it evidence of a serial killer? Is it some sort of cult burial ground? Could it be a fluke dumping ground for some funeral parlor that didn't want to go through with the expense of burying people? I just don't know! There sure are no text book models to rely upon. Do you have any ideas?"

"Us?" asked Lenny.

"Yeah, I'd like to hear your thoughts on this?"

"Uh, well, I, uh, wonder if, maybe these human remains were from some time in the past when maybe there was a plague or something," said Mark.

"But how do you explain the animal bones mixed in?" asked Ellie.

"You've got me there," said Mark.

"Perhaps that cave, or whatever it is, was used by the mob to dispose of some of its victims. All the animal bones maybe come from other animals attracted by the dead bodies. They come along and kill other animals in a fight over the human flesh," said Lenny.

"I don't think so. This doesn't have the look of a mob thing. So far there is no evidence of any of the victims having died from a gun shot or even knife wounds. How about you, Tony? Do you have any ideas?"

"Well, I was thinking, maybe it's a dumping ground for a government biological experiment that went awry. They buried their mistakes and now the opening of the quarry is an unexpected problem. That's why the FBI wants in so they can steer the investigation, you know, cover-up the mistake," said Tony.

"Now I know why you're an author, with an imagination like that," said Lenny mockingly.

Everyone had a good laugh at Tony's expense.

"Hey, you asked for my idea," he protested.

"Well, Tony, the evidence uncovered so far doesn't support that theory. But I'll keep it in mind," said the Chief.

"Would anyone like some more coffee?" asked Ellie.

"I would," said Mark.

"So would I," said Tony.

"Not for me," said the Chief and Lenny.

"How about you, Mr. Pushey?" she asked of Mark's father.

"Yes, I would, thank you very much."

She got up and went straight to the kitchen to make a fresh pot of coffee. When she'd left the room, Gene Pushey cleared his throat and spoke up.

"I believe I know how those bones happen to be in that cave."

"You do?" asked the Chief.

"Yes, I do. I believe the bones of the animals and the humans are the handy work of a legend. According to Indian lore there's a monster that has existed in the Champlain Valley for hundreds, maybe thousands, of years."

Everyone's jaw just about fell to the floor as they all turned and looked at him with anticipation as to what he was about to say.

"Tell me more about this, this monster," said Ed.

"Yeah, Dad, I'd like to hear this," said Mark, as he shot a side-ways glance at Tony and Lenny. Ed noticed the glance and filed it away into his memory for later analysis.

"You see, it all fits. There is an old legend; I believe it's an Abenaki Indian legend. Anyway, they have this oral tradition that has been passed down through the ages which speaks about a creature that lives beneath the surface and preys on living things. I don't really remember all the details. I know, it sounds crazy."

"Dad, enough with the legends. Okay?"

"Go easy on him, Mark. I'm willing to listen to anything that will give me any kind of lead."

"Yeah, Chief, but an Indian Legend. It's like a ghost story. You can't be seriously considering this?" said Lenny.

"Look, I'll tell you something. All of those humans bodies, well, their bones were separated, okay! They were all over the cave. I shouldn't be telling you this, but there were teeth marks on the bones. Something was eating them all right. And I'll tell you something else. There was hardly any blood stains in that cave. Now tell me, where did the blood go? Who or what did this is what I intend to find out. You know, sometimes, ghost stories have a little truth buried some-where in the story or legend. Mr. Pushey, I may just check up on this story."

"Dad, where did you hear about this monster legend?" asked Mark.

"When I was a little boy, an Indian family camped for the sum-mer up the beach from where my father's lake shore camp was located on the Town of Georgia's east shore. I played with the children. We became close friends. At night we would light a fire down on the beach. On one of those nights, one of the Indian children, a little girl, I think, asked her father to tell me and my two brothers the story of "Ne" something or other. Well, he told us this Indian legend, and I don't mind telling you it scared the hell out of me. He spoke of this ancient creature that all the Indians were afraid of that kidnapped humans and ate them. The Indians wore a magic necklace that protected them. They said a white man could not be protected from this creature because he wouldn't believe. I had recurring nightmares for weeks afterwards."

"That's quite a story Gene," said the Chief. "Do you believe it?"

"Look, I sometimes watch daytime TV talk shows. Right now, I'd believe anything's possible."

"Believe what?" asked Ellie as she returned from the kitchen with a fresh pot of coffee.

"Mr. Pushey believes in monsters," said Lenny.

"Monsters, really?" asked Ellie.

She poured out the fresh coffee into their cups.

Chapter 32

Tony and Lenny knocked on the front door of Mark's house. There was no answer. They went down the front steps and headed to the back yard. In the back yard they could hear talking coming from inside the tent. They entered the tent to find Mark and Karl talking about the monster.

"Where's your mom and dad?" asked Tony.

"They've gone shopping. My dad said he needed a new white shirt for the funeral," said Mark.

Lenny looked at Karl to see if the mention of his dad's funeral would get a reaction. Nothing!

"You guys want to sleep over?" asked Mark.

"Naw, we can't. Lenny is sleeping over at my house tonight and my mom wants me to spend a little more time at home. You know how moms are!" said Tony.

"Yeah, I know," said Mark.

Sitting on the edge of one of the beds, Lenny said, "I found out who Louis Germain is. My old man told me that he's an Indian."

Karl sat up in a shot. "Say again?"

"He said that this Germain guy is an Indian. My old man says his name is Louis St. Germain. He lives in that old run down shack on upper Main Street. You guys know the one I'm talking about. It's the house with no paint on it with a barn out back and a couple of horses in the back yard."

"Yeah, I know who he is now! My old man used to tell me stories about how when he was a kid he and his buddies used to tease the horses to get the Indian to come out of the house so they could throw horse shit at him," said Karl.

"That sounds like something my father would do," said Lenny.

"It sounds mean to me," said Mark.

"So, how is this Indian, St. Germain going to help us? We don't even know if he's the actual person the OUIJA board meant and, if he is, why would he want to help us?" asked Tony.

"I don't know, but we've got to do something. That fucking monster has already killed people. For all we know, we could be next. I say we go talk to this guy. What have we got to lose?" said Karl.

"Have you guys thought about telling our parents or maybe telling the police?" asked Mark.

Karl stood up and paced back and forth once, then turned and said while gesturing impatiently, "What do you think we would say to our parents, huh? Are we going to tell them there's a monster and it killed my old man? Do you think they would believe us? I don't think so. Call the police? Those guys trace all their calls—I saw it on Dragnet. They would know where the call came from and pretty soon they would pick us up and grill us, maybe even beat us until we talked. They would say we were accessories to those killings and they would send us to reform school or maybe even to jail, for life! I don't want to go to jail and I don't want to die either. I say we check out this Indian and see if he can help us."

"But Karl, we could call from a pay phone and maybe we could disguise our voices or something," said Mark.

"I don't know, Mark. Karl's right. I say let's talk to the Indian. What have we got to lose? If he can't help us then we can go to the police or something!" said Tony.

"What about you, Lenny?" said Karl.

"What about telling Father Campbell? He would have to keep it a secret because he's a priest. Maybe he could do an exorcism. Maybe there's a special blessing he could give us that would make us untouchable by that monster," said Lenny.

"Get real, Lenny. The priest would tell our parents everything. You know priests and parents are in cahoots. Every time you confess your sins to the priest he goes and tells your parents. If you tell him you checked out a *Playboy* and maybe got a boner or something, he goes and tells your parents. I know because my old man stopped going to church because some priest told his parents he did something bad. So they punished him with an ass-numbing whipping," said Karl.

"Okay, okay, it was just an idea," protested Lenny.

"So, when do we go talk to this St. Germain guy?" asked Mark.

"How about the day after my old man's funeral?" said Karl.

Everyone nodded their agreement.

"Let's go in the house and watch some TV," said Tony.

"Naw, instead let's go over to Vic's Market and buy a couple of comic books, come back here and read them," said Mark.

"Yeah. I think the Red Sox are playing tonight. We could listen to the game on the radio, you know, later after the wake thing," said Lenny.

"Well, what are we waiting for? Let's go!" Karl said eagerly.

As they walked to the front yard on their way to the store, Tony stuck his right index finger up his nose. He dug and dug. "Maybe I'll buy some penny candy," he thought as he explored the inside of his left pocket. It had a generous amount of loose change. Yes, indeed, he would have enough to get some mint juleps and a couple of bazookas, too.

* * * * *

The creature had been listening. He connected with Tony, finding him to be the easiest to reach. He used Tony to listen in on the other boys' conversation. Tony would have no idea the creature was using him. The creature was capable of using any living thing as an instrument. He especially enjoyed using humans to experience their sense of sight.

So these boys were going to talk to the old Indian. That would pose no problem to him. He could easily kill the Indian at any time. He would instead let them have their meeting. He would listen in. It would be interesting to hear what the Indian would have to say after all these years. The Indian would only add to the fear these boys already felt with his tales about Ne Wha Ta. That could be helpful to his plans.

He would continue to turn up the terror level. Terror was his friend. He owned terror. He would use it to keep these boys off balance. He began to make plans.

Outside, deep in the woods, the day's shadows grew longer as the sun set over the distant Adirondack Mountains on the western side of Lake Champlain. The woodland air cooled and the night creatures began to stir as the daytime creatures settled in for the coming night.

Beneath the earth's surface in caves all over northwestern Vermont, bats' internal clocks signaled that nighttime was quickly approaching. Suddenly, as if by command, bats everywhere took flight in a flapping frenzy as they swarmed out of these caves on their twilight journey to feeding areas. In Ne Wha Ta's cave the bats waited. He stood up and sniffed the air. He could hear the bats' shrill peeping sound. He simply thought the word *Go*, which unleashed these bats into a sudden dash for the distant exit, to the surface and food.

He listened as the sound of their fluttering subsided. It was a hot and humid day. A rain shower quickly passed by earlier leaving everything moist to the touch. There would be an abundance of bugs to eat tonight. The bats would return filled and satisfied, and that was good.

* * * * *

"So, Dad, you never mentioned this story about spending a summer playing with Indian children and hearing a story about some Indian legend," said Mark.

Mark's father was driving back home. They all enjoyed the evening at the home of Winooski's police chief.

"I know, son. Sometimes parents don't always tell their children every detail about their own childhood. Some of the things I did as a child I'm ashamed of, and yet other things are just too boring to tell. But that story I told is true, I swear it. And I was scared. Hell, I'm still scared even now as I think about it."

"You still think about it?" asked a curious Mark.

"I still do, sure, especially after the quarry people found them damn bones."

Mark's father pulled the car into the driveway. Everyone got out and headed up the back steps into the house. Pokey was there to greet them and get a scratch behind his ears.

"You boys get settled in. I'm going to take Pokey for a walk. We'll be right back."

"Dad, why don't you let me take him for a walk?" said Mark.

"No, that's okay. I ate too much for dinner and a little walk will help me get a good night's sleep. Now, Tony, if I were you I'd give my pretty young wife a phone call. Let her know you're okay!"

After a moment, Mark's father and Pokey went out the back door. The dog's tail was wagging at a frantic pace.

"He's right, as always. I should call my wife. I'll be right back," said Tony as he headed into the living room to place the call.

"So, Mark, what do you make of your father knowing that old Indian legend long before the summer of 1962? He might know something that could be helpful," said Lenny.

"I don't think so. I really don't want to drag him into this!" said Mark with a slight tinge of defiance.

"Why not, Mark? You know, he may have even had his own encounter with the creature. I think we should talk to him," countered Lenny.

"No, we keep him out of this. This fight is between Ne Wha Ta and us. You remember what St. Germain told us. According to the legend, only those who have brought forth Ne Wha Ta can defeat him. That is a key point we can't lose sight of, otherwise we're just reacting to Ne Wha Ta and he holds all the cards. So let's stop looking for an escape hatch because there isn't one. Let's face it, we're not kids anymore. We've got to take responsibility for letting him out and that means we either find a way to bury him where he will never be able to get out, or we find a way to destroy him," said Mark.

"I suppose you're right," said Lenny.

"Thanks, because we've got to stick together on this," said Mark.

Tony finished his call. He snapped his cell phone shut and was about to go back into the kitchen and rejoin his friends when he heard a voice speaking to him from somewhere inside his head.

"So, human, you and the others think you can defeat me? What makes you think you are clever enough? Don't you understand by now I know each and every move you are planning to make? You'll never defeat me. You must fulfill your part of our bargain. I will have a mate! Only after that, will I consider leaving you alone."

Tony couldn't move. He told himself all he needed to do was call out to the others and the creature would release his hold on him. But his mental calls for his legs to move and his voice to cry out went unanswered. He was overcome with a feeling of helplessness.

"I have had my way with you humans for a very long time. My ancestors did, too. This female of yours is with child. She is proving herself capable of breeding. If you don't bring me a female to breed with soon, I will have to choose one. Perhaps I should choose your female."

Tony strained against the powers of the creature. He felt a well-spring of deep, bitter hatred rumbling to the surface. This anger was raw and powerful beyond anything Tony had experienced before. He commanded himself to break free from the grip of this sadistic creature.

"Noooooooooooo," he screamed at the top of his lungs. Suddenly he felt the monster's grip break away.

Mark and Lenny came running from the kitchen at the sound of Tony's fury. Mark turned on the wall switch and they saw Tony sitting stiff as a board. He was mumbling to himself. "No, no, no, no.....,"

"Tony, Tony, what in the hell is wrong?" asked a deeply concerned Lenny.

"The....the...monst....,Ne Wha Ta....he said he would take my wife for his mate, he'd take her," said Tony as he sobbed into his hands.

"Tony, we won't let that happen. Do you hear me? We won't let that happen to her or anybody. We just need to stick together. He's just trying to divide us," said Mark.

"He's right, Tony! We need to fight this fucker, united," said Lenny.

Tony was still sobbing when he mumbled, "She's pregnant."

"What did you say?" said Lenny.

Tony looked up into the eyes of his friends and spoke haltingly, "My wife, she's pregnant. He...he said he knows she's pregnant. I think he could, ah... he could make her lose our baby. What am I supposed to do?"

Mark and Lenny didn't have an answer. What they had, however, was a greater sense of urgency. Ne Wha Ta once again proved he was capable of anything.

Chapter 33

It was the morning of Bob Sweeney's funeral. There was to be no church service. At the time of his death, Bob had long since given up his belief in organized religion. Instead, there would be only a graveside service. The irony was that Bob Sweeney would be buried in the Catholic Cemetery.

Father Campbell would speak at the graveside service and would, notwithstanding Bob's attitudes and beliefs, bless the casket. The priest bent a few rules in allowing this man to be buried here, but he was sure it was God's will this man's surviving family not suffer any more than they already had. They were, at best, part-time Catholics. Going forward, Father Campbell would redouble his efforts after the funeral to bring them fully back into the arms of their faith and their Church.

The funeral procession was led by a black Cadillac hearse. It slowly made its way up Weaver Street. It made a slow left hand turn as it entered St. Francis Xavier Church's graveyard. The hearse wound its way through the pine tree shaded road that meandered through the graveyard. In the far northern edge of the graveyard was the burial plot for Bob Sweeney. There was a green cloth-covered mound of dirt next to the open grave. There was also a chrome trimmed casket lift straddling the open grave. The grave was eight feet deep, cut perfectly rectangular at three feet by eight feet and was covered around its perimeter by a dark green cloth. There were no flowers at the grave site and no headstone. The hearse stopped approximately one car length past the grave. As the other cars in the funeral procession pulled up behind the hearse, the driver of the hearse, who was also the owner of the funeral home, opened the back door. The flag-draped coffin now awaited the pallbearers.

The pallbearers were all work acquaintances of Bob. He did not make friends easily. He and his wife, Betty, moved to Vermont from Michigan when Bob took a job with St. Johnsbury Trucking, where he worked as a diesel engine mechanic. Because of his temper and drinking problem his wife found it difficult to form friendships on her own. Now she and Karl got out of the funeral parlor's black Cadillac sedan which followed the hearse. She was accompanied by two women neighbors who responded to this Sweeney family tragedy with their usual generosity of time and spirit.

No family members of either Bob or Betty could make it to Vermont for the funeral. All of their relatives were too poor. Bob's parents arranged for a bouquet of flowers to be sent, as did Bob's two older brothers and his younger sister. Betty Sweeney's family sent flowers also. Her father died several years earlier of lung cancer. Her mother sent a bouquet of flowers and called her daughter at least three times a day since the tragedy. Betty's only sibling, a sister, lived in Texas at the moment. Her husband was in the Air Force. She moved around every two years or so and likewise didn't have much money. She sent her sister a small bouquet of flowers along with some rosary beads. In her letter, she said she'd had them for a couple of years. Her letter went on to say the religious store where she bought them reported the rosary had been blessed by the Pope himself.

One of the funeral home's assistants guided the pallbearers in organizing their trek to the grave with the casket. Another employee removed several small bouquets of flowers from the hearse and from the back of the third vehicle in the funeral procession. He quickly placed these modest bouquets in a semi-circle around the grave area starting at the head then along the sides. Gripping the casket handles, the pallbearers moved their feet in a shuffling motion. They gingerly placed the casket upon the burial straps that spanned the open grave.

Several dozen feet away stood a contingent of Army National Guard soldiers in full dress uniform. One of them held a bugle while three others held rifles. In addition, there was a Sergeant who watched as the grieving family and friends gathered around the casket.

The Sergeant turned and gave a command in a firm but respectful voice. The bugle began to play the ever mournful dirge, *Taps*. The sound echoed across the graveyard. A short distance away, the head gravedigger and his assistant respectfully waited in the shadows of a large pine tree to move in after the funeral service to complete the actual burial itself.

After *Taps*, the Sergeant gave orders to the armed men. "Attention..., present arms..., ready weapons..., aim..., fire!" Seven times shots rang out, shattering the solemnity of the moment. Each time, as the weapons discharged, Betty cringed and clutched at Karl, who stood at her side.

After the weapons salute, the Sergeant, along with the soldier who had played *Taps*, stepped smartly together to the coffin and began the time-honored tradition of folding the flag that draped the coffin and presenting it to the deceased's widow. Betty accepted the flag with dry eyes. Her husband spent three years in the active Army and then another six years in the reserves. She always hated guns but she welcomed his monthly absence and the added money his being in the reserves brought into their household.

Everyone now turned to face Father Campbell, who began the graveside service with the sign of the cross. He took out a small bottle of holy water from his suit pocket. He also removed a small black book which he opened to a red-ribbon-marked passage. He began to read aloud abbreviated funeral service prayers. He spoke of the need to embrace the spirit of charity in one's heart. His words soothed the assembled even while his words amused Ne Wha Ta, who listened through the boys to the service.

The priest ended his prayers by blessing the casket which held the remains of Bob Sweeney.

Father Campbell closed his small prayer book and then went to Mrs. Sweeney and Karl. He spoke quietly to her and Karl. Bob

Sweeney's widow dabbed at the corner of her eyes as the priest spoke to her. She nodded a couple of times. The priest gently touched Karl's face and said something. Karl nodded his agreement. Now Father Campbell moved away. Slowly other people approached Betty and Karl and spoke softly to them expressing their final condolences. After a short while, everyone began to drift away to their cars. The funeral director approached Betty and Karl and guided them back to the limousine. As they walked back to the car, Karl looked back at his father's casket one last time. He got into the car with his mother. The black Cadillac soon proceeded to slowly drive out of the graveyard.

When the last car left the graveyard, the two graveyard workers approached Bob Sweeney's casket as it rested suspended over the grave. They slowly cranked the casket down into the ground.

"Click, click, click" was the sound of the casket lift as it lowered the casket slowly into the unlined grave. When the casket was finally at the bottom of the grave one of the workers pulled a pin from each of the three straps that were used to lower the casket. Released from one side of the lift, the straps were now cranked out of the grave from the opposite side.

Once the straps were wound up on the side of the casket lift the two men removed the chrome-covered lift away from the opening of the grave. They began to fill the grave with the two shovels they brought. This grave held no cement liner to preserve and protect the deceased's remains. Soon they finished covering the casket and re-filling the grave. The soil made a small mound over the newly filled-in grave. The men moved sections of sod they had cut out earlier in the day. Next, the deeply green colored sections of sod were placed over the top of the grave. They used their shovels to tamp down the sod. The flowers were repositioned closer to the grave. The gravediggers, their work now done, moved silently away.

They headed to the nearby cemetery shed where they would store the shovels. Later that day they would revisit the graveyard to remove most of the flowers and to cut out and dig another grave. On the wall, near the shed door was a calendar, marked in red, with the name of another dearly departed, the next in line to be buried.

There was a leather bound book hanging on a nail next to the calendar. The book contained the burial plot plan for the entire church graveyard. As time passed, the plot layout was slowly but surely filling in. In fact, both of the graveyard workers had already picked out their own family plot.

Their names were in the book of the dead or soon to be dead.

* * * * *

Karl's mother agreed to let Karl stay with the Pushey family for a few more days. She would be staying with neighbors. They were helping her adjust to the loss of her husband. A couple of them would soon try to convince Betty to go back to her house and sort through her husband's things and try to remove as much as she could be persuaded to part with. Her ability to reach closure would be helped along by these caring and compassionate women.

The morning after his father's funeral, Karl was up earlier than anyone else in the house. Mark's family insisted the boys sleep in the house. Karl hadn't slept well at all. He tossed and turned all night. At dawn's first light he got up, dressed and went downstairs to sit on the front porch. Around five forty-five a squeaky bicycle could be heard making its way up the street. Karl recognized the operator. It was Bobby Oullette, the neighborhood newspaper boy.

The bicycle stooped in front of the Pushey's. Bobby put the kickstand down, walked up to Karl and handed him the neatly folded newspaper.

"Sorry about your dad," said Bobby.

"Thanks."

"You alright?" asked Bobby.

"Yeah, I'm doing okay."

"Well, I've got to finish my route. See yah around."

"Yeah, see yah."

Bobby got back on his bicycle and pedaled away.

Karl unfolded the newspaper. His eyes quickly settled on the headline story. The headline read, *Missing Teen's Car Found*. He read the story slowly so as to not miss a word. The story was accompanied with a photo of the car and two police officers standing next to it—Colchester Police Chief Seltzer and rookie Officer Blair. The story reported how a local hunter located the vehicle and reported it to Colchester police. It went on to report on the efforts to search the immediate vicinity of the found vehicle. So far police efforts had not uncovered any trace of the missing teens. Police sources indicated they didn't believe the teens ran away. The police reportedly had reason to believe the teen's disappearance was suspicious. The story went on to report on the car, its condition and the fact it was found at what was described as a "lover's lane." The story went on to say there had been an organized search by tracking dogs and one tracker's dog turned up missing. Police Chief Seltzer was quoted as saying, "The dog's disappearance was purely a coincidence and was not connected to the missing teens. It just went off on its own chasing rabbits or something. We expect it'll turn up."

Karl pondered the story's details. He looked down the front page and noticed another story which caught his attention. This second story concerned Bremer's Quarry. The story reported the day before there had been two freak accidents at the quarry. In one accident, Oscar Chapdelaine of Milton, Vermont, died when his dump truck fell back into the stone crusher when the approach ramp gave way. Later in the day, another dump truck driver was crushed to death when he got out of his truck to check his quarry load. A large boulder toppled off the truck crushing him with its weight. His name was Octave Beaudoin, formerly of Ste. Pie, Quebec, who was residing in Richmond, Vermont.

Both deaths were considered accidents. Nevertheless, state safety inspectors were planning on reviewing the company's facilities to assess the risk to workers. The story went on to summarize since the quarry's opening in 1944 it experienced only a handful of accidents, none of which led to any deaths. A company spokesperson indicated the company would cooperate with authorities but the company's concern at the moment was for the families of the dead truck drivers. The company announced it was organizing a trust fund for the dead men. On the inside of the front page was another story Karl took notice of. This story reported Charles Letourneau of Winooski was considered missing. He had not returned from hunting and not been seen for a couple of days. Police were treating his case as a missing person's case. They said they were going to begin to interview friends and acquaintances to see if they could piece together a picture of Letourneau's last known whereabouts. Police asked anyone with any information concerning Letourneau's activities on the day he disappeared to come forward to assist with this investigation.

Karl wondered about the "Freak" accidents at the quarry. *Could the monster be involved in the deaths of the two men? If so, why would he?* The answers to these questions eluded him.

What was certain is police from two communities were investigating two separate missing persons cases. Karl was sure his buddies would be panicked by this development. Karl was convinced they left no trace. The police would not be able to connect them to the cave unless they left something behind. He would have to reassure his buddies to be cool and to not panic.

Mmmmm, thought Karl returning his attention to the "freak accident. *Could the monster be causing those accidents to scare the people at the quarry, maybe even shut it down? Yeah, that's it. He's afraid their blasting will uncover his hideout. He is probably trying to stop the quarry from blowing up his cave.*

Karl was deep in thought, when out of the corner of his right eye, he noticed a large black crow had landed on the railing of the porch. It was staring at him and at the newspaper Karl held in his hands. Karl turned and looked at the bird. It looked back at him, turning its head side to side. It preened itself but it did not move.

Karl swept his right hand with the newspaper in it at the bird. "Shoo.....Shoo."

Still the bird did not fly away. Karl was beginning to feel nervous about this bird. He had been in the woods many times. There were crows in these woods. While they tended to be bold birds, they would fly away if they sensed they are threatened. Karl stood up and stared at the crow. It stared back.

"What the hell do you want?" asked Karl.

Still it stared at Karl.

"Are you controlled by the monster in the woods?"

The crow gave him a creepy feeling.

"What do you want from me?"

The bird shifted its feet while its eyes never stopped staring at Karl.

Karl took a step towards the bird. "Shoo, get the hell away from me."

"Karl, is that you?" It was Mark's father.

The porch door opened as Mark's father, wearing his plaid colored bathrobe stepped onto the porch. As he did, the crow took flight right at Karl. He ducked down to avoid being hit by the large black bird. Mark's father was surprised by the sudden appearance of the crow. He took an unexpected step back when he saw the crow fly directly across his porch.

"What was that?" asked Mark's father.

"It was one of the biggest crows I've ever seen. It was sitting over on that railing. I tried to shoo it away, but it wouldn't go, until you came out."

"That's kind of strange. I don't think I've ever seen a crow up close before," said Mr. Pushey.

"Me either."

"What do you suppose it wanted?"

"Well, it was staring at the newspaper for a while," said Karl.

"I thought only parakeets liked newspapers," said Mark's father.

Karl didn't react to the faint effort at humor.

"Do you get it?"

"Get what?" said Karl.

"Oh, never mind," said Mark's father. "Could you hand me a piece of the paper?"

"Sure," said Karl.

He handed over the entire newspaper. Mr. Pushey sat down in the old wicker rocker as Karl sat back down on the front steps. He noticed, in the large maple tree across the street two houses down, a large crow sitting in the upper branches staring back at the Pushey's house.

The crow made cawing sounds. In a moment there were at least five more crows sitting in the same high branches. They all seemed to be looking in the direction of Karl and the Pushey's house.

I've got to get Mark up so he can see this, thought Karl.

Karl went into the house.

Mr. Pushey laid the newspaper on his lap. He leaned forward and bent down a little so he could see down the street. He saw the several crows sitting in the maple tree.

They are acting strange, that's for sure, thought Mr. Pushey as he leaned back and continued rocking and reading his morning newspaper.

Meanwhile, the crows kept watching.

Chapter 34

It was the morning after the dinner with Winooski' Chief of Police. Mark's father took the car because he had a meeting at the VFW. It was the weekly meeting of the officers of Walter Landry Post #23. He was the Treasurer, faithfully holding the position for the past five years. Mark's father said he would be gone until at least two in the afternoon so, if they needed the car, Mark could drive him to the meeting and take the car. He would find a ride home with someone at the VFW.

Mark and Tony were in the living room reading the newspaper and half listening to the television. Lenny was upstairs taking a shower.

"Listen to this. It says here the police investigation into the bones found at the quarry has uncovered evidence which may link some of the human remains to several local cases of missing persons, some going back several years. Final identification will await the results of certain forensic tests to be performed by the Chief Medical Examiner's Office and the FBI over the next several days."

"I think we had to expect that," affirmed Mark.

Tony kept reading the article. The sound of the shower running upstairs could be heard over the low sound of the television. The television show was suddenly interrupted with a screen wide News Flash Message. A serious looking news anchor from the local station WCAX came on the air.

"We apologize for the interruption to our usual morning programming but we have some breaking news. We have a reporter standing by at the scene of the ongoing police investigation at the former Bremer Quarry in Colchester. As viewers know, this quarry is now the focus of an investigation into the mysterious cache of human bones accidentally uncovered during recent blasting at the quarry. Let's go live to our reporter on the scene who is covering this breaking story. Julie Larkin, are you there?" said the television news anchor.

"Yes, I am, Charlie.

"Julie, what do you have for us?"

"Charlie, I've learned this morning some of the human remains lying in the cave just behind me, were taken from a local cemetery. Somehow, unknown to any of the local Church officials there was an apparent systematic stealing of bodies. What has puzzled investigators is just how the thefts were accomplished.

The police will be asking certain families for permission to exhume their loved ones' graves to see just who, if anybody, is buried in those graves. Charlie?"

"Julie, do the police have any theories as to how or why this has taken place?"

"Charlie, one theory is there may be a cult which possibly stole the bodies for some ritual perhaps. How it was done is, right now, a real puzzler for the police. They hope to begin to have some answers to this expanding mystery once they can examine the church grave sites. This is Julie Larkin reporting live from the former Bremer Quarry in the Town of Colchester. Now back to you, Charlie, in the studio," said the beautiful young television reporter.

"Thank you for that report, Julie. We will be bringing you updates as soon as they happen. Meanwhile, this is Charles McMaster bringing you news in a flash. We will now return you to our regularly scheduled programming."

The television screen blinked and in an instant it was reconnected to, "The Price is Right."

"Shit, that is incredible. Grave robbing, is there anything Ne Wha Ta can't or won't do?" said Tony.

"We both know the answer to that question," said Mark.

Lenny came down the stairs wiping his hair with a towel. Mark and Tony told him what they'd just heard on the television. He was as surprised as they were. They went on to discuss this latest development for several more minutes.

Lenny decided he wanted to change the subject, "Guys, I think we should at least get in touch with Karl's widow while we're here. We owe it to Karl. I mean, if his wife knew we had been here and hadn't tried to contact her, how do you think that would make her feel?"

"Lenny's right," said Tony.

"But we don't even know where she is," said Mark.

"I do. I've got her telephone number. I got the number when I called Karl's house and spoke to someone named Marta. She was the one who told me Karl committed suicide. She was house-sitting for Linda. Apparently Linda, her daughter Sherrie, and Bart went to stay with her parents back in Wisconsin," said Lenny.

"Well, what are we waiting for? Let's give her a call. We should just express our condolences, you know stuff like that. We shouldn't mention anything about Karl's suicide. If she wants to talk about it, let her, but let's not bring it up first," declared Mark.

Lenny and Tony agreed.

Lenny placed the call. It rang three times. Lenny spoke to someone and asked for Linda. He identified himself as a lifelong family friend. The person on the other end of the line was a cousin of Linda's. She said she'd get Linda's daughter, Sherrie. Moments later, Sherrie came on the line and Lenny spoke to her. He explained he was with Tony and Mark. She was delighted to hear from them.

Lenny spoke to Sherrie for several minutes as Mark and Tony listened to Lenny's half of the conversation. Lenny learned, to his surprise, that Linda had been suffering from MS for several years. Apparently Karl's death somehow worsened her condition.

Then it was Mark's turn and he spoke to Sherrie. After a few moments of conversation, Mark held the receiver away from his ear and covered the phone's mouthpiece with his hand, "She's crying," he said.

"Yeah, Sherrie, I know. Karl was a strong person. Once he made up his mind, he could be real stubborn," said a sympathetic Mark.

"Uh-huh, yes I will. I'll be happy to contact them for you. No, no, it won't be any trouble. Let me write this down."

Holding the phone to his chest, he asked Lenny to get him a pencil and paper from the kitchen memo pad hanging next to the refrigerator. Lenny quickly returned and handed the pencil along with a small sheet of paper to Mark.

"I've got some paper, go ahead. Okay, yeah! Go on, sure and what was it to say? I see. Yes, I've got it. Yup! Is there anything else? Fine, you can count on me, Sherrie. Please give my condolences to your mom and brother. Why don't I hand the phone now to Tony? Bye for now. Here's Tony."

Mark handed the phone to Tony. Tony began to talk to Sherrie as Mark showed the note to Lenny.

"She wants me to contact this monument company to check on the status of Karl's headstone. She said it should have been delivered by now," said Mark.

"Why don't you call them right after we hang up with Sherrie?" said Lenny.

"I was planning to," said Mark.

Tony spoke to Sherrie for several minutes. Lenny noticed that Tony's eyes were tearing up. Lenny felt a lump forming in his own throat.

"She wants to tell you something she forgot to mention earlier," said Tony, as he handed the phone back to Lenny.

"Yes, Sherrie."

"Lenny, I almost forgot. Dad left a wrapped a package for you. I'm sure he wanted to mail it to you. It has your name on it, but Dad never put your address on it. With the funeral and all Mom and I forgot to look up your address. Look, I'll give you the name and phone number of a neighbor who's looking after our house. She can get the package for you and you can pick it up from her, if that's all right with you?" said a tired-sounding Sherrie.

"Sure, that would be fine. I think I spoke with her a few days ago. She said her name was Marta," said Lenny. "I already have her telephone number."

"Yes, that's her. She called and told me you called. I'll call her right after I hang up. Ah..., I've got to go now. It was so nice to hear from you guys. Maybe, uh maybe, we could get together some-time." Sherrie's voice was cracking up a little. "Dad loved you guys. You all meant so much to him. He... he missed you guys so much." She was crying once again.

Lenny was trying to hold back his own tears.

"Goodbye, Lenny. Please say goodbye to Mark and Tony for me."

Before Lenny could respond the phone went silent.

He hung up the phone with tears in his eyes.

"Sherrie said to say goodbye to you guys."

They all sat in silence for several minutes. Mark spoke first.

"I've got to call the headstone company.."

"Good idea," said a mellow Lenny. "I have to call Linda's neigh-bor. She's going to help get a package for me that Karl apparently intended to send to me."

Tony stood up.

"I'm going to make some coffee." He turned and headed into the kitchen.

Using his cell phone, Mark called the headstone company. It was open. Soon, he was engaged in a lengthy conversation.

The smell of brewing coffee filled the air as Lenny made ar-rangements with Linda's neighbor.

Chapter 35

Mark called over to Tony's house. He told Tony to go get Lenny and meet Karl and him in front of Vic's Market in half an hour.

A half hour later the four young boys were together in front of the store.

"So, what's up?" asked Tony.

"We're going to St. Germain's. Karl and me figure the old Indian may be able to tell us something about our monster," said Mark.

"Our monster?" said Lenny.

"You know what I mean," said Mark.

"Look, we're wasting time. Are we going or not?" said Karl.

That did it.

They set out for the home of Louis St. Germain. He lived in a beat up shack-of-a-house on upper Main Street. The house hadn't seen a coat of paint in years. Weeds abounded around the house. There was a barn out behind the house which leaned to the left. Several pieces of planking were missing from its side. Deeply settled in the tall grass immediately behind the house was the shell of a 1949 Plymouth. It might have been dark green at one time but now it was hard to tell. All four tires were flat.

The four boys stood on the sidewalk in front of the house. They searched for a sign that St. Germain was home. There was no sound coming from the house even though there was a screen door at the front with its inside door wide open.

"You knock on the front door," said Mark to Karl.

"Nah, let's go around back. Maybe he's out back," said a hesitant Karl.

The four boys went around back. There still was no sign of the man. Two large horses stood in the paddock next to the barn. Shade covered much of the paddock from a large elm tree situated just outside the fenced-in area. A swarm of flies flickered around the horses who stood perfectly still except for the constant swishing of their tails. The rapidly warming morning air was filled with the pungent odor of the often soiled ground inside the paddock. The boys noticed an old tractor inside of the barn that appeared to have several of its engine's parts scattered on the barn floor.

Karl went up to the barn and called out for St. Germain.

"Hey, is anybody here?" called Karl. "Is anybody home?"

From behind the four boys came an answer.

"What do you want?"

They were startled upon hearing the voice from behind them. They all turned and for the first time, their eyes took in Louis St. Germain.

He was wearing a T-shirt, along with stained and well worn dark green work pants. He also wore work boots which were so worn the left shoe had a hole all the way through to the steel toe.

In his right hand he carried a large crescent shaped blade. Its sharpened edge glistened in the morning sunlight. He stood five foot six and weighed not more than one hundred and fifty pounds.

His long hair was a mixture of black and gray and was tied in a pony tail in the back by a string with small beads on the ends. He was clean shaven and his eyes were black and firmly fixed on the four frightened boys.

"I asked you boys a question. What do you want?" said St. Germain. His voice was even. It did not betray any emotion.

"We, uh.....need to talk to you. We have some questions we think only you, you know, can answer," stammered a nervous Mark.

"Really," said St. Germain.

"Yeah, we were, well, we heard that, uh ...we were told that you were, uh," Mark was getting flustered.

Tony blurted out, "The OUIJA board told us to come and talk to you."

The stern face of St. Germain slowly melted into a grin. He chuckled at Tony's revelation.

"That's quite a reference."

"Yeah, well it's the truth," said an emboldened Tony.

"If you say so, then it is!"

Louis turned and headed towards the house with the four boys following behind.

"Mister, are you going to talk to us or not?" asked Lenny.

"You boys seem to be doing all the talking. I'm just listening."

He climbed the two badly worn steps to the back porch and sat down on the one wooden chair that was on the porch. It creaked and seemed to strain when he sat on it. He put the crescent blade down behind the chair.

"Well, I'm listening."

"You're gonna think we're crazy," said Mark.

"Maybe I will, maybe I won't."

"I'll let Karl tell you why we're here," said Mark as he elbowed his friend.

Karl took a deep breath and began. "Well, we kind of have a problem. You see, there's this monster that's been sort of after us and we think it killed some people."

Karl hadn't minced his words. He went right to the nub of things!

Louis St. Germain shifted in the chair. "This monster you say is after you, does it live in a cave?"

"Holy shit—that's it! I told you guys he knew stuff," said Lenny.

"Slow down, slow down," said St. Germain as he gestured for the boys to sit down on the weathered porch.

"What do you know about me?" asked St. Germain.

"That you're an Indian," said Lenny.

"And who told you that?"

"My dad told me."

"I see," he said as he closed his eyes for what seemed like several minutes but was really only a short while.

"Are you really an Indian?" asked Tony.

"I am Abenaki, son of Little Thunder and Summer Breeze. I am from the Sokoki-St. Francis Band. We have lived on this land for many, many generations, for thousands of years."

"What does Abenaki mean?" asked Mark.

"It means, People of the Dawn."

"Then what is a Sokoki?" asked a curious Lenny.

"It means, 'People who separated'."

"I never heard these names before," said Karl.

"What do you know about my people? Humph! For you, Indians are savages who hunt and kill. In movies, magazines, even your history books all tell lies about the Indian. If the white man kills Indians it is a good fight. If Indians kill white men it is a massacre."

"I guess you're right. But look, we didn't write that stuff. What we know about Indians is what our fathers told us and that wasn't too much," said Karl.

"Yes, your fathers, I know them well. I remember their coming here to hurt and insult me." He leaned back in his chair and folded his arms.

"Look, we're sorry for that stuff. I know my dad did some pretty mean stuff to you. He was mean to everybody. Shit, he used to beat me. Now he's dead. We really have no one else to turn to. Please, help us, Mr. St. Germain," pleaded Karl.

"Look into your heart. What do you see?" said St. Germain as he looked at a nervous Lenny.

"I don't know how."

Leaning forward, with his elbows now on his knees, St. Germain looked directly at Lenny.

"Close your eyes and tell me what you see."

Lenny did as he was instructed. He closed his eyes. For now he could hear the traffic driving by the front of the house. He could even hear the horses moving in the paddock. Suddenly out of the grayness of his closed eyes, he could see something.

"Now nervous one, tell me what you see."

With his eyes still closed, Lenny spoke.

"I, uh, see my mom. I see my little sister. Mom is holding her."

"What else do you see?"

"My dad, I see my dad. He's got a wise ass look on his face. He's, I don't know, he's trying to take the baby from my mom. My mom won't give him the baby. My mom's crying."

"Don't stop, tell me everything."

"I want to stop," said an anxious Lenny. He was beginning to sweat. His face was tensing up.

"Tell me what is in your heart—look deep inside."

Beads of sweat were now running down his face. Karl, Tony and Mark just watched as Lenny and the Indian explored what Lenny could see.

"I....that bastard, he took my little sister from my mom. She's pleading with him to give her back. He's laughing, he's fucking laughing." Lenny's eyes began to twitch. His brows furrowed with tension. He bit his lower lip. A small trickle of blood was beginning to run down from the cut in his lip.

Mark began to reach out to Lenny but St. Germain gestured for him to not touch Lenny. They all sat still waiting for Lenny to speak.

"He's ....no....it can't be. He's no......no....stop, stop...I'll kill you, you bastard. No! Oh, God!" Lenny's body went suddenly very stiff.

"You killed her. You've.....no...It can't be...no, oh God somebody, please help me, help me. He has no eyes. The teeth, Jesus.....you're not my father.....what are you?"

Lenny's chest was heaving as he strained with each and every breath. He was drenched in sweat.

The boys were watching this spectacle. They began to be afraid for Lenny and themselves.

"Ask him his name," said St. Germain.

"His name....he says his name is....Ne Wha Ta."

"Good, now tell Ne Wha Ta, that on the strength of all your ancestors you command him to leave and return to the hole in the earth he crawled out from. Tell him and mean it."

Lenny's lips moved but there was no sound coming forth.

St. Germain closed his own eyes and he, too, silently moved his lips in perfect unison with Lenny. They seemed to be silently speaking a chant over and over. At the very same moment they stopped and opened their eyes and looked directly at each other.

"Now tell what you saw in your heart."

"I saw fear and I saw death, I think."

"Not death. Ne Wha Ta."

Tony, Mark and even Karl reached out and touched Lenny, who felt clammy and cold, cold as ice.

"I will get you something to drink. Wait here."

St. Germain got up from the tired old chair and went into his house. He soon returned with five chilled bottles of soda pop. He used a bottle opener and handed a bottle to each boy. To Lenny he also handed the extra bottle.

"Here, you will need this."

He sat back down on the chair. He looked away towards the direction of the barn. It was as if he was listening for something. After a while he returned his attention to the boys who were in need of his help.

"You must know the story of Ne Wha Ta. I will tell it to you, but you must not tell anyone else what I tell you unless their lives are in danger. You must all swear on your ancestors' graves to keep this story to yourselves."

One by one, the boys looked at each other and nodded their agreement.

St. Germain looked to the western sky before he began his tale, then, after pausing, he began.

"Long ago, before there were white men, there were only Alnanbal, my people. They hunted, fished and farmed .

Ndakinna. This means, our land. My people were strong and happy. We were at one with the earth. We had many brothers who lived beyond the great western waters, what you call the Great Lakes. They would sometimes get together with other great Indian Nations. There was peace among my people. We had many long houses and great Sachems, too! There was no sickness among my people."

St. Germain paused and stood up, stretched his tired old back and then sat down again to continue his story.

"One day, in the time of summer, a hunting party was formed to go north to hunt for elk. They were gone for over two months. My people didn't know what happened to them. They sent out trackers to search for them. The trackers came back and said the hunting party had vanished. One night, a young member of the long missing hunting party returned. He was bleeding from several wounds. He was tired and frightened and wouldn't let the squaws or the medicine man treat his wounds until after he'd spoken to the Sachem, the Chief. The young hunter was carried to the Sachem's long house where a fire was built. Many Abenaki men gathered there that night. The young hunter, Little White Hawk, told his story. He said the hunting party was surprised one night by another band of Indians unknown to any Abenaki. A fight began and much bloodshed occurred as they fought throughout the night. By morning, where they once started out over twenty men, there were now only three. The bodies of our Abenaki hunters were everywhere along with over thirty of their enemy. This unknown warrior enemy danced to their victory. Then one of the enemy warriors, one who called himself Grey Wolf, the one who killed many of our Abenaki hunters, cut open the chest of one of the three remaining Abenaki. He took his knife and cut out his heart. He took the heart to the camp fire and after adding wood to the fire, so that it roared, he cooked the heart on a stick. He ripped it into pieces and gave some to the others. Then this Grey Wolf called for the prisoners, Little White Hawk and another Abenaki survivor, Swift Bear. He offered to free them, to let them join his warrior band if they would eat the flesh of the dead. They both refused to eat the flesh of the dead. So this flesh eater, Grey Wolf went up to one of his murderous fellow warriors and tore out his heart. The warrior's dead body collapsed on the ground. Grey Wolf ordered Little White Hawk to eat the live flesh or he would kill them both."

"Holy shit," said Mark.

222

"Somehow Little White Hawk escaped while they tortured and killed Swift Bear. These flesh eaters had been tracking and hunting Little White Hawk for almost two moons. He saw them kill and eat other Indians they encountered just as they did to the Abenaki deep in the great north woods. He barely made it to the village ahead of these human flesh eaters. He needed to warn everyone. He was trying to speak of more dangers when Little White Hawk suddenly died."

"The Sokoki Sachem, Chief Great Bear, sent word that all the women and children were to be brought to his long house immediately. As soon as they had been assembled he organized the men to stand watch. The next night, four hunter-warrior flesh eaters entered the village. They went straight to Great Bear's long house. Great Bear and over two hundred Abenaki warriors were there waiting out front."

"Chief Great Bear told Grey Wolf and the other human flesh eaters to stop. Grey Wolf and the others seemed unusually strong and eager for a fight. The Sachem proclaimed these flesh eaters were a disgrace to all men, and that Abenaki would hunt them and destroy them according to Abenaki law. They would be forever called Ne Wha Ta which means, one who is cursed. The evil one, Grey Wolf, demanded to speak before the elders of the Abenaki Sokoki. The entire village turned around and showed their backs to the Ne Wha Ta. Grey Wolf shouted he would have his revenge, that he and his kind were powerful, even invincible. Chief Great Bear asked the Sokoki Medicine Man, who made powerful medicine, to curse the Ne Wha Ta. The Medicine Man chanted a curse that the Ne Wha Ta would no longer be able to live on the surface of the earth. If they were found on the surface they were to be hunted down and killed. He also cursed the Ne Wha Ta to only be able to eat flesh. The curse he spoke also foretold that the Ne Wha Ta should lose their eyes so they could never again see the beauty of our land."

"Grey Wolf and the others left the village with much anger in their hearts. It was later told they had captured some squaws and moved to the north. They lived in caves and were not able to eat anything but flesh. They hated all things human. Soon their eyes failed and they pulled them from their own faces as a sign of their anger. They built tunnels and tried to raise families in their caves. They removed the eyes of their women. They later discovered they could not mate with these squaws. To have children they would have to mate with women who lived above ground. It is told that they tricked others to bring them women to mate. If these women had children, these Ne Wha Ta children would also be cursed. These children of evil ones would have to live underground and their eyes would be useless! If a Ne Wha Ta would be found above the ground, it was hunted down and killed."

"Under cover of darkness they would travel to other places and fill new caves. They were hated and hunted wherever they went. Over many years, after many Sachems had come and gone, the Ne Wha Ta learned to speak over great distances with humans by speaking to their minds. They used this power to trick humans into their traps where they would once again eat human flesh."

"Why didn't the Sokoki destroy the Ne Wha Ta that night?" asked Lenny.

"Yeah, I would have ordered the two hundred Abenaki warriors to at least capture them," said Tony.

"Mr. St. Germain, why didn't somebody do something?" asked Mark.

"They were more powerful warriors, the Ne Wha Tas. The Sachem, Chief Great Bear didn't want to risk anymore blood shed, especially in his village. Later he sent messengers to other Abenaki bands to be on the lookout for these human flesh eaters. The following year there was a great council held in what is called Becancour, near Trois-Rivieres in Quebec. Abenaki came from all over what white men call New England. The council decided to form hunting parties to find and capture the Ne Wha Ta so a trial by the great council could be held. The hunting parties hunted the Ne Wha Ta all during that fall and straight through the following winter. They found one Ne Wha Ta. They captured him and were bringing him to a great council. Word spread, a Ne Wha Ta was captured. One night when no one was looking, the captured Ne Wha Ta killed and dragged off one of his guards. A hunting party followed his blood trail. It led to a cave on the banks of Lake Memphramagog. They were afraid to enter the cave to follow this wounded Ne Wha Ta. They waited outside the cave for two weeks and still there was no sign of the Ne Wha Ta."

"So what happened to him or it or whatever it is?" asked Tony.

"No one knows."

"How long do they live?" asked Mark.

"If they can eat human flesh they can live for over two hundred years. If they eat only the flesh of animals they will live only a hundred years or so."

"If they don't have eyes, how can they see?" asked Mark?

"The old ones don't have eyes but as for this one I don't know. If he has eyes, he won't really need them. Since they live below the earth in the darkness of caves, Ne Wha Ta don't need eyes. It is told that they have developed very large ears. They can hear sound from a very long way away. They also have a very good sense of smell and are very powerful. But their greatest power is their ability to speak to a human's mind and to get inside that mind. They can make humans do things for them. They will use a human as their own eyes and ears."

"What is most important is they hate humans. They have always hated humans. They especially hate Abenaki. We have been their enemy for hundreds of years."

"How many Ne Wha Ta are there?" asked Lenny.

"No one knows. There have been stories over a very long time of reports from all across the earth where men have seen Ne Wha Ta."

"This Ne Wha Ta that is in those woods over there," said Karl, pointing to the north, "wants us to help it find a mate."

"So what do we do about that?" asked Lenny.

"You can not help it find a mate. Once you have done that it will bring another Ne Wha Ta, maybe several into this world."

"Sure, but this bastard has killed several people already. It killed my dad. What's going to stop it from killing us?" asked Karl.

"It does not fear you. It does not need you for food. It needs humans to find it a human mate. You see, all female Ne Wha Ta have never, ever, been able to make a baby. A male Ne Wha Ta needs a human female to mate with."

"I ain't going to bring it some girl to screw, so he can kill her and eat her flesh after he's done with her," said Mark in an unusually crude way.

"Me, either," said Tony. Karl and Lenny nodded their agreement.

"So what can we do? Mr. St. Germain, there must be something we can do. Maybe we could tell the police or the Army or something," said Tony.

"No good! The Ne Wha Ta would only hear the plans and escape through the maze of caves and tunnels that Ne Wha Ta have dug over several hundred years."

"Can they be killed?" asked Karl.

"Yes. My people have heard stories of Ne Wha Ta having been caught and killed. They must be tricked and hunted outside their caves. They are too clever to be caught inside their caves."

"So if we can get this Ne Wha Ta to come out of his cave, and we can see him, then he can be killed," said Karl as he stood up.

"Perhaps, if you are clever enough, but you young ones are dealing with a fearsome monster. One who will know every move you make."

"What do you mean?" asked Tony.

"It may be listening to this conversation now," said St. Germain.

"Then if it can listen to what we are talking about maybe we could write down what we want to talk about," said Mark.

"Yeah, that's a good idea, Mark," said Lenny.

"You are no match for Ne Wha Ta. You have already forgotten what I have told you. It has the powers to be in the mind of a human. It has the power to take over the spirit of a human. It could be using one of you right now to listen to what we say. It could use one of you or another human to destroy your plan."

The boys looked at each other. Was Ne Wha Ta now using one of them? A seed of suspicion was planted into their minds.

"So what does this all mean?" asked Mark.

"It means, we're screwed," said Karl.

Chapter 36

Mark finished his cell phone conversation with the headstone company Linda Sweeney chose to deliver Karl's headstone. Lenny picked up the phone and called the number Karl's daughter, Sherrie, provided him for her neighbor. The neighbor asked Lenny to hold for a moment because she was on another call. She came back on the line after a couple of minutes. She had been on the phone just a moment ago with Sherrie who told her to expect a call from Lenny. He arranged with her to pick up the package Karl meant for him that very afternoon. He told her he would drive over and meet her around one thirty out in front of the Sweeney's house.

Mark called his father to ask if he could get the car. His dad indicated that it would be no problem. Mark said he was going to take Lenny over to his hotel to pick up his car he'd left in their parking lot. He didn't want to leave it there since he wasn't staying there after all. He would park the car in the Pushey's driveway ahead of Mark's father's car in case his father found it necessary to get out.

"I'll be home in five minutes. You boys can drop me back off at the VFW," said Mr. Pushey.

"That would be fine. See you in a while," said Mark.

The guys drove Mark's father back to the VFW. Before they went to pick up Lenny's car, they went over to the Sweeney's. Lenny met a pretty young woman with a small child in tow. The woman let Lenny in with a key that Sherrie left her to use. They were inside the house for several minutes. Mark and Tony sat in the car waiting. It began to snow. Before too long, it was snowing heavily.

Lenny came out the front door. He held a small package in his left hand. The young woman and her child came out of the house right behind Lenny. She locked the front door and they shook hands. Lenny paused, then bent forward and gave her a gentle hug. He turned, waved at the woman and her small child, and now, pulling on his coat collar, headed for the car. He climbed into the back seat. Snow swirled into the car behind him.

"So what's with the hug?" asked Tony.

"Oh, that. I don't know—I just felt....She was so nice to me.....she really liked Karl. She and Sherrie are very close friends. She told me she has trouble sleeping since Karl's suicide. She's worried about her own husband. Geeze, guys, I just felt it was the right thing to do, okay?"

Mark looked into the rear view mirror at Lenny. "Hey, no big deal, Lenny, I understand. There are times I wish I had someone to hug."

"Hey, Mark I'll give you a hug and a kiss, too," said Tony, as he puckered his lips for a big kiss.

"Look, booger, I could never be that desperate, so save those lips for kissing my ass which would appreciate the attention," said Mark with a half-laugh.

Tony and Lenny burst into some good old fashion knee-slapping laughter. At times like this the boys felt as if they were still young teenagers.

Mark slowly pulled the car away from the curb into the winter storm that was beginning to build into a white wash. It took them almost a half an hour to reach the hotel parking lot where Lenny left his car. He got out and brushed the snow off with Mark's and Tony's help. He got in and turned the key. It started up on the first crank.

Lenny took the package he'd picked up from the Sweeney's house earlier and tossed it onto the passenger side front seat.

"I'm not too sure about how she's going to handle in this weather. So why don't you guys go on ahead and I'll take my sweet time. I'll see you back at the house. We can check out the package from Karl later," said Lenny.

Mark looked up at the swirling snow. "Sounds good. Just take your time and drive carefully. Tony and I will swing by the VFW and see if my dad needs a ride home. We'll see you back at the house."

Lenny climbed into his car and adjusted the wipers, defroster and heater. He waved at Tony and Mark as they tooted and drove slowly away into the whiteness of this winter storm.

He searched for a radio station that played oldies and settled on a station out of Plattsburgh, New York. He put his car into gear and slowly pulled out of the hotel parking lot. The winter wind whistled through tiny openings in the corners of the car doors. The whistle of the wind provided a distracting background sound to the radio. He glanced down at the package. It was the size of a shoe box. It was wrapped in brown paper and his name was crudely scrawled on the top. The wrapping was taped with masking tape placed at odd angles to what one would ordinarily expect for a wrapped package.

Lenny reached across the seat and lifted the package. It was light. He shook it a couple of times to see if he could hear anything. The package emitted no sound at all – nothing. No rattle, no tinkle, not even a thump. He put the package back on the seat and contributed his entire concentration to the task of safely navigating the snow slick streets. The all-weather tires performed adequately except he was unaccustomed to driving in such heavy snow. It had been quite a while since he needed to handle a car in such weather. Living in Boston, he'd become dependent upon public transportation. His driving skills were a little rusty. The power of the engine and the car's high speed rear end made for a sporty driving experience, but right now Lenny would settle for not exceeding twenty miles per hour.

It took him almost thirty minutes to safely reach the Pushey's residence. The others weren't back yet. He decided to just sit in the car and enjoy the radio and the weather.

He looked at the package and was about to open it when he decided, since he told the guys he would open it when they got back, he would wait. The wiper blades slowly swept across the windshield. The large snow flakes lightly touched against the glass.

Their unique shapes momentarily held in place when the warmth of the defroster heated glass melted each. In its place was a droplet of water the wiper blade pushed aside with each pass. And so it went for several minutes. Time passed slowly as Lenny laid back and enjoyed the solitude of this winter moment. The music, the car's engine rhythm, the swish-swish of the wipers, the dancing snow flakes and the whistling of the winter wind all combined to have a soothing, almost hypnotic effect. Lenny slowly and contentedly drifted off to sleep.

He entered a dreamscape were he was flying like a kite high above the ground below. He looked around and noticed he was able to move with the speed of not more than perhaps a hot air balloon. He could change direction and altitude by just thinking it so. He tried to recognize the terrain below, but it was no use—it was unfamiliar to him. There were no roads, no houses, only trees. He decided to fly higher to see if he could get his bearings. He climbed higher and higher. He made a slow turn to the left. In the near distance he saw Lake Champlain. There was no mistaking it. He knew the lake's contours even from this height. He turned to his right and noticed he was moving northward at an accelerating rate. The ground moved quickly underneath him. He tried to use his mind to slow down, to stop, to land. It was no use. He no longer controlled this dream-state flying adventure.

Lenny had no idea where he was now. His body began to drift downward slowly towards the forest below. Suddenly he stopped, motionless in the air. He was hovering just above the tree tops. Down below something caught his eye. There was movement. Immediately below there was a fight going on between several Indians. One by one some were killed until only a handful remained. These Indians took knives and cut into the bodies of the slain Indians. He could clearly see what they were doing. They were cutting up the bodies and were proceeding to take bites of various body parts. He watched this horrifying spectacle and felt like he would throw up. He became frightened that these human flesh eaters, these cannibals, would notice him. He tried desperately to use the command of his mind to fly away from this ghastly scene. He couldn't move.

Suddenly one of the flesh eaters looked skyward and saw Lenny. He gestured to the others and they, too, looked up and saw him hovering helplessly in the air. They raised their arms in his direction and now he felt himself descending. He was drifting downward. He tried flapping his arms. Nothing slowed his descent. He could see the detail of their faces now, large furrowed brows, oversized irregular teeth, and large ears. They did not have any eyes. There were bits of bloody flesh hanging from their teeth. Blood also streaked down their hairy chests. Their upwardly thrust arms were muscular and the hands were odd; the fingers were of the same length. They were calling out to him, "Lenny, Lenny, come join us. Be one of us."

"I'm going fucking mad," thought Lenny.

The arms reached out to him, pulling him down, down. He fought with what little strength he could muster, but they were much stronger.

"No, no, no.....," he screamed.

"Lenny, Lenny, you've got to get out of your car," said Tony as he pulled on Lenny's jacket.

Mark was on the other side as he helped pull Lenny from his car. They laid him down in the snow. Mark's father reached inside the smoke-filled car and turned off the car.

Snowflakes by the hundreds fell silently and gently on Lenny.

"Is he going to be okay?" asked Tony.

"I don't know," said Mark.

"Mark, here. Take my cell phone and call 911!" said Tony. He knelt down in the snow and began to check for Lenny's pulse and breathing.

"What do you think happened here?" asked Tony.

"From the color of the smoke and the sweetness of it I'd say it was carbon monoxide."

"But I don't see any hose or pipe stuck up into the car" said Tony.

"You're right. So it must mean there is a leak in the exhaust and it somehow drifted into the car as he sat here. Before he knew what was happening he must have become unconscious from the carbon monoxide."

"Jesus, what do we do now?"

"We wait for help and we pray."

* * * * *

"Can't you do something?" asked Mark.

"Before I answer that, I want you to come with me," said St. Germain.

"Where are we going?" asked Mark.

"You will see."

St. Germain stood up and stepped off the back porch and walked over to the corral.

"You boys wait here while I hitch up the horses."

The four boys sat on the porch and watched him hitch up the horses to the badly beaten old wagon. He walked the horses with the wagon in tow to the back of the house.

"Get in the back of the wagon and hold on. We're going for a little ride."

The boys did as they were told. The horse-drawn wagon pulled out of St. Germain's back yard and took a left on Main Street as it headed north into the Town of Colchester.

"What is that smell?" said Tony as he pinched his nose.

"It's the horse shit or cow shit that he carries around town and sells to people for their gardens," said Karl.

"Man, it smells bad. And the flies, there must be hundreds of them," complained Tony.

"Well, Tony, you know what they say about flies?" asked Mark.

"No, what?" responded Tony.

"Shit attracts flies. Those flies sure look like they just love your sorry ass," chuckled Mark. Lenny and Karl joined in with the merriment.

"Very funny guys, very funny," lamented Tony.

In a few moments the wagon took a left turn off of Main Street, which is called U.S. Route 7 in the Town of Colchester. The wagon entered a narrow dirt road that wound through the woods. It was steep. The old horses strained to pull the wagon up this steep road, but after a couple of minutes they reached the summit of the hill they were climbing. At the top was a large level clearing. Sitting in the center of the clearing was a large green water tank. It rose at least sixty feet in the air. St. Germain stopped the wagon. He climbed down from the wagon and the boys did the same.

"Why'd you bring us here?" asked Mark.

"You'll see. Come with me."

They followed him to the base of the water tower. He circled the water tower for a short distance before stopping at the base of a ladder. This ladder started five feet off the ground but went straight up the side of the water tower. He reached up and with surprising agility for someone his age, scampered up onto the ladder and began to climb.

"What are we supposed to do?" asked Lenny.

"I thought I said to follow me. Are any of you boys afraid of heights?" asked St. Germain.

No one answered.

"Well, then, what are you waiting for?" said St. Germain as he turned and continued his climb.

Karl went first and jumped to reach the last rung of the ladder. He quickly boosted himself up and was soon climbing the ladder. He was followed by Mark, then Lenny and finally by Tony.

When Karl reached the top of the ladder, he looked at the top of the water tank. It gently rose to a flattened center where St. Germain was sitting and waiting. All around the top edge of the water tank was a rail that stood three feet high. St. Germain motioned for Karl to join him at the top. Karl walked bent over and joined St. Germain. They were soon joined by Mark and Lenny. Several moments later Tony slowly climbed onto the tank's top. He looked around and seemed a little pale, nevertheless, he took aim for the others, crawling his way to the center of the water tank. There was a steady breeze blowing out of the southeast at about fifteen miles per hour. Everyone was facing due south. From their vantage point they could see almost all of nearby Burlington. They could easily see all of Winooski. They could also see the Winooski River and most of Lake Champlain.

"Wow, what a view!" said Lenny.

"What can you see?" asked St. Germain.

"I can see Winooski and Burlington," said Lenny.

"Open your eyes and try to see all there is to see, then tell me what you see."

Lenny stood up and slowly looked first to the south, then the west as he continued to slowly turn and looked to the north and finally he looked to the east. The other boys watched Lenny and St. Germain. Lenny sat back down.

"Now tell me what your eyes really see!"

"I....see lots of things. I can see far away. There's a lake, mountains, rivers, woods...and cities and towns. I see roads.....and I see people," said Lenny, as he seemed to be pondering his answer. "I'm....seeing the land of the Abenaki. Am I right?" asked Lenny.

St. Germain nodded his agreement. "With opened eyes you see the land of my people as it is today. I still can see it as it was. And I can see it as it could be." There was a single tear that ran down the right side of St. Germain's cheek. All the boys noticed it but said nothing.

"Why did I bring you here?"

"I think I know," answered Tony. "You wanted us to see the land taken from your people by the white man."

"Almost, but what you see out there," he said with a sweeping gesture from his left hand, "is also the land of the Ne Wha Ta, a land they have claimed for close to a thousand years. My people have suffered at the hands of Ne Wha Ta and now white men have, too. We must be as one in this battle. The land above the earth will never be free until the land below is free of the evil that lives within."

He reached out his right hand, palm side down. Karl placed his right hand on top of St. Germain's. Lenny, Mark and Tony did the same. St. Germain silently mouthed a prayer—an ancient prayer taught to his ancestors and passed down to him through a hundred generations. They were now joined in this struggle as brothers—the common foe of a powerful, devious and talented Ne Wha Ta. There would be no turning back. Their lives would be forever joined and changed by this bond.

Suddenly out of the north came a very large roaring sound that seemed to rush at them from out of nowhere. At a height of approximately eight hundred feet above the top of the water tank passed an F-104 Delta Wing Jet Fighter plane, part of an Air Force squadron based at the Burlington Airport. The plane was traveling around two hundred miles per hour. It was beginning its approach to the nearby airport. Its sound and low proximity startled the boys.

"Rrrrrr....swoosh," roared the massive engine of the aircraft.

"That's friggin' close," shouted Mark.

"You're telling me," said Tony.

"We can go back down now," said St. Germain. "But we must leave in the same order as we came."

He headed to the ladder and soon disappeared from sight.

"Superstitious, isn't he?" observed Karl.

"Can you blame him?" said Lenny.

The boys did exactly as they were instructed and climbed down in the same order as they first climbed the water tank.

St. Germain was waiting at the wagon to take them back to his house. They climbed aboard and rattled around in the back of the wagon as they headed back to Winooski.

When they arrived at St. Germain's house, they jumped down from the wagon and waited as he pulled the wagon to a stop in front of the barn. He climbed down from the wagon, unhitched the horses and led them into the paddock. The horses immediately headed to the water trough to get a drink. He closed the paddock gate and took a bandana from his back pocket and wiped his neck.

"Well, Mr. St. Germain, what do you think we can do to stop this monster?" asked Mark.

"I will think on this. Come see me in a couple of days and we'll see."

"But you'll help us, right?" pleaded Tony.

"I said I will think on this. Now go!"

"All right, we'll check back with you in a couple of days, just like you said. Thanks for talking with us," said a hopeful Lenny.

"Yeah, thanks," said Karl, and Mark and Tony also chimed in with their own "thanks."

The boys headed to the front of the house and turned right to go down Main Street back to Mark's house.

Meanwhile, St. Germain sat down on the chair on his back porch. In his mind a loud message was being broadcast from the monster, Ne Wha Ta, "Keep away from those boys, old one. If I choose, I can kill you at any time! It would be easy and I would enjoy taking your life."

St. Germain closed his eyes and began to hum an old song his Sachem once taught him. He hummed the song and began to rock his body back and forth. Then, he stopped and opened his eyes as wide as he could. He sent a message back at the monster, "You will not harm those boys for they are my brothers. You will come to know the justice of the Sokoki. With the strength of the many spirits of my ancestors I will fight you to the death. I will reclaim this land for my people and all humans. Now go!"

The horses began to rush about the paddock in a panic. Their nostrils flared; their eyes wide with fear. In a nearby pine tree a large black crow took flight and flew northward towards Colchester and the woods beyond Bremer's Quarry.

Chapter 37

Chief Seltzer stood in the middle of a large group of police officers, Sheriff's Deputies and volunteers. The group assembled to conduct the third day of searching for the missing three teenagers. They gathered in the meadow and gravel pit just off of Sunderland Hollow where the teens' car was located. They used this location as a staging area for the ongoing search.

Off to the side of this group was a smaller gathering of relatives of the missing teenagers. They were huddled together. Some of the women were crying.

"Can I have your attention, please?" called out the Chief.

The searchers quieted down.

"We are going to break out into four groups for our search efforts today. Each group will have a search dog and the dog's handler. Each group will also have a two way radio. Now, listen up, you will need to cover your assigned search areas very carefully. Look under branches, under bushes, etc. Look for anything unusual like a pile of branches or stacked wood. If you see an area where the soil has been disturbed, check it out. Also if you see a pile of rocks which seem out of place, check that out, too. Use the metal rods Officer Coulon will give you to poke the ground around any of these suspicious areas."

"Officer Coulon, do you have anything you want to add?" asked the Chief.

Officer Coulon removed his sunglasses and began, "Thanks, Chief. Make sure to bring plenty of water with you. You're going to need it. Today's temperature is going to be in the upper eighties with high humidity. Make sure everyone stays in sight of each other at all times. Also make sure you check back in with the base at the assigned times. Finally, one of our searchers lost his dog on the first day of the search. If you spot his dog, I want you to radio in right away. We'll send his owner out to your location. Don't try to approach the dog on your own; it might just scare him off. I've got photos of the missing teens and the missing dog for each search team leader. If you'll come up now, I'll give the photos to you along with the rest of your gear. Does anyone have any questions?"

Chief Seltzer stepped forward and spoke again, "All right folks—give it your best shot!"

As directed, the crowd of searchers broke up into four groups and secured the various items that Officer Coulon was providing. In a few moments the groups left the staging area. They began to head out into the woods to work their assigned areas.

Grant Blondin, the owner of the missing dog, approached the Chief.

"Thanks, Chief," said Blondin.

"No problem, Grant. I just hope we find your dog for you."

"I know," acknowledged Blondin as he turned, head hanging down and walked to his nearby pickup truck.

Officer Coulon gestured with a nod of his head towards the family and friends of the missing teens. "Do you want me to go talk to them?"

"Naw, I'll handle it. You steer any other searchers that show up into searching the roadside that leads into this place and up and down Route 7 for at least a mile on both sides of the road."

"Will do. Anything else?"

"I don't think so."

"Do you think the search will find anything?"

"I don't think so. There's no hard evidence to lead me to think they're in there. My hunch is they left here with someone. They'll probably turn up somewhere else."

The Chief turned and walked over to the huddled family members and friends of the missing teens. He walked slower than usual. Officer Tom Coulon hoped the Chief was right. Meanwhile a couple of cars pulled into the meadow. More volunteer searchers were arriving. Officer Coulon headed over to the recent arrivals to give them their assignment.

The Chief could see the anxious faces of the family members. He'd spoken with them over the past couple of days. The waiting and not knowing was always tough on the family of the missing. With nothing to offer them but a patient ear, he stepped before them and faithfully did his duty once again.

* * * * *

Mark hung up after making the 9-1-1 call.

"How's his breathing?" asked Mark.

"It's not regular. I don't like his color," said Tony.

"Let's pray for him, that's all we can do," said Mark's father.

Now the distant but rapidly approaching sound of a siren could be heard. In a moment, another siren began to wail. It, too, seemed to be heading in their direction. In less than three minutes since Mark called, an ambulance, operated by St. Michael's College, pulled to a stop in front of the house. A Winooski police cruiser also pulled up across the street from the house. Two EMTs ran to Lenny. A police officer ran into the driveway towards Lenny as well. It was Chief Contois.

Mark's father explained, "We just arrived a few minutes ago and we noticed he was sitting in his car. The car was running. The inside of the car was filled with a soupy looking bluish colored smoke. We opened the driver's door and pulled him out of the car and laid him down."

One of the EMTs asked, "Did he stop breathing at all since you pulled him out?"

"No, we've been right here. Is he going to be okay?" asked Tony.

"We'll know more in a few minutes," said the second EMT.

They strapped an oxygen mask on Lenny. They checked his vital signs and radioed in their findings to the trauma unit at the Medical Center of Vermont in nearby Burlington. They gave Lenny two shots and continued to monitor his condition.

"Can I have his car keys?" asked Chief Contois.

"Sure," said Mark, tossing the keys to the Chief.

The Chief went to the car and opened the door. He bent down and leaned inside the car. He sniffed the air. It smelled slightly sweet with the fading odor of carbon monoxide. He sat on the driver's seat and put the keys into the ignition and started the car. He got out of the car and made sure it wasn't locked and then closed the door. He walked slowly around the car. He knelt down and looked under the driver's side of the car. He got up and did the same on the other side of the car. He went to the rear of the car and looked under it as well. He got up and went back to the passenger side again and crawled under the car. He opened the hood and inspected the exhaust system from that angle as well as the fire wall of the vehicle. In a moment he got up and came back around to the driver's side. The inside of the car was filling up with exhaust smoke. He opened the driver's door and reached into the car and turned it off.

"What did you find Chief?" asked Mr. Pushey.

"It looks like Mr. Drew's car has a crack in the manifold pipe. That crack is right next to a gap in the passenger side fire wall where a gasket appears to be missing. It's not unusual for older cars that are restored for a gasket or two to be missing. With the car parked and the heater fan working it just served to draw in the car's exhaust. I'm sure he had no idea what was happening."

"Chief, it looks like he's coming around," said one of the EMTs.

Lenny eyelids were fluttering. In a moment he opened his eyes. He seemed tired and dazed.

"Mr. Drew, do you know where you are?" asked an EMT.

Lenny just turned his head slowly and looked at the EMT without responding.

"We're going to transport him to the hospital. He will probably be fine but he should be checked over."

One of EMTs returned from the ambulance with a collapsed gurney. The EMTs and the Chief put Lenny on the gurney. They loaded him into the back of the ambulance. With lights flashing it pulled away and headed for the hospital.

"I'll follow over and get an update from the doc. If one of you wants to go along, let's get going," said the Chief.

"I'll go, Chief," said Mark.

"Look, this weather is going to get worse. Tony and Mr. Pushey should stay here and stay off the roads. I don't want to have to investigate another car accident, if you catch my drift. No pun intended."

"Thanks, Chief," said Tony.

"Don't mention it. This is just your tax dollars at work," he said with a wink.

He and Mark headed to his cruiser and soon they were on their way.

Tony and Mark's father started to head into the house when Tony stopped and opened the Lenny's car door and removed the car keys and the brown package he had retrieved earlier at Karl's house. He locked the car and followed Mark's father into the house.

About an hour later the phone rang at the Pushey's. Tony answered it. It was Chief Contois. He said Lenny was going to be fine. He reported Lenny was talking now and seemed to be clearing his head. The doctor told the Chief, Lenny could go home in a couple of hours. Mark was with Lenny. The doctor wanted to wait a bit longer to see how Lenny's reflexes were coming along. He also said he told Lenny to take a taxi home and Mark would ride with him. The Chief had to go, his radio was reporting a fire on Hickock Street. Tony thanked the Chief and hung up the phone.

"Well?" asked Mark's father.

Tony reported on his conversation with the Chief. Mark's father was relieved to hear Lenny was going to be all right.

"Where's the package of Lenny's you brought into the house?"

"I put it on his bed, upstairs," said Tony.

"Good. Now why don't you give your wife a call," said Mark's father.

"Good idea, I will," as he pulled out his cell phone.

He dialed his home phone and after a moment the phone rang. The answering machine soon kicked in. A disappointed Tony left his wife a message. He hung up the phone and went to the bathroom.

Mark's father turned on the television and soon found a local station broadcasting a winter storm watch message. The storm would produce six to ten inches of snow. The weather report droned on.

Mark's father headed into the kitchen and began to organize supper. He would make some homemade soup along with some homemade biscuits.

* * * * *

Chief Seltzer stood in the middle of the tired and drained searchers.

"I want to thank you for your help today. We will conduct one more day's search tomorrow. If nothing turns up we will end the search. I've spoken to the families and they understand. We'll start tomorrow at the same time. We could use your help tomorrow if you're available. Get yourselves some rest."

The weary searchers drifted to their cars and trucks. Grant Blondin, looking sad and disappointed, climbed into his truck and drove away. The families and their friends also drifted away. Officer Coulon spoke to some of the Sheriff's Deputies. After a while, they, too, climbed into their vehicles and left. Only Chief Seltzer remained. He leaned against the hood of his cruiser looking off into the woods. Long shadows were now forming. The sun had already dropped below the tree tops. Twilight would soon be settling in.

Speaking out loud he grumbled, "Damn kids. Don't they know the problems and heartache they've caused? Damn reckless teenagers. I'll have to have a serious talk with them when we find them—

if we find them alive that is!"

He turned and climbed into his cruiser, started it up, turned and drove out of the meadow.

Over a mile away in the coolness of his cave Ne Wha Ta grinned as he listened to the Chief's words.

"Humans are no match for me. They're not as clever as me and don't possess my powers. Humans are weak," said a confident and defiant Ne Wha Ta.

He went over to the pile of bones building up over these many years. He felt among them for a moment and soon found what he was looking for. He held pieces of blood-stained clothes from the teenage girl he killed and had eaten just a few days before. He sniffed them and licked the blood stains. He could still taste her. He could still hear her voice pleading for her life. He enjoyed killing her and eating her flesh. He reminded himself he needed to eat his human victims more slowly, to enjoy the taste of their warm salty blood.

He was getting hungry again.

* * * * *

A taxi cab pulled to stop in front of the Pushey's house. Lenny and Mark got out of the cab. Mark handed the driver a twenty and told him to keep the change. Mark helped Lenny shuffle through the snow and climb the front steps. He knocked on the door. Tony opened the door and welcomed his friends back into the house.

"Jesus, Lenny, how are you feeling?" asked Tony.

"I've got a friggin' migraine headache right now. The Doctor gave me some ibuprofen or some other shit for the headache."

"Sit down and I'll get you some water," said Tony.

Mark's father came in and shook Lenny's hand. "You sure scared us today, Lenny."

"It scared me, too!"

He took out the prescription and poured himself two tablets. He took the glass of water from Tony and took a small sip, swallowing the pills.

"What do you guys think happened?" asked Lenny.

Mark told Lenny about what the Chief found when he examined the car. Lenny seemed relieved to hear it was caused by a broken pipe and a missing gasket. He was amazed he hadn't noticed it on the long drive to Vermont. He surmised the highway speed must have somehow drawn away the poisonous gas before it had a chance to fill up the car's interior.

"Lenny, are you hungry? Would you like me to fix you a bowl of my homemade soup?" asked Mark's father.

"No, thanks. My stomach is a little unsettled right now, maybe later."

The four of them sat in the living room and visited for a short while and then they watched a little television.

Mark's father went to bed a little after nine o'clock.

"Where's the package we picked up earlier today?" asked Lenny.

"It's up in your room," said Tony.

"Let's go see what Karl wanted me to have," said Lenny.

They all went upstairs and went into Lenny's bedroom. Tony closed the bedroom door. Lenny sat on the edge of the bed. He picked up the package and began to slowly and carefully unwrap it. He removed the brown wrapping and lifted the top off of what was obviously a shoe box. Inside, lying on top, were a couple of news clippings. He unfolded the stories and after looking at the headlines he handed them to Tony.

"They're stories about bones having been discovered at the cave. These must be the first stories."

Tony handed the clippings to Mark.

Next in the box was a crudely folded sheet of paper. There were brownish, finger-printed stains on the edges. Lenny unfolded the paper and decided to read it out loud.

"Lenny, I couldn't decide whom to contact first, you, Mark or Tony. I picked you. By now, you've heard about the cave being opened. For the past two days that fucking monster has been talking to me. He's pissed off. He wants me to tell him where you guys are. But I won't."

The writing becomes less legible but Lenny continues, "He reminded me today that he killed my father because I wanted my father dead. Imagine that? He says I was the one who really killed my father. Me! Sure, I hated him, but I didn't want him killed. I can't stop Ne Wha Ta from getting into my head."

The words now are jumbled and barely readable. "He won't leave me alone. He says he's coming for me. He wants her, he aint goin to get her. no wayyy. He;s riht heer. Oooo. Lenee I cantt figth hmm. hee wnts me too gve yuu a messge. itts n dhh bxxxxxxx."

Lenny looked in the box. Inside there was a small plastic wrapped bundle. There was something wrapped up in a rolled up clear plastic wrap. It was stuck together in several places with a reddish brown stained material of some kind. In the center of this wrapping seemed to be two small round objects. Suddenly, Lenny recognized what was inside the wrapping as he peeled back several layers.

It was a pair of eyeballs.

Lenny held the wrapped eyes out towards Mark and Tony.

"It's fucking eyeballs."

He handed the plastic wrapping to Mark.

"I'm going to be sick," as he put his right hand to his mouth and hurried out of the room. He went straight into the bathroom and could be heard losing it in the toilet. Tony looked at what Mark held in his hands. Mark and he looked at one another.

"It can't be, can it?" asked Tony.

"What else could it be?"

"Is there anything else in the box?" asked Mark.

Tony looked and found nothing inside the box, but when he lifted the shoe box cover, he noticed a small envelope taped to the inside. He pulled the envelope free and poured its contents out onto the bed. The envelope contained an Indian arrowhead along with a small leather pouch tied to a leather string.

They both recognized these items.

Chapter 38

Lenny's mother watched as Lenny shuffled up the driveway. It was nearing supper time. Moments ago she noticed she was out of butter. The back screen door opened and Lenny stepped into the kitchen.

"Lenny, honey, would you please do me a favor?" asked his mother.

"Sure, Mom."

"I was hoping you could go to Vic's Market and pick up a pound of butter."

"Sure," agreed Lenny.

She opened her purse, which she kept on the end of the counter, and removed a dollar and twenty-five cents. "In addition to the butter please get a roll of toilet paper. You can keep the change. Now hurry because I need the butter for the mashed potatoes. You know how your father likes his potatoes with butter."

"Okay, Mom, I'll take my bike. I can be back in less than five minutes."

She watched him take his bike out of the garage and hop up on it. Lenny sped down the driveway as he headed off to the store. She returned her attention to the meal she was preparing.

In just over five minutes Lenny came pedaling back into the drive way. He stopped and left his bike, as he always did, at the end of the driveway just off the back porch. He scampered up the back steps and proudly entered the kitchen with a small brown grocery bag in hand. He was huffing and puffing just a little bit.

"How'd I do?"

"Five minutes exactly," she said, knowing it was a lie.

"Really, that's cool. I told you, didn't I? Less than five minutes is what I said and I did it."

"Yes, Lenny. I'm proud of you. Now you go and play for a few more minutes while I finish supper. We should be ready to eat right when your father gets home. And don't forget to wash you hands before you come to the table."

"I won't, Mom," said Lenny as he headed upstairs to his room. He wanted to ask his mom if he could sleep over at Tony's house but he knew from experience she would just tell him to wait and ask his father when he got home. Lenny decided to ask him after supper, after his father had consumed at least a couple of beers.

Lenny flopped on his bed and reached under the far side of the bed and slid a small box forward. He pulled out several comic books. He flipped through them and decided on a particular Batman comic.

A boy can't reread a comic book too many times, especially if it's a classic.

Lenny was deeply into reading the Batman adventure. The stories and artwork were a perfect blend. Each time he would read a Batman comic and explore the comic art frame by frame he would discover some previously unexplored aspect that would intrigue his adolescent imagination. For the moment he was on an imaginary detour.

Meanwhile, downstairs, his mother was finishing up on the supper. She looked up at the kitchen wall clock. The time was slightly past five fifteen. She was beginning to consider how she would be able to slow the dinner down if he was late when she heard the squeal of his car tires as he pulled into the drive way at a faster than normal speed. She watched the car quickly move past the kitchen window on the driveway side of the house when she heard a crashing sound coupled with the screech of the car's brakes being heavily applied.

The next thing she heard was the car door opening and then slamming shut.

Lenny heard the screeching brakes and crashing sound from up in his room. He bolted from his bed. He craned his neck to look to the left of his bedroom window down onto the back of the driveway. He, too, heard the car door slam. Lenny instantly knew these sounds could only mean one thing. Something bad just happened and either he or his mom would be blamed for it.

"Who's it going to be this time?" whispered Lenny. He soon had his answer.

"Lennieeeee....." shouted his father from down in the driveway.

"Lennieeee....., get your sorry little ass down here. Come see what you made me do. Lennieee...., do you hear me?"

Lenny was suddenly filled with dread.

Lenny's mom came down the back porch stairs and cautiously walked over to the end of the driveway. Rudy, her husband, was kneeling down under the front of the car and was sputtering to himself a steady stream of expletives. He quickly got up and got back in the car, started it up and backed it up about ten feet. From out beneath the front of the car appeared Lenny's mangled and crushed bicycle. She nervously twirled the end of her apron in her hands. She pulled the apron up to her mouth to stifle a small gasp.

Rudy noticed her standing there. "Where is that little bastard? Look what he made me do. He knows I always park the car even with the back edge of the house when I come home. Carol, where in the fuck is he? He's going to get his little ass whipped for this, I tell you."

Carol looked at her husband. He was wild-eyed with anger. She had seen Lenny leave the bike standing next to the house. Rudy should have had plenty of room to park the car. Yet he somehow managed to run over the bike. It couldn't be Lenny's fault. *How am I going to diffuse this one?* she thought.

He shouted again. "Lenny Drew, you get out here, now! If I have to come in and get you it'll be a whole lot worse."

The back door to the porch opened slowly. A very frightened Lenny slowly came down the back steps. Lenny could see his bicycle. It was destroyed. He saw the anger in his father's face and saw him begin to remove his belt. Lenny shot a pleading glance to his mother. She, too, looked terrified.

"You get your ass over here and get this fucking bicycle out of the driveway, now!" demanded Rudy in a low growl.

"If I told you once, damn it, I told you a hundred times not to park your bicycle in the driveway. Driveways are for cars, Lenny. You know that. Your fucking laziness has caused me to run over your bike, little man. Don't think for a minute I'm going to run out and buy you another one. You've blown it. You're shit out of luck, little man."

His father was now slapping the folded belt into his palm.

"The bike, Lenny, move it, now!"

Lenny was crying. Tears streamed down his cheeks. He knew his father had plenty of room in the driveway. Lenny clearly remembered parking the bicycle against the house like he always did. He looked at the crumpled bicycle and felt a tiny knot of rage begin to build inside.

Lenny cautiously stepped forward and picked up the bicycle. Its wheels, rims and all were badly bent. The bike's frame was bent in two places. The handlebars were also bent out of shape. The bicycle seat was snapped right of the seat stem.

"Rudy, let's go inside. We can deal with this after supper," said Carol.

He shot her a look that conveyed his absolute disagreement.

"You head inside and get supper ready. Me and Lenny have some business to attend to, and beside he won't be having supper tonight. He won't have an appetite. Now git!"

"But, Rudy," she began to plead.

"You heard me, Carol! Or do I have some business to take care of with you, too?" he said as he continued to slap the folded belt into his palm.

"It's okay, Mom. I'll be all right," said Lenny between sniffles.

Her heart ached for Lenny. She felt helpless. She slowly turned and headed for the house.

Lenny put the broken bike against the outside of the garage. He turned around and faced his father.

"Lenny, this was not a good day to piss me off. Yes, sir, indeed, it was not a good day to piss me off."

Rudy grabbed Lenny by the shirt and dragged him inside the garage. He closed the door behind him. After several moments the horrid sound of leather striking flesh could be heard from outside the garage. Lenny's mom could hear the sounds from the kitchen window.

She heard no voices, only the "smack" sound of each blow. She expected her husband to perhaps hit Lenny at most three times but by her count the blows were up to ten.

Suddenly, her mind simply snapped. She grabbed a carving knife from the kitchen drawer and flew out the back door. She ran to the garage. She heard even more vividly the smacking sound.

She burst through the garage's side door. In the dim light of the closed up garage she saw her son hanging by his arms from the rafter. His shirt was off and was stuffed inside his mouth. His eyes were exploding from terror and pain. Standing behind Lenny was a still fired up Rudy. His right arm poised to swing his belt. The belt with its belt buckle at its end, hung from Rudy's raised arm.

"Get the fuck out of here, Carol! I'm not done with him yet."

"Rudy, what are you doing?" she shrieked, running at Lenny.

"Doing, doing, you have to ask? You fucking women don't know how to raise a man. I'm just giving him a lesson he'll never forget. He'll thank me someday for straightening him out. Now get the fuck out of here."

"Rudy, you untie him right now or I'll...,"

"You'll what, Carol?"

"I'll kill you, you bastard!" she blurted out. This genie was now out of the bottle. She now tried to pull the shirt out of Lenny's mouth but her husband must have wedged it in good and proper.

Rudy stepped out from behind Lenny and shoved her away. She stumbled back against the work bench.

"I see you've brought a knife. How brave. I'm unarmed, Carol. You've got a knife, a fucking knife. I should beat the shit out of you just for that. But I'll give you a chance. Now give me the knife and get back in the house."

"No! You get Lenny down right now," she demanded.

"That's sure is pretty bossy of you Carol! I don't think I like that in you." He took a step towards her and swung the belt. The buckle end of the belt slashed across her face opening a four inch gash which began to bleed. She let out a shriek and put both her hands to her face dropping the knife to the floor. She began to sob. Rudy kicked the knife away into the corner.

"You might as well stay if you're so interested. After I'm done with the little bastard, it'll be your turn. A man can't let his little woman think she's got the upper hand, otherwise all hell breaks out. Right, Lenny?"

Rudy turned to face Lenny. Lenny looked over his father's shoulder and saw the blood streaming between his mother's fingers down her neck. She was sobbing and half kneeling. Lenny seized upon a powerful thought just at that moment. "If I get out of this I will see you fucking dead and I'll spit on your grave."

Carol turned from the sight of her husband and Lenny. She felt pain and she felt rising, unbridled anger. The anger was exploding into rage. Suddenly her eyes focused upon a large monkey wrench lying on the work bench. She quickly picked it up and held it in both blood-soaked hands like a baseball bat. She stepped towards her husband.

Rudy was about to approach Lenny. He was going to have to start over, because his dim-witted wife once again interrupted him and so he'd lost count. He looked up and noticed Lenny looking over his shoulder towards his mother and his look was somehow different. Rudy turned in just enough time to see her swing the wrench. He was barely able to raise his right arm in self defense when he felt the powerful blow of the wrench as it stuck his right forearm. He heard a "snap" sound and knew immediately his arm was broken. It was bent at an odd angle now as he withdrew from his onrushing wife. He tried not to scream but the pain was too intense.

"Geeze....Goddamn it! You've fucking broke my arm, bitch," roared Rudy.

"You get away from us right know or I'll break the other arm and maybe I'll break your fucking skull." Carol didn't recognize her own voice as her rage was still strong and compelling.

He took a step towards her and kicked out at her, catching her in the side. The kick knocked her back several feet. She stumbled down to one knee. He had broken a couple of her ribs. He started towards her. As he got ready to kick her again, she swung the wrench with her right arm as hard as she could. It caught him square in his left side, breaking two or more of his own ribs. With that effort, the wrench flew out of her blood soaked hand and skidded across the garage floor. She was now defenseless. It didn't matter this time. The fight was momentarily out of Rudy. He grabbed his side. Now wheezing, he shuffled to the side door. She collapsed onto the garage floor. She heard the car start up and speed out of the driveway. In a moment there was just the sound of her strained breathing and Lenny's muffled sobbing.

She pushed herself to her feet and staggered over to her son. She couldn't untie the knots of the rope that was used to tie his hands. She spotted the short, step ladder. In another moment she located the kitchen knife. After stepping on the second rung of the ladder, she found she was able to cut Lenny free. Lenny dropped to the floor. He removed the shirt that was stuffed into his mouth. He reached out to his mother and they hugged one another gently. The bleeding on her face glistened in the dimmed light from the side window of the garage.

"Let's get into the house, Lenny."

"Mom, oh, Mom! I love you," he said with fresh tears streaming down his face.

He turned to head to the house. She saw numerous gashes and welts streaked across his small back. Blood streaks ran down to his waist. The welts were swollen. When she saw what her husband inflicted upon her son's back she became weak in the knees.

That's it. He's never going to hurt us again. I'm leaving him and I'm taking the kids with me, silently vowed Carol.

When they got inside the house, the smell of burnt and over-cooked food was everywhere. The dinner was ruined. She quickly turned everything off. The baby was crying in the other room.

"I'll take care of her, Mom," offered Lenny.

She nodded her agreement. He went into the other room and soon the baby was quiet again.

She looked around the kitchen. She decided she couldn't and wouldn't live here anymore. She went into the bathroom and turned on the overhead light. She turned on the water and wet a wash cloth and began to wipe her face slowly so as to not start up the bleeding again. From the medicine cabinet she removed a bottle of disinfec-tant, a box of gauze and a roll of medical tape. She also found a box of Band-Aids. She used the disinfectant and gauze to clean the wound on her face. She fashioned a dressing for her cut face and taped it into place. She wiped the blood off of her hands and removed her blood-stained blouse tossing it into the dirty clothes hamper over in the corner. She put on a clean blouse from the clothes folded on the ironing table. She took two aspirin for her pain.

"Lenny, come here," she called.

Lenny came around the corner. "Let me take care of those cuts and welts. Here, sit on the toilet seat."

She knelt down in front of Lenny and kissed him on the fore-head. She was crying now. Her crying was soft and healing. She didn't sob. The tears, in a steady stream, flowed down her cheeks. Gently as possible she dabbed at the cuts and welts on Lenny's back. She noticed old scars from previous beatings. Lenny hardly winced from her touch. She applied disinfectant to his entire back. Next she gently washed his hands and arms, careful not to rub his swollen and bruised wrists.

"Lenny, I'm going to get you some clean clothes. I'll be right back."

She was gone for just a couple of minutes. She returned and put the clothes on the bathroom counter.

"I'll close the door. Change your underwear and socks and pants. Don't try to put a shirt on just yet. Okay, Lenny?"

She closed the door and Lenny did as he was asked. When he had changed, he tossed the soiled clothes into the dirty clothes hamper. He could hear his mother on the phone. His eyes moved towards the direction of the medicine chest's mirror. He looked at his face. His eyes were red and puffy. The edges of his mouth were red and scratched. He began to see the vague outline of a larger head forming behind his own reflection. This spectral shape displayed long and pronounced ears. It was only a silhouette. Lenny could hear a voice. It was faint at first but it soon became clear.

"Remember, Lenny, didn't I tell you, your friend would be my friend and your enemy would be my enemy?"

"Yes."

"Do you have an enemy, Lenny?"

Without any hesitation Lenny answered. "Yes."

"What do you want me to do about it?"

"I don't care, just stop him."

"Oh, I can stop him all right. If that is what you want?"

"It's what I want."

"Just remember, Lenny I always keep my word."

The shadowy shape faded from view. Its reflection no longer appeared in the mirror.

The bathroom door opened and Lenny's mom came in. She held up a cotton tee-shirt which belonged to Lenny's father.

"Here put this on, Lenny."

"I don't want to. It's Dad's."

"I know, but it's bigger and will be loose fitting. Right now it will be better for you."

Lenny put the shirt on. It hurt to lift his arms over his head.

"Mom, Dad's never going to hurt us again."

"I know Lenny. I know," she nodded.

She gave Lenny a single aspirin.

Carol Drew went to check on her baby, who, it turns out, was sound asleep. She went upstairs to her bedroom and took out a small bag from her closet and began to fill it up with clothes. In a few minutes she came down stairs. She put the bag next to the front door.

"Lenny."

He came from the kitchen with a glass of milk in his hand.

"Lenny, I want you to pack a couple of bags. I've called over to your friend Tony's house. I spoke to his parents and told them a little about what happened. They're coming right over to take you to their house. You're going to stay with them for a while. The baby and I will be moving in with Janice Goodrow. You remember, the nice lady from church who plays the organ during mass. Father Campbell is coming to take me there. I'll be staying there for a while. We might not come back here for a quite some time, so I'd pack as much as you think you can. I'm going to give you the spare key to the house, but I don't want you coming here alone. Do you understand? We need to get away from Daddy and we need to be safe. I'll try to work this out with your father, but right now I don't want him anywhere near you, Lenny."

Lenny nodded and quickly ran up the stairs to pack. Meanwhile, Carol Drew packed the baby's things. After she packed the baby's things, she took her purse and made sure their bank book, check book and household cash were put into her purse. She also checked to see that everything was turned off in the house. She waited in the living room in the chair by the door. Lenny came running down the stairs half dragging two overstuffed bags. At that moment, two cars coming from different directions pulled up in front of the Drew house. Their rides were here to take them away to safety.

Lenny and his mom were both silently crying.

Chapter 39

Tony hung up the telephone. The winter storm of yesterday and Lenny's brush with carbon monoxide poisoning was still fresh in everybody's minds. He went into the kitchen and sat down with Lenny. Lenny was still eating breakfast. Mark was upstairs taking a shower. Mark's father was off on a walk with the dog.

"The current parish priest remembers Father Campbell. It seems Father Campbell married his parents. He believes he is still around. Last he heard, Father Cambell was staying at the Bishop MacGregor's Diocesan Home for Retired Priests and Religious. He said he'd check for us and call us back."

"Good," said Lenny.

"Do you think he'll even remember us?"

"We won't know until we see him."

The phone rang and Tony went to answer it. Meanwhile, Lenny continued to read the ongoing newspaper story about the mystery at the quarry. Near the end of the story located on page 12, in the back of the first section was a new revelation. The story reported police now expect numerous local missing persons cases will be resolvable based upon some of the assembled evidence confirmed to date.

Mark came downstairs from his morning shower. He poured himself a cup of coffee.

Without looking up from the newspaper, Lenny said, "Tony has a lead on where Father Campbell is. We may try to see him today, if we can."

"That would be good. Maybe he can give us some insight into how to deceive that monster. You know something that might let us get close enough to perhaps kill the bastard."

"That's for damn sure. We're going to need all the help we can get. We fooled him once but I doubt we can pull it off a second time."

Tony came back into the kitchen.

"Good news and bad news," said Tony.

"All right, let's hear the good news first," said Lenny.

"It seems Father Campbell is, in fact, living at a home for old priests and nuns. He's been living there for the past eleven years."

"And the bad news?" asked Mark.

"He has Alzheimer's disease."

"How bad?" asked Mark.

"The parish priest didn't know. He did say visiting hours are pretty flexible."

"I say we pay Father Campbell a visit, preferably today," said Lenny.

"I'll check with my father and see if we can borrow his car," said Mark.

"Good. I'd also like to stop by a local body shop and see if they'd be willing to take a look at my T-Bird," said Lenny.

"It shouldn't be a problem," said Mark.

Just then Mark's father and Pokey came to the back door. After stomping his feet a few times, Mark's father came in through the door. Following behind, Pokey immediately headed over to his food dish. He licked up the few crumbs he missed at breakfast.

Mark's dad removed his winter coat and hung it up on the hook on the back of the door.

"It's friggin' cold out there. It must be only ten degrees. That northwest wind is brutal."

Mr. Pushey poured himself a cup of coffee and sat down at the kitchen table, rubbing his hands to get the blood circulating.

Mark explained he, Tony and Lenny would need the car for a while. He told his father about their plans to visit their old friend,

Father Campbell. He omitted the real reason for the visit.

"You boys go on. I've got a lot of laundry to catch up on and with you fellows out of the way I won't be distracted and tempted to spend my time in bull sessions. By the way, would you guys like to try my homemade Mulligan Stew? It's practically made me a legend at the VFW."

"Dad, you've always been a legend, in your own mind of course," said Mark playfully.

The chitchat continued for a while longer but soon the three guys left for their visit with Father Campbell. Mark's father was right, it was brutally cold. The car was slow in warming up.

They decided to make a detour to Leo's Fine Car Restoration Emporium. Lenny was successful in persuading the auto body shop owner to check on his T-Bird. To be safe, the shop owner said he would have to tow the car in to be able to effectively check it out. Lenny gave him his set of car keys. The shop owner indicated the car repairs would take about eight hours of work. They would have to pull the front fender and install two gaskets. One gasket would be installed between the outer fender and the inner fender. The second gasket would have to be installed between the fire wall and the inner fender. He would also check out the exhaust system and replace any needed parts, just to be safe. The shop owner felt that, baring any unexpected surprises, he could complete the work by Tuesday of next week, at the latest. Work was a little slow right now. He believed he could easily fit in the work on Lenny's car around his other work. Lenny signed the work authorization release form. The guys were soon on their way to see Father Campbell.

It wasn't long before they were all sitting in a waiting room at the Bishop MacGregor Retirement Home. A short, old and frail looking Sister let them in. After hearing the explanation of the purpose of their visit, she asked them to take off their coats and have a seat.

The waiting room was a six-sided sun room with four walls filled with windows starting two feet from the floor and extending to within one foot from the ceiling. The ceiling was more than ten feet high. It was covered with a very decorative sculptured tin. The furniture was old. The room had but one decent chair, an old overstuffed chair covered with leather that was badly cracked in several places, along with three other mismatched wooden folding chairs. There was also a small cherry coffee table with two well-worn magazines lying on top. The cover of one was missing. They looked at each other and around the room as time passed slowly.

After fifteen minutes passed, they heard steps coming up the hallway, accompanied by a creaking, repeating sound. Around the corner came a wheelchair pushed by the diminutive nun. In the wheelchair was an old man, hunched at the shoulders. He was nearly bald. His complexion was pale and he was very thin. A dark blue blanket was lying on his lap and he wore pajamas covered over by a red plaid bathrobe. The eye sockets where his eyes once filled the space were deeply sunken. He was drooling onto his lap. The Sister pulled the wheelchair to a stop in the center of the room. The wheelchair was positioned so Father Campbell's visitors could all have a good look at him and he of them, presuming he was capable.

"He's just had his morning bath. I'm sorry to say he has been drooling off-and-on now for nearly a month. This towel on the back of the wheelchair can be used to wipe him every now and then, if you'd be so kind of course," she said with a twinkle.

"Does he, uh, you know, talk and uh...." asked Mark.

Interrupting him, she said, "Oh, he speaks just fine. Sometimes he's as clear as a bell and other times he can go for weeks and not say a thing. Isn't that right, Father?"

There was no reaction. A long drip of spittle ran down from his lower lip and was nearly onto his lap. She quickly wiped it away with the cloth from the back of his wheelchair.

"Well, I'll be leaving you gentlemen to your visit. I've several others to attend to. As you can see, we are kept busy. If you need me for any reason just push that bell over by the light switch. I'll come back in a jiffy and take him off your hands." Turning to Father Campbell she said, "Now Father Campbell, don't you be telling these fine young men about all the carousing and partying you and the others do all day long around here." She patted the old priest gently on the shoulder and soon scooted down the hallway.

Lenny sat forward in his seat. He folded his hands and looked directly at the priest.

"Father Campbell, do you remember me, I'm Lenny Drew?"

There was no noticeable reaction from the shell of a man sitting in the wheelchair.

"Over there is Tony Fredette and Mark Pushey. You remember them, don't you? We've come to visit you. How have you been?" asked Lenny.

Still nothing!

Mark got up from his chair and knelt in front of the wheelchair. He spoke louder than Lenny.

"Father Campbell, we need your help. You must remember who attacked you, terrorized you, who did this to you! We all know you tried to help us before and that monster punished you. Well, the damn thing is back. We need to not just lock him back up this time Father, we need to destroy him."

Nothing!

"It's no use, he's too far gone to be of any help to us," said Mark.

Mark sat back down. They all just stared at the frail old priest.

Tony decided to address the elderly priest.

"Father, he said he wants a mate. He, uh, threatened to use my wife. He's very strong, Father. I don't know if we can stop him. Look, um, my wife's pregnant and that sick son-of-a- bitch......" Tony searched the priest for some reaction and upon seeing none declared, "Oh, what's the use? He can't or won't hear us."

A string of drool began to run off the priest's lower lip.

"Wipe his lip, will you Tony?" asked Lenny.

Tony wiped the priest's lip and sat back down.

Lenny got up from his seat and walked over to the priest. He knelt down on one knee next to the priest and placed one hand on the priest's lap.

"Look, I don't know if you can hear me or understand me right now. I just want you to know, once a long time ago you showed me, no, you showed all of us you cared for us. You tried to defend us. We were just kids. We were scared and you were ready to stand with us. We've never forgotten your courage and your faith. We, uh,....we're sinners in the eyes of God. We know that. We have been and are penitent. This evil must be stopped. If he is successful in mating, he and his kind will terrorize many generations to come. It can't be God's will we let that happen! I believe we have been chosen and you were chosen, too. We've all been chosen to play a part in this struggle. Father, your part isn't over yet. The fact we're all here has to mean something! It just has to!"

Lenny's head bent down. He was discouraged. He was about to get up when he felt a feeble icy grip of his hand. He looked up and Father Campbell was grasping his hand. The priest's lips quivered as he attempted to speak. In a feeble voice he stammered, "It...must...be stopped...now!"

Mark and Tony were out of their seats in a shot. They were all now kneeling next to the priest.

Father Campbell continued, "Use the gun."

"What gun, how?" asked Tony.

Drool was spilling from the Father Campbell's lips once more.

"How, how are we supposed to get close enough to him?" asked Mark.

"Sh......." said the priest, "he's listening."

Father Campbell rolled his head to his left and there it sort of limply hung against his shoulder.

"Father Campbell," said Tony.

"Shake him, Lenny," said Mark.

"No, I don't think that will do us any good. I think we were given all we're meant to have."

Lenny got up and went to one of the windows and looked out into the winter view. After a moment he turned and said, "Let's go."

"That's it, that's all there is. I don't believe that is all he can tell us, Lenny. We have to try to learn more," said Mark.

"Look, guys, we can always come back. He isn't going anywhere. Let's get out of here," said Lenny.

Lenny went over to the bell and pushed it. A distant "ding" could be heard. In a few minutes the Sister appeared and unlocked the wheelchair's brake.

"Well, Father Campbell, it's time to go. Your favorite T.V. show is coming on. It's that Wheel of Fortune with the lovely Vanna White," said the Sister in a merry voice.

The three guys thanked her and said their good-byes to her and Father Campbell. Lenny leaned down next to the old priest and whispered, "We'll come back, soon. Meanwhile, be careful."

To Lenny's surprise the priest whispered back, "There's more than one, Lenny. You be careful!"

"Let's go now, Father. We've got parties to go to and champagne to pour," said the Sister as she turned the wheelchair to start down the hallway. At that moment a loud fart sound ripped out. "Brrrrrippp."

"Why, Father Campbell, have you no manners, in front of your guests and all." She looked over her shoulder, and with a smile, she said to Lenny as he moved towards the door, "It's the broccoli."

Lenny closed the front door, walked over to the car and climbed inside.

"She's a pip, ain't she?" queried Tony.

"She sure is. What do you guys make of his saying to use a gun?" asked Mark.

"He didn't say use a gun, he specifically said, 'use the' gun," said Lenny.

"What gun is that?" asked Tony.

"I know! I'll bet it's the gun you guys removed from the cave. It's Chucky Letourneau's shotgun. You guys remember my hiding it in my garage after you snuck it out of the woods?" said Mark.

"Shit, I remember that. Do you think the gun is still there?" asked Tony.

"I don't see why not," said Mark.

"Let's check it out then," said Tony.

"Hey, Lenny, what did the old priest say to you back there as we were leaving?" asked Mark, looking into the rear view mirror at Lenny, who was sitting in the back seat.

"He just said to be careful," said Lenny.

Mark's and Lenny's eyes met.

Chapter 40

Rudy Drew slowly pulled his car into the driveway. It stank of beer. There were several empty beer bottles on the front passenger floor. The bottles clicked against one another as he pulled the car to a stop. He turned off the engine. He'd spent the night sitting in his car parked next to the Mallets Bay Rollerama. He'd bought a case of beer and despite his broken arm he managed to carry it back to his car. Now, he had drunk it all. He sat listening to his car radio and watched the young couples coming and going from the Rollerama. He despised their holding hands, their giggling and even the occasional kiss.

Most of all Rudy despised himself. He was laid off earlier in the day. As far as his co-workers knew, he was laid off ostensibly because there was less work in his area, which was in the plating department. He was really laid off because the quality of his work had begun to slip lately and in the past six months he called in sick too many times. He wasn't really sick. He was just out somewhere getting drunk. Word of his drinking and his dodging work reached his first line supervisor who decided to send Rudy a message—either shape up or ship out! He spoke to Rudy about his problems before sending him home with a two day, unpaid lay off. He advised Rudy to straighten out his drinking problem or else he would see to it Rudy would be out of a job by Thanksgiving.

By the time Rudy arrived home he'd managed to work up a good lather over his layoff. He was steaming and he was mildly drunk. For Rudy that usually was a dangerous mix. He hadn't planned to tell his wife about his layoff. Instead, he was scheming to slip out of the house each day and head off to work just like always. His plan was to go to Leo's Pub on North Street in Burlington. He would do odd jobs for a buddy of his who owned the place. This way he would still make some money and no one would be the wiser.

"I'll show that bastard," thought Rudy as he pulled into his drive-way earlier this afternoon. He never saw Lenny's bicycle. "Sure I was driving too fast and sure I was a little drunk but that's no excuse for Lenny to deliberately leave his bike where it could be run over."

When he heard the crunch of the bike beneath his tires he lost it. It was not his fault the bike was totaled. Lenny needed to be taught a lesson, just as Rudy's father had to straighten him out once or twice when he was a boy.

The bitch had to stick her nose into Lenny's lesson.

"What's gotten into her lately?" muttered a deeply inebriated Rudy.

He sat drinking outside the Rollerama until closing, drinking and pondering the day's events. His arm hurt like a son-of-a-bitch. He'd wrapped it with some tape and gauze he bought at the Drug Store right after he left the house. He also downed several aspirin over the past six hours. His lower ribs on his left side also hurt, especially when he went to the bathroom to relieve himself of the accumulating amounts of beer.

Rudy never once thought about how his wife was or how Lenny was doing. Only his pain and his problems mattered to Rudy.

He decided to return home. It was three in the morning. He was expecting to head to bed just like always. He would wake up with a splitting headache, that's for sure, along with other pain that right now he was only vaguely aware of. He closed the car door with his good arm. Rudy staggered up the back steps. He tried to pull open the screen door with his broken arm. A sharp pain shot straight up his arm. He had to use his other arm. The back door to the house was locked. Rudy fumbled with his keys and after a few false starts was able to unlock the door. He stepped inside and felt around for the light switch. The kitchen light flicked on and even in his drunken stupor he noticed the supper dishes were still on the table. The dinner was still on the stove. The house smelled bad from the over-cooked and burnt food.

He went into the bathroom and fumbled with his zipper. After a moment he was able to unzip himself. He deposited a generous amount of beer by-product in the toilet. Next he slowly climbed the stairs. He didn't want to wake anyone. He just wanted to get to bed. The bedroom shade in his room was open and moonlight cast a faint light into the room. His eyes were barely able to focus but he clearly could tell no one was in the bed. In fact it was still made. Now he fumbled for the wall light switch. It clicked on. Suddenly he could clearly see he was alone in the bedroom. He turned and walked heavily towards Lenny's room. He turned on a light switch in the boy's bedroom. The result was the same. He stomped back to his own bedroom and with his one good arm pulled open his wife's top two dresser drawers. They were practically empty. Anger was now exploding inside him.

His clouded mind began to break through his drunken fugue. He decided to head back downstairs. He wanted to discover just what other little surprises his bitch had pulled on him. He generally knew what he would find but he needed confirmation of his suspicions. He went straight to the kitchen cupboard to the right of the kitchen sink. There on the second shelf sat a big blue Crisco can. It was where they stored their rainy-day money. There should be over a hundred and fifty dollars in assorted small bills inside. He pulled the can down and removed the lid. It was empty.

He roared, "You fucking bitch." With one powerful swipe from his good arm he sent the Crisco can airborne. It crashed into the refrigerator, which sat in the opposite corner of the room. His anger not sated, he next overturned the kitchen table. Dishes and utensils crashed and scattered across the floor.

He roared once more. "Where in the fuck are you, my love, my sweetheart, you dirt bag?"

He kicked over the kitchen wastebasket and garbage spilled out onto the floor.

He went over to the refrigerator, opened it and noticed it was well stocked with two six packs of his favorite beer. He pulled out a bottle, went to the utensil drawer and removed a bottle opener. Then he sat down on one of the kitchen chairs. After a short struggle he opened the beer bottle and took a long draw of the ice cold beer.

"Yes, sir, Schaefer's the one beer to have when you're having more than one. Isn't that right Rudy?" he asked himself out loud. He frequently engaged in conversations with himself when he was drunk, especially when he was drunk and angry.

"But, Rudy my man, more than one sounds mighty fine, now don't it? You're right! This beer is too good to just leave here. Who knows, maybe she'll come back and throw out my beer. Rudy, maybe then you can break her arm, maybe even both arms. The bitch is long overdue for a tune up. Right, Rudy? Damn right, Rudy, a tune up would do just fine!"

He finished the bottle and retrieved another from the refrigerator. He sampled this new bottle and held it head high as a gesture of approval.

"Rudy, there's only one thing left to do. You've got to find Carol and teach her a lesson she will never forget. You've got to put her back in her place. You can't have her smacking you back. She's in need of some serious ass kicking. The sooner you find her, the sooner you can educate her. And if she begs for forgiveness, Rudy, you can show her how big a man you are. After smacking her a few times, you can have her anyway, anywhere and anytime. Penance is penance, I always say. Power belongs to the righteous. Yes, sir!" said a deeply-drunken Rudy.

He got up from the chair and removed the rest of the beer from the refrigerator. He filled a brown paper grocery bag with the long neck bottles of beer and a bottle opener. Now he headed out to his car with the bag of beer bottles. In a moment, he squealed his tires as he sped out of the driveway. He put the car into drive and stomped on the gas as he raced away in search of his wife and children. He went to several houses of people he thought were friends of Carol. He knocked on their door and rang their bell. No one was happy to see him. A few cursed him for waking them up. No one knew where his family was. The last house was the lady who stopped by Rudy's house from time-to-time selling Avon products. She and her husband were not happy to see a drunken and vulgar Rudy Drew at what was now four thirty in the morning. The husband slammed the door in Rudy's face and said through the closed door that he was calling the police. Rudy kicked their aluminum front door, severely denting it in.

Rudy climbed back into his car. As he closed the door he heard the sound of a police siren starting up from somewhere downtown. It was clearly heading in Rudy's direction. One of the people he woke up in his search for his family actually called the police. He turned on the car, slipped it into gear and quickly sped away. He didn't want to tangle with the cops right now. This was family business.

He turned the corner rather wide and headed west on St. Peter Street. At the western end of St. Peter's Street it intersected with Mallets Bay Avenue. He took a quick right on Mallets Bay Avenue and headed north towards the Mallets Bay area of Colchester with plans to return to the Rollerama. He had just taken the right turn, when in his rear view mirror, he saw the flashing lights of a rapidly-gaining police cruiser. Rudy floored the gas pedal. The speedometer needle began to climb to the right as his speed moved upward past fifty miles an hour.

He took a swallow of beer and then tossed the near empty bottle out the window. The bottle shattered on the cement sidewalk. Rudy, despite the pain, still tried steering with his broken arm. He glanced at his rearview mirror and saw the police cruiser closing in and was within a hundred yards. Rudy's speed was climbing over sixty miles-per-hour as the road began to narrow at the City of Winooski-Town of Colchester border. He pushed the gas pedal further downward.

"C'mon, you bastard. Let's just see if you're willing to try and stay with me," he sputtered out loud.

The roadside mailboxes whizzed by at a dizzying pace. He leaned over to grab another beer. His steering drifted as he leaned to the passenger side of the car and pulled another beer bottle out of the paper bag. Suddenly, the car clipped several mailboxes. Their wooden posts and the boxes themselves exploded from the contact with Rudy's car. He over-steered to reposition the car in the center of the road. The car's swerve caused the rear wheels to begin to fishtail. Rudy needed to firmly grip the steering wheel with both hands. Excruciating pain shot up his broken arm.

The police cruiser had to dodge some of the debris from Rudy's mailbox demolition. This slowed the police chase and the cruiser dropped back just a bit. Rudy didn't notice this. He just pushed the gas pedal down further.

The road dipped down just a bit. Rudy's car went airborne because of his excessive speed. His car reacquired the pavement, slamming down hard. Sparks shot out from under the car as it bottomed out. He was now speeding past a couple of dairy farms. The farmers, who earlier herded their Holsteins out of their barns, were about to lead them across the road to a pasture to graze for the morning. Rudy's car shot past the fenced-in cows. Right behind Rudy in pursuit followed the Winooski police cruiser. Both farmers were very grateful their prized milking cows were not out crossing the road when these two speeding cars came by. The carnage would have been incredible. Both farmers offered up a silent prayer of thanks.

Rudy needed to slow down over the next mile as the narrow road dropped then curved and dipped in several places. He had a very difficult time keeping the car on the road. Twice he could feel the car lift up on one side so that over a short distance, only two wheels were touching the road. He soon came up on "Shipman's Hill." a steep hill which brought the road from out of the flood plain of the Winooski River to a plateau atop a hill which was the home to several large vegetable farms. He navigated the hill and its sharp right hand turn at the top at over fifty miles per hour. At the top of the hill the road straightened out and was flat for over a mile. He pushed the gas pedal down nearly to the floor. He was determined to lose the police officer chasing him. Soon his speed reached ninety miles an hour and was still climbing.

Back when the chase first began, the Winooski police officer radioed the dispatcher to ask for Town of Colchester police to set up a roadblock because he was in pursuit of a drunk driver heading into the Town of Colchester.

They set up a roadblock at the end of the straightaway Rudy was now speeding across. The cruiser was positioned to block the intersection where it merged with a road that came from the right. At the intersection you had only two choices. Take a hard, forty-five degree, right hand turn or take a left hand turn at an angle of approximately seventy degrees. The road Rudy was on displayed a stop sign at this intersection. The Colchester police officer could see the oncoming headlights of Rudy's car. He also could hear the siren of the pursuing police car. The Colchester police car's blue, flashing, strobe-lights were on.

The Colchester officer was standing on the passenger side of his cruiser.

"I hope the fool sees my car and stops in time," said the officer to no one.

In an instant the Colchester officer realized Rudy was not going to stop. The officer sprinted to his right to get off the road and away from the on-rushing collision.

Rudy's tired and bloodshot eyes noticed the police car blocking the road. It was too late to slow down or even to stop. He decided to try and drive to the right of the car in the gravel on the side of the road. He felt he could squeeze through and then somehow miraculously pull off a left-hand turn. Unfortunately he hadn't taken in to account his speed. His car exploded through the intersection at ninety miles an hour. His car snapped the stop sign off at ground level. The sign flew over the top of his car and tumbled across the road.

Rudy's right-side tires caught the gravel. The car began a high speed fishtail to the right. The right-side tires reacquired contact with the road but now the car was sideways. The sudden bite of the tires caused the car to begin to flip over. The car flipped once and then went airborne. As it flew forward it flipped several times before it went crashing into the woods. The car crashed and bounced between trees before it came to a stop on its right side, badly bent as it wrapped around a large maple tree. All the windows exploded or were blown out from the rollovers and the force of the impact.

The Winooski police car came to a stop next to the Colchester police car. The two officers ran to Rudy's car, which was over two hundred feet into the woods. Numerous trees were snapped off from the impact of Rudy's car. A car door was lying on the ground about sixty feet into the woods. Other, less recognizable pieces of his car were scattered in a path of broken trees, which led directly to Rudy's car.

Rudy was pinned in his car. The firewall under the dash was pushed into the front seat area, crushing his legs. The steering wheel was pushed into his stomach. Two more ribs were now broken. His face and neck were cut in several places from broken glass. He was barely conscious.

"I'll check to see if he's alive," said the Colchester officer, as he climbed up on the passenger side of the car. The Winooski officer used his portable radio to call for an ambulance and a fire truck.

"He's alive. He's also pinned in real tight in there. Jesus, you should smell the beer. There must be more than a dozen empties in there."

"That's what I figured," said the Winooski officer.

Just then the he realized he could smell gasoline. He used his flashlight to check the underside of Rudy's car. The gas tank had ruptured. A tree branch was sticking into it. Gas was running down the tree branch and across the underside of the car. He noticed the gas was heading straight for the overheated exhaust pipes.

"Get down from there now!" he shouted to the Colchester police officer. "Gas!"

With that news, the Colchester officer jumped clear of the car. The two of them quickly backed away from the car.

"Can we get him out?" asked the Winooski officer.

"There is no way! His legs are crushed under the pushed in dash. The steering wheel is pushed into his rib cage. We're going to need some help."

"Yeah, well, he's going to need those firemen to get here soon."

Distant sirens could be heard in the early morning stillness.

Suddenly, the gas reached the overheated exhaust pipe. It burst into flames. The fire swiftly retraced the path of the gasoline heading straight into the gas tank. It exploded, igniting the entire car with flames. The officers needed to back further away from the heat of the fire. They each raced to retrieve fire extinguishers from their cruisers, but this fire was way too big for their equipment.

Meanwhile, inside the car, Rudy was barely able to discern where he was and how he got there. Curiously, he could hear a voice speaking to him.

"Rudy, when I talk to you, you'd better listen. You did some bad things to my friend. This is your payback, Rudy. You will never again hurt my friend or anyone else again. Feel the pain, Rudy! Feel the pain!"

"Who in the fuck are you?" responded Rudy.

"I'm your worse nightmare Rudy. With your death, Lenny, your son, will owe me a favor, a favor which I will collect."

"What's Lenny got to do with this? I just fucked up here."

"Doubting humans always amuse me. Rudy, look into the darkness behind your eyes and you will see me."

"I ain't looking at nothing. Ow, my legs fucking hurt."

"Very well, Rudy I'll help you."

Suddenly, Rudy could feel someone's hands touching his face. His eyelids were pulled back. In a squeezing pull his eyes were extracted.

"Rudy, can you see me now?"

The inside of the car was beginning to catch on fire.

Rudy let out a scream. "I won't do it again."

The car was totally ablaze. The rear tires exploded while they were on fire. The back of Rudy's seat was rapidly consumed with fire. His flesh blistered from the searing heat before lighting up and joining the ever growing ball of twisting flames.

Less than a minute later a Colchester fire truck pulled up and the firemen ran towards the burning car trailing hose as they went forward.

"Anyone in the car?" asked the lead fireman.

"Yeah, just one, a male; he's pinned in the front driver's seat."

"Too bad," said the fireman.

"Too late," said the police officer.

It took a couple of minutes before the firemen were able to get two hoses trained on the burning car. By then Rudy was dead. His body was burned to the bone. After covering the car with water, the firemen were able to extinguish the fire in just a few minutes. A second fire truck arrived along with an ambulance, but neither would be needed tonight. The crash scene was investigated for the next hour and a half. The county medical examiner arrived and gave permission to remove the body. While the medical examiner filled out his paperwork, the firemen pushed the charred car back onto its upright position. They pried open the driver's side door with their extraction tools.

The medical examiner walked over to the car and looked inside at the skeletal remains of Rudy Drew. The sickening smell of burnt human flesh filled the inside of the car. The medical examiner coughed twice. The odor was overpowering. He went to his car and brought out a heavy vinyl black bag with a long zipper along one side. He handed the bag to one of the firemen.

"After the police take their pictures, please put his remains in here and use these gloves. You can put the bag in the rear of my van," said the medical examiner.

"Say, Doc, we have a possible identification. The car was registered to a Rudy Drew. We've got an officer heading over to check his residence. If we can locate a next of kin, do you want us to give you a call to set up an I.D.?" asked the Colchester officer.

"No, his remains are too badly damaged. Having a close relative see them like that is not necessary. I will see if we can locate his dental records. I believe I saw a couple of fillings. We'll probably be able to preliminarily I.D. the victim based upon dental records alone. I'll look for blood trace to see if I can come up with a blood type. With that information we'll have our second source and a positive I.D. of the victim.

"Doc, he's no victim. My men tell me he was traveling over ninety miles an hour. He had to be substantially drunk from the looks of his car and he would not pull over. He endangered the lives of some good police officers tonight. We could have just as easily been conducting an investigation into their deaths, so please don't call this man a victim."

"I understand your feelings, officer. In my business everyone's a victim. Consider it just a slip of the tongue. I certainly don't condone this man's reckless behavior, let alone his putting at risk the innocent lives of others."

"Okay, Doc. I just needed to vent a little that's all. I guess I just see too many of these senseless accidents."

The Medical Examiner nodded his agreement and turned heading to his van.

The firemen were filling the black bag with Rudy's remains.

Once the body was totally placed into the bag, which weighed very little, one fireman carried it to the Medical Examiner's vehicle. As the fireman headed towards the van, he failed to notice a single white orb, lying on the wet pine needles several feet from Rudy's car. He was wearing his usual heavy fireman's boots, and when he stepped on and crushed this small white object, he didn't feel a thing.

He had just crushed one of Rudy's eye balls.

He kept right on walking and loaded the remains into the van.

At this moment a tow truck arrived to haul away the wreckage.

Chapter 41

It started to snow again and the wind also picked up. The winter wind was blowing a steady twenty miles per hour straight out of the northwest.

It was 2:10 in the morning. At the intersection of Padden Road and Route 7 there was a small, red, older model Toyota Camry pulled off on the south bound side of the road. The driver was Susan Drapeau, a twenty-seven year old nurse. Her car had a flat right rear tire. She waited inside her car for thirty minutes in hopes someone might drive by and offer her a helping hand. Susan was already late for work. She worked the third shift at the Medical Center in Burlington in the trauma unit.

Due to the late hour and the weather she could expect to sit there for a long time with no assurance anyone would even stop to help.

"I guess I'm going to have to change this damn tire myself. Shit, why did I have to forget my cell phone at home on a night like this?" said Susan.

She stepped out of her car and pulled her coat tight around her neck. She went to the back of the car and opened the trunk. She found her emergency lantern, tried it and found it worked. She set it on the ground next to her flat right rear tire. She removed the jack and spare tire. The spare was one of those temporary spare tires that seem more like a pretend tire, certainly not one that belongs on a real car.

She studied the car's service manual while she waited in the car. She felt reasonably confident and familiar enough with the tire changing process to proceed on her own. She removed a small emergency snow shovel she routinely carried in her car's trunk. Using the shovel, she began to clear the area around the flat tire to try and locate pavement or solid ground upon which she could safely place the car jack.

Deep beneath the surface, over three quarters of a mile away, roaming through the underground tunnels was Ne Wha Ta. He was using all his senses to locate an opportunity for some food.

His senses picked up a trace of a human voice. He now focused his entire capabilities upon that trace. He stopped and listened.

Susan successfully jacked up the car. She proceeded to try removing the hub cap. It easily popped off. She tried to turn the lug wrench to loosen the wheel nuts which held the tire's rim. The wrench slipped off, which caused her to strike her knuckles against the ground.

"Damn," she said.

He heard her loud and clear. In a moment, he was rushing through the underground network of tunnels and caves. He was heading in her direction at full hunting speed.

Try as she might, she was unable to get all five of the nuts to loosen. Three came off easily but the fourth seemed unmovable. She stood up to straighten her back. She noticed a car coming up the Route 7 hill heading north, in the opposite direction. She went to the front of her own car and waved at the car as it drove past her. She could see the other driver and it was an old man. He never even looked in her direction.

"Shit," she said as she returned to the back of her car. Once again, she tried to remove the tire's remaining wheel nuts.

Ne Wha Ta made very good time. He reached the exit to the tunnel that led to the surface. Reaching up, he began to move a large flat boulder which sat over the exit. He moved it back and forth as quietly as he could. He felt cold air rush into the tunnel. Snow swirled around as it descended into his tunnel. He climbed out. He could feel the full fury of this winter storm. These sensations didn't distract him. He was sniffing the air for signs of the human.

Nothing! Then he heard a clinking sound coming from his right about a hundred feet away. His exceptional hearing skill was on high alert. He turned and carefully headed in the dialed-in direction of the sound.

Susan had just gotten the last wheel nut lose. She was proud of herself. Her strength and stubbornness sometimes combined and produced interesting results. She began to crank the car jack lever up and down as the right side of the car slowly lifted up off of the ground. Susan elected to leave her car engine running along with the car radio while she worked on the flat tire. These sounds, while comforting to her, also hid the sound of the approaching danger.

The radio was tuned in to an oldies station. A song by the Vogues was playing. Ironically, it was their hit song, "Turn Around, Look at Me."

The song's lyrics began.

"There is someone, walking behind you, turn around, look at me." The song continued.

The monster encountered and stepped easily over the short fence and snow pile at the edge of the road. He sniffed the swirling air and picked up the trace odor of a female human. He also heard a mix of sounds coming from straight ahead. He was closing in. He was taking a chance spending this much time above ground and so far from the safety of his tunnels. But with this storm and the darkness, with his senses he believed he could risk some exposure above ground for this particular hunt.

Susan never saw him approaching until he was standing beside the car. He was standing within the light radiating from the emergency lantern when she noticed him. She first saw his powerful, hairy feet. She thought, *This must be a dream—nobody goes outside in this weather barefoot.*

Suddenly, he reached down and grabbed her by her coat. In one motion, he lifted her clean off the ground. He held her face close to his and sniffed her. The faint light from the emergency light provided enough light for her to see the face of Ne Wha Ta. The one facial feature that riveted her attention was the deep, empty eye sockets. She let loose with a full-throated scream. There was no one to hear her except her captor.

"You are just what I need," growled Ne Wha Ta.

Susan heard him and immediately exploded into action as she began to kick and punch him with all the force she could muster.

He seemed unfazed by her frantic struggling. He carried her back towards his tunnel. He needed to wrestle her a bit to fit her into the tunnel, but after a moment she was dropped in feet first. She tumbled and slid down inside the tunnel at least sixty feet before coming to rest at the bottom. She was now dazed, bruised, confused and in total blackness.

Meanwhile above her, in the tunnel, Ne Wha Ta worked at moving the large flat boulder back into its resting position covering the entrance to this tunnel. At the surface the winter storm's swirling wind and blowing and drifting snow began to cover up any trace of Ne Wha Ta ever having been on the surface.

Susan's head began to clear. In a flash, she realized she must get away from that monster as fast as possible. She reached inside her coat pocket and found her butane cigarette lighter. She flicked it twice and on the second flick it lit. From this faint light she was only able to see perhaps fifteen to twenty feet around. From above she heard the moving of the boulder into place. She immediately knew she needed to put some distance between herself and that creature. She needed time to think, maybe find a way out, perhaps find some-thing to use as a weapon, anything.

She moved forward, deeper into the tunnel, trying to move as far away as she could. She stumbled as she went. Susan didn't want to look back. The tunnel meandered, taking turns to the right and left. At times it would rise and then it would descend. There were moments she felt she could hear him coming up behind her. She hoped her lighter wouldn't fail her before she could find a way out.

He could hear her moving around ahead of him. He was in no hurry. She was in his tunnels. He knew every twist and turn, every hole and crevice. There was no place for her to go.

She focused all her efforts to stay ahead of her attacker. She tried moving quickly but her vision was limited by the range of the small butane lighter and the fact she didn't want to stumble and drop it. Susan entered a large cave. How large she could not tell but it certainly was high and wide. She moved around its perimeter.

She soon came upon two tunnels branching off of the cave. Susan had to make a decision. She needed to keep moving to either find a way out or to find a place to hide. She was warm from her efforts at fleeing from that thing, whatever it was. She went about twenty feet down one tunnel and removed her scarf. She placed it on the ground. She retraced her steps to the larger cave. By leaving her scarf, she hoped if he chose that tunnel, he would be sold on the assumption she went down deeper into this particular tunnel. This might give her some extra time. Of course, if he simply followed her into this tunnel, her attempt at deception will not have a chance to work. She considered it was worth the gamble.

She kept moving and thinking.

Ne Wha Ta took his time following her. She would not escape, of that he was certain. Before he ate her he would consider the possibility she might be a suitable mate. He enjoyed this chance to hunt her in his element. She might just be mating material after all. He came into one of the large central caves that occurred every half mile or so. Over the centuries, water naturally hollowed out large cavernous areas and even started and or formed many of the tunnels he traveled. He simply expanded them so they were passable, or connected them so they could serve as routes to allow him to range over a wider area.

This large cave had several tunnels branching off of it. He stopped and listened. She was being careful to not make any noise. He tried locking in on her mind. He frequently experienced trouble connecting telepathically with females. This female's mind was strong. He couldn't easily connect with her.

He let loose with a howling sound that pierced the dark silence of the tunnels and cave. The howl echoed and reflected back at him from everywhere.

"I will find you," bellowed Ne Wha Ta.

Deep inside the tunnel she had chosen, she heard his howling echo. She stopped and tried to gauge how close he might be but it was useless. She heard his chilling words. She was about to move along when she noticed the flame on the lighter was flickering forward. That could only mean one thing: air was able to enter this underground labyrinth and was also able to exit. Somewhere ahead of her current position could be an exit to the surface. Encouraged by this observation, she began to move forward.

The creature entered the false tunnel. He traveled a few feet where he smelled her presence. He sniffed the air and then knelt down. He reached towards the female odor certain he would take hold of her. He felt some kind of cloth. He picked it up and sniffed it. The material was a piece of her clothing.

"Did she lose it while fleeing or did she deliberately leave a false trail?" he thought. He decided she was clever enough to try leaving a false trail. On that basis he abandoned this tunnel in favor of the one just next to it. He doubled back and began to track down the other tunnel. He stopped and sniffed the air. Yes, there was a trace of her female odor in the air. He felt certain this was the right tunnel.

Susan moved as fast as she could. The tunnel was moving slightly upward. All of a sudden it opened into another cave. This cave seemed much larger than the other.

Which way should she go?

She glanced at the lighter and it flickered to her left. She decided to follow the air current. After a short distance she came upon a huge cache of bones. She immediately recognized many of them as human. There were also scraps of clothing mingled in with the bones. She held back, losing her stomach. She kept moving. In another twenty feet she saw a human shape standing against the wall. She cautiously approached. As she came to within a few feet, she noticed the human shape was a corpse, a corpse with no eyes. She needed to keep moving.

She began to climb up a sort of natural staircase. The flicker of her lighter was now much more driven by active air currents. There must be an exit somewhere up above. Soon she found she was next to a smaller tunnel, which required her to crawl on her hands and knees. The lighter was flickering more than ever. There was no choice. She entered the tunnel.

At the moment she entered the tunnel, Ne Wha Ta entered his main cave where he stored the trophy stockpile of bones. He sniffed the air. She had clearly come into this cave. The odor was stronger than ever. Which, of the half dozen tunnels that branched off from here did she take?

Before he could decide, he heard her. He could hear movement in the upper cave, located nearly two hundred feet away. It was the cave the four boys some years before had explored for the first time. That small cave did lead to the surface. He would have to move more quickly now. He climbed the cave walkway with cat-like speed.

Susan could feel the air temperature getting colder. She crawled as fast as she could. This small tunnel or cave now moved upward. She needed to move on her stomach. She could hear wind blowing just a few feet ahead. Suddenly she also could hear her pursuer.

"I have found you!"

She scrambled forward as fast as she could. She was close to escaping. So close that her right hand plunged into a small mound of snow at the entrance of the cave. She pushed forward with all her strength. So did the creature.

Her head and shoulders were out of the cave. Just as she was about to pull herself out of the cave, he grabbed hold of her ankles. She tried kicking with all her might. It was no use. With one strong pull, he yanked her back inside the cave. She screamed. He dragged her by her feet, deeper, back down into the inner cave. She tried grabbing onto the side of the cave, but it was no use. She left bloody trails as her fingers were ripped open by the rugged surface of the cave. She wiggled and screamed but she was firmly in his grip. She lost the lighter at the moment of her hoped-for escape. It tumbled past her down into the darkness of the cave. She was now in total darkness. Her head was banged around on the floor and walls to this cave. She was soon cut and scraped in several places.

He carried her to the bottom of the inner trophy-laden cave. Suddenly he threw her to the floor of the cave. She scrambled to her feet and tried to run away. He reached out and grabbed her by her right arm. With one arm he pulled her close to him. His foul odor made her feel like retching. He licked the side of her face.

"I need a mate, a human female who is strong."

Her lighter, somehow still lit, had tumbled to the cave's floor about fifteen feet away. She could see his face and it repulsed her. She spit in his face. He wiped his face with his free hand. She used her left hand to reach up and scratch his face. She dug as deep as she could.

He winced momentarily at this unexpected attack. He snapped at her, biting off her right ear.

She screamed out in pain.

"You fucker," she screamed at him.

She began to punch at his face.

He next sank his yellowed and misshaped teeth into her left hand, biting off four fingers. He reached up with his other hand and pulled her hair back with such force he broke her neck. She died in that instant.

Now, he would have to eat her. She was just food to him.

As he sat and slowly pulled apart her body to devour her, the lighter she used and which brought her to the brink of an escape flickered one last time before it died out. Complete darkness once again surrounded Ne Wha Ta, as he continued to consume his newest victim.

Back on Route 7 a snow plow operator noticed the car off to the edge of the road. He also noticed the emergency lantern lighting up the right side of the car as he pulled up behind the car. He stopped and got out of his truck to see if he could lend a hand. The car and its radio were running. Someone was trying to change a tire from the looks of things. He glanced inside the car and saw a purse sitting on the front passenger seat. This didn't look good. Without touching anything he went back to his truck. Once back inside the cab he radioed his central dispatch.

"Frank, this is Walter. Come back!"

"I got you Walter. What's up?"

"You'd better radio the police. I've come across a pretty suspicious abandoned car."

"What's your location?"

"I'm on the southbound side of Route 7 at the intersection with Padden Road."

"Somebody hurt?"

"Don't know. Someone left this car and its radio running. They appeared to be changing a tire, but now no one's here. There is also a purse left on the front seat."

"Why don't you hold right there while I radio the police. I'll be back to you after that." The dispatcher clicked off.

The snowplow operator didn't like this situation one bit. His stomach was beginning to flip.

"I sure hope the little lady is all right," thought Walter. His stomach, however, betrayed his true reaction. He was afraid something bad happened here.

Chapter 42

On the way back from the rest home meeting with Father Campbell, they discussed with considerable animation the possible options to destroy Ne Wha Ta, the monster from their childhood. They pulled into the driveway, parked the car and went straight to the garage. Once they entered, Mark went up into the loft of the garage. He was up there for perhaps two minutes when he shouted, "I've got it!"

He came down from the loft carrying the very same gun they hid away some thirty five years ago.

"Let me see it," asked Lenny.

Mark handed it to Lenny. Lenny turned it over a couple of times. It was a Remington 12 Gauge pump-action shotgun. There was no sign of deterioration. The stock was in excellent condition. There were two shells in the gun's five shot magazine. In that summer of 1962, no one had ever checked to see if it was loaded. Lenny removed the shells and put them in his pocket.

"We need to get some fresh ammunition, preferably 12 gauge slugs. They have more stopping power," said Lenny.

"You mean killing power," said Tony.

"We hope," said Mark.

"Mark, put it back in the loft for now, We can look for ammunition later," said Lenny.

Lenny handed the shotgun back to Mark, who went back up into the loft and carefully hid the gun in the same location as before.

They left the garage and headed to the house. They'd just gotten inside when the front doorbell rang. Mark already had his shoes off, so he hurried to answer the front door. To his surprise, when he opened the door, he found Winooski Police Chief, Ed Contois and FBI Special Agent, Joyce standing on the front porch.

Chief Contois spoke first, "Hello, Mark. This is Special Agent, Joyce, of the FBI. We would like to come in and ask Tony, Lenny and you a few questions, if you don't mind?"

Mark hesitated and then said, "Sure, I guess so. Uh, come on in." He held the door open for the two men as they stomped their feet to remove the snow. They stepped past Mark and entered the living room.

"Have a seat. I'll get Lenny and Tony."

Mark went into the kitchen where Lenny and Tony were busy raiding the cupboards while water heated on the stove.

"We are going to have some tea, Mark. Do you want some?" asked Tony.

Mark held his index finger up to his lips to indicate to his friends to be quiet. He gestured for them to listen as he carefully whispered to them.

"The police chief and an FBI Agent are in the other room. They want to talk to us."

Lenny pulled on Mark's arm and Tony's arm as well. "We need to be very careful!" cautioned Lenny.

Mark and Tony nodded their agreement. The three of them headed for the living room.

The Chief and Agent Joyce stood up when the guys came into the living room. Handshakes and greetings were quickly exchanged. Everyone sat down.

The Chief spoke next.

"Agent Joyce and I came here today to ask you fellas to maybe give us a hand with this investigation going on up at Bremer's old quarry."

"You're asking for our help?" asked Mark.

"Yes, we are, Mark."

"Excuse me, for just a minute. I was about to boil some water for some tea. Would you guys care to join us? Otherwise I need to turn off the stove," said Lenny.

"Tea sounds great," said Agent Joyce.

"Me, too," said the Chief.

"Okay, give me a minute to add some water, I'll be right back," said Lenny. He got up and went into the kitchen. He added some water to the tea kettle and turned the stove on low. He noticed a very large crock pot sitting in the corner of the counter. He went over and lifted the cover and an exquisite aroma of homemade stew billowed up to greet him. He just noticed Mark's father wasn't home. He was obviously making this great stew. He'd said earlier he was going to do some laundry, but he clearly wasn't home at the moment.

Lenny turned around and returned to the living room.

"The water should be ready in a few minutes."

"That's good," said Chief Contois.

"So, you think we could be of some assistance?" inquired Mark.

"That's right. I'll let Agent Joyce explain it to you."

"First of all gentlemen, what we discuss here is strictly confidential. Agreed?"

Everyone nodded their agreement.

"As you are aware, there is considerable media attention focused upon this case. We wish to carry on our investigation with the utmost dispatch. Rumors, speculation and leaks to the media would only serve to impede our efforts to solve this case."

With a nod to the Chief, he continued. "We took notice in the police report on Karl Sweeney's suicide that just hours before he took his own life he seemed preoccupied with the recent discovery of the bones at the quarry. His wife reported he seemed upset and fixated on these bones."

Chief Contois spoke up next.

"We were wondering if Karl spoke to any of you around the time of his suicide. Did he try to contact any of you?"

"No," responded Lenny, then Mark, then Tony.

"Well, we're a little curious about something then. Karl's widow told us she held a package for you, Lenny, a package Karl wanted you to have. She said she spoke to you about it and you picked it up yesterday," said Agent Joyce.

Lenny blushed at Agent Joyce's line of questioning. He needed to think fast.

"Oh, that package. Sure, it was from Karl, all right. She told me about it yesterday. I thought I just heard you ask if any of us had spoken with Karl prior to his suicide. Naturally, I didn't think the package fit your question, since it came up long after Karl's death."

"Could you tell us what was in the package?" asked Agent Joyce.

"Sure, in fact I'll show you. It's right upstairs. I'll get it for you."

Lenny left and went up the stairs. Mark and Tony shot a glance at one another.

"What in the hell has he got up his sleeve?" thought Tony.

Lenny quickly came back down the stairs and handed the Special Agent the box Karl had previously prepared for Lenny. Agent Joyce opened the box and examined its contents. It was filled with several old comic books. Mark recognized them right away. These were from Mark's own collection, which he had packed away in the closet in the bedroom that Lenny was using.

"Was there a note?" asked the police chief.

"Nope, just the comics," said Lenny with a shrug.

"Why comics?" asked Agent Joyce.

"We use to collect and trade comics when we were kids. These were some of my old comics Karl hadn't returned to me. My guess is, he was trying to get his house in order, you know, before he took his own life. I hear people do that."

At this point Agent Joyce removed a cellular phone from the inside of his jacket.

"I've got a call. Could you excuse me for a moment?"

"Sure," said Mark.

The agent went into the kitchen. He could be heard talking softly into his cell phone.

"I bet there are a lot of reporters sniffing around for a story," said Tony.

"You wouldn't believe. Between the local police stations we have received over a hundred tips from psychics alone."

Agent Joyce came back into the living room. "Now, where were we?" he said.

"Comic books, I believe," said Mark.

"That's correct. Look, I'm going to level with you fellas. Our forensics lab has already confirmed several of the skeletal remains come from local cemeteries. We exhumed a couple of burial sites and found empty caskets. The caskets themselves were torn apart. They are rotted and in some instances have collapsed. We have also been able to identify some remains of some local missing persons."

"Anyone we might know?" asked Tony.

"We're not yet at liberty to say. But we can tell you, some of the remains go back at least a couple of hundred years," said Chief Contois.

"So what does this have to do with us?" asked Lenny.

"When you fellas were young, you played in the woods all around Winooski. You knew quite a few other kids. Did you hear or see anything that seems now to be out of the ordinary? Were there maybe a group of kids into devil worshipping, maybe some adults as well? Could there have been a cult group?" asked Agent Joyce.

"I can't speak for the others but I can say that I don't remember anything that could even suggest a connection to the mass of bones you're now investigating," said Lenny.

"Same here," said Mark.

"Yeah, I agree with Lenny," said Tony.

Just then Mark's father entered the house by way of the back door. He made considerable noise as he stomped the snow off of his boots. Pokey wandered into the living room. He sniffed everyone and accepted pats on his head or a friendly scratch behind his ears.

Mark's father came into the living room. His cheeks were bright red, having just come in from the cold.

"I see we have company," said Mr. Pushey.

Mark introduced the FBI Agent.

"I'd like to continue this chat with you boys but I've got to put some food away and get back to my laundry. Make yourselves at home."

Mr. Pushey left the room.

"Do you think some sort of multi-generational cult conducted human sacrifices or practiced grave robbing?" asked Tony.

"That possibility exists, yes," said the Chief.

Standing up, Agent Joyce reached out and shook hands with the guys. "We've got to get going. We have some appointments to keep. Thanks for your cooperation. Here is my business card. My cell phone number is on it. If you come up with something you think may be of some help, please feel free to give me a call, any time, night or day. We'll have to take a rain check on that tea."

When the front door closed, Tony turned to Mark and Lenny and said, "Any time, night or day?"

Chief Contois started the car. He looked over to Agent Joyce, "Well?"

"They're hiding something!"

* * * * *

The front doorbell to the Rectory of St. Francis Parish was given a good twist by the police officer. A loud "brinnnnnng" could be heard throughout the residence. An older woman answered the front door, holding it open just a little bit.

"Yes, officer."

"Hello. I've been sent by the Chief to deliver a message to Father Campbell. Is he in?"

"Father Campbell is at Fanny Allen Hospital visiting with some of our sick parishioners. We are expecting him back at any time. Would you care to come inside and wait? I'm sure he won't be long."

"No, thanks. I was just told to leave this message for him. Please tell him it's urgent."

"Very well," said the old housekeeper.

The officer gave her the envelope and quickly turned and headed back to his cruiser.

She placed the envelope on the small table next to the door where the mail was usually left for the priests to pick up.

At a little past ten o'clock in the morning Father Campbell returned to the rectory from his daily visit with hospitalized parishioners. He noticed the envelope on the table with his name boldly written on the outside. He stopped and opened the envelope and quickly read the short note that was enclosed.

The priest hurried to his office, removed his formal black suit coat and exchanged it for his casual light-weight black summer jacket.

"Mrs. Lesage, Mrs. Lesage? Where are you?" he half-shouted.

She came from the kitchen area located at the back of the residence. She was wiping her hands with a small white cloth.

"Yes, Father Campbell, what is it?"

"There has been a car accident involving the father of young Lenny Drew. You know him—he's one of my altar boys. It appears his father died this morning in a car accident. I helped Lenny and his mother with temporary placement last night. I'm leaving right away to join the police chief to notify the two of them. So please take my messages. I don't know when I will get back but tell Monsignor Kinney I'll call him later."

"God be with you, Father."

"Thank you, Mrs. Lesage." He sprinted out the front door.

She went to the door and held it open for just a bit and watched as the young priest climbed back into his well-used Plymouth. As his car drove down the long driveway, she made the sign of the cross. She made a mental note to say a special rosary tonight for the new widow and her son. She also planned to offer up a special prayer for young Father Campbell. She admired his gentleness and his charitable spirit. These qualities surely were special gifts.

She closed the front door and went back to her work in the kitchen.

Father Campbell drove straight down Weaver Street. He parked his car on the west side of the street. The street was very steep, so he was careful to angle his front tires towards the curb and to apply his emergency brake. On the opposite side of the street was the main entrance to the Winooski Police Department. The police department was located in the basement of a building, which for years had served as a Congregationalist Church. The city had bought it more than ten years before when the church put it up for sale. It now served as Winooski's city hall, police station and even the city's one room library was located here.

The priest crossed the street and was about to head into the police station when Winooski police chief, Merrill, came out of the station to greet him.

"Hello, Father Campbell, I see you got my message."

"Yes, I did." They shook hands. "Where is the body now?"

"My guess is it's already been released to Lavigne's Funeral Parlor. Do you have any idea where the family is? My boys have been checking around this morning and we haven't had any luck."

"I can help you with that. The family was placed last night with temporary host families. They were in fear for their lives. Apparently the man was quite violent."

The priest and police chief stood on the sidewalk as the priest reported what he knew about yesterday's events at the Drew household.

"She should have called the police. We would have held him on charges of criminal assault. I'm sure the county D.A. would have wanted to press charges. We could have also called in Child and Family Services."

"She has been trying to hold her family together for the past few years. She was afraid to stay with him but was even more afraid of leaving him. I tried, without success, to get them into marriage counseling. I was told to stay away by the husband."

"Well, hindsight is of no use to her now." The Chief shook his head in sadness. "I need to speak to her and her son. Why don't we go together? It would make it easier to break the news to her."

"You're right. But first I need to go to Lavigne's and give Mr. Drew the last sacrament."

"You haven't heard how he died?"

"No, your note only mentioned a car accident."

"You didn't get to talk to Officer Roberge when he delivered the note?"

"No, I didn't. I wasn't at the rectory. I was at Fanny Allen Hospital visiting some parishioners. Why?"

"Father, there's not much left to Drew. His body was badly burned. His car exploded into flames right after his accident, he was traveling over ninety miles an hour. I doubt there are more than twenty or so pounds of charred bones. There certainly won't be any open casket."

"Let's go," said the Priest.

"Are you sure?"

"Yes."

"Okay, it's your stomach. Let's take my car."

They drove the short distance to the funeral parlor. They knocked at the back door a couple of times. It was opened by Oscar Lavigne who was wearing heavy duty black rubber gloves.

"Father, Chief, please c'mon in."

They went inside and followed Lavigne downstairs to the embalming room.

On a stainless steel table with a ridge all around its sides lay an assortment of bones; some even held chunks of burned and blackened flesh. These were the remains of Rudy Drew.

"I was just about to check him over for any items we need to remove before burial. The coroner hasn't confirmed his ID yet but given the details of his death, it has to be Drew."

"Don't let us stand in your way," said the Chief.

The priest opened a small black leather bag and spread its contents out on a nearby counter. He began to softly speak in Latin to anoint the dead. He signed the cross over the skeletal remains of the body and then upon himself.

The undertaker went about his own work.

"Aha! See here, Chief, two silver fillings," he noted as he pried with a small stainless steel utensil at the teeth within the skull. After a moment he proudly removed the two fillings and dropped them onto a tray.

"Now, let's see. Where is that left hand?" He poked around the assorted bones for just a moment.

"Here it is. Just as I expected—the wedding band. It's melted a bit during the fire." He broke the ring finger in two and the twisted piece of gold dropped onto the embalming table. Lavigne picked it up and deposited it on the tray with the silver fillings.

"That's it," said the funeral director.

He stepped back from the table to give the priest more room.

Leaning over towards Chief Merrill, Lavigne said, "As soon as the Padre is done, I've got to wash em' down, you know. It's the smell."

The Chief nodded. He was watching Father Campbell perform his priestly duties.

This young priest is all right in my book, he thought. *He handles himself real good around some pretty tough situations. He would have made a good cop.*

"Have you told the family yet?" asked Lavigne.

"We're going there next," said the Chief.

Father Campbell finished up and placed the holy water and holy oil back inside his small black case. He folded up his stole and fitted it inside the case as well. He zipped it closed, then without saying a word, he went up the stairs and out the back door.

"It seems like the Padre has a lot on his mind, Chief."

"Yeah, that he does, Lavigne. By the way, my guess is the family will be calling on you later today."

"No problem, Chief. Me and Mr. Drew aren't going anywhere" he said as he picked up a bottle of some kind of cleanser which displayed a skull and cross bones label affixed to the side.

"See you around," said the Chief as he headed up the back stairs.

"Later," said Lavigne, as he began to spray the contents of the odor-suppressing disinfectant on Drew's remains.

When the Chief stepped outside he saw that Father Campbell was leaning against the front of the police car holding his head.

"Are you all right?" asked the Chief.

"I am now. I just lost my breakfast over there by that spreading yew."

"I was wondering when you'd get around to that," smiled the Chief.

"I need to get something to drink and some gum to get rid of this taste."

"No problem. We'll swing by Vic's Market and pick up a couple bottles of ginger ale. That'll settle your stomach. It will be my treat."

"Thanks."

They climbed into the Chief's cruiser and headed to the store. Today was going to be a sweltering, sticky-hot day. There was already a humid haze. Afternoon thunder showers were expected as a small cold front was likely to pass through later in the day. The cold front would bring some brief relief from the recent spell of hot and hazy weather that covered the area for the past week.

As they sat in the Chief's car sipping on the ice cold ginger ale, Chief Merrill turned to the priest, and said, "Would you mind if I asked you a sort of personal question?"

"Not at all. If I don't want to answer your question, I won't, but you would understand, right?"

"Sure, sure, what I was wondering, is, what made you want to become a priest?"

"What made you want to become a police officer?"

"Wait. I asked first."

"If you'll indulge me a moment and answer my question, then you'll have my answer."

"All right. I decided to become a cop because I thought I could help people. I thought I would be good at it."

"It's the same with me!"

"I see," responded the Chief.

"And Chief, we also have a couple of other things in common."

"Such as?"

"We both have to face man's inhumanity on a daily basis."

"What else?"

"We both also have to wear a uniform, in all kinds of weather."

With that, the Chief managed a slight chuckle.

The day was getting appreciably warmer. The worst part for both of them was just ahead.

Chapter 43

Ne Wha Ta was beginning to lose patience with Lenny, Tony and Mark. He decided he needed to find some way to get their attention and force their hands. After all, he delivered on his part many times over and yet they failed to deliver on their one obligation, to find him a suitable mate.

He began to focus his energy on old man Pushey.

Gene Pushey, Mark's father, was a widower. He had been living in the same house since his marriage to the beautiful Joan Latimer in 1944. The down payment for the house was a wedding gift from her parents. She died several years ago from breast cancer. He would not, indeed, could not, remarry. His devotion to his wife was unwavering even in death.

Gene Pushey enjoyed reasonably good health. He had a small dose of arthritis. His blood pressure could be better. His eyesight weakened a few years ago, then it steadied so his eyeglass prescription hadn't changed in the past four years. He enjoyed walking. For someone who was approaching ninety years old he was in pretty good all-around shape.

Mark's father added spice to the crock pot stew he was preparing for their dinner. Next, he began to wash the fresh bunch of carrots he'd picked up earlier that morning. He was planning to cut them up and add them to the stew. As the water ran in the kitchen sink, he began to scrub the carrots. His mind began to drift off.

He began to daydream about his childhood. He pictured himself back on a rocky beach along Lake Champlain, somewhere on the Georgia East Shore. In this dream there was a campfire blazing ahead. He felt himself walking towards it. Sitting around the fire were several children. They didn't even react to his arrival. He joined them and sat by the campfire. He looked through the flickering flames and saw an old, white haired man kneeling down and looking slowly around the campfire at the children, he began to speak.

Mark's father robotically continued to wash the carrots.

The white haired old man in this dream began to tell a tale, of a time long ago, about a murderous breed of humans. These humans were led by a horrible man. This man had become an eater of human flesh. He had convinced his followers to do the same. This abominable act began to change these men. They began to lose their human identity. They were shunned by the people of the land, the Abenaki. A curse was placed upon these flesh eaters by an Abenaki medicine man.

Ne Wha Ta has now locked in on Mark's father. The link-up is strong. He is now in control of his mind and his body.

The old white haired man continued to tell his story. He now spoke about the flesh eaters as important beings. They were powerful. They could live much longer than humans. He spoke about their strength.

The other children sitting around this campfire did not react in any way to this tale. They simply sat, staring into the fire. The old man began a chant, a chant to summon the flesh eaters. The children, without moving their eyes joined in the chant.

Young Gene Pushey noticed there was some sort of barbecue spit stretched across the fire. It was turning slowly, yet he saw no one turning it. He tried to make out what kind of meat was on this spit but he could not make it out. The old man took a knife from his waist band and reached into the fire and cut off a piece of meat. He held it on the end of his knife and raised it over his head. The cooked meat was steaming hot. The old man skewered the piece of meat on a sharpened stick. He passed the meat to the child to his left. Expressionless, the child took a bite of the meat. He passed the meat to his left, that child also took a bite. Two more and the meat would be passed to him. He looked back at the meat on the slowly-turning spit. He could make it out now.

It was the headless body of a young human.

The piece of meat was one person away from being passed to him. Young Gene Pushey began to feel sick to his stomach. He began to panic.

Gene looked across the fire at the old man. His appearance had changed. He now had larger, somewhat pointy ears. His lower jaw seemed larger. His nose was a little longer. He smiled at young Gene Pushey. He had a mouth full of sharp teeth.

The piece of meat was passed to Gene. Looking at it, he was revolted. He tried to pass it on to the next child, who ignored him. He turned to his right, to hand it back, but the child was not there anymore.

Mr. Pushey was standing motionless at the kitchen sink glassy-eyed. His pulse was racing at a dangerously high rate. The water continued to run into the sink. A bunch of carrots were held limply in one hand, a potato peeler in the other. He appeared to be in a deep catatonic state.

Meanwhile, in the daydream, young Gene Pushey felt many small hands pushing him down on the rocky beach. He looked up to see the children all holding him down. The light from the campfire illuminated their faces. He immediately noticed their ears were pointy, their noses longer, and their lower jaws were larger. Their grins revealed a full set of very sharp-looking teeth. But the most frightening thing of all—they didn't have any eyes. There were only empty holes where their eyes should have been. The hideous children were trying to force the meat into his mouth.

He struggled to keep his mouth shut. The sightless children keep pushing the meat against his lips. He was terrified. Suddenly, behind their faces, he saw the old white haired man, standing over him. Yet, it was no longer the old man. It was a fierce and evil looking creature. This creature bent down and picked up young Gene Pushey by his throat. He lifted him high above the children. The creature took the meat from one of the mutated children and began to force it into Gene's mouth.

Young Gene Pushey held his mouth shut with all his might. He held his breath, wishing for this nightmare to end.

Mark's father was beginning to sway at the sink.

The Winooski police chief and the FBI agent had just left. Tony headed into the kitchen, drawn by the aroma of the stew. He saw Mark's father drop to the floor. He was blue in the face. He was holding a bunch of carrots in one hand and a potato peeler in the other. His hands were firmly gripping both.

Tony let out a shout to the others.

"Mark, come quick, it's your father! Lenny, get in here!"

Mark and Lenny heard a "thump" emanate from the kitchen. Tony's call now set them into action. They bolted from their chairs and raced into the kitchen.

Mark's father was beginning to writhe on the kitchen floor. Pokey was frightened by his master's behavior. He barked repeatedly.

Mark was quickly at his father's side. "Lenny, call an ambulance."

Lenny quickly pulled out his cell phone and placed the emergency call.

"He's got his jaw locked tight. It seems he's holding his breath," declares Tony.

"Dad," shouted Mark, "Dad, can you hear me? Dad, what's wrong?"

Mark's father's eyes were nearly bulging out of his head. He was now turning a deep blue.

In desperation, Mark slapped his father hard across the face. His father opened his mouth and took a gasping breath like a swimmer coming up for air. He began to stammer. His lips were quivering. His voice was child-like. The voice revealed a terror.

Soon his ramblings were coherent.

"No, no, no get it away. Away.....No, I won't eat it! Take it away, no....no....I can't eat it! It's human!"

The words hit the three of them like a jolt of electricity. Mark looked at the others and seemed suddenly overwhelmed by the power of the words his own father just spoke.

"No, no....I....please not that....what are you? You...you have no eyes." Mark's father was now crying like a baby. Tears flowed freely as his body shook from the sobbing. He curled himself up into the fetal position.

Mark lay down on the floor and held his father in his arms. Mark was also crying.

Lenny and Tony were kneeling on the floor. They were thunderstruck by what they had just witnessed.

The piercing sound of the ambulance siren filled the house. Lenny got up and quickly moved to the front door to let in the now-familiar EMTs from St. Michael's College Rescue Squad. He silently pointed towards the kitchen. The two EMTs, carrying their equipment, hurried into the kitchen.

They coaxed Mark to move aside. They immediately began to examine Mark's father. They dialed into the Vermont Medical Center on their cell phone and began to relay the patient's vital information. Lenny and Tony put their arms around Mark.

"He'll be okay, Mark," assured Lenny.

"I don't know guys, you heard him. You saw how he was."

At that moment Mark's father suddenly regained his senses. He seemed confused and scared.

"Who are you?" he said, looking anxiously back and forth between the EMTs.

"What's going on? Where's Mark, Lenny and Tony? I've got to get up. I've got to finish the carrots. Supper is almost ready."

"Listen, sir, you've had some kind of spell. It seems you might have passed out. We're going to start an IV and transport you to the hospital, just as a precaution. The doctors want to check you over," said one of the EMTs.

"Could you fellas step aside while we bring in the gurney? Thanks."

Lenny helped the EMT bring in the gurney. The EMTs assisted Mr. Pushey up onto the gurney. They strapped him in and wheeled him to the front door. They lifted him up in the gurney and took him to the ambulance, where they placed him inside.

Turning to Mark, one of the EMTs said, "Would you like to accompany him to the hospital?"

"Yeah, I would," said Mark. Before he climbed inside the ambulance he tossed his father's car and house keys to Lenny.

"In case you need the car," said Mark.

"We'll be right behind you guys. We'll see you there," said Tony.

The EMT climbed inside and closed the back of the ambulance. The ambulance lights began to pulsate faster and the ambulance siren began to wail. It pulled away smoothly, quickly turned the corner, disappearing from sight.

Lenny and Tony quickly put out some food for Pokey, turned down the crock pot and then locked up the house. They took Mr. Pushey's car and were soon on their way to join up with Mark and his father.

"So what do you think?" asked Lenny as he drove the car out of the Pushey driveway.

"I don't know. Jesus, Lenny, you heard him. He must be talking about that friggin' monster, right?"

"Yeah, it sure seems that way. Do you suppose, well—could it be, that Ne Wha Ta was trying to kill Mark's father, to sort of send us a message?"

"It's possible, I suppose. But is seems to me if he wanted to kill him he would have. We both know, he could if he wanted. So…maybe he's just trying to get our attention."

"You might be right."

They drove down Main Street and waited for the light at the intersection with East and West Allen Streets.

"Tony, do you miss your parents?"

"Yeah, I do. Losing them in that car accident was hard. I had plenty of friends in college. But even being around people all day didn't help. I still felt alone. It took me a long time to get over it."

The stop light changed to green.

"How about you? How are your mother and sister doing?"

"Well, my mother remarried. She met this guy right after my kid sister graduated from college. He was career Air Force. They moved away right after they got married. Right now they're on a vacation trip to South Korea. My kid sister lives in Madison, Wisconsin. She's married and has a couple of kids. Her husband is a professor at the University of Wisconsin. He teaches agricultural economics."

"So, you're an uncle, eh?"

"Yeah, the kids are growing up fast. They're both in college. The oldest is a senior."

"Family—it sure is important to have."

"You can say that again!"

They drove the rest of the way in silence.

* * * * *

The Chief's police cruiser pulled to a stop in front of Janice Goodrow's house. Yesterday evening Father Campbell brought Carol Drew and her baby here for sanctuary from her violent husband. Janice was a maiden woman in her mid-fifties who, from time-to-time, allowed her home to become a shelter for battered women. Her generous spirit, combined with her warm and friendly personality, masked a toughness that occasionally came to the forefront. She often stood between angry husbands, even jealous boyfriends, hellbent on reacquiring their woman.

Father Campbell went first with the Chief close behind. The Priest was about to knock when Miss Goodrow opened the front door. She welcomed them both and invited them to come in. She took one look at the Priest and the Chief. She came to the immediate conclusion something wasn't right.

"Thank you, Miss Goodrow. How's Carol doing this morning?" asked Father Campbell.

"She's doing all right, I suppose. Right now she's upstairs giving the baby a bath. Is something wrong, Father?"

"Yes, her husband died late last night in a terrible car accident."

"Was anyone else hurt?"

"No, just Mr. Drew," said the Chief. "He was quite drunk and caused a disturbance in the neighborhood. When one of our officers arrived to investigate, he was nowhere to be found. Shortly after he was spotted, another officer tried to pull him over. Mr. Drew took off and our officer was forced to follow in pursuit. Mr. Drew eventually lost control of his car in Colchester and crashed into the woods. The car caught fire before he could be rescued. He apparently died in the fire."

"Where is he now?"

"He's at Lavigne's, what little there is left of him," said Father Campbell.

"Do you want me to break the news to her?" asked Miss Goodrow.

"No, I believe I should be the one. Poor dear has suffered for so long at his hand and now he leaves her one last burden to bear," said the Priest.

"Chief, please have a seat. Father Campbell and I will go upstairs to her. I'll be back after I leave Father Campbell with her. Just call me if you need anything."

Chief Merrill sat on the end of the camel-back couch, removed his hat, and leaned back.

Miss Goodrow and Father Campbell went down the short hallway to the bottom of the stairs. They found Carol Drew sitting on the third stair holding her freshly bathed baby close to her chest. The baby was asleep and Carol was crying silently. Miss Goodrow took the sleeping baby from her and Carol's arms dropped limp by her side. A steady stream of tears ran down her face. Father Campbell took her by the hand and led her into the living room. He sat her down in a Queen Anne wing-backed chair. She remained silent. Her eyes were not really focused on anything in particular. Father Campbell pulled a similar chair close to her. He reached out and held her left hand in both of his.

Miss Goodrow laid the baby down in the playpen in the adjoining room and covered her with a light baby blanket. The baby was still sleeping. Miss Goodrow went over to the couch where the Chief was sitting and joined him there.

"Carol, you heard everything we were talking about?" asked Father Campbell.

After a pause, she nodded her head.

"Carol, sometimes the Creator....," began Father Campbell.

"No, Father. Please don't." Carol put her left hand up to stop the priest. "He's dead. My family is all that matters now." She sniffled a bit and Miss Goodrow reached over and handed her a tissue from the box on the end table.

"Part of the healing process is to be able to come to the terms with the loss, to accept the will of God, to be able to..."

"Father, I prayed last night. I prayed God would take him from me and my family. In my heart, I prayed for his death."

Her tears stopped flowing now. She released the priest's hand.

"Carol, we understand your anger at him, but you don't want to carry that around with you for the rest of your life," said the Priest.

"He's right, Carol. His death is not your fault. Don't blame yourself," said Miss Goodrow.

"I am not blaming myself for anything."

"Mrs. Drew, do you think you could tell me what happened between you and your husband yesterday? If you can't talk about it right now, I would understand," said Chief Merrill.

At that moment, the baby began to cry. Miss Goodrow got up to attend to the baby. Carol motioned to her to sit back down. Instead, Carol herself went and picked up the baby. She brought the baby back with her into the living room. She peeked into the baby's diaper, and finding nothing she sat back down in the chair with the baby on her lap. The baby was wide eyed and bubbling with energy.

"Chief, I can't tell you about yesterday, not without telling you about what living with my husband was really like over the past few years."

"Mrs. Drew, please tell it any way you can."

Taking a deep breath, Carol began her story.

"I think he changed right after our son, Lenny, was born. He visited only once in the hospital. It was deer hunting season. He wanted to be with his hunting buddies. When he came to visit me one time he was so drunk the night duty nurse didn't want to let him near me. He'd brought a drinking buddy with him when he came. They made a scene." She bowed her head and paused for a moment.

"I had no one to drive me and my baby home. I had to call a cab. I made up a story for the nurses and the doctor so I could go home. I always made up stories to cover for him."

She looked away for a moment and the tears resumed. Miss Goodrow handed the tissue box to Carol. The baby tried to take the tissues out of the box.

"Can I hold the baby?" asked Father Campbell.

"Thank you," said Carol, as she handed the baby to the priest. The baby went to the priest and giggled out loud as she was turned around to sit on his lap. He gently moved his legs up and down and the baby seemed to enjoy the motion. Her face was filled with a big smile.

"I loved him. I think part of me still does," she said as she dabbed her eyes with a tissue. "But the rest of me no longer loves him. He destroyed that part of me. He made our family life a living hell. I so wanted to have a happy and loving family. I became too afraid of him. I also became too afraid to leave him. I didn't think I could stand on my own two feet." She sighed. "He broke Lenny's arm when Lenny was seven months old. Lenny was crying and ..."

Carol went on with her story for the next half-hour. Miss Goodrow, during this time, changed the baby's diaper and gave her a bottle of juice.

"And when I was sure he was gone, I untied Lenny and took him into the house to get some things so we could get out of there as fast as we could. That's when I called you, Father."

"I'm glad you did. Carol, you made the right choice yesterday. It might have saved both of your lives."

"No, Father. It saved Rudy's life for a short while. If he'd come back while we were trying to leave, I might have ended up killing him and then where would my family be?"

The Chief studied her demeanor and quickly found he agreed with her assessment. She probably would have killed him. Her husband had pushed her over the edge and there would have been no turning back.

"Mrs. Drew, I think I've heard enough. I want to thank you for taking the time and having the strength to speak to me."

"Father, Chief, can I ask you both a question?" asked Carol.

"Sure," said the priest. The Chief nodded his agreement.

"Is there a way I could skip having a wake? I don't think I could stand there greeting people and receiving their condolences and everything. I just want him buried as quickly as possible."

"I suppose it is possible. It really is your decision. But what about a funeral mass and a grave side service?" asked Father Campbell.

Carol's expression sent a clear message.

Father Campbell then nodded and said, "All right, no funeral mass. We can have just a small grave side service."

"I'll go the graveside service. But that's it," responded a weary Carol

"Carol, we haven't discussed telling Lenny. Would you like me to break the news to him?" said Father Campbell.

"I'd rather we do that together."

"I could drive you both over to where he's staying. But I'm afraid I can't stay. I need to get back to the station," said the Chief.

"I'll look after the baby," said Miss Goodrow.

"That would be wonderful. Thank you."

In a few moments, the Chief, the priest and the new widow left together to break the news to Lenny that his father died last night in a car accident.

What none of them could know was that in his heart Lenny already knew.

Chapter 44

Lenny and Tony walked through the emergency room doors together. Tony asked at the desk if someone knew where the ambulance patient, Mr. Pushey, was. A nurse working near the information desk pointed to the fourth examining room down the left hallway. Lenny and Tony walked down the hall and looked around the opening to the examining room and saw Mark talking to his father, who was lying on a small bed. A doctor and two nurses were working on Mr. Pushey. He was already hooked him up to an electrocardiogram machine and was now in the process of having a second IV inserted into his other arm. A doctor pushed by the two arriving friends.

"Excuse me." Approaching the bed the hurried doctor continued, "Has your father suffered any fugues or fainting spells recently?"

"No, not that I know of."

"Do you know what medicines he takes?"

"Listen, young man, I'm not deaf and I'm not unconscious. You can ask me those questions," said a defiant Gene Pushey.

"All right, Mr. Pushey, talk to me about your medicines," said the young Doctor.

Both nurses were holding back smiles while the second year resident looked into Mark's father's eyes with a small flashlight.

Mark stepped back from the examining table to give everyone more room. Lenny and Tony moved over next to Mark.

Mr. Pushey looked at the three of them standing there. He winked at the nurse to his left to get her attention. She smiled at him.

"You guys go wait in the waiting room. I'll be out in a few minutes as soon as this young boy finishes up with me."

"We'll come tell you what we find out as soon as we have something to report," said the smiling nurse.

"Okay, Dad, we'll be right down the hall," said Mark.

Mark's father started to wave when the nurse caught his arm and pushed it back down.

"Mr. Pushey, you've got an IV in that arm. Please!"

The three guys left and headed out to the waiting room.

"Sound familiar?" asked Tony.

"Wise ass," retorted Lenny.

"So what do they think happened to your dad?" asked Tony.

"They don't know yet."

Mark sat down on the well-worn yellow plastic chair. Lenny and Tony sat across from Mark in equally worn chairs. One of the administrative staff, a young man of around twenty or so approached Mark and asked if he could take a moment to fill out a hospital form.

Mark took the clipboard. He grabbed the pen attached to the clipboard and began to fill out the form. It took several minutes. After he'd completed as much as he could, Mark walked the form back over to the young clerk and handed it to him. They spoke to each other for a few moments and then Mark returned to his seat.

"We can't afford to wait to take on that bastard much longer. I think he is trying to get our attention. Face it. We know he can reach out at any time and kill any one of us, or any one close to us. He won't stop until he gets what he wants. We have to take him on and the sooner the better as far as I'm concerned," half-whispered an obviously wound-up Mark.

"Look, Mark, we all agree here," whispered Lenny. "The real question is how do we do this? We won't get a second chance."

"We've got to lure him out of the cave. There must be something we can come up with to get him out of the cave where we can shoot the fucker," said Tony in a half-whisper.

"What we did back then won't work now. He's smarter. Besides, we know he can also listen in on our plans. We're going to have to find a way to plan this thing, and pull it off, before he can figure out what we're up to," said Lenny in a low voice.

"Remember Father Campbell said, we have to use the gun," said Tony as he glanced around the room.

"Yeah, we know. But is it going to be enough?" asked Mark.

"Maybe it is, maybe it isn't, but one thing's for sure. It has to be at the center of our plans. I can just feel it," said a solemn Lenny in a low and determined voice. "That shotgun is part of bringing this nightmare to an end."

"Mr. Pushey?" asked one of the nurses who'd been working on Mark's father. "Could you come with me, please?"

Mark left with the nurse, leaving Lenny and Tony in the waiting room. After nearly a half hour, Mark and his father appeared from around the corner.

"Let's go, guys," said Mark.

Tony and Lenny got out of their chairs and went immediately over to Mr. Pushey and began to shake his hand and give him a warm hug.

"Are you okay?"

"I don't think they'd be letting me go home if I wasn't."

"Did they figure out what happened to you?" asked Tony.

"The docs all say my ticker is strong and shows no sign of any heart attack or aneurysm. They don't think I was having any kind of stroke, either. They think all I had was a fainting spell. They wanted to keep me overnight for observation but I said, 'Not for me thank you.' They do want me to make an appointment with my own doctor as a follow up just to make sure everything is good to go. That's fine with me. So I told them who my doctor is and they said they'd take care of forwarding their reports to him on what happened today."

Tony shrugged his shoulder. "Well, whatever it was, it sure scared the shit out of us."

"Sacred you guys, damn, how do you think I felt? I had one hellacious scary episode; I don't mind telling you boys. I was having a dream. No, it was more of a freaking nightmare. I felt my heart beating as if it was going to explode."

He looked at the pained expression on his son's face. "Sorry, Mark."

Mark put his arm around his father and together everyone walked out of the emergency room of the Trauma Center at the Medical Center of Vermont.

They all piled into Mark's father's car. Mark took the wheel and set off for home.

The conversation soon turned to the stew Mr. Pushey was preparing. Everyone was very hungry. On the way home, and at his father's suggestion, they stopped at Shaw's Grocery Store and picked up a fresh loaf of French bread. Tony also picked out a bottle of Cabernet Sauvignon. No one spoke about the fainting episode or what Mr. Pushey said during his blackout. As of now, no one wanted to open that can of worms. Even tough, old Gene Pushey preferred to avoid the subject.

They didn't want to broach the subject because they didn't want to be drawn into a discussion that might reveal what was really going on. On the other hand, Gene Pushey didn't want to discuss the incident either. He had a deep dark secret he preferred, for now, to keep hidden. Long ago, he had vowed to take this secret to his grave. Now he wasn't quite so sure any more!

After they parked the car in the driveway, they entered the house to an enthusiastic welcome from Pokey. The dog couldn't seem to get enough pats from everyone. He rushed from one person to another.

"All right, Pokey, you can settle down now. I think he probably needs to go for a walk, unless he's made a mess somewhere," said Mr. Pushey.

"Well, Pokey did you make a mess boy, huh?" The dog sat in front of his master with his tail sweeping the floor at a furious pace. He barked once.

"Mr. Pushey, I'd be happy to take Pokey for a walk. How about it, Pokey, want to go for a walk with me?" said Tony.

The dog looked at Tony and barked once. He ran to the back door and turned in a circle before barking again.

"It looks like you've got your answer, Tony," said Mr. Pushey. "The leash is hanging against the door. I think all you need to do is take him around the block once. Oh, and Tony, you're going to need the pooper scooper and a plastic bag. They're under the sink."

In a moment, Tony and Pokey headed out the back door as the others began to put the final touches to supper.

Upon Tony's and Pokey's return, they all sat down to a much-anticipated dinner.

Lenny proposed a toast. "To the men in this house, may we all live long and prosper, if I may quote Star Trek's Mr. Spock."

Pokey barked twice. With that, Lenny raised his glass to Pokey, "And that goes for you, too, Pokey."

* * * * *

Mrs. Drew and Father Campbell waved to the police chief as he drove away. They slowly climbed up the front steps of Tony Fredette's house. Father Campbell rang the front doorbell. Mrs. Fredette anticipated their arrival and greeted them at the door. Mrs. Goodrow had called ahead and forewarned Mrs. Fredette of what was happening.

"Please come in," said Mrs. Fredette. "I'm so sorry for your loss," she said, as she gave Mrs. Drew a warm hug. "If there's anything I can do, please feel you can count on me and my husband."

"Thank you. You've already done quite a bit by letting Lenny stay with you."

"Oh, that's no problem. He's such a wonderful boy. He's very polite and we treat him as if he's family, which he practically is since he and Tony are so close."

"I know. He really enjoys being here. Tony has been a good friend to Lenny, and, well, he needs that right now."

"I understand. Can I get either of you something to drink? Some ice tea perhaps?"

"Nothing for me, thank you," said Mrs. Drew.

"Nothing for me, either," said Father Campbell.

"Where is Lenny?" asked his mother.

"The boys are out back in the yard. They're tossing a baseball. They are each pretending to be a famous Red Sox pitcher. I don't know which one, since I really don't know much about sports, but they seem to be enjoying themselves," said Mrs. Fredette.

"I'll go get the boys," said Father Campbell. He turned and headed to the back of the house.

Once he left the room, the two women settled down on the living room sofa, sitting there in silence. It was awkward. Mrs. Drew was trying to think about how she was going to tell Lenny, but she also felt uncomfortable being around someone who knew she was now a widow. She knew this awkwardness would be repeated over and over again in the next few days. It would have to be faced and conquered. She so wanted to not be pitied.

Mrs. Fredette felt uncomfortable, too. Last night after she and her husband picked up Lenny they took the two boys out for soft serve ice cream. Throughout the ride she noticed Lenny didn't sit back in the car seat. Later that night, when the boys were getting ready for bed, she walked by the partially open bedroom door. She saw Lenny shirtless. His back was red and raw with several welts and cuts all across his narrow back. He was such a small boy. *How could anyone do that to his own child?* she thought.

Mrs. Fredette wanted to reach out and hug Mrs. Drew. How that dear woman must have suffered at the hand of her husband! A red gash was still visible on her face. And if matters couldn't be worse, poor Mrs. Drew had a young baby to care for as well. Mrs. Fredette looked at the delicate features of Mrs. Drew. One thing seemed to come across, it was an inner strength this woman possessed. A woman can see that in another woman. Mrs. Fredette's instincts told her that somehow, this woman would survive. She would find a way to keep her family intact.

Even though not a word was spoken between the two women, much was communicated.

Their mutual awkwardness was broken when the two boys came bounding into the room followed by the priest.

"Tony, I could use your help in the kitchen for a while," said Mrs. Fredette."

"Sure, Mom."

After the Fredettes left the room, Father Campbell gestured for Lenny to take a seat on the sofa.

"Lenny, your mother and I have some bad news."

"Lenny, come here," said his mother.

She held him close to her. Lenny wrapped his arms around his mother. He stroked her hair. She had a single tear running down the side of her face.

"It's all right, Mom. I think I know. Dad is dead, right?"

She pulled back from Lenny, looked at him and asked, "How did you know?"

"Because I prayed he would be punished for what he'd done to us. God had to have heard my prayers."

"God heard your prayers?"

After a pause, Lenny answered confidently, "Sure he does, that's what I believe."

"Lenny, God hears our prayers, but he doesn't always grant us our petition. He ....," Father Campbell was interrupted by Lenny.

"He's dead, isn't he, right? He can't hurt my mom any more," said a bitter Lenny, as he pushed his slipping, taped-up eyeglasses back up onto the bridge of his nose.

"Lenny, you mustn't be so quick to judge your father," said Father Campbell in a pleading voice. This boy has hardened his heart. The priest recognized he would have a difficult time reaching him but, relying upon the help of the Holy Spirit, he expected to succeed.

Lenny's mom gently touched him on the bottom of his chin and turned his face back to her. "Lenny, it's true that your dad is dead and it's also true he was a mean and hurtful man. But we can't dwell on the bad. We must become better than that. We need to be there for each other. You have a younger sister. We both will now have a chance to show her what love and caring are all about. We also can help each other. We both have a lot of healing to do, don't we Lenny?"

"Yes, Mom." Lenny had tears running down his own face. His mother gently wiped the tears with both her hands.

"I love you, Lenny."

"I love you, too!"

As Father Campbell watched this mother-son moment, he too, had a sentimental lump in his throat. In the back of his mind he noted he just experienced the privilege of watching the Holy Spirit at work.

Chapter 45

The forensic work in the quarry was progressing slowly. Not only were there bones to be carefully removed and cataloged, there was a huge assortment of personal effects mixed in with the bones. There were shoes, socks, hats, shirts, blouses, skirts, underwear, sweaters, etc. Mixed in with some of these personal clothing items were the contents of pockets. There were coins, wallets, car keys, combs, and scraps of paper with faded written notes. There was also jewelry, such as rings, necklaces and watches. There were even a few cigarette lighters, and of course, half-used packs of cigarettes. All these personal items were scattered among the bones. Some of the wallets and other personal items gave the investigators a clear answer as to who the owners were.

State and local authorities, largely following the advice of the FBI, refused to announce to the media, or any inquiring relatives of missing people, any conclusions as to specific identity of any of the human remains.

The FBI assigned their top forensic people to the case. They also assembled, from academia and their own in-house staff, a team of specialists to examine the possible cult and or mass murderer angle. The Director of the FBI, Wallace B. King, asked for and received a daily on-the-scene briefing report prepared by the Agent-in-Charge, Agent Joyce.

On the ground there was also a cadre of local and state investigators, each busy working their individual jurisdictional lines. As with any mysterious case such as this, there was the usual collection of press. The press corps now reached over two hundred people. All the national magazines, national television and cable networks, over two dozen newspapers, as well as several tabloids, so-called news shows and at least fifteen international media sources were represented. The collection of satellite broadcast trucks set up to do their daily live feeds filled the upper level of the quarry.

Local businesses, restaurants, and hotels were happy about the extra business traffic. Because of the official news blackout, the reporting began to focus upon local reaction to the unfolding events. Lately the media had become so desperate they began to interview one another.

This waiting period was part of a ritual that had become a routine part of the landscape for every important news story over the past ten years or so. The public's appetite for news, no matter whether it was real or bogus fostered a media industry hell-bent on scooping the competition. They knew the news blackout would be overcome eventually. It was just a matter of the right amount of money flashed to the right investigator or insider. One's conscience or ego could easily be persuaded the story was coming out anyway. All the media hounds needed was someone to agree to speak off the record, just for background. That one leak would most certainly lead to others. If one person broke the story, then others could justify their own background contribution. After all, if the story was going to come out anyway. why not make a little money on it? Greed became a reporter's best ally these days.

The investigators, knowing the bent of the various media personalities, played their cards carefully. Initially, they preferred the media to just go away. If no one broke or leaked the story of the investigation, then some, if not most, of the media, would withdraw and take up the chase of the next big, breaking story. They could not afford to wait just as they could ill-afford to walk away empty handed. On certain occasions, investigators sometimes leaked the story directly either to advance certain investigative initiatives or, as is more often the case, to advance some aspect of their own personal career.

This investigation into the mysterious cave filled with human remains contained all the classic tensions. So far there were no leaks, but it was just a matter of time.

Meanwhile, no one took any unusual interest in the fact the quarry was located directly under the main flight path into and out of the Burlington International Airport, which was also the home of the Green Mountain Boys, Vermont's Air National Guard Tactical Defense Squadron. An assortment of aircraft flew over the quarry at heights that ranged from a thousand feet to fifteen hundred feet depending on the aircraft and prevailing wind conditions. Each and every day dozens of commercial as well as military aircraft flew directly overhead.

Deep beneath the earth, Ne Wha Ta often listened to the various humans who now swarmed about the quarry. He decided, as long as this investigation went on, his "friends," who he was trying to persuade to bring him a mate, would be likely held back by this spectacle. Ne Wha Ta needed to find something to bring a halt to this investigation and to allow him to focus on completing his recruitment efforts at locating a suitable mate.

He came up with a solution.

At the Burlington International Airport, sitting on the tarmac just outside the Air National Guard readiness hangar, were two F-16's. The fuel tanks were always topped off. Each plane carried a full complement of air-to-air missiles. On a moment's notice, the pilots for both planes could scramble from their readiness quarters and inside of one minute be airborne. In less than four minutes, after full throttle, they could easily be stationed off of the New England coast ready to make contact with the "enemy." As a unit, they were deservedly proud of their readiness response.

It was seven-thirty at night. Two pilots had just started their turn on readiness watch at six o'clock. Their duty would continue for a thirty-six hour rotation. The scramble alarm suddenly sounded, as it did at least every other day throughout the Cold War period and since. The pilots ran the short distance to their waiting planes and swiftly climbed aboard. They already wore their flight suits. Their personal helmets were waiting for them in the cockpits. Generators, used to keep the engines on standby, were already being disconnected. The whine of the engines began immediately. The pilots received a radio message they were cleared for immediate takeoff. The flight canopies were lowered and locked as they turned their planes left and then left once more before turning right onto the runway. Without a pausing, they immediately began to accelerate down the runway to takeoff.

Tonight, one of the pilots, a fourteen year veteran, Lt. Colonel Steven "Scrappy" Duclois, began to hear a voice speaking to him. This voice was not coming through his headgear. This voice came from inside his mind. He was unaware he was no longer in control of himself or his plane. He continued to pull back on the joy stick, as he accelerated his jet's engine up to three hundred miles per hour. He otherwise operated all the controls as he always did.

As the planes cleared the runway, his flight partner and wingman, Lt. Colonel Ed Dempsey, spoke to his leader, "Scrappy I'm on your right, we're looking good."

There was no response.

"Scrappy, have you got your ears on?"

No answer from the radio, as Scrappy's F-16 began a maneuver which was not part of the usual mission routine. In an instant Lt. Colonel Dempsey recognized his leader was in trouble.

"Scrappy, what's wrong? Talk to me!"

Lt. Colonel Steve Duclois couldn't speak to his wingman. He was busy having a conversation with a mysterious voice inside his head.

Pilot Duclois turned the plane slightly to the northwest. His elevation was approaching eleven hundred feet. His speed was accelerating past three hundred miles per hour. His landing gear was still down and locked. He reached out and flipped a switch to activate his full complement of missiles.

He looked ahead and could easily make out the brightly-lit work area of the quarry, which was less than a mile away. It was straight ahead and closing rapidly. He pushed the throttle to full ahead. His afterburner ignited as his engine went full and hot. Finally, he put the plane into a steep dive towards the quarry.

"Steve, what's wrong with you? Say something, damn it!"

There was a clatter of voices screaming into the pilot's headsets.

"He's armed his arrows," said a bewildered ground controller. "What's going on here?"

"Oh, God! No!"

Lt. Colonel Dempsey watched helplessly as the F-16 flew straight into the top of the quarry wall slightly to the east of the cave. The explosion of the crash, combined with eight fully armed missiles exploding, lit up the evening sky. The ground rumbled as if a major earthquake just struck. Plane debris, jet fuel and thousands of tons of rock fell to the quarry floor.

The few investigators inside the cave were fortunately at its entrance. They scrambled as they pulled back from the cave. Debris dropped all around them as they ran for cover. A motor home that served as the headquarters for the on-site investigators was hit by several large pieces of debris, crushing the vehicle. The flaming jet fuel, JP-4, a highly flammable grade of fuel, ignited the motor home whose own fuel tanks now ruptured, bursting into flames as a secondary explosion. Other vehicles, two pick up trucks, also caught fire and soon burst into flames. A large fissure opened near the front center of the cave. From underneath a D-4 bulldozer, three state police criminalists watched as the roof of the cave they were just inside of moments before collapsed in one large earth shaking roar. A roiling wall of dust cascaded straight at them from the collapsed cave.

The explosions created a series of concussions, which propelled towards the assembled broadcast vehicles and their satellite dishes. Many of these were knocked over from the first concussion wave. Others, not knocked over, had their satellite dishes twisted out of position.

Lt. Colonel Ed Dempsey circled his plane around the devastating scene on the ground. He was stunned and in a state of shock.

His earphones were abuzz with ground chatter. He could not listen to them.

Not now.

He circled again and again.

"Colonel Dempsey, this is Commander Dupont. Do you copy, airman?"

Finally Dempsey's attention was alerted.

"Uh, yes, Commander. Over!"

"I suggest you return to base immediately."

"Commander, but...,"

"Airman, this is a direct order!"

"Yes, sir!"

Lt. Colonel Dempsey pulled his F-16 around and flew south to begin his wide turn to make his landing approach. As he flew past the quarry for the last time that night, he could see the flashing lights of several emergency vehicles quickly approaching the crash scene. He hoped there were not many others hurt by this senseless tragedy. Back in the recesses of his own mind he began to sort through his memory for any tidbit of information which might have indicated his flight partner was unstable. There must be an explanation. Right now that explanation eluded him. He was a highly trained professional. His training told him that what he'd just witnessed was not caused by a mechanical malfunction. The crash of a fully armed F-16 with its weapons activated was a deliberate and deadly act by the pilot.

"Why Scrappy, why?" said a puzzled Lt. Colonel Dempsey.

* * * * *

Lenny went back outside with Tony while Mrs. Fredettes and Father Campbell sat in the Fredette's living room with Mrs. Drew.

"Mrs. Drew, I want you to know how sorry I am about your family's loss," said Mrs. Fredette. She was trying to be polite. In her heart she felt deep sorrow for what Lenny's father had put his son and wife through.

"Thank you."

"Mrs. Drew, my family would be happy to have Lenny stay with us for as long as you see fit. We enjoy his company and he is a good friend to our son, Tony."

"Under the circumstances, I don't know. Lenny should be with his family. I, uh, just don't want to impose. You understand?"

"Mrs. Drew, if I may. I believe Lenny, for the near term, would be comfortable here with the Fredettes. He already spends a great deal of time here now. This way his transition from recent events would be supported by the stability that would surround him here. This would allow you the time to re-adjust yourself. You would still be available to him and him to you. I am merely suggesting a few weeks of nurturing and healing for all of you. Mrs. Goodrow will spend whatever time with you that is necessary to assist you until you find you can move back to your own home. Even then, she, I and others will pitch in and help you along the way."

"Mrs. Drew, please allow us to help," said Mrs. Fredette.

Looking down into her lap, Carol Drew decided to put Lenny's needs ahead of her own need to have him close by.

"I understand, and I accept your generous offer to allow Lenny to stay here with your family. Lenny and I will be better able to support one another when we can focus on each other, including his little sister. But I want you both to understand. I will focus all of my energy to rebuild our lives. My children have been and will continue to be the center of my life. I want my family back together again as soon as possible."

"That's what we want for you as well," said Father Campbell.

"I know."

Later, Mrs. Drew said good-bye to Lenny, Tony and Mrs. Fredette. Father Campbell walked her back to Mrs. Goodrow's house. Along the way they discussed the burial ceremony. They also discussed her financial situation. Father Campbell agreed to arrange having Mr. Ready, a retired Insurance Executive who was a faithful parishioner, join the two of them at an appropriate time at Mrs. Drew's home to examine her personal financial affairs.

The burial ceremony would take place tomorrow morning sometime after the daily mass schedule.

When they arrived at Mrs. Goodrow's, they sat down to enjoy some lemonade. Father Campbell called the rectory to get a message to the cemetery foreman to have a grave ready for tomorrow morning. The burial plot would be at the back of the graveyard where the plots were not yet assigned or spoken for. The priest called the undertaker to advise him of Mrs. Drew's decision to forego a wake and to proceed straight to a burial service. The undertaker asked if there was going to be any newspaper announcement for the local newspaper's obituary page. After checking with Mrs. Drew, it was agreed a short and inexpensive obituary could be placed. The priest and the undertaker composed it over the phone in a couple of minutes. Father Campbell excused himself at this point and indicated he needed to get back to the rectory as soon as possible because he had a couple of marriage counseling sessions to conduct before dinner. Father Campbell left to retrieve his car, which was parked a short walk away near the police station. Carol Drew felt relief that she could be alone with her baby for a short while. Carol thanked the priest and said good-bye as he headed out the front door. Mrs. Goodrow also left to do some quick grocery shopping. Carol went into the bedroom and looked in upon her tiny daughter, who was asleep in the bassinet. The shades were pulled down and a window fan was humming in the window facing the back yard. The baby was lying on her back. She had kicked her baby blanket off. Carol carefully replaced it over the sleeping infant.

"My beautiful baby, you will not have to know what it was like, living with your father. Your older brother, Lenny, has known and thank God he has survived. I promise you will be raised in a household of love and happiness. We may not have much, but we will have one another, and that's enough."

Carol Drew lay down on the bed next to the bassinet and in a moment, she, too, fell fast asleep.

Chapter 46

The Fredette family and Lenny arrived at the cemetery a few minutes before nine in the morning. They were the first to arrive. After a moment, another car pulled into the graveyard of St. Francis Xavier Church. It was driven by Mrs. Goodrow. Lenny's mother stepped out of the car carrying her baby daughter. They joined up with Lenny and the Fredette family. A couple cars arrived and parked in the street outside the cemetery. About a dozen people headed straight for the final resting place for Rudy Drew. In this group were the Pushey family and Mrs. Sweeney, who herself was recently widowed. Her son Karl waved at Lenny, who smiled and waved back.

An elderly couple, the Gauthiers, also arrived. They attended every funeral they could. As parishioners, they somehow felt it was their duty. They were both in their eighties.

Shortly past nine o'clock, a single black Cadillac hearse slowly made its way into the cemetery. It pulled alongside the grave site. The parish's two grave diggers stood their usual respectful distance. The undertaker opened the back of the hearse and the men in attendance, even Father Campbell, lent a hand carrying the lightweight casket to its place just over the grave. Father Campbell read a brief passage from the Book of Psalms about a weary journey. He asked everyone in attendance to look into their hearts and to ask for the help of the Holy Spirit in finding forgiveness for the sins of Rudy Drew. After a brief moment of reflection, Father Campbell spoke again.

"May God grant Rudy Drew, everlasting mercy and forgiveness! For our Creator sent his only Son to die upon the cross for our sins....,"

The grave diggers watched the service come to an end. No one approached the coffin. There were no flowers, no flag draped over the coffin and little to no mourning from what they could see. The assembled quietly made their way to their vehicles. Soon everyone left. The grave diggers went about the business of burying the dead.

One of the grave diggers nodded at the casket and said to his partner, "I hope when they come and bury me, someone cares, eh?"

"Yeah, I heard he was one mean bastard."

Their work proceeded mostly in silence. This time the two men didn't feel like joking around. They simply wanted to get the burial over with as soon as possible.

* * * * *

The Salt Lake City, Utah television meteorologist adjusted his tie as the station's producer held up five fingers then four, three, two then one as he pointed to the weatherman. The red light went on underneath the camera signaling it was live.

"Hello. This is a Channel 7 weather bulletin. This just in from the National Weather Service: the winter storm we've been expecting out of the northwest has begun to merge with a low pressure area that was stalled over the central Rockies. This storm has the potential to dump a lot of snow over our viewing area. Let's go to our weather map so we can see the scope of this impending storm."

Against the green-wall backdrop, the weatherman pointed to an image of a colorful satellite overhead video image of the forming storm. The image was displayed on a nearby monitor just out of sight of the camera. This allowed him to coordinate his gestures with the imagery being broadcast to viewers at home. The rest of his report was filled with the usual technological jargon of his trade. In simple layman's terms, what he had described for his viewers was a storm; he now boldly predicted could become the "storm of the winter." He forecasted a total snowfall that could exceed thirty inches in Utah's valleys, with perhaps as much as five or more feet at higher elevations. The storm had already dumped six inches outside of Tony Fredette's Utah home.

Kelly Fredette watched the storm bulletin and grew a little concerned. She didn't want to stay home alone. Their home was built in a secluded part of Ogden, in northern Utah. She was at least thirty miles from her hospital. Pregnant as she was, she was concerned if she were to start premature labor, she might not be able to reach help in time. She decided to call her friend Liz Carlisle to see if she could come over and wait this storm out with her and her husband and their lovely little daughter, Cody. Their home was only two miles from the hospital.

Liz thought it was a splendid idea. She even offered to drive over and get Kelly. Kelly wouldn't think of it. She told her friend she would pack a few things, give Tony a call back east to let him know where she would be and then she would drive herself over. She would be over in less than an hour. Her friend Liz made her promise to drive carefully and to wear her seatbelt, which she naturally agreed to do.

Kelly quickly packed. Before heading out the door, she tried calling Tony at the number he left her. Her phone line was full of static. She tried redialing again. The result was the same. She decided she would try calling him later from Liz's house. She went out the side door into the garage. Kelly locked the house door and climbed inside her four wheel drive Nissan Pathfinder. Reaching up to the passenger visor, she pushed the garage door opener, which signaled the garage door to slowly lift open.

Kelly pulled out of the garage and immediately needed to turn on her windshield wipers. She closed the garage door and slowly made her way out of her driveway. She headed over to her friend's house. Kelly kept her speed to less than thirty miles per hour.

The fierce storm lashed at the car. The car rocked with the force of the wind pushing against it. She encountered only two other vehicles along the way. The snow was presently falling at the rate of one inch per hour, with the main brunt of the storm hours away.

After nearly ninety minutes of slow driving, Kelly pulled into Liz's driveway. She struggled to push against her car door to keep it from slamming against her as she removed the two bags of her things she brought along.

The snow struck her face and stung as it made contact. She trudged up to the side door, which quickly opened as Liz reached out and took Kelly's bags.

"Come on in."

"Thanks for letting me come over, Liz."

The two women embraced. Cody came skidding around the corner in her footed pajamas. She rushed over to Kelly and gave her a hug around her legs.

"Hey Kelly, want to see what Mama and I are making in the kitchen?" said Cody.

"Not right now, dear. Mama is going to take Kelly to the guest bedroom and help her get settled. Then we can go back to the kitchen."

"Let's get the baby settled."

"Later, Honey," said Liz as she rolled her eyes to Kelly.

"I can't wait to have my own. Liz, she's so cuddly."

"You'll get your chance, Kelly, and from the looks of things it won't be too long."

"I know! I seem to be blowing up like a birthday balloon."

With that, they both laughed and hugged once more.

"Liz, I tried to call Tony from my place, but the cell phone couldn't catch a signal. Would you mind if I used your phone? I've got my phone card."

"You can use the phone in your room."

"Do you think this storm will knock out power?" asked Kelly.

"If it does, we're still all set. Frank had an emergency generator installed after the last storm. You know Frank, he has to have his television so he can watch college basketball, fly fishing, and bowling. Anything that passes for sports, Frank will watch it."

"It could be worse, you know," chipped in Kelly.

"I know! It's just that sometimes I think the only way he'll look at me is if I'm wearing hockey pads or a football helmet."

"Look, girl, you've got to use your imagination. How about wearing that football helmet and nothing else? If that won't work then maybe he's beyond hope. I'd give it a shot."

"Say, you've given me an idea. I'll dig out his hip waders and wear them with a garter belt. I think I even know where his favorite fishing hat is. It will be a perfect match. Frederick's of Hollywood will have nothing to match this."

"Liz, if it works we may have stumbled upon the solution to the loneliness all sports widows experience. This could lead to clothing catalogs, magazines, talk shows and maybe even advice columns."

"We sure do have over-active imaginations, don't we?" giggled Liz.

"Liz, you know my motto, any way and every way."

They laughed so hard that tears came to their eyes.

Just then, they heard the side door open and Liz said, "That must be Frank. He called earlier and said he was getting out of work early."

"Is my car in the way?"

"Not to worry. Frank will take care of it."

Kelly went on to the guest room and began to unpack. In a moment, Frank and Liz appeared in the doorway of the guest room.

"Hi, Kelly, I'm glad you came over. Liz and I would have been worried about you. You should be fine here. Can I have your car keys to move you car? I'm going to put it inside the garage along with Liz's car. I'm going to pull my car up to the garage door so I can snow blow behind it when the storm is over."

"Thanks, Frank. You both are so kind. I do appreciate you having me over." Reaching into her purse, she located her keys and handed them to Frank.

"Great. I'll be right back."

"Have you called Tony yet?"

"No."

"Well, girl, what are you waiting for?

Chapter 47

The explosion from the plane crash was felt several miles away. The explosion rocked the Pushey house, which was less than three quarters of a mile away. At the Pushey house everyone was settled into the living room to watch the television game show, *Jeopardy*. They had just divided into teams. Lenny and Tony were set to compete against Mark and his father.

The three television game show contestants were just being introduced to the television viewing audience when Lenny noticed from out a north facing window, a flash of very bright light burst into the sky. Before he could say anything the concussion shock wave from the explosion shook the house. That was followed by a "boom" louder than the concussion explosions at a Fourth of July fireworks show.

"What the hell?" declared Tony.

"There's been an explosion, nearby, to the north. Just a second ago I saw a flash of light, out this window," said Lenny, nodding in the direction of the northeast-facing window.

Without their overcoats, they all quickly went out the front door onto the front porch. The porch faced northeast. From the porch they could clearly see a huge billowing fireball climbing into the nighttime sky.

"It looks like that's coming from the quarry," said Mark.

"I think you're right," said Tony.

"What do you think caused it?" asked Mark's father.

"No way of telling from here," said Mark.

In a moment, a sideways glance went around and everyone immediately headed back into the house to grab their coats. They were going "ambulance chasing."

Mark drove the car. As they pulled out of the driveway, they could already hear the Winooski Fire Department responding to the explosion with their three trucks. From a distance other sirens were heard, seemingly all headed to Winooski. Mark turned up Weaver Street and headed north past St. Francis Church on up the hill past the cemetery. At the very top of the hill they all could see a huge fire filling the night sky. There were even more explosions pushing the fire higher into the sky. There was no doubt now, whatever happened, it happened at the quarry. They took a right and came down to a stop light on Main Street. A police car and an ambulance flew by heading north on Main Street. A few hundred feet past where Mark was stopped, the police car and ambulance took a hard left hand turn and sped up the hill into the quarry. When the light turned green, Mark drove across Main Street and pulled into the parking lot of Winooski High School.

"Let's park here. We don't want to get in the way of the emergency people," said Mark.

"Good idea. It's only a short walk from here, anyway," said Lenny.

They all climbed out of the car and headed in the direction of the quarry. Right after they jogged across Main Street, several more emergency vehicles arrived and sped into the quarry property. One of the vehicles was a huge fire truck from the Burlington International Airport. It was labeled, BIA Emergency Service, with large black letters painted on its large white tank which also was labeled, "Fire Suppression Foam."

When they reached the crest of the hill leading into the quarry, they looked down onto a scene which resembled a movie set. There were several fires going on across the entire north side of the quarry.

The menagerie of television broadcast vehicles were all pushed together. Some were overturned, while others had their satellite dishes twisted out of shape. There were people running about everywhere. Smaller explosions boomed from across the quarry. The various fires lit up the scene and created a flicker effect. Several more vehicles pulled into the quarry. It was getting crowded. Behind them a couple of hundred onlookers somehow managed to enter the quarry with many more en route.

Rumors began to sweep through the gathering and growing crowd.

A state police car pulled to a stop in front of the crowd. Two officers got out of the car. The driver reached back into his car and withdrew a microphone. With a loud click it turned on.

"Ladies and Gentlemen, we have to ask you to please leave the area. Your presence will only hamper the work of emergency personnel. We are concerned for everyone's safety, so we're going to insist you leave. Now!"

There was a lot of grumbling from the crowd but in general people understood. Slowly they began to retreat back down the hill. Mark, his father, Lenny and Tony, left the quarry. They stopped, every few feet, to look back at the unfolding scene below.

They made it back to the car. Mark started up the car while his father turned on the radio, which was broadcasting the news of the huge explosion at the quarry they'd just left. The radio announcer reported, "This has just been handed to me. There is now a confirmed report, a Vermont Air National Guard F-16 Fighting Falcon crashed into the north side of the former Bremer Quarry located in the Town of Colchester. The F-16 had just taken off from the Burlington International Airport. We do not, I repeat, we do not have any word about the pilot. We do not know if he ejected from the aircraft before it crashed. We also do not have any information about any casualties on the ground. Our remote broadcast unit is on its way now to the crash scene. They will, I'm sure, be in touch with us as soon as they can. Meanwhile, I repeat, an F-16..."

Mark's father turned the radio off.

They arrived back home. They went into the house and Pokey jumped up to greet them. Mark took the dog for a short walk. Lenny went into the living room to turn on the television. Mark's father headed into the bathroom and Tony pulled out his cell phone to call his wife, Kelly.

The phone rang at his house in Ogden, Utah. After a couple of rings, a recorded message came on the line, "I'm sorry, the number you have dialed is not in working order at this time. Please hang up and try again." After a pause, the recorded message repeated. Tony hung up and redialed, figuring he must have misdialed the first time. The same recorded message greeted him as before.

"Damn."

"What's wrong?" asked Lenny.

"There's something wrong with the phone line between here and Utah. I'll try back later. Maybe it will have cleared up by then."

The local television channel had interrupted its normal programming to cover the important plane crash story. While the north side of the quarry was actually in the Town of Colchester, the newscaster referred to the crash scene as the former Bremer Quarry located on the north-west side of upper Main Street in Winooski.

Mark and his father joined Lenny and Tony in the living room. There was now live remote television broadcasting from the quarry. They were able to watch the coverage of the crash from the comfort of Mr. Pushey's living room.

Tony tried several more times to call his wife, Kelly. The recorded message was the only response he got. With each succeeding call Tony grew more frustrated and even more anxious.

* * * * *

The morning after Rudy Drew's burial, Tony and Lenny headed over to Mark's house. They went into the back yard and stepped into the tent. Karl was still asleep. Mark was not in the tent. Tony went over to Karl. He looked down at his sleeping friend and said,

"Who wants to kiss the sleeping princess and wake her from her eternal sleep?"

"Not me," said Lenny with a giggle.

"Well, I'll do it."

Tony leaned over and planted a wet kiss on Karl's forehead. Karl shot out of bed like a rocket. He furiously rubbed his forehead.

"What the hell was that?"

Tony and Lenny laughed uncontrollably as they fell to their knees holding their sides.

Just then Mark sauntered in and wondered what all the laughing was about. Upon hearing what happened Mark mockingly pretended he needed to throw up.

From inside the Pushey house, Mark's mother could hear the boys' merry laughter. She was pleased, as any mother would be, upon hearing her son and his friends enjoying themselves as only children can do.

After the laughter subsided, Karl spoke up, "We have to go back and see Mr. Germain. I think he can help us make a plan we can use to stop the monster. Remember, he told us to come back after he had a chance to think about helping us. Well, I know I have some questions now that I've had some time to think about what he told us before. I bet you guys have questions, too. What do you say?"

"I'm in," said Mark.

"Me, too," said Lenny.

"Sure," said Tony.

With that settled, they left the tent and headed back to Louis St. Germain's house.

They went straight to the back yard. There they found St. Germain feeding his horses.

"How are you doing?" asked Tony.

"I'm doing fine for an old man."

"That's good."

"Mr. St. Germain, we need to talk to you some more about you know who. Remember you told us to come back in a couple of days after you had a chance to think about things," said Lenny.

"You don't need to talk in code. If Ne Wha Ta wants to listen he will." St. Germain looked the four boys over. He reached out to Lenny and put his hand on Lenny's shoulder and said, "Like your friend, you, too, have lost your father. I'm sorry for you. You must now be strong for your family, eh?"

"Yeah," said Lenny.

"Okay," said Karl, "Look, we have some questions and we were hoping you'd have the answers we need."

"Humph."

St. Germain opened the paddock gate and stepped inside while holding a large bamboo rake. He began to rake clean the paddock. The boys all climbed up onto the paddock fencing to sit.

"Can Ne Wha Ta bleed?" asked Mark.

"Yes, he is after all still mostly human."

"Can he really be killed?" asked Tony.

"As I have spoken before, many have tried. It has been told that it has been done, but the stories are of long ago."

"That doesn't answer his question" said Karl.

"If he can bleed, then he can be killed."

"How come you haven't tried to kill him?" asked Karl.

"I am Sokoki Abenaki. I kill only to eat, and then only enough for my needs. I would kill if my life was threatened, but it is not."

"Why can't you help us kill this monster? After all, he has killed my father and many others," said Karl. He was clearly getting annoyed with St. Germain.

"Part of what I know about Ne Wha Ta is legend passed down to me by my father and his father before him, many times removed. It is said, Ne Wha Ta chooses those to help him mate, he chooses others to release him from his prison beneath the earth and it is also said only those that Ne Wha Ta chooses, those who he allows to get close to him, can kill him. Knowing this, Ne Wha Ta uses his powers to weaken those he chooses so they are not able to destroy him."

"You mean he chose us. How did he do that?" asked Mark.

"The four of you were trying to enter his world. I'm sure he examined your fitness to serve him and decided instead of eating you, he would use you for his purposes."

Mark jumped down from the paddock fence into the paddock area, which caused the horses to trot to the other side of the paddock. Mark appeared agitated as he said, "Now, wait a minute. You're saying he figured we were four suckers he could just order around. Is that it?"

St. Germain stopped raking the paddock for a moment. He looked at the four boys.

"Ne Wha Ta must figure four young boys could be frightened into doing what he wants. Look, anyone, even four men, could be frightened by this creature. It is what he does. He and his ancestors have been doing this for hundreds of years."

"All right. We can understand that, but does he ever leave that cave? I mean, couldn't we set a bear trap or maybe a hole with spikes in it?" said Tony.

"Yes, he can leave the cave. He's always been able to leave. But I doubt he would, except to seek food. Remember, because of the curse, Ne Wha Ta has become a creature of the darkness within the earth. He is uncomfortable being above ground. I doubt he would come out during the day. But at night, that's different."

St. Germain resumed his raking. He was nearly finished.

"What if we can get him to come outside? Then we could kill him," said Tony.

"How, dork? He's a friggin' monster, remember," said Mark.

"Well, if we can't kill him, can we trap him or maybe bury him back inside the cave so he'll leave us alone?" asked Lenny.

"Hey, that's it," said Karl, hopping down from the paddock fence. "What if we find a way to bury him in that cave? We might even get lucky and kill him at the same time!"

Tony jumped in with his own enthusiastic observation.

"Yeah, it's like putting the genie back in the bottle. You know, like we saw in that movie, the Seventh Voyage of Sinbad."

"Wait a second," interrupted Mark. "He just got done telling us the monster can get out of his cave any time he wants. That must mean he's got other exits. So, even if we close up one, he can still get us. We're still screwed."

Lenny asked their mentor Louis St. Germain, "Is Mark right?"

St. Germain didn't answer right away. First, he stepped out of the paddock, hitching the gate behind him. He put the rake inside the barn. In silence he walked over to his back porch and settled into his wooden chair. It creaked from his weight as he filled the chair.

The four boys looked at one another quizzically as they followed him to the porch. They each found a place to sit and waited for an answer.

"Well?" asked Lenny.

Finally, St. Germain spoke softly so the boys had to lean towards him to hear. "He believes you are weak. He is counting on you behaving like boys. If you behave like men, if you stand up to him and show no fear like a Sokoki Warrior, then and only then, will he leave you alone! Can you kill him? Maybe, but he must know your time for that is not right. Can he be driven back underground? It is the only question for which you have an answer!"

"So we might be able to drive him back into his hole. But if we can't kill him, won't he just keep on killing—maybe even finding some others to find him a mate?" asked Mark.

"He has chosen you, and only one of you can bring him a mate. That is how it is. Until you die, his choosing you has bound him to you in his efforts to mate and continue his kind."

The four boys sat back and let these words sink in. Their role in this struggle was ordained. They now knew the limits of this struggle. What were they going to do now?

Karl stood up and walked over to St. Germain, extending his hand to him. They shook hands. The other boys did the same.

"Thanks for all your help," said Lenny.

"Yeah, thanks," said Tony.

"Wait. Before you go, I have something for each of you."

St. Germain rose from his chair and headed into the house. He returned in an instant. He had four leather string necklaces with a small leather pouch hanging from each. He draped one around the neck of each boy.

Into each boy's right hand he placed a stone arrowhead.

"What are these for, Mr. St. Germain?" asked Lenny.

"The arrowhead is a symbol of a warrior. A warrior is always given a sacred arrowhead by his Sachem before heading out to do battle. It means the warrior carries with him the power of his village. The necklace carries a special potion. All my ancestors wore one of these. They were blessed by a Sokoki Medicine Man. Whoever wears them carries the spirit of my people, the spirit of many generations. These things I give you will not protect you from Ne Wha Ta. These gifts are only meant to bring you wisdom and courage to face your journey.

"Gee, thanks," said Lenny.

"Thanks, Mr. St. Germain. This is cool," said Tony.

Mark looked at his arrowhead, "Yeah, thanks."

Karl instead looked away, to the north, in the direction of the cave. "Mr. St. Germain?"

"Yes."

"We're going to need these, aren't we?"

"Yes."

"Thanks," said Karl, as he ran off to join his friends.

Chapter 48

The morning following the crash of the Vermont Air National Guard F-16 was filled with chaos. The U.S. Air Force and a number of other organizations and institutions, including the National Transportation Agency, each flew in their respective teams of specialized crash investigators. They immediately clashed with the FBI and other investigators who'd been engaged in the ongoing investigation of the human bones uncovered in the cave at the quarry. The crash of the F-16, the fire that followed and the collapse of the cave all contributed to a confusing overlap of bureaucracy that simply boggled the mind. By mid-morning various federal, state and local officials were in each other's faces and tempers were exploding everywhere.

Meanwhile, below the earth's surface, a few hundred feet from the disaster scene, Ne Wha Ta enjoyed the chaos and confusion he created. Humans were so controlled by their technology and their institutions that, at times, they became less human, often forgetting their instincts and senses. Their rising tension amused him.

Humans believed they grew more powerful with each succeeding generation. Their power came from their toys. They were wrong. They themselves were growing weaker. He, Ne Wha Ta, and his forefathers had proven, they and they alone grew stronger with each generation. He must not fail. His kind must continue to live and stalk humans for generations yet to come. Once boys, now men, the chosen ones must fulfill their destiny to bring him a suitable breeding mate. His seed would produce a Ne Wha Ta even more powerful than him, of this he was certain. It was his added curse he was without a Ne Wha Ta female to give him companionship. A human female would provide him something far more valuable—a child!

Ne Wha Ta now began to form a plan to bring this waiting game to an end.

* * * * *

Kelly Fredette picked up the phone on the end table in the living room and dialed the number for Tony. The phone line was nothing but static. She hit the automatic redial button and nothing changed. Still static.

"What's wrong, Kelly," asked Liz.

"I still can't reach Tony. The number I've been calling the past several days doesn't seem to work. It's all static."

"Why don't you try your cell phone?"

"I've tried but I can't get a signal!"

Kelly tried the cell phone once more. This time she got a recorded message that the number was out of service at this time.

"No luck. Damn it! This time there's a recording that says the phone number is temporarily out of service."

"Well, you can try later. With the storms we get around here in the winter, there's always some kind of interference with the phones, computers, and power."

Cody was sitting quietly on the couch with the two women, her little head turning to each person as they conversed with each other. Finally, when the adults paused in their conversation, little Cody saw her chance and spoke up.

"I don't know about you two, but I'm getting hungry."

Liz and Kelly looked at Cody and broke into huge smiles.

"All right, young lady. What do you suggest we have for dinner?" asked her mother.

Cody folded her small arms and held her right hand under her chin as if she were deep in thought, which of course she was.

"I've got it. Pizza!" Cody exclaimed with both arms fully extended.

"Okay, but we have to make it ourselves. No store bought pizza for us, right?" asked her mother.

"That's right, no store pizza. Can I help?"

"Of course you can help. After all, it was your idea," said her mother.

"Let's get started, Mommy. I'm really, really hungry," said Cody, pulling on her mother's arm.

Kelly and Liz each took one of Cody's hands and headed off into the kitchen to make homemade pizza.

Liz's husband, Frank, had settled himself in the den and turned on the television. As usual, he began to channel surf. From the kitchen came the sound of the three pizza chefs preparing "pizza surprise."

Frank finally settled on CNN. The day's news was covered and repeated on the half-hour. He decided to flip through a stack of sales catalogs, which were sitting on the coffee table. The catalogs were another habit of Frank's. He hadn't yet met a catalog he wasn't interested in.

The television newscaster deviated from the usual monotone delivery to announce a breaking story that just come in. At first Frank didn't give the television his full attention, until he heard the words, "Winooski, Vermont."

Frank thought for a moment, "Say, isn't that where Kelly's husband is?"

Using the television remote he turned up the volume.

"We are going live to our on the scene reporter, who will fill us in. We apologize for the report coming to you by phone, but apparently our on-the-ground affiliate's broadcast truck has sustained serious damage from this plane crash. Now we take you to Andrea Foley. Andrea, can you hear me?"

"Yes, I can, Bob."

Frank called into the kitchen, "Liz and Kelly, come quickly. There's something you've got to see."

Liz looked at Kelly and said, "It's probably some silly sports story like some guy winning money for shooting a basket from half court."

"It can't hurt. Let's go," said Kelly.

They wiped their hands on their aprons and Cody, watching every move they made did the same on the little apron her mother gave her to wear. They all hurried into the den.

"We have unconfirmed reports the pilot did not have time to eject. He'd apparently just taken off from nearby Burlington International Airport on a routine training mission when he apparently lost control of his aircraft. His F-16 crashed into the quarry wall about a thousand feet behind me," said the reporter as she looked, out of pure habit, towards the distant wall behind her position. "The crash scene is now illuminated by several still burning fires and an array of emergency spotlights panning across the crash scene."

"Andrea, isn't this the same quarry we've been covering in connection with a mysterious cave that was discovered there?"

"Yes, Bob. What you are referring to is a cave that quarry workers uncovered recently, which is reported to contain dozens of human remains. Federal, state and local police have been working down inside this quarry for the past several days since the discovery. Apparently the F-16 crashed into the top of the quarry wall just slightly to the east of the cave."

The reporter paused as she listened in her ear piece to an incoming report.

"I've just received a report which appears to indicate the cordoned area around the cave entrance has been destroyed and that the cave itself may have collapsed."

"Andrea?"

"Yes, Bob."

"What about casualties?"

"That's a good question. We've been trying to get some official word on that for the past several minutes. At the moment I can only tell you there are several ambulances here and as of yet, none of them have left although I should add that it's still early. We can see many people down below carefully looking through the enormous amount of debris."

"Thank you, Andrea. Ladies and Gentlemen, we've been listening to Andrea Foley speaking to us live from Winooski, Vermont, where apparently an Air Force F-16 crashed right after take off. We don't have confirmation as to the condition or the identity of the pilot. We also do not, as yet, have any word about any casualties on the ground. We will keep you informed about this breaking story as soon as more information becomes available."

Frank hit the television remote control mute button.

"Isn't that where Tony is?"

"Yes. He went to Winooski several days ago," said a worried Kelly.

"I'll bet that's why you haven't been able to reach him by phone. The crash must have knocked out the telephone system or something," said Liz.

An unconvinced Kelly nodded her agreement.

"Sure, a crash like that probably knocked down lines or sent some kind of magnetic wave from the explosion which screws up things like phones," said Frank.

"Mommy, are we going to make my pizza?" pleaded Cody, as she tugged at her mother's arm.

"Not now, honey. Kelly and Mommy want to watch this."

"No, it's okay. We can go and make pizza. Let's go," said a worried Kelly.

They left Frank to the television. When they turned to leave the room, he turned the volume back up and decided to watch the news for anything which could help Kelly know her husband was safe.

When Liz, Kelly and Cody reached the kitchen Liz said, "Kelly, why don't you try calling him again?"

"Thanks, I will."

This time Kelly used the kitchen wall phone and dialed Tony once more.

Static!

* * * * *

Mr. Pushey went to bed at around ten o'clock. The three guys sat in the kitchen. Tony was still trying to telephone his wife, Kelly, and was growing more concerned as the night wore on.

"Shit," said Tony as he flipped his phone closed.

He sat down at the table.

Mark spoke up. "I'll be right back."

He ran upstairs and in a moment he was back in the kitchen carrying a well worn paper bag. From the bag he pulled out a yellow faded thin rectangular box. It was the OUIJA board game.

"Jesus," said Tony.

"Where did you get this?" asked Lenny.

"C'mon, you know me. I never throw anything out."

Mark opened the board up and placed the OUIJA game piece on the board.

"Who wants to go first?" asked Mark.

"What do we want to ask it?" asked Lenny.

"I don't know, how about asking about a plan to deal with Ne Wha Ta?" said Mark.

"Let's do it," asserted Lenny.

Meanwhile, Tony was preoccupied about his inability to reach his wife.

Lenny and Mark sat across from one another. They reached out to the OUIJA game piece and gently placed the tips of their fingers from both of their hands onto the top of the piece.

"Is Ne Wha Ta listening right now?" asked Mark.

The piece began to move in a small circle. It moved over to the place on the board which was marked "no" and stopped.

"What do we need to kill Ne Wha Ta?" asked Lenny.

Again the piece moved in a small circle then it moved across the board stopping over the letters "G...U...N...S."

"It must have meant gun, like in shotgun. You know, the one we took from the cave," said Mark.

"Will we be successful in destroying this Ne Wha Ta?" asked Lenny.

The game piece quickly moved over the spot marked, "yes."

"Which one of us will destroy the monster?" asked Mark.

The piece moved over and stopped at the letters: ."..a...l...l."

Tony jumped in at this point. "Where's Kelly?"

The game piece spelled out the word, "s..n..o..w."

"Is she okay?"

The piece moved around then began to spell out the message, "n..e..e..d..s.....y..o..u."

"I asked if she's okay, damn it," said Tony, as he slammed his fist on the kitchen table.

"Let me ask a question. Is Kelly alive?" asked Mark.

Tony stared at the piece as it moved around the game board. The planchette stopped over the spot marked, "yes."

Tony got up from the table and headed into the living room "I can't take any more of this. Jesus we're communicating with a game board."

Mark looked at Lenny and said, "I've got another question."

"All right, let's hear it," said Lenny.

"After we destroy Ne Wha Ta, will Mark, Tony and Lenny still be together?"

The piece quickly moved over the board to the spot marked, "no."

From the living room, they heard Tony call out to them. "Come here."

They left the OUIJA game in the kitchen and hurried into the living room. The television was on.

"I decided to check out the 24 hour weather station since the OUIJA board said snow. Look!"

The weather newsman was describing a severe winter storm that was blanketing Utah. It was reported as having the potential to become the storm of the century as far as Utah was concerned.

"He said this storm had already dumped over thirty inches of snow over northern Utah. It's still snowing with wind causing drifts approaching twenty feet high," said a nervous Tony.

"I had no idea," said Lenny.

"Jesus, I've got to go back. My wife is alone, I just know it.

She's pregnant and she needs me and where am I? Here, when I should be with her."

"Look, Tony, let's try and figure this out. What about friends? Could she be with friends?"

"I don't know. I can't get a call through."

"Tony, you can't leave now. Don't you see that is just what he wants you to do," pleaded Mark.

"Mark, remember I told you he threatened my wife and baby? What do you want me to do? I've got to know she's okay."

"How about getting in touch with Chief Contois? I know he'd help. Maybe he can get a message to the authorities out in Utah. They could check in on Kelly. Tony, it's worth a try," said Lenny.

"How do we reach the Chief? He's probably all tied up with that plane crash?"

Lenny looked Tony straight in the eye and said, "I know how."

He went into the kitchen and after a moment returned with the phone book.

"Who are you going to call?" asked Tony.

"Not me, you're going to call," said Lenny.

"Who am I calling?"

"You're calling the Chief's wife."

Several minutes later Tony hung up the phone.

"She understands how I feel. She said she will page him and when he calls in, she'll get him to call me."

Mark replied, "That's great. Now all we have to do ....."

The phone rang. Tony answered it. To his surprise, it was Chief Contois on the line. That was quicker than he could have hoped. Tony explained his fear for his wife's safety. The conversation went on for a couple of minutes and then Tony hung up.

Mark and Lenny waited in the kitchen for him to report on his conversation with the Chief.

"Well?" queried Lenny.

"I gave him my Utah address, phone number and cell phone number. I apologized for bothering him. He said it was fine. He didn't have very much to do right now since there seemed to be an army of experts swarming and battling over the crash scene."

"He asked for the names of the neighbors and one or two friends. I could only remember two friends. Her biking buddy Julie and her shopping buddy Liz. He said he'll get in touch with the authorities out in Utah and that he's sure they'll check it out for me. I also gave him this number to have them call here if they can locate her."

"So for now, all we have to do is wait!" declared Mark.

Chapter 49

After leaving Louis St. Germain, the boys stopped at the sidewalk in front of his house.

"I've got an idea. Follow me," said Karl.

The four boys walked the short distance to the entrance to Bremer's Quarry. Heading into the quarry property was a light gray stone dust road. There were several grooves in its hard surface. Every five minutes or so a huge dump truck carrying six cubic yards or more of crushed stone left the quarry, slowly coming down the steep hill with its air brakes hissing all the way down to Main Street. Soon another empty truck slowly climbed the steep hill for a refill.

Beneath the stone Bremer Quarry sign was a small metal sign which indicated trespassing was forbidden and violators would be prosecuted. The boys followed Karl, who was already walking up the hill. When the boys reached the top of the hill, Karl stopped as he took in the site of the huge quarry. It had sheer rock walls climbing in places to over a hundred and eighty feet from the floor of the quarry. Near where they stood were numerous piles of crushed stone reaching over fifty feet high. Each pile represented different size stones ranging from pea size all the way up to softball size. At the center of this sprawling facility, standing on metal stilts, stood a huge, stone-crushing machine. It was at least forty feet high. It had a huge hopper at its top. Leading up to it was a ramp that led to a platform suspended out over the hopper. From the floor of the quarry, assorted rock pieces were loaded into dump trucks by a large diesel shovel that sat at the bottom of the quarry floor. The stone it loaded into the dump trucks was destined for the hopper at the top of the stone crusher.

One by one, dump trucks would back up the ramp and onto the platform. From there they would lift and dump their load into the hopper. Then the truck would drive off the ramp and another would immediately take its place. The stone crusher made a huge noise as it crushed its load into the desired sized stone pieces. From the base of the hopper there was a huge conveyor belt that carried the crushed stone out to the assembled piles of stone. There the conveyor deposited its load to the top of the pile in an endless stream of stone.

Shouting to be heard, Tony asked Karl, "Why are we here?"

"I'm looking for Mr. Mackenzie."

"Why?"

"Cause he has something we're going to need!"

Also shouting, Lenny asked, "What's that?"

"We need some dynamite!"

The other boys all looked at each other with a sense of bewilderment.

"Over there," Karl said, as he pointed towards the familiar pickup truck of "Bud" Mackenzie.

Karl gestured for the others to follow him as they headed off to find Bud Mackenzie.

They soon located him. He was carrying a box clearly marked 'dynamite' on its side. He lifted it into the back of his pickup truck. He noticed the boys heading his way. He removed his Bremer Quarry hat and used a blue handkerchief to wipe the perspiration from his forehead.

"Hey, boys, what are you doing here?"

"We needed to talk to you," shouted Karl.

Pointing to his ears, Bud gestured that he hadn't heard Karl.

"We need to talk to you," shouted Karl once more.

"Okay. Look I get a break in ten minutes. You boys wait over by that trailer and I'll be right back. If anyone asks what you're doing here just tell them you're friends of mine and I said you could wait next to the trailer."

"Great, thanks," shouted Karl.

Karl and the boys walked over to the trailer and sat on the ground in the shade of the trailer. They watched as Bud loaded another case of dynamite into the back of his truck. He climbed inside, turned the truck around and drove away. The boys could see his truck driving along the top of the quarry's wall. It kicked up a dust trail as he went. He stopped the truck at a spot along the quarry wall directly above the diesel shovel busily working from its place on the quarry floor. Bud got out of his truck and emptied several boxes from the back, which he placed on the ground. After this was done, he climbed back inside his truck and backed it up so for a moment it was invisible from where the boys sat. It soon reappeared as he retraced his route back down inside the quarry and came to a stop next to the trailer. Dust filled the air in a cloud which surrounded the stopped truck. Bud got out of his truck and gestured to the boys to follow him inside the trailer. Just as they were about to enter a huge whistle went off. In a matter of moments, all sounds stopped inside the quarry as all machinery ceased to operate, except for the now idling diesel motors of the assorted heavy equipment.

"What happened?" asked Mark, this time without shouting.

"It's break time. It's a fifteen minute break. We get two a day. We have one in the morning and one in the afternoon. Since we work with some pretty dangerous things, we need the breaks to make sure we can maintain our sharpness on the job. Come on inside."

The four boys followed him inside the trailer. It was cool inside the air conditioned trailer. There were two other men inside. Bud introduced the men to the boys. He told the boys they were construction engineers. Since Bud only remembered Karl's name he introduced him and Karl introduced the other boys. The four boys sat on the gray metal folding chairs placed around a folding table while Bud pulled up a chair for himself.

"So, you said you wanted to talk to me. Here's your chance. What's on your mind?"

Karl began. "We've been exploring a cave near here."

The other boys had no idea where Karl was going with this, so they just sat and listened.

Bud nodded.

"Yeah, it's kind of a small cave with some kind of opening way in the back which seems to lead to another larger cave. Anyway, we were checking this cave out and we were wondering if you guys find caves when you're blasting here at the quarry?"

"Sure, we find caves, or sometimes tunnels. We really don't have any time for spelunking."

"What's that?"

"That's the name for someone who likes to explore caves. You see, when we dynamite around here, we loosen up the rock for the machinery. Any caves we might open up would be too dangerous to climb into. The rock walls, after they have been dynamited, sometimes have a delayed reaction. The rock has been fractured by the explosives I've placed into the holes we drill. Sometimes when we move a piece of the wall from below, after the wall's been fractured, a whole section will come crashing down. It's dangerous work. Right guys?" said Bud to his co-workers at the other end of the trailer.

"Whatever you say, Bud," one shouted back.

"You boys really shouldn't be exploring any caves anywhere near this quarry. The underground shock waves from our dynamiting often travel several hundred feet and could easily destabilize a small cave. It could cause it to collapse."

"Really!" declared Lenny

"Oh, yeah, easily!" replied Bud.

"How can there even be caves? It looks like that rock outside is pretty solid," said Mark.

"That's easy. The sub-surface geology is remarkably uneven. It has numerous layers of stone all formed at different times over millions of years. These layers are made up of material that also differs in composition. Some layers are harder than others. When water works its way through these layers it softens and carves out caves in the softer material. Hey, I'll bet you guys didn't know that back in the times of the dinosaurs, this part of the country was under hundreds of feet of water."

Tony spoke up. "That's a lot of water. Where did it all go?"

"Well, some of it receded as it became part of the polar ice caps. Quite a bit of it just worked its way down through the layers of rock. Then a whole lot of it went deep inside the earth beneath where we now live when this area was hit by a huge earthquake nearly 20 million years ago. That earthquake opened up huge cracks in the rock layers and a lot of water simply drained down inside the earth's crust. Some geologists think about a mile or so below where we are now sitting there's a lake of water which is several times the size of Lake Champlain.

"Wow," said Tony.

"Thanks. We've got to get going now," said Karl as he pushed himself away from the table.

"Don't mention it." Bud got up from his seat and looked at his watch. "Wait a minute," he said.

He went over to a cabinet and pulled open a drawer. He removed some things and came back over to the boys, who were still sitting at the table.

"Here, you guys can each have one," said Bud as he placed four pieces of stone on the table.

Tony picked up one of the pieces and examined it for a moment. "What are these lines? They kind of look like a drawing or something."

"Sort of! Those lines are the fossil imprints of a trilobite. It's one of the earliest creatures to leave a fossilized imprint. Those fossils are the trace remains of trilobites which existed in the ocean which covered this land over 200 million years ago."

"Gee, thanks," said Tony.

The other boys quickly chimed in with their own thank you as well.

Outside, a horn blasted again signaling to everyone the break was over. In just a moment the clatter of quarry machinery filled the air.

"You boys have to leave now and don't go wandering around. Please head straight back out the quarry road. And watch out for the trucks."

"We will. Thank you," said Karl.

"Oh, and stay out of caves, especially any of the caves that are near this place. A cave can be a dangerous place, especially if you don't know what you are doing."

"We know," said Karl.

Bud held the trailer door open and watched as the boys left. He continued to look on as they walked up the quarry road. They walked to the side of the road so as to not be in the way of the trucks. He could see the boys passing the fossils back and forth.

"You know those boys?" asked one of the guys from the inside of the trailer.

"Yeah, two of them lost their fathers this summer."

"They die?" asked one man.

"Yup, both are dead and buried," declared Bud.

"Now that's a shame."

"Sure is."

* * * * *

While the boys were at the quarry, St. Germain drove off in his old Ford 150 pickup truck. He drove north on Main Street past Bremer Quarry. He took the same left turn as earlier when he took the boys to the Winooski water tank. He pulled his truck to a stop in the shadow of the water tank. He slowly climbed up the tank's ladder to the roof of the tank. Just as before, he carefully climbed across the sloped roof to the flat center of the tank's top. At the very center was a hatch that when opened, allowed one to get inside the tank. Once a year a State of Vermont water quality engineer from the state's Office of Public Water Safety would enter the hatch and examine the inside of the water tank for evidence of corrosion or any other matter that could affect the safety of the municipal water delivery system. The inspection seal was still attached to the hatch's locked latch.

St. Germain sat next to the hatch and slowly looked around the Champlain Valley which stretched out before his view. He remembered the many stories his mother and father told him when he was a young boy. He remembered his grandfather and grandmother and the words of wisdom spoken to him in the tongue of his people. For the next several minutes he mentally reviewed his entire extended family. He was the last of his band, the last Sokoki of the Winooski River Valley, the last Sokoki who was a direct descendant of the great Sachem White Cloud. These memories brought him much sadness. His eyes welled up with tears.

He reached into his pants pocket and pulled out an arrowhead and a small leather pouch on a leather string just like the ones he gave the boys.

Louis St. Germain stood up and spread his arms wide. In one hand he held the arrowhead. In the other hand he held the small leather pouch. He first faced the South, then, he turned and faced the North. After pausing, he turned and faced the East and then finally he turned and faced the West. Now facing due west he began a soft chant. He was praying to his ancestors and to the great Sachems throughout all time to protect the young boys.

He prayed for them to have courage and he prayed their great struggle would end in success.

The pastel blue sky was filled with numerous billowy clouds. His shadow reached out from where he stood and rippled across the water tank's hatch cover. As time passed, the sun was occasionally obscured by one of the many clouds that dotted the sky. St. Germain could feel the warm sun, and the light summer breeze that gently tossed his hair about.

He was certain his prayers would be heard. St. Germain's arms began to feel weary. The sun brought on a slight headache. He put the arrowhead and medicine pouch back into his pocket. He enjoyed coming up here. He liked the solitude and the view. He was pleased he brought the boys up here. They needed to know and understand the majesty of the land his people called their home for many, many generations. The power of the medicine he had given them could only be enhanced by their appreciation of his people and their struggles with the Ne Wha Ta.

He was about to leave, when he heard a sound that immediately gripped him in fear.

"Caw...Caw."

He used his peripheral vision to check the area. High in a tall pine tree to his right sat a black crow. He was enormous even as crows go. He was looking right at St. Germain. The crow ruffled his wings.

"Caw...Caw."

This sound came from directly in front of him. He once again tried to not look directly at the crow. This one was also sitting in the top of a very tall pine tree.

"Caw...Caw...Caw."

Yet more crow calls came from several directions. He now stood straight and looked at the tree tops of the numerous trees that surrounded the water tank. The trees were full of large black crows.

He heard a flapping of wings. He ducked down just in time as a large crow missed his head and landed on top of the water tank's sealed hatch. This crow turned, upon landing, and cocked its neck to the right and then the left as it looked St. Germain over.

St. Germain tried to shoo the bird away but it would not budge. He didn't like this one bit. He decided he needed to get down off the water tank and the sooner the better. He turned his back on the crow sitting on the tank's hatch and began to set his sights on locating the ladder. He spied the top of the ladder now only forty feet away. Before he could even take a step towards it, however, he heard the beating of wings near his head. In a moment he was being attacked by several crows. They pecked at his ears, his checks, his forehead and the top of his head. He tried swatting them away but each time he struck a crow a disabling blow another would fly into this battle and take the other's place. In less than a minute he was bleeding from several wounds to his head and face.

"Caw...Caw," screeched the crows sitting in the tree tops. There were now more than a hundred gathered and yet still others were flying in and joining their voices in a rising chorus.

St. Germain was engaged in fighting off at least a dozen crows. One of them managed to peck at St. Germain's left eye. In that brief instant, his eye was plucked out of its socket. The triumphant crow flew away with its trophy.

"Caw...Caw..Caw."

St. Germain was brought to his knees as he cried out in pain. "I, a Sokoki warrior, call upon my ancestors to drive you away!"

The birds continued their attack. It was just a matter of a moments before he lost his right eye to the attacking crows.

At that moment, the birds suddenly pulled back from their attack. Most returned to the nearby tree tops while others sat on the hatch cover.

St. Germain decided right then he wasn't going to die on his knees. He knew who was behind this attack—Ne Wha Ta.

At the top of his lungs, he cried out. "Ne Wha Ta, you are a coward. You could not face me like a man. You need these birds to do the fighting for you. Ne Wha Ta, you will not have your way. You will die, Ne Wha Ta!"

St. Germain knew the birds were still around even though the only sound he could hear was the sound of the breeze in the trees. His face and head were streaked with the freshly stained lines of his own glistening blood. As if on cue about twenty crows took flight and headed straight for St. Germain's head and face. The others in the nearby trees joined in an enthusiastic cheering concert of competing "Caws."

The attacking birds succeeded in getting St. Germain to begin to back up. Without his sight he was helpless. He was now less than ten feet from the edge of the water tank. He was not even close to the ladder that might have led him safely down from the water tank. At five feet from the edge, he was still slowly backpedaling. The birds were relentless in their attack.

He felt his right foot slip off the edge of the water tank. St. Germain now lost his balance and fell backwards off the water tank. Silently he fell towards the ground. He crashed into the windshield of his own truck. Mercifully the glass cut his carotid artery as his upper body plunged through. In a brief moment, he was dead. His legs stuck out of the windshield. All the crows in the overhead trees immediately took flight and silently slipped away deep into the surrounding woods, to wait and watch.

Chapter 50

At the top of the quarry road, Karl turned to the others and said, "I've got another idea, but first we need to get a couple of things."

"What things?" asked Lenny.

"What idea?" asked Mark.

"You'll see," said Karl.

Tony was paying little attention to the conversation. He was looking back at the quarry. He was amazed at the sheer size of everything here. It seemed everything here was huge. He stuck a familiar finger up his nose as he continued to survey the scene.

"Hey, Tony, c'mon," said Mark.

The boys headed down the quarry road and turned right onto Main Street. About a half an hour later they were back at Mark's house. Mark's mom made a heaping plate of peanut butter and jelly sandwiches, served with cherry Kool Aid, and slices of fresh cantaloupe.

The boys ate heartily. After lunch Karl asked Mark if he could locate a pair of wire cutters and some electrical tape.

"I think so. I'll go check my father's work bench in the basement. I'll be right back."

In a moment he returned with the two items.

"What are you going to need these things for?" asked Mark.

"I don't want to tell you guys, yet. You're going to have to trust me, okay?"

"So, what happens now?" asked Lenny.

"We have to go back to the quarry."

"What for?" asked Lenny.

"You'll see."

"Well, let's go," said Mark.

With Karl leading the way, the four boys headed off to the quarry. This time, Karl turned to the south side of the quarry. He led them up North Street. At the dead-end of upper North Street he and the other boys traveled up the side of a small hill. After crossing under an old barbed wire fence they moved northward through some tall grass to another fence. Beyond this second fence was a dirt road which circled the upper perimeter of Bremer's Quarry. Instead of crossing under the second fence onto quarry property Karl chose to follow the perimeter by staying just outside the fence.

After they'd traveled a couple hundred yards, Karl motioned for the boys to get down in the tall grass. He gestured for them to stay put and to keep quiet. Tony, Mark and Lenny sat down as Karl went on ahead. He crept low as he moved along the fence. He stopped and seemed to be watching something just across the fence. From where the boys sat, they could hear the many sounds of the quarry, which was just beyond the other side of the fence.

About fifteen minutes passed before Karl crept back to his friends' location.

"Tony, what time do you have?" asked Karl.

Looking at his wristwatch, Tony responded, "It's about ten minutes before two."

"Great, we're just in time."

"In time for what?" asked Mark.

"We're in time to try and steal some dynamite," he said with a sense of firmness.

"What are we going to do with dynamite?" asked Lenny.

"I think I know," said Mark. "You want dynamite to try and blow up the monster's cave, right?"

"Close," said Karl. He looked around as if he were checking to see if anyone else could be listening. "I want to crush him inside it."

"How are we supposed to do that?"

"I don't know yet. But look, remember what Mr. Mackenzie told us this morning about how unstable the rock is around here? Didn't he say any cave near the quarry could collapse from a dynamite explosion? Well?"

"I see. We use some dynamite to get the cave to crush the monster. But how are we going to get him to be in the cave when we dynamite it?" asked Mark.

"I haven't figured that part out yet."

"Do you know how to use dynamite?" asked Tony.

"Yeah, when did you learn how to use dynamite?" asked a skeptical Lenny.

"Just now, I was watching Mr. Mackenzie set up some dynamite in holes that were drilled into the rock. I think I got it figured out."

"So, how are we going to get this dynamite?" asked Tony.

"Easy. In a few minutes the quarry will have its afternoon break. If he leaves and goes back down to the trailer we can sneak inside the quarry and steal some of his dynamite. I think I've figured out a way to take a couple of sticks without him knowing any are missing. Just get ready to follow me."

The four boys crept along the fence and waited in the tall grass just outside the boundary of the quarry. Almost on cue, the quarry horn blasted out its one long blast signaling the beginning of the afternoon break. Bud Mackenzie stopped his work and made sure he hadn't left any sticks of dynamite lying out on top of the ground. In a moment he backed up his pickup truck and turned it around. He headed down the perimeter road to the engineer's trailer.

When the truck was out of sight, Karl slipped under the barbed wire fence and crept along the ground to an area where there were several holes drilled into the rock. Protruding from each hole were two wires—one white wire and the other was a black wire. The other boys also slipped under the fence and crept forward and joined Karl.

Karl gently pulled on a pair of wires coming out of a hole to his right. The wires would not budge. He moved to another hole and tried again. The results were the same. He tried two more holes with the same results. Finally on the next hole he was successful. He pulled and pulled until there was at least twenty feet of wire lying on the ground. At the end of the wires he extracted from the hole, were two sticks of dynamite taped together. He pulled out his wire cutters and cut the wire several feet back from the dynamite. He taped the ends of the wire with the electrical tape they'd brought along.

"Here, take this back under the fence and don't touch the wires together," he said to Lenny.

Lenny froze and didn't respond at first.

"Lenny, we haven't got a whole lot of time, so move your ass."

"Tony, bring me that long piece of rock over there and several smaller ones, too. Mark, check the other holes and see if you can pull out another couple sticks of dynamite."

Tony retrieved the pieces of rock. Karl used a piece of electrical tape to tape up the cut ends of the two wires. Next he taped a piece of rock to the end of the wires and stuffed it back down the hole. He dropped a handful of other rocks down the hole as well. He tugged on the wires and found the rocks were now firmly wedged in place.

Mark motioned to Karl. He had located another pair of dynamite sticks. Karl crept over to Mark and repeated the process. In a couple of minutes they were all back under the fence and moving away from the quarry with the stolen dynamite in tow. Karl wrapped the loose wires around each pair of dynamite sticks. He put each pair inside a small brown lunch bag and both bags were placed inside another larger grocery bag.

Before they reached North Street, they stopped and sat under a wild crab apple tree. Each boy picked a couple of small green apples. While the bitterness of the apples was expected, it nevertheless didn't prevent the eye-watering pucker they each experienced with the first bite.

"So, now what?" asked Mark.

"Well, I figure we're going to need some more wire and some kind of battery to connect to the wires and .....,"

"That's not what I meant."

"What?"

"What's your plan?"

"I told you, I haven't figured that part out yet. Look, with this dynamite, we've got a chance of crushing that bastard. Does anybody have a better weapon?"

"So, we've got some dynamite. Now we need a plan so dynamite can do what you say. We need to get going before he figures out what we might do. You know how he can get into our heads and shit, right?" said Lenny.

"Okay, so let's head over to Mark's and work on a plan and get anything else we might need," said Karl.

"Wait a minute. You're going to bring that dynamite over to my house. What are you, nuts? What if it accidentally blows up or something? Jesus!" protested Mark.

"What do you want us to do? We've got to hide it somewhere. We only need to hide it for maybe a day or two. We can hide it behind the garage," said Karl.

"Yeah, if it was going to explode it would have blown up by now," said Lenny with a forced tone of certainty.

"All right, I guess it'll be okay, but I'm not going to carry it," said Mark.

"Don't worry. Tony's going to carry the dynamite," said Karl.

"What?" exclaimed Tony. "No way! I say we do odds and even, on three, one, two, three!

In a moment, after a couple of rounds of odds and even, Tony lost. He became the designated porter for the stolen dynamite after all. So for now, he picked up the paper bag and followed along as the boys proceeded back to Mark's back yard tent.

Meanwhile, back at the quarry the afternoon break was over and Bud Mackenzie returned in his pickup truck. He was unaware someone had removed four sticks of dynamite and rewired his charges. The rewiring would later prove to be inadequate when the charges would be detonated. Only half of the charges Bud Mackenzie planted would explode.

* * * * *

It was two-thirty in the morning and the storm had not lessened yet in intensity. Everyone was asleep at the home of Liz and Frank Hawley. In a light sleep Liz heard a banging sound. She quickly sat up in bed.

"Bang, bang, bang."

She leaned over and shook her husband awake. "Frank, there's someone at the front door."

"Liz, you're dreaming. No one would be outside at this hour in this storm..."

"Bang, bang, bang."

Liz and Frank hurriedly hopped out of bed. After grabbing their robes, they shuffled down the hallway toward the front of the house. A hallway light went on. Standing in the doorway of her bedroom was Kelly.

"What's going on?"

"Someone's at the front door," said Liz.

The three of them arrived at the front door and Frank unlocked the door as the two women stood behind him pulling their robes tight around themselves.

The winter storm's wind elected to gust at that moment and the door blew wide open. Frank caught it before it slammed against the wall. Standing in the open doorway was a tall figure. He was silhouetted by headlights from his vehicle which was parked in the driveway with its lights on. The snow swirled about and flew into the foyer.

"Sorry to bother you folks at this hour," said the shadowy figure. "I'm Officer Casey. Is this the Hawley residence?"

"Yes, it is officer. Please come in," said Frank Hawley.

The officer entered. Frank closed the door behind him. Liz meanwhile had turned on the foyer lights and the lights in the living room.

"Is something wrong, officer?" asked Liz.

"I'm trying to locate a Mrs. Kelly Fredette. Would either of you have any idea where she is?"

With those words Kelly's stomach immediately tightened into a knot from dread. Her mind was suddenly filled with ominous images about her husband Tony. It just had to be bad news. Since she was unable to reach Tony, she had a growing fear something dreadful had happened to him.

Haltingly she spoke up. "I'm....ah.., Mrs. Fredette."

"We've been asked to locate you by local law enforcement authorities in Winooski, Vermont. I've been instructed to assist you in getting a call through to your husband. If you don't mind I have a portable emergency telephone in my truck. I'll be back in a moment and we can place that call. Now if you'll excuse me."

With a nod he went out the front door and headed to his truck.

"Boy, Tony must have some pull," said Frank.

"I think it's romantic," said Liz.

"Oh, yeah, well, you ask that young police officer when he comes back if he thinks risking his life on a night like this is romantic?" said Frank.

"No, no you're right," said Kelly. "Tony must really need to speak to me."

The front door opened and with it came a blast of frigid air and another dusting of wind-driven snow. The officer was carrying a briefcase-sized bag that he placed on the foyer chair. He unzipped the bag and opened it to reveal the field phone inside. He turned a switch to the on position and a number of dials lit up with their yellowish glow. He lifted the phone- like receiver and spoke into it.

"Base, this is Mobile Four. I repeat. Base this is Mobile Four. Do you copy?"

They could only hear his side of the conversation.

"I've located the subject, Mrs. Fredette."

Liz elbowed her friend, "Now you're a subject."

"Yes, she's ready for the call. I'll hold." He put his free hand over the phone microphone and said, "It should only take a couple of minutes."

"Can I make you a cup of coffee, officer?" asked Liz.

"Thanks, ma'am. That would be great."

"Have you been searching for me for long?"

"Yes, ma'am. We've been trying to locate you and a few others due to family emergencies for the past few hours. Whenever the land line phones and cell phones go out we get a few wellness check-up calls. That's what we call them. It's no problem. We're glad to help, after all, its part of our job. Wait a minute," he listened now to the phone handset.

Kelly's hands were sweating.

"We've got your husband on the line, Mrs. Fredette. Here he is," said the officer as he handed her the phone handset.

"Hello, Tony. Is that you? I'm fine, really. I know the phones are all out."

The conversation continued as Frank, Liz and the police officer headed into the kitchen to allow Kelly some privacy. Liz handed the officer a hot cup of coffee, which he gladly accepted.

"I heated it in the microwave," said Liz.

"That's okay, as long as it's black and hot."

"How bad is this storm?" asked Frank.

"Well, if it continues as they're now saying, we could be looking at least at another twenty four hours and another twenty to maybe thirty inches of snow. I'd say that most things around here will be closed for a few days."

"So how are you able to get around in your truck?" asked Liz.

"I call it a truck but it's really an arctic cat machine. Just like the ones you see up at the ski areas. We break them out in weather like this. It's really the only way to get around."

"Do you have family?" asked Liz.

"Yeah, a wife and twin daughters. They're two years old."

Kelly was still talking to Tony. The officer was eager to get home himself. He finished the coffee and now that he had completed this last assignment, he would be free to go home.

After a few minutes Kelly came into the kitchen to join the others.

"Everything okay, Mrs. Fredette?" asked the officer.

"Yes, and my husband and I both wish to thank you and the other officers very much. We're both humbled and grateful you'd make such an extraordinary effort to help us out during this terrible storm."

"No problem. I know I'd want help to find my wife and family to make sure they were safe, especially if she was pregnant. Well, I've got to go so you folks take care and just wait out this storm. Don't go and try to drive around in this weather. If something does happen and you folks need to get to the hospital to deliver that baby, just contact the police station. Local phones are working. We'll get someone out here real quick to transport you safely to the hospital."

With that he headed to the front door and left after handshakes and thanks all around. They watched as the officer maneuvered his arctic cat out of the driveway and back onto the road.

Suddenly a small voice was heard from behind them.

"Mommy, what's going on?" said Cody, as she rubbed her eyes with fisted hands.

Chapter 51

Mark put the bag with the dynamite inside an old pillowcase he brought from the house. He tied the pillowcase end into a knot. He hung the pillowcase on a nail on the back inside wall of his garage. It was dark in that corner of the garage and the old pillowcase hanging against the wall didn't seem too out of place considering all the other things hanging along the back wall.

"There, that should do it for now," said Mark.

"Yeah, putting it in here is better than outside where it could get wet," affirmed Karl.

The four boys headed into the back yard tent.

Karl spoke up. "We still need more wire and we also need a battery to connect to the wire."

"I think I can come up with the wire," said Tony. "My dad has a couple of rolls of wire which looks just like the wire hooked up to the dynamite. He uses it to fix electrical stuff."

"Do you think you could get a couple hundred feet of it?"

"You mean to keep?"

"Of course, to keep. What else did you think I meant?"

"I don't know. I'm sure he'd miss that much wire!"

"Look, how about after we set off the dynamite, we roll up what wire is left and you can put it back? We probably won't lose that much with the explosion."

With that explanation Tony felt much better.

"I guess that's okay."

"Now, what could we use for a battery?" asked Karl.

"How about a car battery?" asked Lenny.

"Too big to move around," responded Karl.

"What if we tape a bunch of batteries together?" asked Mark.

"I don't know if that will work," said Karl.

"What about a car battery from a small car?" asked Tony.

Lenny and Mark laughed at Tony's suggestion.

Karl didn't laugh. Maybe, just maybe, his suggestion could work.

"I think Tony is right!"

Lenny and Mark looked at Karl, and then, with jaws wide open, they glanced over at Tony, who now proudly displayed a big, shit-eating grin.

"Let's go over to Eddie's Garage on Main Street. See if he has a used battery from maybe a Volkswagen. That ought to do it!" said Karl."

"When?" asked Lenny.

"Right now. Tony, you go and get your dad's wire and meet us back here. Lenny, you and Mark come with me. We're going to see if we can get a car battery, real cheap."

The four boys broke up and headed off on their respective missions.

Ten minutes later Lenny, Mark and Karl were standing outside Eddie's Amoco Auto Service Center. As cars entered or exited the gas station a familiar "ding, ding" sound could be heard. A young boy with blond facial fuzz moved from car to car pumping gas, checking the oil and washing the windshield of each customer's car that pulled into the station to purchase gasoline. He was wearing gray, pin striped overalls with a red and white Amoco patch over the top left shirt pocket.

The distinctive smell of gasoline lingered in the air.

The blond haired boy gave the boys a hostile glance.

Karl turned his back to the gasoline pumps. "I'll go inside and talk to the owner. You guys wait here."

Karl strolled past the blond haired boy, who tried his best to not acknowledge Karl. The boy was very skinny, and the overalls appeared to be way too big for him.

Lenny and Mark stood on the sidewalk and waited as Karl indicated. They could see inside the station's office window. Karl was talking to a huge, bearded man. The man wore faded, dark green coveralls. The man wiped his hands with a rag which at one time may have been white. All the while the conversation continued, the man wiped his hands. Karl gestured over his shoulder to the outside. The man nodded and then he shouted out the front door in the direction of the boy who was busy pumping gas into a badly dented aqua-colored Ford Fairlane. The car had seen better days.

"Bobby, hey, Bobby, after you're done with that fill-up, I want you to git somethin' for me," said the huge, hand-wiping man.

In a few moments, the boy finished with his Ford customer. He strolled slowly into the station office. He received some obvious instructions from the huge man because he went inside the garage area and then reappeared carrying a wrench as he went out the far side of the garage around the corner to the station's back yard. The huge man handed a small wooden box to Karl.

The phone must have rung because the huge man could now be seen speaking into a phone as Karl stood nearby. After a couple of minutes, the boy stepped around the far corner of the garage returning from the rear yard. He was carrying a small car battery. He went straight to the station's office where the huge man holding the phone with both hands nodded towards Karl. The boy put the battery inside the wooden box Karl was holding. Karl gave a nod to the huge man, who waved in return. Karl stepped out of the office carrying one used Volkswagen car battery inside a small wooden box.

His two friends ran over to join him. As they walked away with the battery, the station's bell rang, "ding, ding!"

The blond haired boy pulled a heavily-stained rag from his back pocket and wiped his hands as he approached a two toned Chrysler Desoto.

"Fill'er up?" he inquired with a slight smile.

Meanwhile, about a mile north of the gas station, high upon a hill overlooking the Bremer's Quarry next to Winooski's Water tank, sat Louis St. Germain's pickup truck. Sticking out of the truck's windshield were the legs of St. Germain, who had died a few hours earlier. The temperature was ninety two in the sun and in the upper eighties in the shade. Two crows moved across the truck's hood. Their feet scratched the surface as the big, coal-black birds tried to steady themselves. They were picking at the flesh of the two legs which protruded through the windshield. One pulled free a large piece of flesh, then it flew away into one of the nearby tall pine trees. Another crow flew out of a nearby pine tree and skidded to a stop on the truck's hood. This bird also pecked away at St. Germain's flesh. The eager, hungry, scavenger crows had already reached and exposed bone.

Dozens of small silvery colored flies buzzed everywhere.

A solitary crow flew down out of a nearby pine tree. He landed on the driver door's edge since the window was rolled down. He cocked his head first to the right then to the left as he surveyed the inside of the truck. He hopped down inside and began to peck at the face of St. Germain.

* * * * *

Tony hung up the phone and let out a huge sigh. He looked drained. Mark and Lenny heard the phone ring. Mr. Pushey answered the phone and then knocked on Tony's door to tell him it was a call for him, a call from Utah. Lenny and Mark stood in Tony's bedroom doorway.

Mr. Pushey went downstairs. It was nearly seven o'clock in the morning. He had already stepped out to take Pokey for a walk. It was a cloudy overcast day and winter darkness was slow to give up its grip.

"Well, are you going to keep us in suspense?" asked Lenny.

"She's all right. She decided to go and stay with her friend Liz. Apparently this storm is really bad. She said everything may be shut down for days out there. She also said the officer who found her was risking his life."

"Jesus! It must be some shit-ass of a storm?" asked Lenny.

"You just can't imagine what a fierce winter storm is like in Utah. It is worse than anything we've ever seen around here. The winds and the snow drifts are just unbelievable."

"So, you're stuck here for a while?" asked Mark.

"Yeah, so let's make the most of it."

"I think you should let the Chief know his assistance worked and that Kelly is safe." said Lenny.

"You're right. I'll call his house and speak to his wife in a few minutes. You know what? I'm incredibly hungry!"

"The man's got his appetite back."

The three guys shuffled out of Tony's bedroom and headed down to the kitchen to root around in search of something to cobble together a breakfast. It seemed they were all quite hungry.

Mark located a box of pancake mix and was soon cooking some delicious looking pancakes in the large skillet on the stove.

Mr. Pushey opened the back door and Pokey shot through the door and went to each one for a scratch and a pat. The dog headed straight for his food dish and quickly snapped up the dog food Mark had put out for him. Mr. Pushey removed his coat and began to rub his hands together.

"Smells great," said Mr. Pushey.

Mark handed him a cup of coffee and Mr. Pushey put it on the table. "This will have to wait, the bathroom comes first."

Mark's father headed off to the bathroom. He was gone for just a few moments and then the familiar sound of the toilet flushing followed by the sink running could be heard from the hallway off of the kitchen.

Soon everyone was seated around the kitchen table enjoying the freshly made pancakes.

Tony reported again on his earlier call with Kelly. This time he added more detail. His description of winter weather in Utah was even more graphic the second time around.

He excused himself and left to place a call to the Chief's wife to thank her and the Chief for assisting him in connecting with his wife.

Mark got up and poured himself another cup of coffee.

"Anyone need a refill?"

"Not for me," said Lenny.

"Nope," said Tony from over his shoulder as he left the room.

"How about you, Dad?" asked Mark.

"No, thanks. My tank is full."

Mark sat back down and realized no one had the newspaper yet. It hadn't yet arrived at its usual early morning time. Mr. Pushey called the newspaper to report the late delivery. They assured him one would be delivered by mid-morning.

"I'm going to check to see if the damn paper has come. If it still hasn't arrived I'll just have to call them again and give them a piece of my mind!"

He was up again and soon returned with the paper. The front page was totally devoted to the plane crash from the previous day.

Before anyone could begin to read the newspaper Mark's father nervously looked everyone over than spoke up after clearing his throat.

"I've got something important to tell you boys." He had their attention. He had piqued their curiosity as well. "I've been keeping a terrible secret all my life, and now, I've just got to tell someone. I never, ever thought I would be breaking a vow to keep this to myself. But after what happened to Karl and what's been happening around town lately, and what I think you boys are up to, well, I have no choice but to spill the beans."

The room was totally silent.

* * * * *

A black Plymouth Valiant pulled up next to the three boys who were on their way back to Mark's house. Mark was carrying the wooden box with the used Volkswagen car battery inside, while Karl and Lenny walked alongside.

Karl recognized Father Campbell's car immediately. The priest got out of the car and approached the three boys. Mark was relieved to have a chance to put the heavy car battery down. It was his turn to carry it and he was finding the load difficult to bear.

"How are you guys doing?"

"We're doing fine," responded Karl.

"What have you got there?"

"A used car battery. We're borrowing it from Eddie's Garage," said Lenny.

"I see, and just what are you going to do with this battery?"

"We're planning on building something that needs a big battery," said Karl.

"And what is that something?" said the priest, as he folded his arms and leaned against his car.

Tony blurted out, "It's a secret."

"Yeah, a secret," echoed Mark.

"Oh, a secret! I see!" said Father Campbell, nodding his head and grinning.

The three boys felt uncomfortable not telling the priest the entire reason for the battery. After an awkward moment of silence Father Campbell spoke again. "Well, look. The reason I stopped is because I was going to look you guys up. I've got tomorrow off. I had been planning on hooking up with Brother Phil from Don Bosco's. He is planning to take a few boys over to Ausable Chasm tomorrow. I was hoping we could join him. You'd like him a lot. He's an amateur geologist and archeologist. He's got a hundred stories. We'd be gone all day, and the trip is on me. So what do you say? Do you want to go?"

The other boys looked at Karl for some kind of signal as to how to respond.

Karl glanced at the others and then answered the priest "Yeah, it would be cool."

The others, almost on cue, nodded their agreement.

"Good. I'll pick you up at Mark's house around eight o'clock tomorrow morning. Please invite your friend, Tony, to join us. We should be back by seven o'clock tomorrow night. After we go through Ausable Chasm, we'll be going swimming at St. Anne's

Shrine in Isle Lamotte. If we have time, we're also going to go fossil hunting."

"We'll be ready," promised Karl.

"I've already spoken to your parents and they all said it's fine with them."

With that, Father Campbell turned and got back into his car. He started the car up and tooted his car's horn as he pulled away from the curb.

"We're going to put off our plans for just one day. The day after tomorrow we'll try and kill that monster," said Karl.

"Why not do it today?" said Lenny.

"Because, guys, we need to think this through! We don't want to make a mistake, right?" said Karl.

"So," said Mark.

"So we can work on this while we're on this trip. Look, we'll be a long ways away. Maybe this monster can't reach our minds that far away. It gives us a chance to plan a surprise."

"I'm all for it," said Mark.

Lenny quickly agreed.

"Let's get going," said Karl.

Just then Tony came jogging into view. He quickly joined up with the other boys.

Mark explained about the priest's invitation to join in on the trip to Ausable Chasm. Tony was all excited about that. It would be a new adventure and Tony enjoyed adventures, especially a trip to a place he'd never been before.

Tony explained he had been successful in rounding up plenty of electrical wire.

Karl grew a bit impatient with this street corner jawing so he urged everyone along.

"C'mon, guys, let's get going," said Karl as he turned and headed off in the direction of Mark's house.

Tony and Lenny followed along. Mark brought up the rear. He needed to carry the car battery to the corner of North and Hall Streets, then Tony would take over and carry it the rest of the way.

It was a hot and sticky day. Enormous, dark bottomed, summer storm clouds were building in the West. There would most likely be afternoon thunderstorms.

Lenny noticed the building storm clouds. He would welcome their arrival. He was half hoping to be able to listen to this afternoon's Red Sox game. The Sox were playing on the road against the dreaded New York Yankees. The Yankees were starting red-hot Ralph Terry against the Red Sox number one pitcher, Gene Conley. Maybe the guys would be interested in a card game inside Mark's tent. Being inside a tent during a rain storm on a hot summer afternoon and playing cards with your buddies is about as good as it can get.

"Hey, Tony, it's your turn to carry this box," said Mark.

"Gee, it's my turn already?" said Tony.

"No shit, Shakespeare," said Mark.

The boys moved along the street and eventually reached Mark's back yard. They put the car battery inside the garage. The house was locked up. Mrs. Pushey must have gone shopping with one of the neighbors. Mark must have forgotten his house key in his other dungarees. The boys were hot and thirsty. Mark headed over to the back yard hose and turned on the water and each boy took a turn drinking from the hose. The water was cool and refreshing. In a few moments, Tony playfully turned the hose on Mark and then Mark took the hose from Tony and sprayed him with it. He also sprayed Karl and Lenny. Soon they were all drenched from spraying each other. Their wet clothes stuck to them. They eventually settled down and sat at the picnic table under the shade of the large maple tree. A summer breeze out of the Southwest began to dry off the boys.

"Do you guys want to play some cards this afternoon?" asked Mark.

Lenny quickly agreed as did Tony and Karl. Lenny then spoke up and asked if the guys would be interested in listening to the Red Sox game at the same time.

"Sure," said Tony.

"I don't care, as long as we can listen to some rock and roll after the game," said Karl.

Somewhere off in the distance a roll of thunder could be heard.

* * * * *

"I don't know how to begin," said Mark's father.

There was no reaction from Tony, Lenny or Mark.

"I have been sort of listening in on your conversations since you've been staying here. Now mind you, I didn't want to listen in, but some of the secret things you've been discussing have reminded me of my own long-held secret. So instead of beating around the bush I'm going to say it straight out."

He took a deep breath. Obviously he was struggling with this. Nevertheless, he continued to tell his story.

"Many years ago, when I was a young man, probably twelve or thirteen years old, I used to spend a great deal of time at a summer camp my father rented. This camp was somewhere in the northern islands of Lake Champlain. Staying next to this camp was an Indian family. They were Abenaki. Their name was St. Germain."

Mark, Lenny and Tony looked aghast.

"Were these people related to old Louis St. Germain who use to live up on Main Street?" asked Mark.

"Yes, it was one and the same family. There was the mother, I think her Indian name was Summer Breeze, and her husband whose Indian name I can't remember. They had three boys and one daughter. Louis St. Germain was the youngest boy. He was around eight or ten. His sister was maybe nineteen and his two other brothers were older. Well, one summer I was wandering down the beach and I came upon a path which led away from the beach. It went back into the woods. I followed this path and it stopped at the bottom of a small hill. The hill was maybe two hundred feet high. Being a curious young boy, I started to climb up the hill. About half way up I spied a cave. It was covered with branches and so I moved them out of the way and I climbed inside."

"Did anybody know where you were?" asked Lenny.

"Nope, at least I didn't think so at the time. Well, anyway, the cave wasn't very deep and I couldn't see because there was no light and I didn't have any matches or flashlight. I started to back out of the cave and when I got outside Mr. St. Germain and Summer Breeze were standing there. They pulled me up by my shoulders and then they both looked at me for the longest time without saying a word. They led me back down the hill and then back to their camp. The father told me I must come to his camp that night after everyone else had gone to sleep at my camp. He said my life depended on it. It scared the dickens out me, I don't mind telling you."

"Later that night, I slipped out of my room and headed over to the St. Germain's place. They took me out to the beach and we went a short ways up the beach until we couldn't be seen by anybody. They started a bonfire. His whole family and I sat down and then Mrs. St. Germain..."

"Summer Breeze?" said Tony.

"Yes, Summer Breeze began to tell me about this monster that lived deep in the earth. She said it waited to catch little boys so it can lure them into its cave and then kill them and eat them. At first I just thought they were just trying to scare me."

Mark, Lenny and Tony's facial expressions were unanimous in their conveyance of surprise.

"Mr. St. Germain asked me to look at him, which I did. Now he was sitting directly opposite me so I had to look at his face through the bonfire. He started to describe this monster and while he did I swear, I could begin to see the face of this monster that supposedly lived beneath the earth. The face was hanging there in the fire. The creature didn't have any eyes. He was hideous. He had a mouthful of sharp teeth and large pointy ears. His skin was very white except for his hands and feet which were somehow slightly darker. Now I looked at the other St. Germain kids and they were looking straight into the fire, but their eyes were not moving. I was really scared at this point."

"Did this monster have a name?" asked Lenny.

"Uh-huh. He called it Ne Wha Ta."

"Ne Wha Ta," repeated Mark.

"I know. I heard you boys talking this week and I know some of your story. I think I know why you've all come back here."

"Why do you think?" asked Lenny.

"I believe you each returned here to kill that son-of-a-bitch."

"But you just said you thought it was just a mirage in the bonfire," said Mark.

"I know son. But there's more. You see, what I was told that night scared me for sure, but it also did something else. It got to my curiosity. So a couple of days later I was back at that cave and this time I brought along a flashlight. I was in the cave only a few minutes when I sort of blacked out. Next thing I woke up and I was in a different cave. I couldn't find my flashlight. Then I heard someone or something coming towards me. I started to pull back, when two hands reached out and grabbed me. It was Louis St. Germain and his sister. I think her Indian name was Summer Moon, but I could be wrong about that. They whispered to me so I knew who it was and then they told me to be real quiet as they began to lead me out of that cave. It was completely dark. I couldn't see a thing for quite a while, but I knew we were climbing up. Then I saw a small spot of light. They pushed me ahead of them. At that moment, I heard this horrible roar or growl. It just didn't sound like a human or any animal I knew. I knew it was coming from somewhere behind me. I kept moving towards the light. Someone or something was surely gaining on us!

Mark's father paused. He had developed a sniffle. He got up from the table and used a paper towel to blow his nose. His eyes were noticeably watery as he sat back down at the table.

"Go on," urged Mark gently.

"Okay, before I could get to the exit from that cave, I heard a woman's scream. The scream went on and on. It echoed all around me. I didn't want to turn around and yet I couldn't bring myself to climb out of the cave. The woman's scream stopped. I heard sobbing and pleading in a language I didn't understand. But I knew I recognized the woman's voice. It was Summer Moon and she sounded like she was pleading for her life."

Tears were now flowing down Gene Pushey's face. The horror of that summer had come back to him and he felt the pain all over again.

Swallowing, he continued, "Then I heard the voice of one of the older St. Germain boys. He must have gotten past me without my noticing. He and someone or something sounded like they were fighting. I heard rocks crashing from inside the blackness of the cave. I turned around to go back. I wanted to help them. I really wanted to help. Before I could get too far I heard Summer Moon's voice call out to me to get away. She tried to say something else when I heard a sound like a small branch snapping. Then the older St. Germain boy let out a cry I still can remember. There was a terrible sound of fighting going on. I didn't know what to do, so I crawled out of the cave and just sat and waited. Young Louis St. Germain slipped out of the cave right behind me. He was as wide-eyed with fear as I was. After a couple of minutes the older St. Germain boy, whose name I later learned was Walter, crawled out of the cave. His Indian name was Grey Owl. Walter St. Germain had cuts and bite marks all over him. I asked him, "Where is Summer Moon, where is she?" He didn't answer me. He just started walking down the hill back towards the lake. Louis and I ran after him and I kept asking him, "where is she, is she okay?" He said nothing and just kept on walking. But I knew what happened to her. That monster, Ne Wha Ta, killed her. After that, the St. Germains stopped talking to me. They all acted like I didn't even exist."

"But it didn't end there. That monster started to talk to me in my dreams, sometimes during the night and even during the daytime. He has been torturing me for over sixty-five years. I have been afraid to tell anyone because they'd think I was crazy. I tried to apologize once to Louis St. Germain but I chickened out. Then one night he pulled up with his horses and wagon, right out in front of the house. Now, I hadn't spoken with a St. Germain in years. Then he did the damnedest thing. He walked right up to me and he placed these in my hand."

Mark's father removed his right hand from his pants pocket and placed an Indian arrowhead and a leather necklace with an attached small leather pouch onto the kitchen table.

"For the first time since that day in the cave he spoke to me. He said I'm not to blame for what happened. That Ne Wha Ta planned it all. He said his sister's spirit was free and she was with her people in the land of sunshine. He told me one day I would learn of others who will have these things. He told me that the others and I will be a powerful match for Ne Wha Ta. He also said it would lead to a mighty battle and it would be my one and only chance to avenge his sister's death. I was to not try this on my own for I would only fail. I was supposed to wait until others came along."

"I listened in on you fellas and I know enough to know you're the ones Louis St. Germain told me I should wait for. So I want you to know, whatever you're planning, I want in."

"Shit, dad! Why didn't you say something before?"

Chapter 52

Father Campbell arrived at Mark's house at five minutes to eight in the morning. The morning air was cool and still. He arrived in a bright yellow school bus. The bus driver opened the door and Father Campbell bounded out. He started for the front steps when the front door swung open. Mrs. Pushey held it ajar as the four boys exited. They all seemed in good spirits.

"Good morning, Mrs. Pushey," said Father Campbell.

"Good morning, Father!"

"Hello, boys. Are you ready?"

"Yup," answered Tony for everyone.

Each boy brought along a backpack. In it they packed a towel, their swim suits, a couple of comic books, and gum. They also brought along a couple of soft drinks and brownies Mrs. Pushey baked last night. Karl packed a small note pad and a couple of pencils, while Lenny packed his portable transistor radio.

They were the first ones on the bus. They each chose a separate seat. Father Campbell spoke privately with Mrs. Pushey for a moment. She handed him some additional brownies. With a wave, he turned and climbed aboard the bus. The driver let out the air brakes and with a few creaks and rattles the bus pulled away. Mark knelt on his seat and waved to his mom. Mrs. Pushey waved back. She turned, climbed up the front steps and went back inside.

Father Campbell spoke up. "We've got to drive over to Don Bosco's in Burlington. We'll be picking up Brother Phil and some of the boys from there."

"How many others are going?" asked Mark.

"I think Phil said about twenty, or so."

"What is Don Bosco's?" asked Tony.

"It's a home for boys who have been in trouble. They live there and go to school in the area."

"Are they juvenile delinquents?" asked Tony.

"Not quite, Tony. They're just boys whose parents can't handle them. They're not really bad boys, they try and act tough, but inside, they're just boys. You don't have to hang out with them. They won't cause you any trouble. Besides, Brother Phil and a couple of other Brothers will be coming along. They're going to look after the boys from Don Bosco's."

Tony simply nodded.

Karl and Lenny said nothing as they looked out the bus windows. Mark moved into the seat next to Tony and the two were soon giggling over something.

Fifteen minutes later, the bus pulled into the circular driveway of Don Bosco's Home for Boys. The Boys' Home was a large, rambling stone building which sat back on the western side of North Avenue in Burlington, Vermont. In the back, the land quickly dropped down over a hundred feet to a beautiful beach at the bottom of the slope. The Boy's Home overlooked Lake Champlain. Standing outside the building were twenty three boys and four adults. The adults were all standing together and laughing at something. A couple of boys were horsing around and shoving each other. The rest of the boys were quietly standing and waiting. These boys were not smiling.

After the bus stopped, Father Campbell stepped off and went over to the adults and began shaking hands. One of the adults gestured to the Don Bosco boys to begin boarding the bus and they all stepped forward and began boarding. The first ones on board were the oldest of the group. These boys were sixteen or seventeen. A couple of them needed a shave. From the back to the front of the bus it soon filled up by age, the oldest in the back and the youngest in the front. The youngest were around twelve years old. No one sat next to Karl or Lenny.

Father Campbell and three of the four other adults stepped on board. Soon Lenny and Karl had seat companions. Brother Phil sat with Lenny. Sitting with Karl was Brother Frank. Sitting in the seat directly behind the bus driver was Father Campbell and Brother Julius. The brothers were members of the Society of St. Edmund. The Society had been running this Don Bosco Home for the past fifty-one years. The home could handle a maximum of fifty boys. At the moment it housed forty-five. The older boys were working summer jobs today and thus could not join in on this trip. Two other boys were confined to their rooms. They would be looked after by Brother Robert who remained behind. The boys were caught smoking two days before in the woods down by the lake below the home. Their punishment would last for seven days and would include completing household chores for eight hours a day. They would also receive counseling and of course would spend some time in contemplative prayer.

The bus, now fully loaded, pulled out of the driveway and headed south on North Avenue. In a few minutes the bus pulled onto the dock in front of a huge ferry boat. The bus was waved on and it crept aboard slowly and carefully. Once secured, the driver opened the front door and everyone got out.

All the boys were allowed to exit the bus. They were reminded to be on their best behavior and when the boat docked, in about an hour; they were to be back on board the bus for a head count.

Without further discussion everyone got out of the bus. Lenny, Tony, Mark and Karl got off together and immediately went to the front of the boat where they staked claim to a couple of the built-in seats. The ferry boat's engines were rumbling below deck. The water immediately around the boat was deep and dark. The sky above was cloudless. A gentle south-westerly breeze brushed against their faces. A dozen seagulls screeched overhead.

"This is really cool," said Mark.

"How deep do you think it is, Karl?" asked Lenny.

"I don't know."

"I'm going to find out," said Mark as he got up from his seat and headed over to the guy who guided the bus and assorted cars onboard. The boat suddenly began to move forward as it pulled away from the dock. Mark caught up with the man and spoke to him for a couple of minutes. He pulled out a folded piece of paper from his back pocket and handed it to Mark. Mark saluted the man, who smiled and returned the salute. Mark scampered back to his friends.

"Who was that?" asked Karl.

"He said he's the Forward Steward."

"Sounds like it's important," said Tony.

"Sounds like, doesn't mean that it is," said Karl sarcastically.

"Anyway, he gave me this," said Mark.

"What is it?" asked Lenny.

"He said it's a map of the entire bottom of Lake Champlain."

"Cool, let's check it out," said Tony.

Mark unfolded the map. It was a bit of a struggle, because as the boat moved across the lake, this motion only added to the windy conditions. In fact, the air felt chilly. Karl held one side of the map and Mark held the other side.

Karl studied the map for a moment. "Look, it says here, back at the dock, the water was seventy feet deep."

"How do you know that?" asked Tony.

"Because it says so right here!" he said, pointing at a spot on the map. "See, it even has the route the ferry boat is taking marked in red," said Karl, as he traced the line across the map.

"Gee," said Lenny.

Mark pointed to another spot on the map. "Right here it says the lake is three hundred feet deep and we're going to go right over it. Holy cow!"

"What's the deepest part?" asked Mark.

Everyone scanned the map to find the deepest point.

"I've got it," said Karl. He pointed to a couple of spots in the northern area of the lake known as the Champlain Islands.

"It says right here the lake is three hundred and ninety five feet deep. Holy crap!"

"What's so holy?" asked Father Campbell as he strolled towards the four boys.

"We were just looking at this cool map of Lake Champlain," said Lenny in an obvious attempt to provide cover.

"I know, this lake's pretty amazing, isn't it," said the priest, letting the boys off easy.

"It sure is," said Tony.

"Wait until you see Ausable Chasm."

"How long will we be there?" asked Mark.

"I think we'll spend about three hours or so there. Then we're going over to St. Anne's Shrine on Isle LaMotte, which is one of the Vermont islands. We'll have lunch there. The brothers and I have made a bunch of sandwiches and we've brought a couple of watermelons. We can swim there all afternoon or some of you can tag along to a fossil hunting site near the Shrine Brother Phil knows about. Then we'll have a barbecue with hot dogs and hamburgers. After that we'll head back home."

The priest got up and walked away, leaving the boys to enjoy the rest of the ferry boat ride.

"Father is a nice guy," said Tony.

"Yeah, he's also a good friend," said Lenny, as Mark and Karl nodded their agreement.

The boys sat quietly and took in the view as the ferry glided across the calm waters of Lake Champlain. In a few minutes they could make out the docking area the ferry was heading towards. The boat horn sounded a small "toot."

A couple of men on the boat dock stood by with ropes. They tossed them to the ferry crew, to tie up the boat when it docked.

The ferry boat's engines began to rumble as the Captain guided the boat into its berth. A metal ramp was lowered down onto the flat deck of the boat. Everyone began to hurry to their vehicles. The boys moved through the maze of parked cars on the deck and climbed back inside the school bus. They were the last ones back inside the bus. Some of the Don Bosco boys glared at the four boys, but Lenny, Karl, Mark and Tony chose to ignore the stares. After a quick head count was taken, the bus started up. The driver slowly moved the bus forward and off the boat. He put the bus into second gear as it climbed a small hill on the way out from the ferry boat landing. Soon the bus was moving along a state road on its way to Ausable Chasm. It took less than twenty minutes to reach the much-anticipated scenic wonder. The parking lot was filled with cars from many different states. There was a large colorful sign next to the entrance which announced that next to Ausable Chasm was the at-traction known as the Ausable Wild Animal and Amusement Park.

The bus pulled into a parking space at the far left of the parking lot which was reserved for buses. The driver put the bus in park as air brakes let out a "hiss." He turned the bus off. Brother Julius stood up and asked for attention. Soon it was absolutely quiet on the bus.

"You all have been assigned to one of the Brothers. Please try to stay together. We will be leaving here," he looked at his watch, "at twelve forty-five sharp. Don't be late. Now have fun and please respect everyone you meet. After all, you're representing Don Bosco's of Burlington. Now, let's go."

With that cautionary message having been delivered, everyone piled off the bus. Karl, Lenny, Mark and Tony waited for Father Campbell. He gathered them up and they all headed for the park entrance. Father Campbell and the four boys were the last ones from the bus to enter the park. Father Campbell paid for their ad-mission. They were each handed a colorful brochure which included a detailed map they could use to guide them as they explored this natural wonder.

Father Campbell explained the Chasm was a sort of northeast-ern version of the Grand Canyon, only on a smaller scale. The boys slowly read the guide pamphlet as they carefully made their way down the wooden stairs. From below they could hear the sounds of a river rushing along. The sound grew louder and louder as they descended deeper into Ausable Chasm. The rock ledge to their right was wet. Moss or ferns grew across the rock's face. The wooden steps were wet, and at times, slippery.

They finally reached the bottom. They each turned around to see just how far they had descended. They had climbed down at least two hundred feet. The swiftly-moving water rushed with a roar past them. There were railings in some places to discourage the wanderers amongst those who chose to explore this beautiful natural wonder. However, most of the river's edge was left accessible which added to the excitement of the chasm.

The boys were moving slowly along the water's edge, stopping every few feet to read the posted signs or their pamphlets. Father Campbell stayed back on purpose. He wanted these boys to explore the chasm without his help. He admired their resilience and their sense of adventure. It reminded him of his own youth.

Father Campbell was taking in the sights when he heard someone whisper his name.

"Father Campbell, Father Francis Campbell!"

The priest turned around to see who was trying to speak to him. Behind him, there wasn't anyone within fifty feet. The roar of the rushing water made normal conversation next to impossible. Whoever was calling to him would need to be within five feet to be heard.

He shrugged it off as just some sort of a momentary fugue. He started to read his pamphlet when he heard the voice again.

"Hey, Francis, what's the matter? Are you too good to talk to someone like me?"

He spun around fully expecting to see someone standing immediately behind him. Nothing!

The closest person behind him was at least fifty to sixty feet away and it was a pair of older women who were busy taking pictures of the Chasm.

He turned and looked ahead. All he could see were the four boys who were beginning to put added distance between themselves and his own location.

He craned his neck, looking up the sheer rock surface to see if perhaps someone was hiding up in the rocks and was playing a practical joke on him. Still nothing!

He decided to put it out of his mind as he moved along to catch up to the boys. He finally caught up to them. They were standing on a huge flat rock and were tossing small rocks into the water trying to skip the rocks across the swirling surface to reach the other side.

"What do you think of this place?" asked the priest.

"This is really cool," said Mark.

"Yeah. Hey, Father, watch me make this skip, and hit the other side," said Lenny.

His toss failed to deliver on its promise. Karl said he could do better, as did Mark and Tony.

As the priest watched the boys the mysterious voice called to him again.

"So, Padre, you like to let humans think you and your religion can save them. Well, too bad it's a lie!"

Father Campbell wasn't going to look around this time, for he realized where the voice was coming from. It was a voice coming from inside his mind.

Who is behind this? thought Father Campbell.

"Who is behind this, you ask? It is curious, that you, of all people, would have to ask that question," said the voice inside his mind.

Smiling at the boys, the priest tried to not let on to what he was experiencing.

Are you the devil? thought the priest.

"Are you asking me if I'm evil? Is that your question, Padre?" said the mysterious voice.

Back in his underground cave, Ne Wha Ta was enjoying playing his usual mind game with this holy man. *After all, a holy man is just another medicine man,* thought Ne Wha Ta. Given what he and his ancestors had been through, he had reason enough to deeply hate holy men or medicine men, whatever they chose to call themselves.

If you are Satan then I command you to leave and return to your own place. I command you with the power of.......

"You command no one......Do you hear me.........No one!" shouted Ne Wha Ta into the mind of the defenseless priest.

The power of this voice rocked Father Campbell. He held his head with both hands. It felt like his head would explode.

"Are you okay?" asked Karl

"I'm..ah...fine. It's just... a sudden headache."

Father Campbell looked around for a place to sit. He spied a flat rock back from the water's edge. He went over and sat down. He fumbled around his coat pocket and found a small vial of aspirin. He took two without water. The dry, bitter taste caused him to momentarily shudder.

The boys were ready to move along the Chasm trail. Father Campbell followed behind. For the next ten minutes there was no sign of any mysterious voice. Father Campbell was about to dismiss the episode when the voice spoke to him again.

"Do you think you can get rid of me with your medicine? Well, let me tell you, your medicine is useless against me."

You're just a figment of my imagination, thought the priest.

"So now you think I'm some kind of mirage. What happened to the devil? Why did you give up on that theory so quickly? Hmmm! I happen to think I'm worse than your so-called devil. Once you get to know me, you'll agree."

Why did you pick me?

"Oh, but that's the question, isn't it? Maybe I'll reveal myself to you at some point and then again maybe I won't. We'll just have to see."

Are you of this world?

"I am of this world and part of it as well."

"Hey, Father, are you coming?" shouted Lenny.

"Yes, I'm coming."

Lenny turned to Karl and said, "Father Campbell doesn't look too good, does he?"

"Yeah, he looks a little pale. Let's hang back with him, you know, in case he needs a little help."

The two boys waited a bit for the priest to catch up.

Father Campbell moved at a brisk pace now. He walked up to Lenny and Karl and gestured for them to move along. In a short while they all came around a corner and met up with the Brothers and the other boys of Don Bosco's.

Brother Phil was speaking to everyone about the geological features of Ausable Chasm.

The four boys all sat down. They listened along with the others to Brother Phil's description of the forces of nature which created this natural wonder, thousands of years ago. He gestured to the various lines of rock that ran parallel to each other.

"These layers were formed millions of years ago." His voice droned on in the consciousness of Father Campbell.

The priest sat down next to Brother Frank. Trying not to be noticed, he pulled out his rosary beads and held them closed up in his right hand. He began to silently pray.

Two elderly ladies now passed by. They stopped to take a photo of Brother Phil and he obliged by favoring them with a big smile.

Soon the lecture was over and the group began to move along through the Chasm. They were moving towards an area opposite a series of caves which could be seen across the swiftly-moving river. According to the pamphlet guide, one of these caves was named by the Indians that first discovered the Chasm. It was named, "Devil's Door."

Karl noticed the name in the pamphlet and pointed it out to the others.

The boys stopped to examine the caves across the river. There was a separation now between them and the other boys from Don Bosco, as well as a separation from Father Campbell and Brother Frank, who was walking along with the priest.

Karl motioned for the others to walk close together.

"I think I know how we can trick Ne Wha Ta to come out of his cave. We'll bring him a woman. And when he comes out to get her, we'll dynamite the cave, crushing him."

"We can't bring him a woman, Karl. You know what St. Germain told us. We just can't bring him a woman to screw. That would be just crazy," said Mark.

"Yeah, we can't do that, Karl."

"Did I say that we would bring him a real woman?"

"No, but..." said Tony.

"That's right. I've got a plan. Now listen in."

Karl went on to explain his plan to his buddies. Soon a smile swept across their faces.

"It might just work," said Lenny.

"It has to work," said Mark.

"It will," said Karl with his usual certainty.

Meanwhile the priest was busy praying. He nodded every so often as Brother Frank spoke to him. He really didn't hear a thing Brother Frank was saying. He just wanted to pray as intently as he could. He didn't want to leave any part of his consciousness open to another conversation with the entity that had chosen to confront him. He prayed for strength and for courage. He prayed to the Saints, to the Holy Spirit and anyone else he could think of.

He tried to dismiss the feeling at first but there was no mistaking it now.

He felt the unmistakable grip of fear filling his insides like a long, cold drink of water. He felt a chill take hold of him. His teeth began to chatter.

Ne Wha Ta could also sense the priest's building fear. The creature truly enjoyed this aspect of his power over humans. He had only just begun. He enjoyed playing with the priest. He needed to drive home to these boys that the time of playing was over. He would use this holy man, this medicine man, to send a powerful message. No one, not even this human who sets himself up as a holy man, is beyond the reach of Ne Wha Ta.

"Holy man.....can you swim?" asked Ne Wha Ta with a mocking tone.

Chapter 53

The conversation around the kitchen table was getting ramped up.

"Look, I don't think it's a good idea," said Mark.

"You're not going to talk me out of it," said Mark's father.

"All right, let's just assume for a moment you can be of some help. This friggin' monster is playing for keeps. I mean, look, any one of us, maybe all of us could be killed," said a pleading Lenny.

"I know, boys, I know. I've thought a great deal about this and I know in my heart that I must do this. I've led a full life already."

Looking each one square in the eyes, he went on. "My conscience has been burning with guilt. If you won't let me in on this, then I'll have to try something on my own."

"Jesus, you're one stubborn old geezer," said Tony with a chuckle.

"I'll take that as a compliment."

"I guess he's in," said Lenny.

"Shit," said a frustrated Mark.

"So, guys, what's our plan?" asked Mark's father.

"Dad, we don't have a plan."

"Oh, I see!"

"We do know one thing. Somehow we need to use the shotgun that we hid in your garage's loft back in 1962," said Tony.

"And how do you know this?"

"Because when we visited Father Campbell the other day he told us the gun was to play a part in stopping this monster," said Tony.

"I can't believe one shotgun would be enough," said Mark's father.

"Me, either," said Mark.

"Well, for the sake of argument, let's say the gun is a part, maybe even a small part. The bigger problem is getting that monster to come out of the cave and fight. He has to be drawn out so we can see him and he doesn't have the advantage of darkness," said Lenny.

"Remember, we tricked him once before. I don't think he's going to be easy to fool again," said Mark.

"I don't understand. You mean to say you once tried to kill him, and you lived to tell about?" asked a surprised Gene Pushey.

"Yeah, we damn near killed him all right," said Mark.

"Tell me about it?"

"You tell him, Tony. You're the story teller here," said Lenny.

Smiling, Tony sat back in the chair and looked at his partners, now including Mark's father, and began to tell him about that twilight encounter many years ago.

"It was a hot afternoon when Karl Sweeney wrote out his plan. He's the one that came up with our strategy. He wrote it out on paper and handed each of us our part. It was sort of scripted out like a play..........."

He continued for the next half hour telling Mark's father everything he could remember. Lenny and Mark occasionally provided a filler comment along the way.

"That's really quite a story," said Mark's father.

"Yeah," said Tony.

"What I don't understand is why he just doesn't kill you. He could, you know, if he wants to."

Lenny attempted to explain. "Based upon what St. Germain told us and what we've come to learn on our own, we figure the Indian curse he and his ancestors have been under won't let him kill us. He can make us kill ourselves like he probably did with Karl. But, because he chose us to help him acquire a mate, he can't kill us himself. He has to try to get us to bring him a mate. If we bring him one, then I suppose all bets are off. At that point he'd probably kill us."

"Like Karl?"

"Yeah, like Karl. Sure, Karl killed himself. We think the monster just mentally tortured Karl to the point he committed suicide," said Mark.

"Hmmm," said Gene Pushey.

"What are you thinking, Dad?"

Gene Pushey got up from the table and said, "Anyone interested in a fresh pot of coffee?"

"Dad, I know you. Give it up. You've got an idea, right?"

"Maybe I do!"

"Well, we're all ears. Let's have it," said Lenny.

"First, let's have some more coffee, while I tell you what I have in mind."

* * * * *

As Brother Frank spoke, Father Campbell tried with all his might to close off his mind to this invasion. It was no use.

"Your legs are under my control, holy man."

"I believe in God the Father Almighty..." prayed Father Campbell.

He couldn't feel his legs, yet somehow they were moving. He was walking towards the river. Brother Frank's voice was fading into the background. He stopped on the edge of a large rock which hung out over the rushing water.

"Holy man, I can make you jump into this river. All the boys can watch you drown. Maybe even some of them would be foolish enough to jump in and try to save you. Well, holy man, where are your spells and magic potions? Now you must know your so-called magic is powerless to stop me. I am Ne Wha Ta. I am feared by all humans. I have great powers."

While Ne Wha Ta was busy boasting, Father Campbell was busy praying with every ounce of his being. He could feel the muscles in his legs again. He knew he didn't have much time, so he strained and finally broke away from the mental grip of this unseen torturing entity. Father Campbell turned away from the water's edge without anyone taking any special notice. He even managed to force a smile for Brother Frank as they resumed their journey through Ausable Chasm.

Ne Wha Ta was caught off guard by the ability of the priest to break free from his mental grasp. This struggle would be especially satisfying. No one had ever broken free from him before. He firmly resolved it would not happen again.

"Holy man, I said, HOLY MAN...." he sent a powerful call out to the priest.

Father Campbell suddenly grabbed for the sides of his head. He pushed his hands against his temples. He felt pain in every part of his head.

"Father, you in some kind of pain?" asked Brother Frank.

The priest couldn't answer. His jaws felt as if someone were squeezing them inside a vise. His ears rang and his eyes felt enormous pressure from inside his head.

Brother Frank helped Father Campbell to sit down.

"HOW DARE YOU....HOLY MAN."

Father Campbell focused what mental strength he could muster and sent back a message of his own.

YOU ARE NOTHING BEFORE THE POWER OF THE CREATOR!

Ne Wha Ta felt his own sense of pain. He stumbled back against the damp moss-covered cave wall. In a brief instant he was filled with blind rage. He now focused upon the man's beating heart, a heartbeat he could hear beating inside the chest of Father Campbell. Ne Wha Ta reached out his hairy muscular right arm. His powerful fingers closed slowly, as Ne Wha Ta mentally squeezed the distant, beating heart of the priest.

Father Campbell suddenly felt a sharp pain in his chest. Now his left arm felt numb. These were some of the classic signs of a heart attack getting underway. He knew, however, this was no ordinary heart attack—he was in the death grip of an unseen demon.

His mind was racing. *Who or what is this demon and why is he attacking me? How can I fight this? Will I die? Oh, God, the pain, the pain! It is too much!*

Brother Frank didn't like what he was seeing in Father Campbell. His complexion was turning ashen-gray. He was sweating even though the deep floor area of Ausable Chasm was no more than a chilly sixty-eight degrees. He decided to go for help.

"Father, you wait right here. I'm going to get some help. I'll be right back. If you want, you can lie back against the rock face." With that, Brother Frank bolted to find help.

At that moment, the priest made a decision totally out of desperation. He decided to speak to this demon.

Speaking out loud in a halting way, since he was feeling unbelievable pain, he called to the demon in the name he discerned. "Ne Wha Ta, why have you chosen me?"

The creature heard him. This human was different. Ne Wha Ta decided to not kill him just yet. He responded, "Because you are like all the other Holy Men. It was your kind that cursed my ancestors."

Barely able to breath and in danger of losing consciousness, Father pressed on with another question.

"There are other Holy men here with me. You haven't attacked them. So I ask again, why me?"

Ne Wha Ta decided to loosen his grip on this human. While he didn't let go completely, he lessened the pressure.

"You are the one who is the protector of the four boys. I need them to fulfill their obligation to me. So far, they have resisted. With their protector gone, they will realize they must find me a mate. They will have no choice."

The sharp pain in his arm was receding and he felt his breathing returning to near normal.

"What have these boys done to you? Did they free you from some bottle or something?"

With that last question Ne Wha Ta laughed.

"You humans are so ignorant."

At that moment Father Campbell could see Brother Frank and Brother Phil running along the tourist path towards him.

I wish to continue speaking to you, to learn, maybe to understand, thought Father Campbell. For a moment he wasn't sure if his message had gotten through. The Brothers were approaching fast. Then, he felt the painful grip on his heart being fully released.

"I will think about your request, Holy Man. But don't think you can trick me or even escape my reach. We will speak again."

Upon hearing those words, suddenly his heart ached no more. The pain was completely gone. Father Campbell did feel a deep soreness, but for the moment he managed to survive this encounter. As the huffing and puffing Brothers arrived, he decided not to tell them anything—at least, not for now.

* * * * *

Ne Wha Ta was intrigued by this human. Not since the curse had been placed on his people had his kind ever had such a "conversation" with a human. As he pondered this phenomenon, it occurred to him he might need a back-up plan. Perhaps this human might accommodate his needs and help him find a mate.

All of a sudden his mind reacted to a conversation he monitored on a fairly regular basis. He locked in on the thoughts and conversation going on between the owner of Bremer's Quarry and Bud Mackenzie.

"C'mon in Bud. Pull up a chair," said Edgar Bremer. At the age of sixty-one, Edgar Bremer possessed the rugged appearance of a man in his late forties. He was tall, slightly over six feet tall, lean, with a full head of salt and pepper hair. He liked wearing tan work clothes and was seldom seen without his hard hat.

Bud strolled into the owner's office and picked out a chair whose leather was faded and cracked in places. He sat down and crossed his legs. He wore dungarees to work, along with a white tee-shirt. He also wore heavy duty, steel reinforced-toe brown colored work boots. Bud was a bit dusty from his work that morning with the driller out on the southwest face of the quarry wall. They would soon be bringing down over a thousand tons of quarry rock with their next blast. He had planned this one very carefully. There were two hundred and forty dynamite sticks strategically placed to achieve the objective of dropping to the quarry floor nearly a quarter acre of surface rock.

"Thanks for coming down."

Bud wondered, *Is he goin' to lay me off or fire me? Shit, he hardly ever talked to me before.*

"Bud, I've got some good news. Yesterday I bought the Longe brothers' farm and the Gamelin farm as well. Together that's over three hundred acres abutting our west and north boundaries."

"Jeezs, that's a lot of land, boss."

"I know and it cost me a pretty penny, too. I'm hoping to get the crushed stone contract for the northern stretch of Interstate 89 from Richmond to the Canadian border. That's over forty-five miles of highway. I'm talking millions here!"

His eyes were wide with excitement.

"That sounds great, boss, but what did you want me for?" asked Bud, hoping to press the obvious.

"Bud, I need to know if I can pull this off. I gambled with this land purchase. I need to move fast. I need to know how deep we can go and bring out class "A" stone for crushing. I need to know if we have any geological and or hydrological problems and how we might work around it. I also need to expand the production, maybe doubling our present delivery runs. I will need you to find good men to bring on board so we can move our production capacity up to a level were we can deliver on this Interstate 89 contract."

Bud's head was swimming with all of his boss's questions.

"Why are you asking me to work this all out? You've got engineers and estimators who should be able to handle those questions."

"Because, Bud, I don't want some technical crap. I've got my balls hanging out here. I picked you because I know your reputation for calling it as you see it. No bull shit. Am I right?"

"Yeah, I guess I have a tough reputation."

"I want to make you Plant Foreman. So can I count on you to work with me on this?"

"You bet! I wouldn't miss it for anything. When can we start setting off seismic charges on the property you purchased?"

"Tomorrow you can start on the Longe property. No one's living in the house any more. We can move on-site to the Gamelin property no earlier than September first. They will have moved out by then."

"Okay, I'll have some preliminary estimates on the sub-strata's depth by late next week."

"Fine, just keep me directly informed."

"I will and that's a promise!"

Bud got up from his seat and started for the door, when his boss called out to him. "Starting right now I'm going to raise your salary by seventy five hundred per year. After I get the sub-strata report I may up it even more."

"Thanks, boss."

The two men nodded towards one another. Bud stepped out of the office into the bright mid-day sun with a huge smile on his face.

Damn, my salary is going to thirty two thousand five hundred dollars a year, maybe even more, thought Bud. *With overtime I could be making...*

Deep inside the earth, inside a cave on the Longe property, Ne Wha Ta immediately recognized he was facing a serious threat to his home, the home of his ancestors. This threat could not be tolerated. He must act, and soon. He needed to completely shut down this quarry once and for all.

* * * * *

"Now listen, because I will only say this once. I don't want to give that monster any chance of listening in and learning about my plan before we've had a chance to spring it on him."

"All right, Dad, so what's your plan?" said Mark.

Leaning closer for emphasis, he whispered, "I think he's growing frustrated and perhaps he's losing his grip on his powers."

"What do you mean?" asked Tony, as he leaned in.

"It seems to me he's so intent on getting a mate, and he's intent on getting you boys to do the deed. Am I right? He's not expecting someone else to be lurking in the background so to speak?"

"You mean you?" asked Lenny.

"Not just me, but someone else."

"Who?" pressed Lenny.

"First, let me lay out the basics of my idea, then you'll understand why I think we need someone else to pull this off."

The guys all nodded their agreement, and with that, Mark's father continued to explain his strategy.

"We will need to contact him and agree to meet him outside his cave. We will agree to bring him his mate. In other words, we promise him what he wants to hear. We tell him we have a woman who is willing to be his mate. He will believe it, trust me. We make him promise he'll leave you guys alone after you bring him the woman."

"But what if he wants to make some kind of contact with her before we supposedly bring her to him? Won't he know this is just a hoax?" asked Tony.

"I thought about that. I propose he be allowed to contact her just once, just to confirm she's a real woman."

"Great. Now who are we going to get to pose as the woman who is willing to mate with him?" asked Mark.

"Karl's daughter, Sherrie, has agreed!"

"Dad, are you out of your mind?" protested Mark.

"Maybe, maybe not. Look, I took the liberty of calling her after I returned from the hospital following my so-called fainting episode. We enjoyed a long conversation. While I didn't know everything about your battle, I was able to convince her that Karl was driven to take his own life. She agreed to come here to hear the rest of the story and to decide for herself if she wants to risk helping to avenge her father's death. I couldn't very well have asked Karl's widow to help given her problems with MS, but I assure you his daughter Sherrie is very, very motivated. "

"Jesus, Dad, you're something else."

"Now that we are past that, let me tell you the rest of my plan. She won't really be brought near that cave. All we need to do is let Ne Wha Ta probe her mind to confirm our planned offering is real. We will agree to meet him at his cave, but he must come out of the cave to take her. I'm going to wear a disguise and play her part. You guys will be pretending to have brought her, I mean me, to him. When we get him outside the cave, we will use that shotgun and blast him to hell."

"It all sounds a little weak to me. Why won't he figure it's a trap and just not come out?"

"Because we are going to piss him off so badly that he will become totally enraged and out of control. He'll be too angry to do anything but come straight for us. He'll want to rip our heads off, I guarantee it."

"But one shotgun, how's that going to stop him?" asked Tony.

"Ah, that is the question, isn't it? Well, we will need more firepower, that's for sure. We'll need killing power that would be certain to bring him down and it must be a total surprise."

"What kind of power and who's going to provide it?" asked Mark.

Mark's father sat back in his chair and took a long sip on his coffee. He smiled and said, "You're just going to have to trust me on that."

"Trust you? Trust you? Shit, it all sounds crazy," said Mark.

"I don't know," said Lenny, as he leaned forward. "It does make some sense. I for one believe maybe fate is a part of this. It does seem to hang together. The St. Germain family helping two generations of Pusheys has got to be more than a coincidence."

"Look Mark, if I told you who and how I plan to spring this attack on the monster, then he would eventually learn the most important part of our plan and then he'd defeat it. No, it has to be this way. The less you guys know, the more of a chance we all have. I'm not on some suicide mission here. You all saw what happened with that plane crash at the quarry. It's just a matter of time before he decides to kill you all off and find someone else to trick and maybe find a mate after all. We can't let him succeed. It's got to stop now!"

"Your dad's right, Mark," said Tony.

Mark ran his hands through his hair. He seemed thoroughly frustrated. With resignation clearly in his voice he said, "I hope for all our sakes this works, because we'll never, and I mean never, ever live to try killing him again. This will be our last chance!"

Chapter 54

"How are you feeling, Father?" asked an obviously concerned Brother Phil.

"I'm...a little sore," said the priest.

"Do you think maybe you're having a heart attack?" asked Brother Frank.

"No, I don't think so. I....ah, I've had a bad cold and I think it just settled into my lungs. I also have asthma and that could account for the tightness. It might simply be a reaction to all the moisture and dampness. I'm sure I'll be fine when I get to the top."

"Well, nevertheless, we will walk along with you, won't we Brother Frank?" asked Brother Phil.

Brother Frank nodded his agreement. The three men then stood up and headed down the path. About twenty minutes later they reached the exit to the park. Everyone else had already exited. The boys were all standing around outside the bus waiting to leave.

Brother Phil directed all the boys to board the bus. The other Brothers and the priest boarded last. Brother Julius did a head count to confirm everyone was aboard. Once that fact was confirmed he advised the bus driver to proceed. The driver had earlier opened all the bus windows, so as the bus moved out of the parking lot of Ausable Chasm, fresh air poured into and throughout the bus.

The bus turned to the north as it left the parking lot. The bus would take everyone across northern Lake Champlain at the Rouses Point Crossing. From there it would proceed to the Shrine of St. Anne located on the western shore of Isle Lamotte. There the boys could swim, join Brother Phil in a fossil hunt or just hang out in the picnic area. It was a weekday, so the Shrine would have very few people for the boys to disturb.

During the ride to the Shrine, Father Campbell did not experience any contact efforts on the part of the entity that had tortured him earlier. The priest did not try to make contact on his own. His own mind, however, was racing with thoughts.

Is this entity Satan? Is the entity an agent of possession? Am I losing my mind? Could this all be some kind of hallucination? Am I being tempted or tested by an Angel? What is going on? Will it happen again? What should I do? Who should I tell?

Father Campbell tried to listen to the Brothers. They each tried to engage him in conversation, but while he nodded and smiled, they knew he was holding back something he wasn't yet ready to share with them.

Gradually the Brothers left him alone.

Finally, the bus pulled into the shaded parking lot at the Shrine. The boys were all eager to exit the bus. Brother Frank organized the boys so those interested in a fossil hunt could go with Brother Phil, and those interested in swimming could go with Brother Frank. Brother Julius brought along some horseshoes. He even managed to round up three other players.

The four boys who came along with Father Campbell all decided to go on the fossil hunt. They planned to go swimming later in the afternoon.

The bus driver brought along a chaise lounge. He set it up in the shade of a large pine tree. He faced it so he could enjoy the view of the lake. There was a gentle breeze blowing in from the south west.

Father Campbell walked slowly over to the Shrine nestled in a grove of tall pine trees. There were several benches nearby. He selected one in the shade. He sat down and removed a small black book from his back pocket. The book, the *Daily Office*, was a compilation of meditation prayers. It appeared his copy got a lot of use, as its edges were badly curled.

He opened it and began to read silently. After he turned his first page over, he could sense the entity was reaching for him. He did not fight its efforts.

"Holy man, I have decided to let you live for now. You can be of value to me."

Speaking out loud, Father Campbell responded. "How could I be of value to you?"

"You are one who has power over four young humans. You know which ones I speak of."

"Are you referring to Lenny, Mark, Tony and Karl?"

"They are the ones!"

"What have they got to do with you?"

"They, Holy man, owe me a female to mate with. I chose to reveal myself to them. I could have easily killed them but instead I chose them to find me a female human to mate with. They have resisted me. I even promised them, their friends would be my friends, and their enemies would become my enemies. I killed for them."

"Killed? Who?"

"Three young humans who showed disrespect, another young human who threatened them and I also killed the male parents of two of them."

This news startled the priest but he kept his composure.

"Why can't you leave them alone? They're good boys."

"Good....Good, you believe they are good? Holy man, you should know the young humans wanted, even asked their parent humans be destroyed."

"But you just said you would be the friend of their friend. Well, I'm their friend and yet you have tried to kill me. It seems you are a liar. How can I know what you say is true?" said Father Campbell.

"As their Holy Man, you are their protector. You would not let them die!"

"I see. Now you want my help to convince them to bring you a female human to mate with. Maybe I should even find this female for them, is that it?"

"Yes. I will leave you all alone once this female is brought to me."

"You lied before. Are you lying now?" demanded the priest.

"I am tired of your questions. Now go and be their true friend, Holy Man, and get them to bring me a female to mate."

"No," asserted the priest

"NO! You dare to deny me HOLY MAN. I have the power to kill you in an instant. I WILL KILL YOU." Ne Wah Ta's anger now exploded.

"No, you won't, because if you do, these four young boys will be much too scared to help you. I have learned from you. I have learned you can't force them into helping you. If you could, you would have done so already. No, evil one! You somehow are prevented from procuring a mate except from a willing human, a human you chose without knowing if they would come through on your demand. You are stuck with the ones you chose. I'm right, yes, I'm right!"

"Holy Man," said Ne Wha Ta, "maybe killing you would make it harder for them to come to me and fulfill their destiny to bring me a mate. "But,......HOLY MAN," shouted Ne Wha Ta into the mind of the priest. "You can still help me send a convincing message they must fulfill their part and bring me a mate. Yes, you will serve me after all."

Father Campbell didn't understand at first what was happening. He could feel the muscles in his arms and hands suddenly responding to some direction not his own. His hands rose slowly to his face. He watched as his thumbs and index fingers formed two pairs of pincers. At that very moment he somehow knew what was coming. He prayed with all his might. In his heart, he knew his prayers would be futile.

Father Campbell pulled his own eyes out of their sockets. Blood streaked down his cheeks. He wanted to scream but forced himself to hold it in. The pain was nearly unbearable. He didn't want any of the boys to see him like this.

"Dear God Almighty,....," he began to pray, but at that moment, he collapsed onto his left side on the bench.

A short distance away, the bus driver stood up from his chaise lounge and stretched. He looked around the area. He could see several boys swimming, others playing horseshoes. Further down the beach he could barely make out a cluster of boys picking through rocks along the rocky shore. He couldn't see the priest. Sitting back down, he decided to take a nap. He pulled his baseball cap down over his eyes and went to sleep.

* * * * *

Bud Mackenzie spent the past hour and a half with Walter Kosloski. He was the man who operated the driller which drilled holes into the rock at precise locations Bud identified. The locations were important to enable Bud to determine the amount of dynamite he needed to bring down a piece of the quarry wall.

Bud told Walter all about Mr. Bremer's plans. Walter was excited, anticipating the potential of overtime pay. The afternoon horn sounded, signifying it was time for the afternoon break. The two men sat in the shade of a small maple tree next to the fence which previously marked the boundary of the Longe brother's property. Their respective thermoses were filled with something cool to refresh them on this hot summer day.

Several minutes passed, when Bud began to hear a voice inside his head. He was startled by this experience. He turned to look at Walter to see if the voice was his. Walter leaned back against the tree and had pulled his hat down over his eyes and was trying to catch a little nap before the break was over.

"You must go to your truck," said the mysterious voice.

At first, he believed it was some kind of trick. But then he found he couldn't resist the voice. He felt himself drifting off into a dream-like state. He stood up and began to walk to the truck.

"Now take four sticks of what you call dynamite and prepare them to explode with what you call a fuse. See that it is set for ten seconds. But don't explode it yet."

He did just as he was told. Bud was aware of everything he was doing even though he was powerless to stop.

"Get inside your truck and wait for the horn to sound. When the horn sounds I want you to drive your truck along the road which follows the quarry wall."

The quarry horn sounded at that moment. Walter sat up and pushed his hat back on his head. He noticed Bud was in his truck and the truck was running. Bud started to put the truck into gear when Walter shouted over to him.

"Where're you going?"

Bud looked over at Walter but didn't really seem to look at him. Walter would later say that he thought Bud appeared to be in a trance.

Bud responded with one word, "Dynamite."

Walter watched Bud drive off in a cloud of dust as many small stones were scattered by the truck's spinning tires.

Meanwhile, down on the quarry floor, Mr. Bremer was also in a trance-like state. He was walking slowly towards the dynamite storage shed. The shed stood about a hundred and twenty feet away from the quarry wall. No other buildings were allowed near this shed. At that moment the shed contained over two thousand pounds of dynamite, eleven hundred blasting caps, and thirty two hundred feet of wire used to string the charges together. There were also several hundred feet of fuse cords with different burn rates.

Mr. Bremer kept walking directly towards the dynamite storage shed. The outside of the corrugated metal shed was liberally covered with signs warning of the dangerous material within and for unauthorized people to keep out.

Bud, as one of the employees assigned a truck, was now driving his at nearly thirty miles per hour when he heard the voice for the last time. "Light the fuse and drive as fast as you can, Bud. Drive the truck off the edge and crash it into the dynamite shed."

Everything in his mind told him to stop, but he couldn't. He pulled out the truck's cigarette lighter and lit the fuse of the dynamite he had placed between his legs. When the fuse was lit, he dropped the lighter onto the truck's floor. The fuse was now rapidly burning down. He put the gas pedal to the floor and the truck surged forward. After a few seconds it went airborne at two hundred and fifteen feet above the dynamite shed. The truck's engine still roared because Bud had the gas pedal pressed to the floor. The truck plummeted straight down towards the shed.

Mr. Bremer was about fifty feet away from the shed when the truck crashed through the shed's roof. At the precise moment the truck crashed into the shed, the dynamite, between Bud's legs exploded, which in turn caused a second explosion as the entire inventory of dynamite, blasting caps and other items exploded.

Walter watched Bud drive off in the truck. He watched in utter surprise and horror as the truck veered off the quarry wall's edge. Next he experienced a moment of silence as the truck disappeared from view. He started to run toward the edge, when he felt a huge rumble which shook the very rock surface he was standing on. The ear-splitting sound of the explosion reached him next. Then he saw a huge fireball billowing upward from the quarry floor. The fireball created a cloud of dust, now spiraling upward from the explosion. It was forming a massive mushroom-shaped cloud. Getting back to his feet, Walter slowly approached the very edge of the quarry wall to look down into the quarry itself. What he saw below was almost beyond belief.

Where the dynamite shed once stood there was now a crater blasted into the rock-hardened quarry floor which had to be fifteen feet deep and over fifty feet across. There were several pieces of heavy equipment overturned from the force of the blast. The engineer's trailer was lying upside down about a hundred feet or more from where it once stood. The quarry office building was flattened by the explosion. Many workers were running about helping their co-workers, some of which were either injured or were trapped in the rubble. He looked around for any sign of Bud's truck. He really didn't expect to spot any sign and his instincts were right.

There was no visible trace of Bud's truck.

* * * * *

"Brother Phil, come quick. Something has happened to Father Campbell," said the small boy who was wide-eyed and out of breath.

Brother Phil looked around at the eleven boys who joined him on this fossil hunt. He called out to them. "Boys, we've got to go back immediately. There's been an accident. Let's hurry!"

The eleven boys stopped picking through the rocks along the shore of the lake and followed Brother Phil in a run back to the Shrine of St. Anne. The four boys, Lenny, Mark, Tony and Karl joined in the sprint back. No one had any idea what might have happened to the priest.

When all the boys arrived back at the Shrine, they joined up with the others, who were standing under a maple tree. There were whispered conversations between the boys.

Ahead of them, the three Brothers, the bus driver, two women and another man, who looked like he may be a priest as well, were huddled over someone lying on a bench. A siren could be heard from somewhere off in the distance. The siren sound was becoming more and more audible.

The person lying on the bench was not moving.

Karl pushed his way through the crowd of boys and stopped at the front of the group. Behind him one boy whispered to another. "He's not moving, I'll bet he's dead."

Lenny, Tony and Mark now pressed forward and stood next to Karl. Brother Julius, with a clearly frightened look about him, moved away from the group around Father Campbell and walked towards the crowd of boys.

"Please, stand back. Please!"

Lenny ran right past him towards the bench where Father Campbell was lying down. A loud siren blared from the Grand Isle Ambulance Service as it skidded to a stop in the gravel parking lot. The group standing by the priest had their attention momentarily distracted with the arrival of the ambulance. Their heads turned towards the sound of the siren so they didn't notice Lenny running to the bench.

Lenny stopped next to the bench. He looked down at his friend, Father Campbell. The priest's face was covered with a white handkerchief. There were two bloody stains over the place which was covering his eyes. There were other streaks of blood staining the handkerchief, which was sticking to Father Campbell's face. Lenny looked to see if the priest was breathing.

He was!

At that moment Karl scooted up next to Lenny and then Mark and Tony arrived as well. Each boy could plainly see the stricken priest lying on his back on the bench.

Brother Julius turned around and shouted to Brother Phil. "Brother Phil, for God's sake, the boys..."

Brother Phil turned away from looking over at the ambulance and saw immediately why Brother Julius had called out to him. He quickly stepped around the bench and spread his arms as if to shield the priest from the boys.

"Boys, this is nothing you should see. Please go wait over by Brother Julius."

While looking at Father Campbell, Lenny spotted blood on his right hand. Lenny squatted down and looked at the priest's left hand, which was hanging over the side of the bench near the ground. Lenny tapped Karl's leg. Karl squatted down and looked. He immediately spotted what caught Lenny's attention. Father Campbell's left hand, between his thumb and index finger, was pinching a squished bloody eyeball. A couple of sand flies were crawling across his blood-stained hand.

Brother Phil pulled Karl and Lenny to their feet and started to push them back. The four boys reluctantly cooperated.

The ambulance driver and an assistant rushed to the priest's side. The Brothers spoke in hushed tones to the adults gathered around the priest. The driver stood up and asked Brother Frank to give him a hand as they ran back to the ambulance. In a moment they returned with a stretcher. Stepping back, the adults and children watched as the ambulance driver and his assistant picked up Father Campbell and placed him upon the stretcher. The white cloth had been removed for a moment by one of the EMTs, but now Brother Frank placed it back over the face of the priest. The ambulance driver folded Father Campbell's arms across his chest and then strapped him onto the stretcher. The adults followed the stretcher to the rear of the ambulance. Father Campbell was loaded into the back of the ambulance. Brother Frank, followed by the one of the EMTs, climbed up into the back to be with Father Campbell. The other EMT, the ambulance driver, climbed into the ambulance's cab. Almost immediately the siren was turned back on and the ambulance lights began to flash. The ambulance backed up a short distance and pulled around as it quickly moved out of the parking lot.

Brother Julius and Brother Phil approached the crowd of boys.

Brother Julius spoke in a hushed tone.

"Boys, it seems our good friend Father Campbell has suffered an accident. He is on his way to the hospital. I ask each of you to join Brother Phil and me in prayer. Please come with me."

Silently everyone, including the bus driver, the other priest who, it was later learned, worked at the Shrine and the other adults followed along. Brother Julius stepped behind the wooden pulpit of the outdoor church as everyone else filled in the benches, being careful to avoid the bench that a few moments before was occupied by Father Campbell.

Brother Julius solemnly began to pray.

"Let us bow our heads in prayer. We pray to the Saints, to Mary the Mother of Jesus our Savior, and to God our Creator. We pray for their help for our good friend Father Campbell. All powerful Lord we......"

Lenny leaned over to Karl and whispered, "It was no accident."

Karl nodded his agreement.

Mark whispered to Karl. "What did he say?"

Karl turned to Mark and Tony and quietly said, "Lenny said it was no accident."

Mark looked at Karl. "Ne Wha Ta?" he said with a knowing look.

"Yup, it has to be!"

"Damn it," responded Mark.

Chapter 55

Mark paced the floor inside the airport waiting area. Sherrie's flight was late. The overhead monitor blinked that the arrival of her flight was on time, but its scheduled arrival was now fifteen minutes overdue. Mark was nervous. He knew Ne Wha Ta's powers and expected that somehow the monster had learned of their plans and done something terrible to Sherrie Sweeney.

Through the floor to ceiling windows at the arrival gate he was able to see only a small portion of the airport's runway.

A large passenger plane moved past the windows down the runway on the far side of the airport. In a couple of minutes the passenger gate representative of United Airlines Commuter Line announced the arrival of the flight Mark was waiting for. He blew out a puff of air to settle his nervous breathing. Several minutes later passengers were exiting the arrival gate and exchanging greetings with family or friends who had come to greet their arrival. Mark was beginning to wonder if Sherrie had indeed made this flight when he finally spotted her.

Sherrie was carrying a small overnight bag in one arm and her purse in the other. She was wearing sunglasses even though the day was a typical gray overcast mid-winter day. She recognized Mark and smiled an ice-melting smile at him. She was wearing a powder blue long sleeve cashmere sweater with a cowl neck. Her blond hair was tied back in a pony tail. She wore dungarees that, while some-what faded, fit her as if she'd grown into them. She had an L.L.

Bean lightweight jacket tied around her waist. She was drop dead gorgeous and had a model's complexion. Karl's daughter possessed all the natural beauty of her lovely mother, Linda. Sherrie was deeply devoted to her father Karl and was reported to be as equally stubborn as he.

Mark waved to her and she half ran to him. When she reached him, she put down her overnight bag and threw her arms around his neck and gave him a hug that brought a small amount of pain to the back of his neck. Mark was not going to complain about her vigorous greeting.

"Mark, thanks for picking me up."

"No problem. Do you have any other luggage?"

"Yes, as a matter of fact I do. It's only one piece. Do you mind?"

"Of course not," replied Mark with a smile.

"Gosh, it's so good to see you, Mark. How have you been?"

"I'm doing okay," he said with a lack of conviction in his voice.

"How's your father?"

"Dad's fine. He's a tough old bird."

"I can't wait to see him again. How are Lenny and Tony? I heard that Tony's wife is expecting. Isn't that wonderful?"

Sarcastically Mark answered, "I guess my Dad can't keep a secret."

"Hey, go easy on him. He's very special you know."

"I know. Geesh, Sherrie you look fabulous, if I may say so."

"Thanks, Mark," she responded with a hint of melancholy in her voice.

"Miss your Dad, huh?"

With a heavy sigh, she looked up at the ceiling of the airport terminal and Mark could see her swallow hard. Out from under her dark sunglasses a single tiny tear ran down her cheek.

"Uh-huh!"

"Me, too," said Mark. He turned away, because at that moment he felt, he, too, might cry.

"There's my luggage," said Sherrie pointing to a large piece of rectangular black canvas covered luggage.

"I'll get it."

With the luggage in tow they headed out of the terminal and walked out to the nearby parking lot while neither said a thing.

During the ride back to the Pushey residence they spoke only briefly about light weight matters such as the weather and her flight out. They both purposely avoided the hot topic which was the reason she'd flown out here in the first place. It was getting late in the day. Long shadows drifted across the roads and a few snowflakes fluttered about.

Even before the car came to a full stop, Mark's father was pulling open the door on Sherrie's side. Lenny and Tony were also outside to welcome her. Pokey was there, too, jumping up and twirling around with excitement. Sherrie's spirit responded to this warm and energized welcome with a burst of enthusiasm. When Mark finally stopped the car, she seemingly burst from the car and went to each member of her welcoming committee to properly hug each, including Pokey.

The merry group then proceeded to gather up her things and head inside the house.

Lenny carried her luggage to the remaining spare bedroom, which had been specially cleaned by Tony and Lenny earlier in the afternoon. Mark's father offered her some hot cocoa, which she accepted. It was heaping with miniature marshmallows.

Soon everyone was seated in the living room. The casual conversation died off and there was a moment of uncomfortable silence.

Sherrie broke the tension and spoke up. "I want everyone to understand something. I came back because I believe in my heart my father did not deliberately take his own life."

"We all believe that, too," said Lenny.

"There's more," she said. "Mr. Pushey, you told me over the phone something evil had driven him to commit suicide. Well, as it happens, I already know something about that."

Lenny, Tony and Mark were stunned. Mark's father knew what she was about to say because she previously revealed this secret to him when he called her and invited her to join them in this so-called crusade.

"My father left an audio tape which was probably meant for one of you. I found the tape the night of his funeral. I haven't shared this with anyone else. I found it hidden under his pajamas. I was looking through his things just to remind myself of him. Anyway, since he had this tape seemingly hidden, I hoped he might have left me a message, some kind of explanation of why he had left Mom, Bart and I. Needless to say, I was angry at him for what he'd done. No, I was much more than angry."

Sherrie was sniffling as she told her story. Tony rose and returned with a box of tissues which he placed next to Sherrie.

"Thanks. Well, I, ah...I played the tape and what I heard terrified me. I had no idea my Dad was being pursued by this thing, Ne Wha Ta. I cried all night long. I didn't know if anyone else knew what was going on. I didn't go to the authorities because I would have expected them to label my father as some kind of psychotic. It was bad enough he committed suicide, but to add madness on top would have twisted everyone's memory of him. I have prayed every night since that I could find a way to clear my father's name. When you called, Mr. Pushey, it was like a weight was lifted from my shoulders."

"Did you bring the tape with you?" asked Mr. Pushey.

"Dad, hasn't Sherrie gone through enough already?"

"No, Mark, I want you all to hear my dad. It's okay. I've gotten over the pain of hearing his voice. Really, it's all right."

"Where is it?" asked Lenny.

"It's in my purse," she said as she reached down inside her purse and removed the audio cassette. "Here."

Mr. Pushey took it from her, stood up, and headed into the kitchen. "The cassette player is in here."

With those words everyone followed along and went to the kitchen. They each chose a chair at the kitchen table as Karl's voice filled the room.

"This is for Lenny, Tony or Mark. Uh...It's about one-thirty in the morning. I've had to get up because I keep having nightmares. You guys understand what I'm talking about. That fucker is back. He's been dropping in regularly for the past two weeks. He's pissed off and said I'm going to have to bring everyone back together. All this shit is so damn tiring. I haven't had more than two hours sleep per night for the past six days. I don't want to let Linda or Sherrie or even Bart know a thing about this monster. Damn it all, today he almost made me drive over a couple of kids walking home from school."

The tape kept running with no sound to be heard except for a low level tape hiss.

"Is that it?" asked Mark.

Before she could answer, Karl's voice was broadcast once again by the tape player.

"Oh God... when will this end? No, I won't help you. No, I refuse. Why can't you just let me live my life in peace? No, I will not. Oh, Jesus that hurts.......Oh....G..od! You....can go take a flying fuck for yourself....Oooooooooooh. I...can't I just can't .... no, leave her out of this. No, you can't... ,I won't let.....Oooooh no.. This nightmare has got to end. It's just got to," said a desperate and distraught Karl.

For several more minutes the tape replayed the sounds of Karl sobbing deeply. Suddenly his sobbing came to a stop. Now, a voice Sherrie had never heard before this tape recording, spoke. It was a voice that everyone else in the kitchen had more than a passing familiarity with. From having played and replayed this tape, Sherrie knew each word by heart. She steeled herself for what she knew followed.

"You are sooooooo weak. You will regret this. I will take your life. I will then destroy everyone you have been protecting. Your wife, your children, and I will save for last your friends. I want them to know I'm coming. I want them to see the trail of blood I will leave. It will be your fault, Karl. This whole thing is your fault. Now think about this because when I return Karl, I will use you. You will be my personal instrument to destroy your family. Their blood will be on your hands. You have denied me my right to a mate. For too long you have stood in the way of my need to bring to life another of my kind, to extend my family's heritage, to extend the curse. I, Ne Wha Ta, and my ancestors must have another to carry on our bloodline. It is time! I will have my revenge!"

Everyone in the kitchen sat in stunned silence. The tape was still playing. Karl's distressful breathing could be clearly heard. Then his voice was heard once again.

"No fucking way!"

* * * * *

Everyone was herded onto the bus for the ride back to Don Bosco's. Brother Phil phoned ahead so someone would be there to pick up the four boys Father Campbell brought along on this fateful trip. Lenny sat with Tony and Karl sat with Mark. The windows on the school bus were pulled down so that inside the bus it was windy as the air swirled throughout.

Karl took a small note book and pencil out of his backpack. Karl started to write notes that began to fill a couple of pages. He then drew a couple of diagrams on the note pad. He ripped up some sheets and reworked the material. He refused to let Mark see what he was working on.

Meanwhile, in the seat directly in front of them sat Tony and Lenny. Lenny sat next to the window. He sat silently staring out the window at nothing in particular. Tony looked over at his friend and knew Lenny was thinking about Father Campbell. Everyone knew Lenny admired the priest. Tony noticed there were tears running down Lenny's face.

Before he could say something to Lenny, Karl interrupted with, "Hey, guys, listen up."

Karl leaned over the back of Lenny and Tony's seat with his note pad in hand. Mark sat up and was hanging onto Lenny's and Tony's seat back.

"I've got it figured out. We're going after him tomorrow. I don't think we can wait any longer, because too many people are in danger. We have got to seal him up in his cave and pronto."

"So how are we going to pull this off?" asked Tony.

"Here's how," said Karl, as he handed his notepad to Lenny. "I've made these notes and I also drew some pictures to kind of show how it has to be set up. So, what do you think?"

After flipping through the notepad, Lenny handed the pad to Tony and said, "It could work."

"You bet your ass it could work," said an excited Karl.

Tony handed the notepad to Mark. Mark had a turn to examine Karl's plan.

When Mark finished, he looked up. The other boys were all looking at him for his reaction. He smiled one of his best shit-eating grins ever. That immediately set off satisfied grins on each boy's face.

They all sat back contemplating the mission which now lay before them. Each privately resolved to faithfully complete this challenge. They were united in their bond to bring to an end this monster's grip on their lives.

Meanwhile, Ne Wha Ta was focused upon communicating with the stricken priest. He tried to get inside the priest's mind by sending numerous sacrilegious messages. Unknown to Ne Wha Ta, his attempts to mentally torture the priest were short circuited by the influence pain had upon the now sightless priest. Father Campbell was alert enough to know he needed to survive this attack. This monster could very well be Satan himself. Until he could safely confide in a senior and trustworthy priest, Father Campbell would try to lock out Ne Wha Ta by embracing the pain he felt. Never before had he ever experienced the headache he now was experiencing.

The ambulance driver was driving as fast as he dared. Meanwhile, in the back of the ambulance with Father Campbell was Brother Frank. Father Campbell could hear him praying through the haze of his pain. Father Campbell did not dare to confide in Brother Frank. He could not take a chance and perhaps risk harm to Brother Frank.

The ambulance's siren was switched off, as the vehicle pulled to a stop at the back side of Fanny Allen Hospital in Colchester. The emergency facilities, while adequate, were not as impressive as those of the larger nearby hospitals in Burlington. However, this hospital was the preferred one for the priest, given the fact his trauma condition was deemed non-life threatening. Being a Diocesan priest meant you were treated at the most "affordable available facility."

Father Campbell was wheeled into the hospital emergency area. Standing at either side of his gurney were two nuns in their full nursing habits. The taller of the two spoke softly under her breath, "Jesus, Mary and Joseph," as both nuns made the sign of the cross.

Finally, Ne Wha Ta gave up trying to exact dominance over the mind of the priest.

* * * * *

"Now you know why I wanted in on this," said Sherrie.

"Geesh, Karl must have been pursued by Ne Wha Ta for quite a while," said Tony.

"That's over. We must prepare for our own battle with this monster. If we don't move soon, then none of us will be safe," said Mark's father.

"Dad's right."

"So we have this plan and now we have Sherrie on our team. What else will we need?" asked Lenny.

"The plan is not yet ready. I have to go and speak to someone first. When I return, we'll set our strategy into motion," said Mr. Pushey.

He got up and grabbed his overcoat and headed out the door. Pokey padded along behind him but was prevented from following out the back door.

Sherrie and the guys watched Mr. Pushey pull his car out of the driveway and drive down the street.

"Well, we'd better get started on dinner. Anyone care to help?" asked Mark.

"I will," said Sherrie.

"Me, too," said Tony.

"Count me in," said Lenny.

I guess no one wants to be alone right now, thought Mark as everyone headed into the kitchen. *It's because we have some time to kill,* he thought. The irony of this point brought a smile to his face.

* * * * *

Karl was already sweating from the weight of the car battery he was carrying. He was carrying it inside the same wooden box the gas station owner had given him along with the battery. Inside the box was a roll of small gauge copper wire that was over one hundred and fifty feet long. He also brought along a folding knife and the four sticks of dynamite with the blasting caps still attached. He didn't want anyone else to carry this material. It was dangerous and he didn't want anyone else to get hurt. The other boys followed at a short distance behind. They entered the woods at the end of Pine Street. After they'd traveled a couple of hundred feet into the woods, Karl stopped and put the box down. He wiped his forehead with his clean but stained handkerchief.

"After what happened yesterday I didn't think we'd be able to tackle this today," said Lenny.

"Same here," said Karl. "My mother was really strung out over what happened to Father Campbell."

"You can say that again. My father and mother must have asked me a hundred questions," said Mark.

"Same here," said Tony.

Karl bent over and picked up the box. With his right knee, he boosted it up so he could get a good grip on it.

"Want me to carry the box for a while?" asked Lenny.

"No, it's okay. Look, from now on as we head to the cave and until I give the signal, we need to try and think about something besides what we're going to do. We don't want this Ne Wha Ta to get a whiff of our plan before we have a chance to spring it."

"So what do you want us to think about?" asked Tony.

"I want you guys to pray!"

They all nodded. Karl picked up the box and continued to head deeper into the woods. At the pace he was setting, they could expect to be at the cave in about thirty minutes. It would take a few minutes to set things up and then they could try to kill Ne Wha Ta. He hoped his plan would work.

* * * * *

The early heat of the day had already begun to cook the early morning air into a hot soupy kind of swelter. There was a huge dark swarm of flies settled on the rotting flesh of St. Germain. They would occasionally take flight whenever a crow landed on the truck door and hopped inside the truck to peck at the flesh. The incidence of crows or any other animal arriving to take away some of his flesh had declined dramatically since he had died. The rotting flesh had become too ripe for most scavengers, except, of course, the flies and the maggots.

It would be nearly four more weeks before his remains would be discovered.

* * * * *

St. Germain's body was discovered by an employee of the City of Winooski's Water Department. The following day a two sentence article reporting the gruesome discovery was carried on page 3 of the local newspaper.

Body of man found yesterday in his vehicle parked beneath the City of Sinooski's Water Storage Tower. Police are investigating.

Chapter 56

"You say all this is true."

"I swear to you upon my dead wife's grave," said Mr. Pushey.

"If it is, why don't I just arrange to have a search of these caves made? I'm sure we could draw him out."

"That won't work. Please, you got to believe me. This is the only way. We can't afford any mistakes."

"All right! Let's suppose I buy into this, even though I have my doubts. When do you expect to try and pull this off?"

"Tomorrow afternoon."

"That doesn't leave me much time does it?"

"I know."

"Well, all I can say is, you'd better be right or I'm going to look pretty foolish."

"I'm not worried about looking foolish, I'm worried about being able to stay alive," said Mr. Pushey.

Something in his voice and his eyes were convincing and compelling at the same time. The two men shook hands. Mr. Pushey got up from the chair in the den and with a nod he moved swiftly to let himself out.

* * * * *

Karl stopped and put the heavy wooden box down. He wiped his forehead again. Karl gestured to the others to stay put until he'd finished with his work and gave them the signal. He also gestured to them to keep praying. It was important to keep their minds busy.

Karl picked up the box. Heading in a semi-circle, he pursued a wide berth away from the cave's entrance. He carefully kept to the wooded side of the hollow. In a few minutes he was climbing the steep rocky face of the hill which towered over the cave. He slid along the smooth surface until he reached the large flat rock that was balanced at the summit of the hill directly over the entrance to the cave. He set the box down and then he took out the dynamite.

Down below and across the hollow the other boys could see Karl at work. They were all busy watching and praying.

Karl was sweating heavily. His hands were drenched in sweat. He wiped his hands on his dungarees several times. Karl took out the roll of wire and unrolled quite a bit of the white coated copper wire. He took the folding knife from the box and cut the wire once he figured he had rolled out about half of the wire.

Karl stripped the end of the cut wire and carefully wrapped it around the white wires that protruded from the blasting caps, which were themselves stuck inside of the ends of the four sticks of dynamite. Next he stripped the end of the wire that was still wrapped around the roll. He unrolled a few feet of this wire and very carefully wrapped this wire around the black wire which was also extending from the blasting caps. When he was through with this step, he noticed his hands were shaking.

With sweat running down his back, Karl kept working. He began to slide slowly backwards, unrolling one wire from the roll and pulling the other wire along. He moved back nearly ninety feet when the wire connected to the dynamite's white wire came to an end. He placed it under the box to hold it in place. He cut the wire that was on the roll and stripped it to expose the copper underneath. He carefully wrapped this wire around the positive terminal of the car battery. With that task completed, he started to lift the battery out of the box when the other wire slipped out from under the box. The weight of the car battery helped keep it under the box. The wire began to slide away from Karl. In an instant he let go of the car battery and reached out his left hand to catch the wire before it slipped away. Karl looked down at his sweaty hands and wondered if his moist hands touching the one wire and the car battery at the same time could accidentally set off the dynamite. It didn't and Karl was deeply relieved.

Karl took the unconnected wire and stripped it to also expose the copper wire underneath. When he was done he tied the wire to the wooden box. With this dangerous part done, he wiped his hands once again on his dungarees.

Karl tried to stand up so he could signal his buddies. He found his legs were like rubber. He had to push himself to his feet in order to wave to the guys who were watching him from across the hollow.

It was time.

* * * * *

Mr. Pushey removed his winter overcoat and hung it up on the wall pegs behind the back door. Pokey padded over to him and received a scratch behind his ears then trotted away to settle back down in his usual place.

Everyone except Sherrie was sitting in the living room waiting for him. He had been gone for nearly an hour. They were beginning to worry about him.

"She's upstairs taking a shower," said Lenny, anticipating Mr. Pushey's question.

Mark's father sat in his usual chair. Looking around the room before he spoke, he said, "We do it tomorrow afternoon."

"Will you have everything you think we'll need?" asked Tony.

"Yes, I just took care of that."

"What about Sherrie?"

"What about her?"

"Is she going to be in on this?"

"I am not completely sure, probably not."

"Probably, what do you mean?" asked Mark.

"It depends on tonight. And, it depends on Ne Wha Ta."

"What are we going to do tonight?" asked Tony.

"We are going to have a conversation with Ne Wha Ta. We must set the bait, so to speak. If he bites, then we will have a small advantage tomorrow."

"And if he doesn't?" said Lenny.

* * * * *

Lenny, Tony and Mark saw Karl wave. Upon seeing the signal, Lenny moved out to take up his position. He crept along the left side of the hollow until he reached the side of the rocky hill. He was going to listen for the approach of Ne Wha Ta.

Mark also moved to his position. He went over to a medium tall pine tree and started to climb. He climbed up to a spot about twenty feet off the ground. He had a clear view of Karl and Lenny and he could also see Tony.

Tony pulled his backpack off. He reached inside and pulled out a copy of the June edition of *Playboy*. His hands were sweating heavily. He flipped through the magazine and reached the centerfold. He unfolded it and held it up in front of his face to block out any view of the cave or of Karl or Lenny. Tony looked at the half-nude figure and studied her ample and seductive shape. It didn't take him long to have her image solidly in his memory. Now, for the hard part. He called out loud to Ne Wha Ta.

"Ne Wha Ta, look what I brought you. Isn't she a beauty? Come out and get her. She's all yours."

Lenny listened, with his left ear pressed firmly against the rocky surface.

"Hey, I thought you wanted a woman. Well, here she is," shouted Tony.

The boy's voice reached the ears of Ne Wha Ta. He listened to what Tony had to say.

"So the young male has given in and brought me a female," thought the monster. He decided to enter this male's mind and make sure. He gently probed and just as he was told, there was a human female there. She didn't seem afraid at all. That was good!

"You have done well, my friend," said Ne Wha Ta to the mind of Tony.

Tony almost lost his concentration. He was caught off guard by the suddenness at hearing Ne Wha Ta speak to him. He struggled to regain his focus on the *Playboy* centerfold. For once in his young life focusing on a nearly nude woman was proving to be a struggle. Nevertheless, he reacquired his concentration.

"She will meet my needs, young one."

"Come and get her." said Tony

"No, send her to me."

"I can't."

"Why?"

"Because, she's ...uh... shy, yeah, she's shy."

"Shy?"

"Look, I brought her here, but I can't make her go inside the cave, okay! Only you can do that."

"I will speak to her."

"No... no, I mean, can't you tell she's hot? She wants you. Why not come and get her?" His heart was pounding at a furious pace.

The other boys were all watching and waiting.

Ne Wha Ta had been moving towards the cave's entrance during his conversation with Tony. The entrance to the cave was not quite in Lenny's field of view. He kept listening for any sign of an approaching Ne Wha Ta.

Karl waited at the top of the hill carefully focused on Mark. Mark in turn tried to keep an eye on everyone else. No one was watching the front of the cave.

Ne Wha Ta had been waiting for this moment for over a hundred and forty years. He made a fateful decision to move ahead and take this female. He had waited long enough. He was lying on his back and was beginning to slide himself out of the cave.

Tony's hands were shaking as he held the centerfold up before him. Ne Wha Ta was no longer speaking to him. He thought, "What's he waiting for?"

Ne Wha Ta was nearly all the way out of the cave when Lenny spotted him out of the corner of his eye. He'd somehow missed hearing him coming.

Lenny turned quickly and waved in the direction of Mark. At that moment Mark also spotted the monster exiting the cave. He began to wave at Karl.

Ne Wha Ta couldn't see anything since he was sightless. Nevertheless his instincts were always tuned for survival. He sensed something was moving to his left, followed almost immediately by sudden movement behind him across the hollow. He heard something moving along the rocky surface high above him. It was a trap.

When Karl noticed the wave coming from Mark he reached out with his right hand, and touched the bare copper wire to the negative terminal, which now completed the circuit. A large earth-shaking explosion shook the rocky hill.

Ne Wha Ta was scampering to reenter the cave.

A low rumble began as the thirty five ton rock broke free from the surface of the hill and began to slide down the rocky face of the hill. It was heading straight for the cave's entrance.

Ne Wha Ta barely reached the safety of the cave when the rock crashed down. It pushed several feet into the ground, sealing up the front of the cave. Numerous pebbles and sand cascaded down the rocky hill. In a moment, everything was still.

Karl had ducked down behind an elm tree. He stood up and looked at Mark. Mark gestured with a thumbs-up sign before he began to climb down from the tree. Lenny hesitatingly moved to the front of the cave and stood in front of the large rock. In a moment he was joined by the others.

They were smiling and slapping each other on the back.

"We did it! Damn! We did it!" exclaimed Lenny.

"Yeah, we did," said a very happy Karl. "Let's get the hell away from here."

At this moment the boys were the happiest they had been all that summer. They turned and headed back home. They would have to celebrate.

Ne Wha Ta rushed to the deepest part of his network of caves. He had just escaped his first real brush with death.

His chest was heaving rapidly. He was filled with rage. He

screamed at the top of his lungs. Only the thousands of bats that lived inside the caves and tunnels of his domain heard his fearsome scream. He raced about his cave, reaching out for anything he could get his powerful hands on. He picked up thigh bones, skulls, even boots and shoes. He flung these about in a fury of explosive anger. With his anger not yet spent, he raised up huge boulders often several hundred pounds apiece and flung them across the cave to smash against the pile of discarded human and animal bones he had been stockpiling over many years. He screamed again and pulled hair from his chest. Nervous bats fluttered everywhere. At last, his anger began to subside. Exhausted, he collapsed on the floor of the cave, his fists clinched tightly and pressed against his temples.

After several quiet moments Ne Wha Ta began to focus his mind to his near brush with his own death. He mentally debated his next course of action. Ne Wha Ta stood up and began to pace the floor of his domain. In a low but fearsome voice he debated his options.

"I-- I will have my revenge for this!"

He would have to wait for just the right moment. Now would not be the right time. He would fulfill the tradition of the Ne Wha Ta to sire a child with a human female brought willingly to him by humans of his choosing. His mistake was in choosing humans too young to truly appreciate his awesome powers.

He vowed to himself, the next time he would be patient.

They would have left by now thinking they had triumphed over him. This could be turned to his advantage. The next time he approached them they would be surprised and unsettled by his having survived their youthful attack. He would break their collective power and yet use them to have a female mate.

His voice bellowed throughout the cave and surrounding tunnels. "I am Ne Wha Ta! I will have a human female! They will bring one to me or I will destroy everything they know and love. I promise this on the graves of my ancestors!"

His impatience had almost cost him his life, but never again would he make such a mistake.

Chapter 57

Sherrie came downstairs after her shower. Her hair was still damp and the sweet smell of her shampoo filled the air in the living room. Lenny, Tony, Mark and his father were all waiting for her arrival before they began. Sherrie elected to sit cross-legged on the living room floor.

Mark's father began to explain what needed to be done next, and how they all needed to be on guard. This phase of their efforts to trick Ne Wha Ta must not fail. After a few moments of discussion, they were ready to begin.

Mark was elected to make the initial contact. He spoke out loud. "Ne Wha Ta,....Ne Wha Ta, speak with me, now!"

It was Mark's father's idea, that for this contact, everyone should be assertive, not belligerent. This change in attitude was hoped to keep Ne Wha Ta just a little off balance. The key was to try to appear convincing in their collective interest to bring this struggle to an end, at whatever the cost.

Mark heard Ne Wha Ta's answer almost instantly.

"I am here. I have always been here, waiting."

"There are others here with me. They also want to speak to you. Use me, to speak to them all."

In a moment, Mark was knocked backwards onto the couch. His eyes rolled up into his head, showing only the whites of his eyes. Mark's eyelids fluttered rapidly.

In a gravely voice, Ne Wha Ta used Mark as a temporary vessel to communicate with the others. As Mark's lips began to move, he sat back up and his eyes focused intently on everyone in the room.

Ne Wha Ta's voice broke the silence in the room.

"I see Tony, and Lenny, heh, heh. It is nice of you both to come home."

He looked at Mark's father and stopped, seemingly puzzled.

"I know this old one. You are the parent to Mark."

"Yes, I am. I am also the one you almost killed one summer many years ago before I was saved by St. Germain's daughter."

Mark, filled temporarily with the spirit of Ne Wha Ta, squinted at his father before breaking into a wide grin as the monster spoke. "I remember that time. She fought fiercely but no human can be a match for my strength and powers. Her flesh was special." Mark was licking his lips in an obscene manner.

"Ne Wha Ta, do you know who I am?" asked Sherrie.

Mark turned and looked down at Sherrie. His eyes narrowed as he zeroed in his gaze upon her.

"I know who you are. You are the female spawn of Karl. He was so proud of you and wanted the best for you. I can provide what he wanted for you, little one. I am the best of my kind," replied Ne Wha Ta through Mark. Mark now grinned at this comment, as Ne Wha Ta seemed to enjoy this dialogue.

Sherrie skillfully hid her bitter emotion at what she had just heard. Her anger could come later.

"We are going to make you an offer you can't refuse, Ne Wha Ta. I am prepared to mate with you. I am no virgin, but I am fertile enough to have a child. To bring an end to all the pain you have put my family through I will, fulfill your foul and evil demand, but I, too, have demands. We will mate, as you put it, only once. I will give you your child, but on three conditions. First, you will not come near me any time after we mate. Second, you will release me to go to have your child, which I agree to deliver to you. Third, you will leave all of us and our families alone after this, forever."

"That is your offer! That is your offer! Why should I agree to this? Why is it something I can't refuse?"

Mark's father spoke next.

"Listen, carefully Ne Wha Ta. If you don't agree, I and Lenny,

Mark and Tony are all prepared to take our lives tonight. We believe based upon your curse, with our deaths, you would have to start all over in finding a human or humans to help you find a mating partner. How much time do you have Ne Wha Ta, how much time do you have left to fulfill your destiny?"

The monster was intrigued by this proposition. This female was not some paper image, she was flesh and blood. Better yet, she was Karl's daughter. How fitting! Could he trust her or them? He quickly left Mark's mind and mentally leaped from Tony to Lenny, to Mark's father and finally to Sherrie. He was searching for any sign of a plot, a trick, a deception. Finding none, he returned to occupy Mark's mind once more.

"How is this to be done?" asked the monster through Mark.

"First, where do you want us to meet you?" asked Lenny.

"You must come to the cave where we first met. The cave where you tried to destroy me! You do remember where it is?" asked Ne Wha Ta.

"Yes, we remember. But it was closed up when we dropped a huge rock on the cave's entrance," said Lenny.

"I have taken care of that. The rock has been destroyed."

"So, tomorrow, we will all come to your cave. The cave you first made yourself known to my father and the others. I will join you to get this disgusting thing done. Then we will all leave. I refuse to live in that cave, especially with you. I will live here, while your spawn develops. After its birth, it is yours. My part will be done, as promised," said Sherrie with an air of defiance.

"Very well, I accept this. But I warn each of you. If I find a trick, or plot, planned against me, you will not have to take your own lives. I will do it for you, after I kill every one, each of you cares for, even that dog. Do not think you can defeat me. Tomorrow is set. It is the day my ancestors will at last have their line extended by yet one more generation."

"Before I go, I have a message for Karl's little girl." Mark's eyes tried to focus upon Sherrie. "I will have a surprise waiting for you tomorrow."

With those words Ne Wha Ta released his grip on Mark and Mark fell back onto the couch. He was in a faint. His pulse was racing. He was clammy to the touch. Drool was spilling from the edges of his half-opened mouth.

Everyone else looked at each other. No one smiled, no one spoke, but each knew the other was thinking the same thoughts at that moment. They were all thinking the price of failure this time was too high. Failure was not an option anymore.

Sherrie also wondered about the surprise he had promised her, as did Mark's father.

Gene Pushey went to his bedroom, closed the door and made a call.

* * * * *

Mark's father checked his watch for the umpteenth time. He was nervous and couldn't get himself settled down. He took Pokey for a walk not only this morning but again after lunch. He even made lunch for everyone, but no one ate.

A winter storm had begun earlier in the morning. The radio weather forecaster indicated this storm would produce intermittent snow squalls. Accumulation was not expected to amount to any more than three to four inches. The city's snow trucks drove by earlier and dropped salt and sand on the street. Not much snow had actually fallen yet.

The shotgun salvaged from the front of Ne Wha Ta's cave back in 1962 stood against the wall over by the back door. It was fully loaded with four rounds in its magazine and one in the chamber. The five shotgun shells were slug loads designed primarily to bring down their target from up close. The gun possessed what is often described as stopping power. The gun's thumb safety was engaged.

Tony had called his wife earlier. They spoke about his being able to come home soon. Tony only hoped it would be so. Mark was generally quiet, as was Lenny, who couldn't seem to sit down. He kept pacing from room to room. Sherrie spent the last half hour composing a letter to her brother and her mom. She licked the envelope and went upstairs to lay it carefully upon the center of her bed. A yellow post-it note was stuck on the outside of the envelope which said, "Please do not open, forward to the addressed party."

Sherrie came down the stairs and went into the kitchen. Everyone was putting their overcoats on. Mark's father knelt down and gave Pokey a hug. The dog's tail wagged vigorously at first and then stopped. The dog let out a small soft whine. It was as if it sensed something bad might happen to its master.

"Stay, Pokey, stay," commanded Gene Pushey. His voice was slightly broken.

Mark's father picked up the shotgun and headed out the back door. The others followed.

"Dad, don't you want to lock the door?"

"No," responded a determined Gene Pushey, without looking back.

The five of them trudged up the street heading northward. At the end of the street they moved across a small field in the direction of the woods that lay just beyond. There were rabbit tracks everywhere. Snow began to fall. The wind began to pick up as well. There wasn't a tamped down path to follow. They had to break through the nearly three feet of winter snow as they went. Lenny was in the lead, followed by Tony, Mark, Sherrie and then Mark's father.

The woods were quiet.

High overhead in a pine tree sat a solitary large black crow. Its head turned from side to side as it seemed to be trying to get a better look at the five humans trudging through the snowy woods below. Its small coal black eyes fixed upon the humans as it studied each one as they passed below. Everything seemed as it should, so the crow took flight and quietly moved up in the sky and turned to the north. Its mission now complete, it was now free.

Mark's father noticed the crow take flight. He waited until the crow was safely out of sight before he stopped. He shifted the shotgun to his right arm. He was carrying the gun concealed under his long, faded army coat. As an added precaution, he would keep the gun concealed until the last possible moment. He hurried to catch up with the others, since he had fallen behind. As he went, he kept a watchful lookout for any other creatures that might have been sent to spy on them.

The snow crunched under their feet. The falling snow made a soft swishing sound as the flakes tumbled through the pine trees on their way to the ground.

After a hike of nearly forty-five minutes, they reached the side of the hollow the guys remembered from that summer so long ago. The snow was falling heavily. Visibility was down to less than a hundred feet. It was almost three in the afternoon and in the hollow deep in these woods it was already settling into early evening's twilight.

The large rock that fell down from the rocky hill above and thought to have crushed Ne Wha Ta was lying in pieces on the ground in front of the cave. It had somehow toppled, no doubt assisted by the efforts of the monster and the effects of the renewed dynamiting at Bremer's Quarry. To the left side of the cave entrance stood a pine tree about ten feet tall.

Slowly they crossed the hollow until they stood about seventy-five feet in front of the cave. Standing in the front were Lenny, Mark and Tony. Directly behind them were Sherrie and Gene Pushey. The gun was still hidden beneath his long coat.

"Close enough," whispered Mark's father.

"Okay, guys, let's get it over with" said a determined Sherrie.

Lenny shouted, "Ne Wha Ta."

His own voice echoed back to him. There was no sound. There were no mental connections from the monster. There was nothing but deep silence.

"Again," said Mark.

"Ne Wha Ta, we're here."

From inside the cave came their response.

A gravely voice bellowed to them, "Send her to me."

They didn't answer him. No one moved.

The voice returned, only louder and more commanding. "I said send her to me, NOW!"

Lenny responded, "No, you must come out and prove to us you do not mean to hurt her."

Laughter sounded from inside of the cave.

"Karl's spawn, I have a gift for you," and with that a long hairy arm extended from the cave and knocked over the small pine tree which stood at the left of the cave's entrance. It had been stuck in the ground to conceal something which Ne Wha Ta now revealed to everyone.

It was Karl Sweeney. His corpse was standing upright with his arms folded across his chest. His disfigured head from the suicide was turned slightly so it was exposed for them to see. Snow had built up on the shoulders of his dark suit. His skin color was ashen gray and his cheeks were shriveled and sunken.

Sherrie put her hands to her face and began to sob.

Mark shouted at the top of his lungs, "You fucking bastard."

Ne Wha Ta once again managed to gain the upper hand. He had thoroughly surprised them. Their minds were swirling.

The monster spoke again. In a mocking tone he said, "It is only right he should be here to celebrate this day."

Lenny felt the arrowhead inside his right pocket. Mark and Tony had tied theirs to their necks. They each wore the small medicine token Louis St. Germain had given them over forty-five years ago. Mark's father also carried his own arrowhead and medicine necklace. Sherrie brought nothing but her own courage and powerful need for revenge.

Mark's father spoke in a hushed voice. "We must stay focused. He wants us to be out of control. Let's not forget why we're here."

Simultaneously Sherrie spoke between sobs, "For my father's sake and everyone else that he killed..."

"Come to me, human. You offered a deal which I have agreed to. My loins await the pleasure of your human flesh."

"You bastard, this deal is off," said Lenny, mustering as much anger as possible.

"Yeah, you can just hang it high. We're out of here," said Tony.

"NO…"

"It's no longer up to you. You're just an animal. We won't be a part of helping you have your little Ne Wha Ta. Let's go," said Mark.

The three guys turned their backs on the cave's entrance as they shielded Sherrie and Mark's father.

Mark's father and Sherrie looked past their shoulders and could see the monster finally pull out of the cave.

Sherrie whispered, "He's out."

The three guys turned around so now all five of them stood face to face with the legend in the flesh, Ne Wha Ta.

He stood at nearly six-and-a-half feet tall. He had long pure white hair tied back. His ears were pointy and very large. His jaw protruded from the base of his face. He had a long narrow nose and sunken eye sockets where eyes should have been. His large muscular body was very hairy. His skin appeared pale. He had enormous teeth. He stood before them, feet apart, with his long powerful arms at his side, with his hands clenched tightly into fists.

"You will never make it out of the woods alive." Pointing with the unusually long index finger of his left hand, he commanded, "Karl's most precious one, come to me."

Sherrie could feel her will slip away as she began to step forward towards the monster.

Lenny moved in front of her, wrapped his arms around her and tried to run across the hollow with her in his arms. He'd traveled only twenty feet when he fell to the ground with her in his arms. He was now gasping for breath and pulling at his throat.

Ne Wha Ta stepped forward a couple of steps. Sherrie stood up and began to once again go to him.

This time Mark ran at her and knocked her to the ground with a football style tackle. Ne Wha Ta stepped forward another step as Mark grabbed at his chest. He was feeling enormous pressure on his heart. Lenny's breathing had begun to improve.

Sherrie broke free from Mark and stepped towards Ne Wha Ta. They were now less than thirty feet apart. Tony moved towards her, but before he could do a thing, he clutched his head and fell to his knees. Ne Wha Ta took another step towards Sherrie and she towards him.

The monster spoke to Mark's father. "So old one do you think you alone can stop me?"

"No, I know how powerful you are."

"Good, you may wait here while I take her inside. Do not worry if you hear her scream. It will be because I will have given her pleasure no human could ever possibly provide. She will be sent out after I am through with her."

Sherrie walked past Gene Pushey in a trance like state. Ne Wha Ta turned his back on Mr. Pushey as he proceeded to put his left arm on Sherrie's shoulders. They were both no more than fifteen feet away when Gene Pushey raised the gun out from under his long coat. He quickly placed the butt of the gun into his shoulder and took aim.

"Ne Wha Ta, prepare to die," said Mark's father.

The monster quickly turned and dropped to his knees in a defensive move.

The trigger was pulled but nothing happened. The safety was still engaged. Before he could release the safety, his head exploded with pressure. Ne Wha Ta stepped towards him to kill him and the others. The monster was no longer in the bargaining mood. He took a step from his crouched position towards Gene Pushey.

A shot rang out. The monster stopped moving.

Another shoot soon followed the first.

Suddenly, Gene Pushey regained use of his mental faculties. He slipped the safety off.

The first two shots came from above the cave and had struck Ne Wha Ta in the back. He'd turned to try and locate the source of these shots. He was bleeding from two bullet holes in his upper back.

The shotgun fired its first slug. It found its mark, the right shoulder area. The monster roared in pain. He spun around to face the shotgun when he was struck with a shot from both weapons. The second shotgun slug tore into the right side of his face, ripping his ear clean off. The other weapon's bullet hit him in the back of his left thigh. He screamed. No longer interested in the human female, his grip on her mind was released. Sherrie awoke from her trance. Realizing what was happening, Sherrie dove to the ground to get out of the way. The shotgun roared twice more with shots that found their target. This time the shotgun slug ripped into his stomach. The other shots clipped his right arm and grazed his right side. He desperately started crawling back towards the cave.

Several shots ripped into him from above, slowing his crawl. He roared out in pain. A trail of his blood stretched behind him in the snow.

Mr. Pushey walked toward the monster. He placed the shotgun next to his head. Feeling the cold steel next to his skin, Ne Wha Ta turned his face to the gun just as it fired. This last shot finally killed him. His body collapsed into the snow as blood flowed freely from his many wounds.

From above, someone descended and jumped down off the rocky hill to stand next to Gene Pushey.

"Thanks, Chief."

"I would have never believed it unless I saw it with my own eyes. He's one ugly son-of-a-bitch."

"Ugly, once deadly, and now thanks to your help, he's a dead legend."

Sherrie, Tony, Mark and Lenny stood with Chief Contois and Mark's father.

"I'll have to turn the body over to the FBI, but other than that, I think we'll probably be able to shut down this investigation," said Chief Contois.

"What's going to happen to the body?" asked Sherrie.

"That's a good one. I really don't know. I suspect the Feds will probably want to take it to Washington. Who knows?"

Snow continued to fall.

Epilogue

Lenny had been back to work for several months. It was now August and it was hot and steamy in Boston.

He was sitting at his computer and furiously pounding at the keyboard. He seemed obsessed to finish whatever he was working on. After a few moments, he leaned back in his chair and stared at the monitor. He had turned the air conditioning off and opened the sliding doors to his balcony. A slight breeze pushed against the floor length, sheer curtains.

He took the computer's mouse and moved the cursor up to save the document he was working on. He clicked the mouse and the save function was executed instantly.

Somewhere in his condominium a radio was playing. It was set to a Boston Oldies Radio station. A caller from Revere had just made a request for a song from 1962. It was Ray Charles' "I Can't Stop Loving You."

The song played softly in the background. Soon the words came into focus.

He got up from his computer and picked up the sweaty glass of bourbon sitting on the cork coaster on his coffee table. The computer's words stared at him from the screen.

"I was only back from Vermont two weeks when the nightmares began. At first that's all I thought they were, nightmares. But then the voice was inside my head during the day. The strange telephone messages....computer messages and then a month ago it happened. I had a conversation with another one. It was Ne Wha Ta's sister. She has been living here, in Boston, in caves and tunnels, even the subway system, since at least the mid 1800s. She has been hounding me for days. She said instant death would be too good for me. She wants me to suffer, painfully. Her brother's spirit came to her in a dream and told her everything. She has vowed to get to each of you, to avenge her brother's death. Will this nightmare ever end for us? How many are there?"

Lenny was about to send the above message as an e-mail to Tony. He started to reach for the keyboard to enter the keystrokes when he suddenly dropped his glass of bourbon onto the tiled floor. It shattered at his feet. He reached up for his head with both of his hands and gripped his head at the temples. He staggered about the room, knocking over lamps and stumbling over furniture.

"Oh, God, please leave me alone! Please. Oh no. That hurts so much! No, I won't tell you where she is! No, you will not! I won't give in. I won't!"

Lenny fell to his knees. His throat was showing signs of someone or something strangling him. He began to turn blue from the lack of oxygen.

"You can't have Mark's father either, you bitch!" he said through clenched teeth.

With some effort Lenny stood up and staggered to the balcony. He suddenly was looking up at his hands which were raised in front of his face.

"Noooooooo!"

Lenny made a sudden decision. He couldn't stand the torture any longer. He knew through him this new Ne Wha Ta would try and reach the others and destroy them, too. There was really no other choice for him. He had to deny this monster, just like its brother, any chance of using him or his friends to secure a mate. His only weapon was his own life.

In an instant, his eyes were removed by his own hands. Searing sharp pain now exploded throughout his head.

Blood gushed from his eye sockets.

"Bitch," he screamed. His decision now sealed.

Lenny took two quick steps towards his balcony's railing as he lunged over the rail. He fell silently to his death.

As his body lay crumpled and broken in the hedges, upstairs in his condominium, his computer's keyboard keys and mouse moved in harmony. The mouse selected a file, "click." Then the mouse selected delete, and it clicked for the very last time.

Lenny's message to warn the others was wiped from the screen.

Lenny's only remaining message to the others was this—his empty eye sockets would serve as his message.

Would it be enough?

Acknowledgments

My deepest appreciation for all her support and encouragement goes to my wife and best friend, Anne. Without her love and wisdom my life's journey would be missing out on her creative passion, her sense of humor, her generous heart and her deep forgiving love.

My appreciation is extended to my three sons who are technologically and creatively talented light years beyond their dad. Your contribution to my writing career is immeasurable. They all also take after their mother!

My two daughters-in-law and my three granddaughters are so very important to me that words cannot sufficiently convey my sentiments. I love each and all very, very much!

My own parents played an incredible part in shaping my drive and curiosity and in giving up so much to make my life better than their own! Eternal thanks, Mom and Dad!

I am deeply humbled and inspired by my faithful readers who invested resources, time and interest in my first published novel, *Evil Agreement*. The feedback, encouragement, and support I received from everyone means so much to me. Your enthusiasm is the fuel I draw upon to drive my storytelling. I am in your debt!

This acknowledgement declaration would be seriously incomplete if I didn't take the time to give thanks to the many authors whose writings and talent have served to inspire me. To the true King of Horror Fiction, Stephen King, know that you sit at the pinnacle of my most favored writers. Close behind are writers such as Ray Bradbury, Anne Rice, Dean Koontz, Nora Roberts writing as J.D. Robb, Tom Clancy, Brad Thor, Brad Meltzer, Vince Flynn,

Ken Follette, George R.R. Martin, J R.R. Tolkien, Samuel Clemens, Stephenie Meyer, Steven Emerson, David Baldacci, Deborah Harkness, James Patterson, Rick Robinson, Don Helin, Karna Small Bodman, Dan Brown, and many, many others, too numerous to mention.

Last but not least, I wish to acknowledge my publisher and her excellent and talented staff. Cathy Teets, President of Headline Books is a true professional in every sense of the word. Her knowledge of the business side of the industry is a true asset that I have frequently drawn upon for wisdom and guidance. She has always come through for me in ways that help me become a better writer.

About the Author

Richard L. Hatin was born in Burlington, Vermont where he attended area schools graduating from St. Michael's College in 1971 with a B.A. in English Literature. He went on to a successful career in local and state government until 1974 when he was recruited to join the U.S Department of Housing and Urban Development (HUD). He worked for the New England Office of Community Planning and Development. He retired as the Deputy Director of the New England Office of Community Planning and Development in 2010. During his government career, Mr. Hatin wrote several articles for regional and national publications serving the interests of those involved in Community Renewal.

Mr. Hatin served on the boards of many local, state, and national organizations as well as served as an active volunteer in the community. He has received numerous local and state awards for his service to youth. He has also contributed numerous articles to state, regional and national youth sports publications.

Hatin's first novel, *Evil Agreement*, was released in 2012.

He is a member of the International Thriller Writers, Mystery Writers of America, and the New Hampshire Writer's Project.

He lives with his wife, Anne Marie, in Hooksett, New Hampshire and together they have three sons, and three granddaughters.

For more information visit www.RichardHatin.com and www.PublisherPage.com

Also by Rickard L. hatin

In Sutton, Vermont, in 1843 a coven was formed devoted to Satan. The cabal of devil worshippers was recruited by Satan's ever loyal servant, the purely evil Moloch.

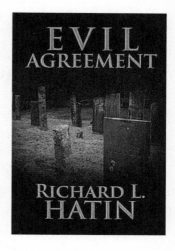

One coven member broke rank. She and her family were soon slaughtered by fellow coven members out of revenge for frustrating their promise to Satan and his covenant of promised unimaginable rewards. Somehow an infant child survived. This child was hunted relentlessly by the other members without success. Now the descendants of that first coven, several generations later, are closing in on the last descendant of the infant that had escaped that fateful night.

The hunt is on! The long ago **Evil Agreement**, the Malum Pactum with Satan, may at last be fulfilled. All they need is to get their hands on the long ago lost member's descendant, Aaron Bailey, to make whole their deeply evil coven; and fulfill their ancestor's hideous bargain with the devil.

Aaron must learn of his hidden past, forge new alliances and with aid from an unlikely source, perhaps have a chance to bring an end to this madness; and even live to tell about it!

The fulfillment of the **Evil Agreement** is getting oh so very close! And then..........!

Forthcoming Books by Richard L. Hatin

"It was mid-summer in 1187 and the Knights Templar were hiding in Jerusalem, which was surrounded and under siege by Salazin's forces. God was displeased with some of the conduct of these "Soldiers of God."

God sent his most faithful warrior, St. Michael, to speak with a small group of the most devout Knights. He recruits them to become special warriors, truly devoted to God, and now tasked with fighting the forces of evil led by Satan anywhere in the world.

These newly recruited Knights of St. Michael were also imbued with unique powers or gifts they had to learn to master. These gifts could be passed down through the ages to their descendants and could only become active once the descendant agrees to become a Knight. Then, these new recruits must be trained and taught the ways of the Knights of St. Michael.

The latest recruits are now being hunted by forces loyal to Satan. Killing them before they can be trained by the few remaining and active Knights is a priority for Satan's minions. This is the time when the Knighthood is weakest.

This battle has gone on for centuries and never before has evil been this close to destroying the "Soldiers of God."

But there is a secret force that not even Satan's own army of followers can easily defeat and that weapon has decided to join in the fight on the side of the new recruits.

"Let the battle begin!"

Janet Olson, a happy, carefree thirty-one year old woman lives with her mother and father in Northwood, New Hampshire. Janet works part time bagging groceries at a local supermarket. She is developmentally challenged and loves her family, especially her twin nieces and nephew. She enjoys her job and most of all she likes to draw in her composition notebook. She enjoys doing her drawing while sitting upon a

THE VISITOR
AT JANET'S MOUNTAIN

RICHARD L. HATIN

granite outcropping, nicknamed "Janet's Mountain." Her life is simple and orderly until one day, she receives and unexpected visitor at her "mountain." This visitor announces that Janet has been selected by God to deliver a message to the world and to validate her selection; Janet is given the power to heal!

Why Janet? How can she possibly spread God's message? Can she handle the attention, the pressure? How do her family, neighbors and community react? What about the media's reaction. How does her church handle this situation? What is the Vatican's response? Just who is the visitor, and what exactly is God's message? Janet's story will change the world and perhaps even you!

This is a powerful and inspiring story that will deeply connect with your emotions from beginning to end. This story is how one unlikely person can suddenly fill a deep need in the lives of many, many people; perhaps even yours!

Young Stanley Bolinski was raised by two drunken and abusive parents. While lying upon his deathbed, his grandfather gives him a gift that will truly last a lifetime. Stanley's grandfather relinquishes his own dark angel of death to now look after his grandson. From that day forward, a bond is formed which soon blazes a trail of death and destruction throughout Maine, New Hampshire and Vermont, along with a side trip through the steamy jungles of the Vietnam War.

Mark Atkinson, investigator with the Cold Case Unit in New Hampshire, develops a theory to help solve a series of seemingly unsolvable murders. His dogged determination places him on the trail of a brazen killer whose body-count numbers seem to be growing by the day. Mark and a team of talented colleagues close in on a prime suspect, and his evil companion, the dark angel. Much more than mortal justice for the victims and their families is on the line. Eternal justice is also at stake.

Just who is hunting who in this pulse-pounding thriller?